A FAE DESTINY NOVEL

A KINGDOM OF SOULS AND SHADOWS

For Austin —
I do believe in
faeries!
Leslie O'Sullivan

LESLIE O'SULLIVAN

A KINGDOM OF SOULS AND SHADOWS
Far Destiny, Book 1

CITY OWL PRESS
www.cityowlpress.com

Cover Design by MiblArt. All stock photos licensed appropriately.

Page Edges by Painted Wings Publishing Services.

Edited by Lisa Green.

For information on subsidiary rights, please contact the publisher at info@cityowlpress.com.

Paperback Edition ISBN: 978-1-64898-443-3

Hardback Edition ISBN: 978-1-64898-447-1

Digital Edition ISBN: 978-1-64898-444-0

Printed in the United States of America

ALSO BY LESLIE O'SULLIVAN

Rockin Fairy Tales:

Pink Guitars and Falling Stars

Gilded Butterfly

Wild Azure Waves

Crimson Melodies

Emerald Spire

***

Behind the Scenes:

Hot Set

Press Release

Not to Scale

PRAISE FOR LESLIE O'SULLIVAN

"*Pink Guitars and Falling Stars* is an interesting take on the story of Rapunzel...O'Sullivan has definitely nailed the initial animosity between Justin and Zeli. As they become closer, the relationship jumps off the page and morphs beautifully. There are awesome love scenes with a lot of description which pull the reader right in and keep a tight grip... A fascinating remix of a popular fairy tale with some very sexy differences. One to add to the e-reader and to be read list!" — *InD'tale*

"*Hot Set*, by Leslie O'Sullivan, is a contemporary love story that creatively infuses modern concerns with the nostalgia generated by a period television show. The Irish setting was fantastically romantic, and I thought the cast of characters was refreshingly practical for a group involved in show business." — *Reader's Favorite 5-star review*

"As full of heart and soul as the music it describes, *Crimson Melodies* drew me in with a fresh take on a classic tale, masterfully combining celebrity and monster romance vibes to give me everything I wanted and more!" — S.C. Grayson, author of *Beauty and the Blade*

"Submerging readers into a fantastical world, *Wild Azure Waves* is a love story swimming with music, mysticism, and magic." — *InD'tale*

"*Pink Guitars and Falling Stars* is a fast paced and very engaging read, with a constantly evolving main character and a colorful cast. The adventure wraps up nicely, and ends with a hint of what is next in the Rockin' Fairy Tales series. This is a great read if you are looking for an action-packed modern fairy tale with aspiring rock stars who fall from the sky." — *Paranormal Romance Guild*

"*Gilded Butterfly* is a unique and magical mashup of fairy tales, Shakespeare, and lore, unlike anything I've read before. At its heart, is a beautiful story about family, the destructive power of chasing fame and money, and the healing power of love. The twists, turns, and magic sprinkled throughout create an engaging story that brings a new kind of fairy tale to modern Hollywood." — *Megan Van Dyke, author of Second Star to the Left*

"With wickedly clever wordplay, fresh and lovable characters, and an utterly unique take on a classic fairytale, *Pink Guitars and Falling Stars* is one of the swooniest romances I've ever read. You'll be cheering for B.A.S.E. jumper Justin to help Zeli escape her tower in the heart of Hollywood's twisted music industry and fall equally hard for their chosen family on the Boulevard. A romantic, heart-in-your-throat read!" — *Sarah Skilton, author of Fame Adjacent*

"Leslie O'Sullivan's narrative style in *Gilded Butterfly* celebrates truth, love, and heritage, and reads as pure poetry from the opening line until the end." — *InD'tale*

"*Pink Guitars and Falling Stars* reads like glitter and stardust, like a song of the heart set free and realizing every dream." —*Fairrryprose*

Pink Guitars and Falling Stars is a winner of a 2023 Gold Author Shout Reader Ready Awards "Top Pick."

Hot Set is a 2023 Holt Medallion Winner for Mid-Length Contemporary.

Hot Set and *Press Release* each received the 2024 Author Shout Recommended Read Reader Ready Award.

For my brother, Rick, who dances beyond the Veil.

CHAPTER I
THE CAROUSEL

Inside everyone's head, including mine, lives the dream of traveling to impossible places. Near the Artists' Gate of Central Park, I pass a lamppost my lifelong friend, Colleen, swears is the entrance to Narnia, her personal fantasy terminus. Neverland tops my list. So far, no red-haired boy in a green felt hat has knocked on my window with an invitation to fly across the Atlantic. Even if Pan bothers to show, one look at me, and he'll zoom away. Adjunct college professors nearing thirty have already hit the expiration date for eternal youth. No matter. It's best to avoid the risk of running out of Faerie dust off the coast of Newfoundland.

My breath coalesces into a tiny kitten-gray cloud as a patch of ice ambushes me. With a *whoop* followed by moves worthy of a contortionist, I avoid plunging into a crusty mound of snow. My performance spooks a pair of wrens pecking at buds on the branch above me.

Ice is a villain.

After an adjustment to my cross-body bag, I trudge deeper into the frozen park. Lose the ice and snow already. It's the first day of spring or Éostre as my grandmother called it.

"*Éostre is a fortuitous time, Ella. Rise up to catch it.*"

I cling to her sayings and stories since they're all I have left of the woman who adopted and raised me. On the way to her favorite winter solstice celebration, she had a terrible fall on devil-sent ice and was gone. Based on a directive I had no part in, she was cremated before I made it to the city from my apartment upstate in Kennard Park. I never got to see Máthair again to say a proper goodbye. Since that awful day, time has become more construct than reality for me, as frozen as the Central Park lake. The last three months have been one prolonged sorrowful heartbeat, reverberating through my hollowed-out soul.

On the path to the carousel, bare branches of trees float above my head in a pearly haze while birds carry on a grand conversation with squirrels. I do love Central Park's fierce hold on nature despite being penned in by buildings tall enough to blot out the sun.

A glint of light on the bridge ahead catches my eye. I remember one of the dream flashes I had as a kid where a buck with silver antlers carried a nymph over those very stones beneath an iridescent dome. I pause a moment, reliving the vivid daydream, one of many visions illustrating my past. Today, no kingly beast breaks through the fog.

"Maybe next time," I tell the trees and chase the mystique of daydreams away. Forget Neverland or Narnia. My grandmother, Máthair, would insist this morning's scene is the misty realm of her ultimate Irish vacation destination, *Tír na nÓg*.

The words I'll never hear from her lips again sting. *"Someday Ella my girl, you'll fly over the hill of Tara through the gates of Tír na nÓg to live forever young among the Faeries."*

I hope she made it there.

I'll be content to meet up with Colleen without slipping on another patch of devil ice.

I take the turnoff to the carousel. Canvas covers its brick pavilion. When I slip inside, a V-shaped shaft of light sneaks past me to reveal a carved swan serving as the side of bench seat. Milady swan's black eye shoots me a savage glance for disturbing the inhabitants' winter sleep.

"Aim that attitude somewhere else," I scold as if she's one of my incoming freshmen.

I drop onto her bench seat. A scant glow trickles under the bottom of the canvas, painting alternate strokes of light and shadow across slumbering beasts. I lean back and soak in the presence of the carousel. The sensation of being encased in a prismatic sheath hails the onset of a dream flash that comes swift and furious. Vibrations within the wooden shells of animals wake around me. In front of the swan, a fierce black horse wears a saddle in the shape of a lion. The great cat's roar resonates through my bones. I imagine it leaping free to lord over the squirrels and rabbits of Central Park.

Air thickens as I give over completely to the vision. Pages of an illuminated manuscript fan inside my head like a flip book to reveal the true story of every beast on the carousel. Behind me, armored plates on a war horse beat a tattoo as the loyal steed carries his knight into a battle lost in time. I revel in this altered reality. Colors smear across the inside of my eyelids as I will creatures to tear free of golden poles and vanish into their stories.

In my fantasy, I leap upon a war horse to join the escape and gallop through the park. A strand of my pale white-blonde hair that shines gold from the kiss of a rising sun catches in an eyelash. The horse banks to the left, my body to the right. I'm thrown into the air, destined for a bone-shattering fall. My eyes snap open to a world where horses are painted wood.

I open the notes screen on my phone to capture every detail of this dream flash. Like all the others, action lingers inside wavering, multi-colored boundaries. The rainbow casing takes on different shapes, sometimes a tunnel or a giant bubble for the length of the flash. I've delved too deeply into Irish myths and folktales not to wonder if there very well might be more to this world than we're comfortable with. I choose to live by the rule it's safer not to be tempted beyond the confines of reality as many in the stories were. More often than not, they did not meet cheery endings. Best not to chase a Faerie down a well if you can't swim.

Today's dip into the imaginary will become one of the poems and stories along with the others I've transformed from a lifetime of these wild visions.

"Colors burst. Horses cry. Bonds dissolve..." My poetry generator is stuck on prosaic. I need a fiery sunset over the Hudson River to inspire a shift into my creative brain.

A scratch at the canvas makes me jump. "Colleen?" No answer. If she were trying to scare me, I'd know. Colleen has zero giggle control. A branch then. Another reminder I'm just an ordinary woman trespassing on a carousel in the middle of a giant city to avoid the inevitable.

The calendar reminder on my phone dings, startling me. I've got three hours to clear the last of my personal items from the rooftop apartment attached to the sky-high greenhouse of Times Square's Royal Crown Hotel where I grew up. As produce manager, my grandmother transformed the unlikely garden into something extraordinary. She coaxed the most stubborn plant to grow regardless of the season. Butternut squash soup in mid-summer—unheard of. Fresh seedless watermelon and watercress soup at Christmas dinner—sorcery. The restaurant at the Royal Crown, the Jewel, keeps its five stars because of Máthair's nothing-less-than-magical green thumb.

Kept.

I can't fathom the new caretakers maintaining the level of my grandmother's excellence. Turning over her beloved garden to anyone feels like a betrayal.

My entire childhood and the last of Máthair's belongings I haven't given away since she passed are boxed and ready to join me in my faculty housing at Kennard Park University. Tonight, a new family will move into the place my grandmother called home for nearly forty years.

"I can handle this. Do you hear me, swan?"

Is it bad luck to lie to such a majestic bird, even a wooden one?

The close air makes my nose itch, my stubby nose Máthair called a Faerie kiss in her way that made everything sparkle. I puff a breath strong enough to make strands of hair blow across my face, tickling, torturing. Colleen has come at me more than once with scissors to solve my flighty hair issues. I hold out a piece to examine it and play my game, blaming feathery hair on my mother, and the strange colored freckles, more gold than brown, sprinkled across my skin on my father. Why not? I have no clue what my parents look like. Wishing Mom had stuck around long enough to teach me how to deal with these ridiculous locks that defy clips, spray, and even braids is a childish pipe dream.

"Ellie?"

For half a second, I swear it's the swan, but Colleen's head pokes through the gap in the carousel's shroud.

"Over here."

She wiggles through the opening to join me, waving an envelope in my face. "It came to my parents' house. You forgot to change your address."

I stare at the letter as if it will come to life as the carousel animals did and fly at me. "It's not an oversight. The results were supposed to arrive before I went back upstate for the new trimester. I didn't want to risk Máthair finding it."

Colleen smacks the envelope against her palm. "I've told you a billion times, Martha wouldn't have cared about a damn DNA test."

I flinch, still not used to hearing my grandmother referred to in the past tense. Shame bats me like the beat of a swan's wing. Máthair worked so hard to snuff the dark inklings of abandonment I felt from time to time, especially in my teens. She wrapped me in boundless love and gifted me her Irish heritage, which she swears is also mine. Adoption is a funny thing. Other people write your script. Still, it's unsettling to have a void in the place an origin story should be.

This envelope may hold the first step toward finding the people who made Ella O'Dwyer.

"Are the results going to change your life? Will you ditch your plan to become a tenure-track Celtic studies professor if you're Flemish?"

I stare past her at the lion saddle. "No, but self-definition does require at least minimal truth."

"I'll give you that." Colleen flicks her auburn hair like a cowboy's lariat. "Before I hand this over, let's discuss my compensation for helping you move out of the apartment."

"Don't say it." I pat my ears and hum to drown her out.

She pulls my hand away. "Commit to the study trip."

Frigid air stings the inside of my nostrils. I know I should jump at the opening to be one of the faculty to represent Kennard Park University on the graduate studies spring break trip they're sponsoring to Ireland. The coveted spots filled quickly with an impressive roster of masters and PhD candidates from top universities. Attaching my name to the trip will beef up my already decent chance at snagging the last remaining full-time position in my department. I'll take any edge I can get. I'm sick to death of piecing together enough money from tutoring and online consulting about all things Irish to supplement my paltry adjunct salary. Upping my ante with the faculty committee assigned to choose a top candidate is the smart move.

Colleen pretends to type. "I pop Ella O'Dwyer in the last blank faculty spot on the trip roster, and it's a done deal. We will have a blast together."

Colleen is the staff events coordinator for our department. The overseas junket is her brainchild. She's going on the trip not only for free travel but also to wrangle logistics, thus the daily encouragements for me to accompany her.

"C, you know this trip tragically exceeds my limits. The long plane flight, mixing with a group of strangers, functioning in a different country—"

Too busy. Too big. Too not me. Only my small digs in Kennard Park, the Times Square rooftop apartment and greenhouse I grew up in, as well as my tiny corner of Manhattan receive the Ella O'Dwyer rating of safe, familiar landscape. Ireland is well—daunting and massively outside my comfort zone.

"Have I mentioned the new professor hire from Boston, Jeremy Olk, confirmed as trip lead? Honey, you don't want to pass up a face-to-face with that bottle of intellectual hot sauce."

I scoff. "You mean the intellectual hot sauce who stole my position?"

"Did he though? Who cares if he snatched one of the two openings first? I'm confident the other one has your name all over it." She grins at me. "Ahh, I see it now, his-and-her monogrammed professor towels in your bathroom."

I nudge her. "Stop already."

Colleen possesses an annoying penchant for matchmaking.

"Think practically. If you make nice with this Olk guy, he could be an asset. Especially if he gives the committee a glowing Ella critique after the study trip." She taps her bottom lip with my envelope. "Professor Sauce starts after spring break, so vacationing together before then is the perfect opportunity to win him over."

I shake my head. "Are you his P.R. person? And it's not a vacation."

"Fine, *working trip*." She grabs the phone from my hand and fiddles with it. "If my persuasive powers are lacking—" She thrusts the screen in my face. "Behold your dream man."

In his profile picture on the trip link, Jeremy Olk is kinda perfect. He's a serious professorial type, possibly close to my age, with round glasses a few years out of style. A lock of hair that I suspect plots a thousand ways to stray out of place, sneaks down the center of his forehead. I'd be lying if I didn't admit there wasn't an instant snippet of attraction on my part from the picture. I may cast Professor Sauce as the new leading man in my late-night, steamy professor fantasies.

Colleen grins. "Ireland's looking greener, isn't it?"

While she gloats, I take the opening to retrieve my phone and envelope. Instead of ripping it open, I stare at my name through the clear window.

Colleen snugs in close and throws an arm around me. "I'm sure the test worked this time, and all will be revealed."

I lean into her. She's been through three failed DNA tests with me that claimed tampered or insufficient samples. It's as if the universe is in cahoots with the analysis company to keep me from knowing who I am.

I nudge my bestie. "I need to open this alone. I'll meet you at the apartment in an hour, and we'll pack my life into your car."

Colleen kisses my cheek. "Whatever it says, you're still my Ellie." She slips through the carousel's cover.

I listen until the crunch of her feet on the dwindling snow disappears then leave the sanctuary myself. The morning sun has broken through to reflect off any piece of ice it can reach. Even though it plays a part in the lovely prism of crisscrossing light around me, ice remains my enemy.

I rip open the envelope. Bright red letters shout at me.

Unable to process sample.

The letter falls from my hand onto the snow.

CHAPTER 2
THE LAWYER

The freight elevator in the Royal Crown Hotel groans like a cranky over-sleeper slogging out of bed in the morning. I've learned to ignore the shakes and shimmies guaranteed to scare first-time riders shitless.

The doors slide open onto my version of paradise, Máthair's rooftop greenhouse. The interim gardener has done an admirable job these three months, encouraging the garden not to give up with the passing of its mistress. My gaze drifts past rows of raised beds to the far end of the green glassed-in wonder that stretches between Forty-Eighth and Forty-Ninth Streets above Times Square.

I move slowly down the center aisle, a march of farewell, working hard to stave off tears as the scents of herbs and loamy earth wrap me in memories of my grandmother. Outside the glass walls, my eyes tilt to the clouds. Scattered black lines fringe the bottom of gray bulging layers. Máthair read the clouds. *Neladoract*, she called it, cloud divination.

"Ask the sky a question with your heart. Watch. Listen. Feel. If you're meant to know, the clouds will tell ye, a stór."

A stór, my treasure. I'd give anything to hear my grandmother call me her treasure one more time.

I stare at the sky and swear the air stills around me. On this first

Éostre since her passing, the clouds wear black lace to mourn Máthair. The sorrowing sky keens to honor her loss, echoing the ache in my heart. Soon these clouds will weep rain or snow to complete the tribute.

I reach the far end of the greenhouse. Outside the doors, a line of Máthair's apple and citrus trees flank a grand open exterior used for exclusive parties. New buds rise along branches unlike the frozen trees down in Central Park. Bird call erupts from the tiny orchard. Feathered thieves peck at awakening blossoms. These damn birds will not ruin my grandmother's prizes.

I move to shove the door open and shoo them, but my body stiffens. This threshold might as well be the lowered portcullis of an ancient castle. Inside the greenhouse is safe territory, but it's been years since I ventured onto the open rooftop. Out there, the sensation of falling will drench me like spray from a waterfall.

Stumbling to pull the chain dangling just inside the door, I start the warming fans among the trees. The squeal of blades sends the flock into the sky. They soar together with the discipline of a fighter squadron, following the same path as the traffic below as they turn the corner and disappear into a tunnel of gray monoliths.

A wave of dizziness wrecks my balance. I support myself on a raised bed of rosemary and thyme. My grip knocks something through the wooden slats of the bed. It hits the floor with a *ting*. A flat circle of silver rolls in front of my boot, spinning on its end.

I'm transfixed, watching the blur as the gauzy feel of an oncoming dream flash tickles my consciousness. Threadlike spears of light appear to emanate from the twirling metal disk, rising toward my outstretched hand. The sound of a single note played on a far-off violin is barely noticeable, fighting its way through the never-ending parade of sirens on the street below. After an eternity, the spinner falls onto its side. The *plunk* of metal against the floor chases away the leading edge of the dream flash as my senses return to the smell of herbs and the normal background sounds of Times Square.

I pick up the object and lay it on my palm. For a moment, I swear the coin pulses warm against my lifeline. It's the size of a quarter and smooth as polished glass. Flipping it, I see black marks cut into its surface. After a squirt of water from a nearby spray bottle and a rub on my sleeve, the symbol is easier to read. I tilt the coin so it catches the strings of sunlight cutting through the green glass above me.

At first, I think it's a cross, but it's closer to a plus sign. A spiral rests within each of the four right angles. There's a silver circle in the center of the symbol. Definitely Celtic. I'll Google it later. For now, I close my fingers around the coin that must be one of the many carefully placed talismans Máthair swore made her plants thrive. Maybe this one will help me thrive.

"Ella O'Dwyer?"

A cry of surprise bursts from my lips, and I nearly drop the coin. Instinctively, I back away from the short, stocky man with bowed legs striding down the center aisle toward me. My hand searches for any gardening tool left in the nearest bed.

He raises both palms and comes no closer. "I didn't mean to frighten you, dear. I'll keep my distance."

I shouldn't be so jumpy. The man never would have been given access to the greenhouse without careful scrutiny from the hotel. "Who are you?"

The man pulls off a knit cap to reveal a shock of wavy hair the color of dark rubies. "I'm Timothy Yew, Martha O'Dwyer's lawyer."

Máthair's lawyer? Confusion breaks through fear as my eyes flick over him. With ruddy cheeks and the dusting of gray stubble across his chin, he's more farmer fresh off a day of plowing than lawyer.

"There are no words to do justice to a sadness such as losing your grandmother, so I won't try to speak 'em."

His accent is so like Máthair's, a knife plunges into my gut.

"Martha and I knew—" He swallows. "Each other from St. Malachy's. We've been goin' to the same mass for years. I'm the one took care of her legal doin's, power of attorney, final wishes, and such." A sheen of tears brightens his eyes when he says *final wishes*. One small droplet meanders down the length of his long, straight nose before he wipes it away.

"It's been three months. You could have called or emailed."

The lawyer wrings his hands then dabs his chin with a knuckle. "It took a bit of doing to finalize all Martha's wishes." He nods at the wall of French doors that lead into the apartment and stammers. "All I had was the phone for your place. When no one returned my calls, I checked with the hotel, and they said you'd be by today to clear out."

From under his herringbone wool overcoat, the lawyer produces a bulging manila envelope and holds it out to me. "This explains the particulars of how Martha wanted things to go."

I stare at my name printed on the front of the envelope for a beat, baffled at what "particulars" wait for me inside before taking it from him. There's an awkward pause as if he's waiting for me to open it. I force a smile. "Today isn't a good day to tackle this." I nod at the envelope. "Is there a way to get in touch with you if I have questions?"

His smile is warmer than mine. "Aye...yes. I've left my card inside."

"Thank you." I really can't deal with legal crap right now. My emotional energy reserves are occupied with leaving the only home I've ever known.

Timothy Yew fusses with his coat, peeking at me through his lashes and waiting for me to add to the conversation. When I don't, he straightens. "I'll say my goodbyes then." He heads down the row but pauses to turn back. "I'm woefully sorry for your loss. Martha was a special person." Respecting my obvious unease, he retreats down the row. The click of the odd farmer/lawyer's Sunday shoes against the floor grows faint as he reaches the elevator.

As soon as the doors close and I'm alone, I clutch the envelope of secrets to my chest. A thought punches through the riot in my head. Is there anything in here about my parents? Maybe the latest failed DNA test isn't my dead end.

I hurry to the apartment and step inside. Instead of the familiar aroma of Máthair's baking, all I smell is dust. It's a gut punch not to see a cream-colored linen napkin with a border of green and gold harps beneath an expertly stacked pyramid of soda bread cookies on the dining table. My eyes land on the watercolor of a fox floating in a burst of colorful splatters, leaning against the tower of cardboard boxes near the French door entrance. It's an ugly thing. I fell in love with it at a street fair in SoHo so my grandmother bought it for me.

Sorrow stabs my chest then radiates through my body. I'll never go to a street fair with her or taste my grandmother's lovely soda bread cookies again.

Will the packet from Timothy Yew bring comfort? My throat feels as rough as rope when I swallow. If memories of her cookies drive me to the brink of collapse, who knows what the contents of the lawyer's envelope will do? I suck it up, hit the light switch, and unwind the string from around the tab on the back of the packet.

Inside the oversized envelope are three smaller ones. I shake them onto the table. Two are document-sized, but it's the tiny one I tear open first. A simple silver band slides onto the tabletop. It's the ring Máthair never took off her left hand.

I raise the silver band to the Waterford crystal light fixture hanging above me. Etched in the metal are two words. Strange. I'd always thought the marks were a pattern or design. The second word looks like *orm*, but the first word is hard to make out. It could be *teach*. Damn, it's probably in Irish. I curse myself for not being more diligent in practicing past the rudimentary knowledge of the language I've needed in my work. Máthair spoke Irish to me my whole life in bits and pieces, but the words on this ring are elusive. I pull out the coin I found in the greenhouse and hold it next to the ring. They go well together.

I slip the band onto the ring finger of my right hand and kiss it. "I'll never take you off." I close my fingers around the disk Máthair lost among her plants. "You neither." I'll turn it into a necklace. Máthair's ring and coin. My treasures.

The next envelope bulges enough to rip part of the side seam. A passport slides out. I wrestle the packet of papers wedged in the envelope free, the culprits of the tear. A letterhead from my grandmother's bank is on a statement of accounts. I shove it aside to peruse other secrets Timothy Yew and my grandmother kept from me.

I sweep a finger over the documents and stop under the name.

Eala Duir

"Wait. What?"

These aren't mine. Timothy Yew screwed up. I flip open the passport. Next to a picture of me, there's my address in Kennard Park and that name again.

Eala Duir

Digging and sifting through the pile of papers on the table doesn't turn up a single item with Ella O'Dwyer on it. I grab one document so quickly; it slices the pad of my finger. While sticking it in my mouth to avoid bleeding over everything, I gape at another piece in this tangle of *what the hell*. It's a birth certificate for *Eala Duir*. Martha O'Dwyer is listed as my adoptive parent—no hint of the two who made me.

I press the heels of my hands against my eyes as if that will erase the weirdness strewn across the table. When I look again, nothing changes. A ball of ice grows in my stomach.

I open the last envelope to get the freak show over with. A ticket to Ireland spills out, a note folded over it. On the front is my name, my real name, Ella, in Máthair's swoopy cursive.

Ella,

If you're reading my letter, I've passed on but not my love for you, a stór. Forgive me for leaving you without saying things you should be knowing. Your true name is Eala Duir. I took it from you when I made you mine, and now I'm giving it back. Free your spirit, my darling Eala. A glorious life beyond our rooftop or your bitty school town awaits. I'll be asking one final favor of you. Follow the inscription on the ring I've left you. When you do, you'll understand why you must. Go to Ireland. Go and ye will be found.

All my love in this world and the next,
Your Máthair

"Free my spirit?" I smack the note on the table and howl at the crystal above me. "I don't want a glorious life."

My fingers grip the edge of the table and the paper cut bleeds.

Go and ye will be found?

I'm running through an untamed forest with branches of anger, despair, and confusion clawing at my soul.

"Eala Duir?" I know enough Irish to translate the ridiculous name. Swan Oak sounds like a municipal cemetery. I'm not Eala Duir.

A slithering sensation runs along my spine.

But I am.

Was that the name my birth parents gave me? I leap to my feet and pace around the table.

"Too many secrets, Máthair."

My gaze returns to the pile of papers. A bank statement pokes out. I grab it, crumbling the edges as I read the balance and process a crap ton of zeroes. Eala Duir is worth a hundred thousand dollars. There's a post-it with a username and password. I punch the bank's website and then the details into my phone, and there she is. There I am. Eala Duir owns a tidy nest egg, a far cry from scraping-out-a-living Ella. Is this the result of our frugal life of thrift store clothing and budget vacations? I'm sick. Did Máthair deprive herself to create a dragon's hoard for me?

I back away from the table as if the papers will leap up and strangle me.

Shadows drape the apartment from a bank of gray clouds floating above the garden. Out the window, flickers from the gargantuan electronic billboards in Times Square reflect off greenhouse glass. Today, Éostre, the spring equinox, is supposed to herald the end of the dark part of the Celtic year, but for me, the darkness of the unknown is just beginning.

I stare at the unreadable words on the silver band around my finger. The woman who claimed I was her treasure left me nothing but an Irish inscription and an envelope packed with revelations.

The groan of the elevator snaps me from my daze. Colleen wheels a cart to the open apartment door. "Let's get the party started. I coerced a couple of the bellhops to help…" She takes one look at my face and rushes over. "Oh, Ellie. I didn't mean to be thoughtless. This must be shit for you." Her arms wrap around me, and she squeezes as only Colleen can.

When she releases me, I point wordlessly at the papers.

"Your passport. Perfect." She fans the air with it. "You can't use a missing passport as an excuse not to go on the trip."

"Open it."

"Why? So I can tell you your picture isn't as horrible as it probably is?" Colleen does a double take when she opens the passport. "What the hell?"

I flap the birth certificate at her. She snatches it from my hands. Her eyes widen as she reads it. Before she puts it down, I hand her Máthair's note.

"Eala—ow-la." She tastes the sound of my real name. "Guess I'll have to call you Owlie now instead of Ellie."

"Please don't." I study her as she continues to skim the paper. "I can't believe she kept this from me."

Colleen crinkles her lips. "Maybe she was waiting until you snagged the permanent position at Kennard Park to share this." She drops into the chair opposite me and leans on her elbows to stare me down. "We all know you can only handle one life change at a time."

"Who I really am isn't a life *change*. It's my life." Lifting my hand close to her face, I show her the ring. "And then there's this."

Colleen grabs my hand and holds the silver band to the light, twisting it to read the engraving. *"Teacht orm?"*

"Do you know what it means?" Colleen, unlike me, was more attentive to her Irish language classes in high school and college.

Her face drains of color. "I do."

"Tell me what it says. I think it could be something Máthair wanted me to know."

Colleen's gaze drops to the note from my grandmother and then slowly lifts to meet mine. My skin prickles at the intensity in her expression.

"It means find me."

CHAPTER 3

THE SWAP

When I was six, Máthair took me to Vermont on one of our rare vacations out of the city. The maple syrup farm I loved. The converted toboggan run turned alpine slide terrified me. We slid and slid without any way to gauge how long it would be before hitting bottom. The same nauseating sensation claws at my chest now as our plane buffets its way across the North Atlantic. Each time I'm close to drifting off, a cart rattling down the aisle, or an overloud conversation snaps me back to the reality that I'm trapped in a metal tube playing chicken with gravity.

The next sleep killer is Colleen's soft whisper. "Are you awake?"

I must be pulling off a halfway decent job of faking sleep for her to ask. Guilt drives me to open my eyes to slits. Colleen is my rock, the friend holding my hand through the soul-ripping job of leaving my Manhattan rooftop apartment behind and the mindfuck of swapping Ella O'Dwyer for Eala Duir. She insisted the info from Timothy Yew makes up for my failure at passing DNA tests. At least I have my authentic name to trace after I suffer this trip to Ireland.

I couldn't punch holes in Colleen's insistence that taking on the duties of the Irish study trip is key to edge out my competition for the last full-time faculty position I want so badly. Truthfully, her logic is only half the reason I finally gave in and agreed to obliterate my comfort zone. The *find me* message on Máthair's ring and her final request in the letter that I go to Ireland sealed the deal.

Colleen crouches in the aisle, nudging me with her elbow. She abandoned her middle seat next to me an hour ago to bop down the cabin and socialize with others in our group. "I need you to do a seat swap."

My eyes pop open the rest of the way. "Why?"

"I'm clicking with one of the PhD candidates from Boston. I'd like to keep clicking, but I'm sick of standing in the aisle. Come meet Charlie."

I suppose one aisle seat is the same as any other, and once I assume my official duties as co-tour leader, I'll meet this Charlie person anyway, especially if Colleen is *clicking* with him. When I undo my seat belt, she chirps like a finch. "I knew you loved me."

"Am I that obvious?" I hug my backpack, a wave of unease washing over me as I vacate the tiny cocoon of my aisle seat. "Lead on to...?"

She points toward the front of the plane. "Thirty-four B."

A tall twig with spiky chocolate brown hair, presumably Charlie, waves his arms above his head. I freeze. B—shit. That's a damn middle seat.

I grab the nearest seat back, earning a dirty look from its occupant, a middle-aged man with an almost perfectly circular bald patch. My jostle tears his attention away from the exploding helicopter scene playing on his tablet. Who in their right mind watches air disasters while on a plane?

I release his seat as if it burned me. "Sorry."

Helicopter guy acknowledges me with a glare and pissy grunt before returning to his airborne mayhem.

I grab Colleen's hands. "I can't do this. Charlie's in a middle seat. I'm sorry. It's too close to the window." I only do aisle seats, as far from a window as possible. Looking down at the ocean, or worse land, as a frame of reference to height is unthinkable.

Colleen pulls me into a tight hug. "It's okay, sweetie. I scoped it out. The guy in the window seat is asleep, and most of the shades in that section are down. No triggers."

Of course, my bestie has her swap case prepared. Judging by the level of her frenetic energy and the way her Charlie guy shimmies into the aisle, they may be a match ordained by the spirit of St. Patrick himself. Just because I drift in a gray haze of unease, doesn't mean Colleen is obligated to join me.

We work our way down the aisle toward Charlie who's approaching at double my speed.

"Hey Eala, I'm Charlie," he says as we execute an awkward, cramped slide-by in the aisle. "Thanks for swapping."

I'm so concentrated on staying steady on my feet, all I manage is a rapid head nod. Luckily, the passenger in the aisle seat used Charlie's exit to head to the back of the plane for snacks or a personal pit stop. I squish into thirty-four B and attempt to jam my backpack under the seat in front of me. There's so little room I can't lean far enough to shove it into place. A foot nudge is required to complete the task. As advertised, shades in the rows around and across from me are lowered while people sleep. I understand why the buzz of a Charlie/Colleen convo would not be welcome here in the snoozy section.

The guy in the window seat wedged his coat against the side of the plane as a pillow. Round-framed glasses park crookedly atop tousled hair. The light is too dim for me to tell if it's brown or black. A few strands stick straight up from the crown of his head like feathers. Add the gentle curves of his features, a smallish nose, and light beard stubble scattered in the vicinity of a round chin, and he gives off a slightly scattered, non-threatening vibe I can deal with. Due to my last-minute arrival at the airport, I had zero time to meet anyone. No clue if he's with our group.

When I reach to twist the air nozzle in my direction, my leg bumps a file folder balanced on window guy's knee. Luckily, I catch it before the stack of papers inside slides free.

"Charlie, how different you look in this light."

"I'm so sorry." The fire running across my cheeks probably brightens the cabin. I hold the rescued file out to him.

He runs a hand through his hair. "Clearly those are scintillating enough to put me right out." There's the tiniest hint of an Irish lilt hiding under his Boston accent. "Please—feel free to grade them."

"I traded seats with Charlie." I thrust the file into his hands. "I hope that's cool."

His lower lip curves into a slight pout when he smiles. "It's a dream come true. Charlie didn't sit still for two minutes together since takeoff." He flips the folder open and squares its contents before offering me his hand to shake. "Jeremy Olk."

I'm so surprised, I don't move. Colleen can be wily. Charlie wasn't her solo motivation to get me out of my seat. She took the first opportunity to connect me with my new colleague before the hubbub of our full itinerary is set in motion. Colleen knows my wish list for the ideal guy. Clearly, she believes Jeremy Olk checks all the boxes. Maybe he does. "The study team lead."

His smile widens. "The very one."

This guy looks younger and far less serious than his picture online. "But you're so—"

I chomp on my tongue before I say he looks too young to be my job-stealing nemesis.

"Not professorial?" He chuckles. "Believe me, I've heard it before."

Did he start college at twelve? I'm dying to ask how old he is. "So, it's technically Dr. Olk?"

He smiles at me. "Is it wrong how much I enjoy the sound of Dr. Olk or Professor Olk? Both titles quantify the life of academia I've always dreamed of."

The life of academia I've always dreamed of.

Colleen's matchmaking may just garner a five-star review from me this time.

His hand lingers in the air between us. I clutch it and hope he can't feel mine shaking. "I'm Eala Duir, but you can call me Dr. Duir or Professor Duir since we're swapping titles."

In our shared life of academia.

He squeezes my hand, squinting at me through the dim light of the cabin. "Duir?"

"Apologies. My name on the trip rosters was listed as Ella O'Dwyer. I've only recently switched to my legal name."

Grasping my hand between both of his, he smiles. "Ella O'Dwyer, yes. I understand we'll be colleagues as of next quarter."

I'm tempted to ask him to clarify what he knows of our collegial relationship. Does he mean adjunct Duir to tenure-track Professor Olk, or might someone on the search committee have let something slip during his welcome tour of the Celtic Studies department? I'm embarrassed when I realize we're still holding hands and start to slip mine free from his very warm, soft fingers.

He doesn't let me retreat, tightening his hold as he leans closer. "For the record, I prefer Eala Duir to Ella O'Dwyer. Such a name would sit well on the daughter of an Irish chieftain." His warm breath dances across my cheek.

I could get used to Jeremy Olk holding my hands. It's been so long since anyone flirted with me, I forgot what a rush it can be. In the next moment, said rush dies a grisly death when Doctor/Professor Olk slides the window shade up. We break through the clouds as expanses of blue ocean and distant fingers of green land splash across the earth below.

I grip the armrests. I shut my eyes tight enough for tears to form. The cabin spins and tilts. I'm vaguely aware the occupant of the aisle seat returns, stealing my chance to move farther from the window.

Máthair swore I'd outgrow my fear of heights, but I'm as fragile now as I was that day on the rooftop when I was eight and had one mother of a dream flash.

A flock of birds circled above Máthair's apple trees on the roof. They were enchanting. Wings commanded the air beneath to hold each creature steady in the sky. My own arms floated up and down to mimic the birds, and then a voice on the breeze called to me.

"Come. Come."

I ran, intent on following the birds into the sky. Only the impact of Máthair's body knocking me against the low wall surrounding the rooftop kept me from going over the edge. Awareness returned like a fist to the jaw. The sense of falling ignited tremors in my body so intense not even my grandmother could soothe me. Máthair raged at the birds as she cradled me in her arms.

I never walked onto the open-air rooftop again. Instead of sending me to join the clouds, that dream flash would have sacrificed my body to the unforgiving concrete of Times Square.

Jeremy Olk gently clasps my arm, shaking me in a different rhythm from the shockwaves running along my spine. "Eala? Do you need help?"

I barely form the words. "I'm...afraid...heights."

His voice is gentle. "We're about to start our descent to Shannon Airport. You're safe."

As long as we avoid wind shear and sudden engine failure.

Despite his efforts, I continue to shut down. Red flashes blaze through my consciousness.

"Listen to my words. Paint them with your mind." Jeremy takes my hands in his, thumbs sliding back and forth across my skin in time with his voice. "I am a wind of the sea, and I am a wave of the ocean."

The steady current of his voice begins to dilute the edge of my panic.

"I am the eagle on a cliff. I am a tear of the sun."

It's as if my skin is being warmed by his words. Fear continues to dissipate.

"I am a turning in a maze. I am a salmon in a pool. I am a lake on a plain."

In my mind, I paint a still lake, a *lough*, centered in a tapestry of emerald puzzle pieces, each with a dark green outline.

Steady breaths move in and out of my body. I have not turned to mush. My seatmate's scent of damp wood after a rain surrounds me. He smells of earth and ground, places to plant your feet and not fall.

"Take a small risk, Eala Duir, for a big payoff. Open your eyes."

Carefully, I accept his challenge.

He stares intently, probably waiting to see if I'll keel over. Since CPR isn't required, he continues. "Who spreads light on the gathering hills?" He gestures out the window. "Who can tell the ages of the moon?" His face glows in the light of morning. "Who can tell the place where the sun rests?"

The plane glides toward Shannon Airport, and I don't slink under the seat in front of me. A countryside of jade, ochre, and gold spills across the world. Houses dot a few of the patchwork squares.

He releases my hands and smiles. "Welcome back."

There's familiarity to his chant I can't quite place. "Your words—where are they from?" I want to remember them—summon them when I need a dose of soothing magic.

"It's a poem called the *Song of Amairgin White-Knee*." Our team leader chuckles at the baffled look on my face. "Ole Amairgin was once a chief ollam of Ireland, a historian, storyteller, sage."

I swipe a sleeve across my forehead, checking how big a sweat stain soaks the fabric. The sting of salt leaves my eyes. "Of course. I know him. I recognize it now." I circle a finger around my head. "Sorry, I won't be up to full capacity until we land."

"I can keep going. I'm a bit of an *ollam* fanboy."

I settle in my seat, unexpectedly calmed by Jeremy's presence. Lightheadedness and jitters are replaced with a desire to keep chatting with this man. "There's a fandom I can wrap my head around."

He sighs. "The world's chieftains could use talented *ollams* at their sides these days." Jeremy Olk's Irish undertone rises to the surface. He pats the file folder on his lap. "Sadly, no potential *ollams* in the bunch."

"Those are poems?"

He flips open the cover. To my surprise, the work is printouts of handwritten sketches mixed with words.

"Attempts. The last assignment I must suffer through before I turn in final grades from my stint at Pogon U." The stream of air from his lips riffles his bangs. "I'm elated to trade that dreary campus and its dreary students for Kennard Park University." He holds a hand to the side of his mouth to whisper. "Its nickname was *Póg Mo Thóin* U."

A laugh explodes from me. "Kiss my ass, U? I can't wait to hear what you'll come up with for Kennard Park."

"I don't intend to mock the benefactors that rescued me from K.M.A.U." He winks. "At least not right away."

I gesture at the stack of work in his lap. "You're old school, huh? Shunning the ease of online grading?" In the light from the window, I study the black and brown streaks competing through his hair. Below nicely shaped eyebrows, the same mix of color shines like dark liquid in his eyes. He's monochromatic without being dull.

Before he catches me studying him, I focus on the poem at the stop of the stack. At the bottom of the paper is a sketch of the same symbol imprinted on Máthair's coin that now hangs around my neck on a silver chain. I pluck the paper out of the file and point to the drawing. "So, *ollam* fanboy, do you know what this symbol means?"

Olk slides the glasses from atop his head into place and squints at the four spirals nested in the angles of a plus sign. "If memory serves, it's the Celtic sign for strength."

Strength. I won't turn that down. Pulling the necklace away from my throat, I show Olk the symbol. "It was my grandmother's."

He eyes it and nods. "A fitting gift for a journey."

I return his paper without reading the poem. He busies himself slipping the folder into his messenger bag and hums as if enjoying a private joke.

Following suit, I snug my backpack farther under the seat in front of me with the hope my near panic attack hasn't left a bad taste in his mouth. I find myself eager to cozy up to Kennard Park's newest Celtic studies professor and replace this flaky first impression with one that becomes a name worthy of an Irish chieftain's daughter.

Máthair's ring shines on my finger as wheels bump onto the tarmac.

Find Me.

I whisper to my grandmother. "I'm here." If only I knew who or what I'm supposed to be looking for.

CHAPTER 4
THE CHANCER

Colleen chatters as we move through the main entrance pavilion of Blarney Castle. Whenever I envisioned an Irish castle, it rose from a profusion of greenery through mists to touch crystal blue sky. A visitor center with ticket windows and a line of tourists did not factor in my mindscape.

My friend flits her hands at hummingbird speed. "Charlie Moser is THE sweetest. He's gone to the bus to get my puffer vest."

The riot of mulberry and fuchsia flowers that greets us on the castle side of the main entrance chases away the fatigue from our overnight flight and subsequent bus ride to get to our first Irish destination. "So, they don't only do green," I say, taking a dozen pictures with my phone before I stop. What's the point? Who am I going to show these to?

"So...Professor Olk—discuss. Easy to talk to, adorable, and totally rocks a history chat. Not boring at all. He's going to get snapped up fast."

Jeremy Olk's narration from Shannon Airport to Blarney Castle did come off as enchanting as a grand King Arthur and the Knights of Camelot tale. His talk of chieftains and passion against the Anglo-Norman invasion beats a crusty recitation of dates and historical VIPs. He's a bit of an *ollam* himself. "Poor guy probably doesn't get many chances to gush over Celtic studies in the wild."

She smiles slyly. "His eyes have plenty of gush for you."

"Slow down there, C. Let's not turn this trip into a social mixer."

I'm sure my cheeks add a new shade of pink to the clusters of flowers shivering in the breeze. "After his first impression of me, he's probably worried about the university's liability if one of their adjunct faculty dies from a panic attack in the air while co-leading an international study trip."

I do appreciate the added benefit of Doctor/Professor Olk being a mesmerizing storyteller so I'm able to fade into background noise most of the time. I'll intervene here and there to make a positive impression that will hopefully get back to the hiring committee. Playing second fiddle will leave me space to work on Máthair's enigmatic *find me* directive.

As we walk along the path near River Martin, the reality of Blarney Castle exceeds my mystical expectations. It does indeed rise from the trees as if planted rather than built. The brownish-gray walls of the tower house slant inward, giving the illusion of a castle tall enough to joust with clouds. Bold sunlight splashes against walls where ancient stains meander down stone. Clumps of living green scruff have taken hold across the castle. The soles of my feet tingle with ancient energy that percolates from deep within the ground, echoes of paradise shattered by battles and conquests. I search for a private bench or path to ride out the possibility of an oncoming dream flash.

My mental traipse into the past is interrupted by a rowdy bunch of teen guys, all wearing orange t-shirts with the same school logo. They swarm us like a cloud of midges, killing the onset of my shift in reality.

Charlie breaks through the haze of Irish, ear-flicking boyos and their back-and-forth jibes to catch up to Colleen. "Here ya go, lassie," he says, holding the hoodie for her to shimmy into. His arms wrap around her from behind. "Warm?"

A few orange shirts mutter insults in Charlie's direction.

I nod at the retreating hoard. "I don't think they appreciate your go at the local accent."

Lagging behind the rest of the group, one of the orange shirts grunts at my statement. I'm tempted to blurt *What's your problem?* until I picture a look of disdain on the face of the hiring committee for representing

Kennard Park University by snarking at the locals. The grunter is older than the teens, probably the teacher who drew the short straw to chaperone the school trip. When I glare at the guy's back, guilt stings as if I'd been the recipient of one of the ear-flicks I just witnessed. He has a pronounced limp and looks miserable. I can't help but notice a very nice set of broad shoulders as he zips his peacock blue jacket then flips the collar up. I'm glad I didn't go smart ass American on him.

Colleen pats the hands that cradle her against a skinny chest. She and Charlie are a grasshopper canoodling a honeybee. "You sounded Scottish, Charlie. Put more *oi* into it."

"Oi, Coilleen."

She takes his proffered elbow, and they head toward the castle. Colleen may be going home with a bigger souvenir than she budgeted for. Since she's staff, not Kennard Park faculty, and Charlie's a fully formed adult postgrad, there's no impropriety to their budding attraction for me to waggle a finger at.

Charlie and Colleen linger at the bottom of a grass covered slope below the castle's entrance, waiting for me. There's no force on the planet that will get me to climb one hundred feet of twirling stairs to hang upside down off a roof and kiss the Blarney Stone. I focus on my map, and then point. "I'm heading over to the Rock Close then the Poison Garden. I'll meet you at the bus."

Colleen tugs Charlie up the incline to join the line waiting to enter the castle and calls over her shoulder. "Have fun. Catch me a fairy."

I continue on, forfeiting the gift of eloquence offered from smooching a rock. Bordering the path is a line of stalks, each topped with a mauve ball of petals that gives them the appearance of floral lollipops. Máthair would plunge into the foliage and grab cuttings. If she were walking next to me, she'd say, *"Flowers are the song of seasons."*

My heart thumps in my chest like the clapper of a church bell at the thought of my grandmother. Sorrow fades when I pass through the narrow stone passage leading to the area of the castle grounds called the Rock Close. Clumps of giant rhubarb leaves encroach on a wooden boardwalk. I need a basket of paint swatches to begin to name the myriad greens surrounding me. A waterfall breaks into five distinct streams and cascades through ivy and ferns to spill onto a puzzle of stones.

Along the path, shadow overpowers light for dominance in this primordial realm. Trees overhang the path in a protective canopy while exposed roots writhe and twist over rocks like ghostly remains of the snakes St. Patrick shooed off the island. The place has more of a dream flash vibe than real time. I check the farthest reaches of my sight, searching for the iridescent sheen that identifies my waking visions but find nothing.

To my right, a cluster of flesh-colored tree trunks bends and stretches toward the sky. What are they reaching for? The sun? Or maybe a fragment of time past. Beyond them is a plaque that reads:

"It is indeed a fairy scene, and I know of no place where I could sooner imagine those little elves holding their moon-light revelry."
Crofter Croker 1824

Am I in the presence of unexplained spirits? In the scant space between a gnarled trunk and the massive stone of a dolmen megalith intended to be the portal tomb to a different world, an industrious spider builds a web the size of a warrior's shield. Droplets of dew like diamond chips cling to threads.

I want to absorb the otherness of this place. Pushing my sleeve to the elbow, I move my arm into light and then shadow, testing the rise and dip of air temperature. Freckles on my arm shift from golden brown to dark amber when the sun can't reach them. Máthair tested for rain this way. When the difference was marked between sun and shadow, she knew clouds were coming. We'd open the slats in the greenhouse roof for plants to catch the rain.

Farther along the path, a collection of moss-covered stones called the Druid's Circle teases the air with subdued energy. I assume the countenance of a druid gliding through a place of power and mystery.

Go and ye will be found.

"Have I found what you wanted, Máthair?"

How will I know? Is this pull of nature and the past fighting the insurgence of a modern world her message—a world that doesn't appreciate her stories of Faeries and magic? The urge to return to my grandmother's greenhouse and get lost in one of her tales hits hard.

My hiking boots crunch on a gravel and dirt path as I leave the circle behind, keeping an eye out for grad students who may be in search of a fact or two I can provide. Stray leaves and twigs litter the ground before me in an artful collage. I wind my way to a sign marked *Druid's Cave*. Only echoes of sunshine touch this part of the Rock Close. The cave opening is black against stingy slate gray light, and I can't see inside. My hand goes to the charm on my necklace.

Strength.

Do I dare go in? At least it's grounded. No steps to climb. The heart of Ireland may be inside, waiting for me to sync the beats of my own heart to its rhythm. How can I walk past without at least a peek?

Máthair would want me to.

The crooked stone entrance wears a scraggly beard of ivy. The day darkens the closer I move toward the opening, and my nerve wobbles. Maybe just a step inside is enough to appease the Sidhe, the otherworld Máthair believed in. I lay a hand on the cool bulging rock forming the entrance slit and focus on the uneven ground so I don't trip.

It's silent here. Peaceful, not frightening. The lingering wisps of unease disappear, and I embrace the gloom. My mind feels clean and boundless. If I find a nice rocky perch in the cave, I'll sit for a moment to capture impressions of the Rock Close in my head to jot down later in my journal.

"You're too weak-kneed to climb to the top of the castle, but you'll plunge straight into the dwelling of spirits?"

My head snaps up. His voice is so close, I feel warm breath slither through the chill air. I backpedal, stumbling out of the cave's mouth straight into a puddle and bite my lip to keep from screaming. When I spin to escape the presence in the cave, a hand closes around my upper arm.

"Wait. I didn't mean to spook ya." It's the limping grunter with the great shoulders from the student group.

I pull free of his grasp. "No, just to insult me."

He's a few inches taller than me. This guy is the antithesis of grasshopper Charlie with a mop of nut-brown hair twisting into thin, springy curls. His solid frame suggests a strength barely hampered by the limp.

We lock gazes even though I can't see his eyes through the sunglasses he wears. He stares down his long, straight nose at me, assessing. I'd be insulted if I wasn't distracted by the sweet look of his rounded cheekbones and full lips nearly as mauve-colored as the lollipop plants.

I'm the first to break the staring contest. When I back away to put more distance between us, he scratches his neck as if those ringlets itch. "Watch out for roots." He points at the ground. The trunk next to the cave is a collection of thick ropy strands that rise to split into high branches as well as spilling across the ground in an unruly tangle.

I sidestep a gnarled tendril as he moves with me. It's beyond creepy to collide with a stranger, no matter how attractive, in a dark cave, who then decides to follow you. Not to mention, the guy wears sunglasses in a stretch of forest as dim as twilight.

"Going to give the castle another go then?" His mocking tone is maddening. The farther he sticks his nose in my business, the greater the sense I need to get away. He grunts. "Shame to come all this way and—"

"It's none of your business if I skip the castle. Leave me alone." I walk with purpose along the path, clueless where I'm headed. A stone with the profile of a witch makes me regret the direction I chose. I'm going deeper into moss-covered everything instead of the open grounds near the castle.

He catches up, limp and all. "American gal, your friends would be back that way." His accent draws me to this stranger despite the warning klaxons going off in my head. The sound of it reminds me of my grandmother singing or storytelling when her lilt rang with such clarity, I glimpsed a Máthair from the past. With a start, I remember someone else with a blend of old and new language.

Máthair's lawyer.

I whip out my map and pretend to plan a route. I don't want to think about Timothy Yew or talk to a rude Irish schoolteacher. "I'm not finished here." Thankfully, a few people are drifting our way, so I'm not alone in a possibly enchanted forest with the farthest thing from a prince I can imagine.

"Why bother with this castle if you skip the Blarney Stone?"

I shake the map with a crack. "Again, not your business. Please go away."

He picks at the curls covering his ears. Irritation colors his words. "It's biscuits to a bear stepping on Irish soil if you're not going to climb towers."

"Biscuits to a bear?" I want to slap a hand over my mouth at my accidental invitation to prolong this conversation.

He speaks slowly as if I'm the idiot. "A—waste—of—time."

I force myself to ignore his lovely accent and strong, unapologetically masculine jaw. "What's the local phrase for jerk?" I focus on the map and strut past him. Instead of leaving well enough alone, I turn back. "I didn't see you climbing the castle stairs either." Immediately, my mind flashes on his limp as my gaze falls to his leg. "I'm sorry. That was uncalled for." When I get the nerve to look at his face, I notice the deep dimple in a chin that tilts up instead of down.

He waves me off. "Whanker or *amadán* will do."

"What?"

"Or call me a jerk. It translates fine." I give a curt nod and attempt to leave again. Máthair dropped a lot of *amadán* bombs on people she labeled fools. I should have remembered the word. "But I prefer you be calling me Sion."

The weird phrasing intrigues me. Is he messing with the American gal? "Fine. Hey, Sion, quit following—"

He stops and cocks his head. "You said it right." Who knows if he might actually be looking straight at me through the sunglasses? "Most Amerrrricans say Shahhhhhn not Shun."

The condescending tone he uses on *Amerrrricans* tempts me to copy his students' head-flicking on him. I make a shooing motion instead. "Time to go back to your cave and wait for someone else to insult."

Still, he follows. "Fair enough, but you should bite down and get your round Amerrrrican ass up a tower or turret while you're here."

I step onto the wooden boardwalk leading out of the Rock Close and whirl on him. "Get your Irish ass away from me."

Charlie surges around a bend of giant ferns. "Whoa, buddy!" He points a string bean finger at Sion. "I heard what you said to Eala. Sod off."

I move shoulder-to-shoulder with Charlie and low-talk. "I believe sod off is an England thing."

Sion doesn't back off. He juts a chin at my protector. "No worras, you rawny bugger. I'm insult fluent in Irish, English, and Amerrrrican."

Charlie moves closer to Sion. I swear I smell the ozone of toxic masculinity wafting around Colleen's conquest. Charlie makes a low sound in his throat. Shit, less than a few hours in country, and I'm about to be responsible for an international incident.

"Let's go, Charlie. Sion can go back to his cave or lurk under the castle murder hole."

Sion laughs. The genuine warmth in the sound and curl of his lips softens me a little toward him. He tilts his head. "You've no need to kiss the stone, Eala, is it? You've already got a spicy gift of gab."

To my surprise, Jeremy Olk rounds the corner with Colleen. My new colleague throws a protective arm around my waist. "Everything all right, Eala?"

Sion hangs back, held in place by a trio of glares. Being pressed against Jeremy's body is as comforting as his poetry reading. The heat rippling through me has ideas beyond comfort. I lean into him. "Yeah. Just exploring."

Convinced I haven't been abducted by the Fair Folk, our team leader focuses on Sion. "I only agreed to take you on as a local guide, Mr. Loho, as a favor to a colleague of mine."

This would be a good time for Sion to lose the sunglasses and be a smidge contrite. Instead, he yanks at the bottom of his dark peacock padded jacket until it covers his jeans to the knees and lifts his chin.

Jeremy's posture goes rigid. He takes a step toward Sion, breaking our lovely side hug. "A gesture that can easily be rescinded."

Sion presses those rosy lips together as if caging his reply and then nods, curls bobbing. "Understood." Our newest trip mate has the good sense to exit down the boardwalk, sunglasses still on duty.

Jeremy Olk and Charlie move off to jabber over a sign marked *Seven Sisters* near a small circle of standing stones.

Colleen fusses over me. "When we told Professor Olk you'd gone to the Rock Close, he semi-freaked, practically yelling '*not the Fairy Glade,*' and bolted." Colleen fans her face. "Then I stressed, thinking the Fairy Glade was a place tourists get mugged."

"Relax, this isn't a sketch neighborhood in the city." I raise the map. "I did want to check out the Fairy Glade."

Doctor/Professor Olk's head snaps up. "Hey partner, ready to head to the bus?" He tosses me a smile.

Partner.

Oh, so many ways to interpret the word.

I peek over my map at Sion, who limps through the passage leading out of the Rock Close. I want to write him off as a sour apple, but he pokes my curiosity. Questions burn in my chest. Why was this local *amadán* so offended over my pass on kissing the Blarney Stone? What earthly difference does it make to him?

As we emerge from the Rock Close, my sight lingers on Sion's broad back and the fit of his jacket tapering to what looks like a trim waist.

It starts to sprinkle, and Sion disappears into his hood. We've almost caught up to him as we near the entrance pavilion. The breeze sends a few of his rogue curls dancing.

Máthair's voice cuts into my tumbling thoughts.

"Now that man is a song to be sung."

My grandmother may have embraced the benefit of the doubt for strangers, but I'm not her. Sion Loho is welcome to keep his distance, and I will do the same.

CHAPTER 5
THE SHEEHOGUE

Charlie carries Colleen's bulky travel backpack as the three of us stroll along a street in the postcard perfect village of Rowan Bend where our group stayed last night. I'm mesmerized by the variety of colors splashed across buildings. We pass façades of canary, teal, and blood orange. No matter the color of each wall, the trim around every window and door is shiny white. Some places we pass wear their vibrant coats of color from street level to the roof. Others shift to brick or stone above gaily painted ground-level floors.

Colleen chirps as we pass a pub called McClendon's. "That's where Professor Olk took us last night." She imitates Olk. "To soak in local flavor." She nudges Charlie. "Everyone was crazy friendly, right?"

"Aye, that they were," says Charlie, still working unsuccessfully on his Irish accent.

I skipped dinner to sleep and let Colleen cover local flavor for both of us. I've been sleeping a lot since I lost Máthair, and my life turned into a watermelon dropped from a rooftop.

"Gimme yours too," says Charlie, motioning to my backpack.

I'm afraid the added weight will snap his spine. "I'm good, thanks."

Colleen flits ahead of us to stop in front of a calendar-worthy storefront. "Here we are."

Two mullioned picture windows rest on square panels of dark cherry wood. Above the door is a forest green rectangle stretching from one side of the windows to the other with raised gold letters spelling out *A. Sidheóg*. Bricks rise above the sign past a single second-story dormer window overlooking the street. Curtains of ivy spread from roof to ground.

Colleen opens the door for a ladened Charlie onto a wide room more tavern than pub. I nearly trip on the uneven flagstone floor near the threshold. The stone floor covers the space from window to window and back to the bar. Off to the left, a more modern wood floor extends beyond what must have been the original square footage of the pub into a room filled with rows of long tables.

We add our packs to the rising mountain of luggage in a corner. Charlie pokes a toe at a neon orange backpack near the edge of the pile. "We'll look like a circus trekking to the campsite later."

"I hope midgers don't eat us alive," says Colleen, wrinkling her nose.

"Máthair said summer is when *midges* bite," I say, emphasizing the correct pronunciation of the winged nuisances. "Hopefully, they're still doing whatever midges do in the spring."

"Not keen on living rough this evening, ladies?" asks Charlie, draping an arm over each of our shoulders. He's a sweet guy, but this professor being on huggy terms with a grad student I've just met crosses a line for me. Huggy terms with a fellow professor though...

The rafters of the pub are full to bursting with memorabilia. There are vintage radios, a wagon wheel, enameled road signs, a bicycle, and even a single Wellington boot. It's a museum where the curator threw everything in the air and let items settle where they may. Behind the bar is an eclectic patchwork of mirrors hung together to make one giant looking glass. Above the line of non-matching stools, hang equally mismatched mini chandeliers that scatter yellow light across the top of the bar. Climbing the wall on either side of the mirrors are shelves sagging under rows of liquor bottles, interspersed with an old typewriter, black and white pictures of men in military uniforms, a violin, and sports trophies.

Colleen follows my gaze. "It's not exactly hoarding—"

"Ambiance," says Charlie. "History."

"Stories," I say, glancing at an old menu handwritten on a rectangle of slate. We're in the midst of a living scrapbook. Máthair once told me nothing is random in an Irish pub. Every old clock or war medal belongs there as a remembrance of patrons who contributed their own unique flavor to the place.

"You go to a pub for folks, Ella. Walkin' in the door is becomin' part of a family."

Colleen experienced that last night. My twinge of regret for missing a chance to hang out with Jeremy subsides when a stronger jolt reminds me even though I can handle facing a full lecture hall, a roomful of strangers in a social situation drowns me in anxiety. Mingling on this personal level lacks the invisible barrier teaching to the masses affords. One of the many reasons my initial instinct was to avoid the trip.

Our group crowds together at tables overflowing with food. My trip mates cram down slices of bacon or rashers as Máthair called them, tomatoes, mushrooms, sausage, beans, black pudding, and eggs like it's their last meal. The three of us tuck in at the end of a bench and fill our plates from heaping community platters. My goal is to connect with at least one new person every hour to build rapport with the group and hopefully earn some positive evals. Food is always a good conversation starter.

Charlie pops to his feet again before he's settled when one of his friends hails him. "I'll be right back, Flutterby." He kisses Colleen's hair.

I watch Charlie cross the room with his electron-level energy, and then raise an eyebrow. "Hair kissing already? Flutterby?"

Colleen's eyes get dewy as they follow Charlie. "We stayed up way too late last night and got slap happy. When he tried to call me butterfly, it came out wrong." Her face lights at the memory. "I haven't clicked this hard with anyone in...well ever. Maybe you won't be the only one finding a snuggle honey over here."

"A little more subtle on the matchmaking please. I'm a dignified faculty group leader."

"I can do subtle," she says with a grin.

I shovel a forkful of sausage and potatoes into my mouth, gearing up to smile supportively at the line-by-line recitation of Colleen and Charlie's evening when a figure in the doorway stops me mid-chew.

Morning sun backlights Sion Loho's hair. It's not all the nut brown I thought it to be yesterday at Blarney Castle. The color is merely a topcoat blanketing—

I clasp the scarf around my neck. The one Máthair made me for Christmas. Its brandied melon color matches the undertones of Sion's hair as if the yarn had been dyed to match. The autumn glory of his curls glistens and gleams like the reflection of an amber moon on the water. Lyrics from one of Máthair's folk songs come to me.

"While nature with ringlets his mild brow adorning,
His hair Cupid's bowstrings and roses his breath."

Even though she constantly hummed and sang her never-ending repertoire of old Irish songs, I'd only hear the notes of that particular song when she was alone, tending her garden. As her voice roamed across beds of beloved plants, her eyes would drift to the clouds and for those few moments she'd retreat into a memory kept all to herself. For all my adoptive grandmother shared, there were depths of a lifetime before me she locked away.

Like a tiny spark, the title of the song glows in my memory as I study Sion. *"Dear Irish Boy."*

Sion is ruggedly attractive overall with shadings of a gentler appeal: ringlets and bowstrings like the song. He's a contrast to Jeremy's more refined good looks.

The forkful of delicious breakfast heading into Colleen's mouth drops with a clatter onto her plate when she catches me watching Sion in the doorway.

"Are you nuts? That guy is dear Irish nothing."

I flush, realizing I spoke the song title aloud.

I concentrate on cutting my sausage into smaller bites. "It's the title of a song I was trying to remember." A song whose sweet sentiments definitely do not match the rude Irish man in the doorway.

Colleen's foot nudges me under the table none too gently. She nods toward the bar where Jeremy Olk sits on a stool, chatting up a rosy-cheeked, barrel-shaped man with a laugh loud enough to fill the room. "La, don't waste any of your attention on that rude wood chip when the personification of your dream man sits at the bar. Per your specifications, I might add. Complete with round professor glasses."

She's got a point. Staring at Sion is a waste of my time. My chest tightens. Then why is it hard to switch my gaze from this annoying temporary addition in my life to the man who has the potential to be someone interesting?

Looking at Colleen is a safe alternative. "La? That's where you landed on my name?"

"I'm not going to call you Owlie." She purses her lips and gives me a look of disapproval. "And you won't let me call you Ellie anymore."

I take a breath in and out. Ella O'Dwyer vanished with Máthair. I'd like to think they're together in *Tír na nÓg*, partaking in whatever Faeries do in the land of eternal youth. Eala Duir is the one left behind—again.

"Did you catch the red bow tie Professor Adorbs was wearing at dinner last night?" Colleen taps the back of my hand. "Look. He's actually got a red handkerchief sticking out of his jacket pocket." She gives her chest a quick pat over her heart. "Red, the color of love."

"Or blood." I blow out a breath. "You're too much."

"I'm just trying to keep you on track," she says, kissing my cheek.

I point my fork at her. "You may encourage, but not embarrass."

As I look at Jeremy, the idealized future I've always dreamed of pops into my head—a small life in an old house on the outskirts of a New England college town. My professor husband and I watch through the picture window of our kitchen nook as deer saunter through the backyard. After we finish breakfast tea and homemade biscuits, we don matching wool coats and plaid scarves to walk under crimson and gold leaves on our way to teach classes at the university. As a pair of PhDs, we'll call each other *doctor* as we hold gloved hands and swap anecdotes of student antics.

Colleen leans closer. "He's thirty-eight by the way. I asked him last night while he was asking me quite a few questions about you." She raises her finger. "No arguments. Who cares if he's a couple of years outside your ridiculously rigid dating range?"

I bite into a piece of toast.

Colleen shakes her head. "You act a hundred years older than you are anyway." She refocuses on Olk. "A meeting of the minds is ageless."

"What did you tell him about me?"

"Calm down. I gushed with finesse. I firmly believe if the attraction is going to stick, it should be organic."

Olk turns our way and smiles a greeting. Colleen waves and lowers her voice. "I'm just saying, if Charlie wasn't in the picture, Prof Olk would definitely be on my 'defile me in Ireland' list." She touches a finger to her bottom lip. "That bow mouth is perfect for kissing." Her head tilts to one side. "The upper lip is a little thin, but I'll bet he knows how to compensate."

Thankfully, Jeremy turns to the bar and sheds his jacket. He rolls up the sleeves of a scarlet and brown flannel button down, revealing wiry yet solid forearms. It appears Professor Sauce works out.

"Make that top of my 'defile me in Ireland' list," says Colleen.

"Your what, Flutter?" asks Charlie, sliding onto the bench next to her.

Colleen snuggles against his side. "My never mind." Her face squinches, changing from gooey to salty as Sion claims the seat across from Charlie to sit next to me. "There are plenty of seats in the other part of the pub," she says, tossing her head at an already crowded section of the room.

Sion chews on a twig sticking out the corner of his mouth as he gestures toward the bar. "This here's the mess hall. That way's the pub." He nods at the jolly fellow who chatted up Jeremy earlier. "Ole Robbie knocked out a wall and converted the other part of the old place into this soup kitchen for school groups such as yours." He nods approvingly. "Genius way to fill the tourist lulls when it's not St. Patrick's Day, Beltane, Samhain and the like." He leans his arm on the table and beckons us closer with a crook of his finger. "You want to see a real pub? I'll take you for a drop of drink." A distinct whiff of alcohol comes off the twig stuck in his mouth.

"You smell like a pub," says Colleen, wrinkling her nose.

Sion extracts the sliver of wood and waves it at her. "Whiskey on a stick. Best thing for toothache."

"Cut the guy some slack, Flutter. He's come to apologize."

I study the complex pattern of potatoes and eggs on my plate. Colleen *humphs*. "At your suggestion, I'll bet."

The table creaks when Sion presses his hands flat, leaning in. "Of my own accord."

I decide to join the conversation in the spirit of diluting Colleen's overprotective side. "It's actually me who owes Sion an apology."

Charlie and Colleen goggle-eye me. The only person not surprised is Sion. In fact, he doesn't meet my gaze at all, his focal point landing somewhere in the vicinity of my right ear. No sunglasses rest on his long straight nose this morning. Wavy bangs flop over his brows except where a stubborn curl sticks behind his ear, exposing a thin, V-shaped expanse of ruddy forehead. His lashes, a beautiful shade of burnt cinnamon mixed with cayenne, hood the glint of gemstone hazel eyes I can't seem to pull my gaze from.

I clear my throat. "Sion, that crack about you not climbing the castle was mean-spirited, and I'm sorry." He still won't engage me eye to eye, so I turn to Charlie and Colleen. "That's why you heard him being rude to me." I am willing to defend Sion Loho to atone for my lack of compassion. He can make peace with his own nasty comments.

"And I'm sorry for spooking you in the cave as well as the ample ass comment."

I'm tempted to put my hands on either side of his face and force him to look me in the eye while he apologizes. It's unnerving being talked around and not to.

"And then acting the maggot after."

"Ugh," says Colleen is disgust.

It's not the maggot reference that unsettles me. I've heard the phrase from Máthair plenty of times. A pang of grief knifes through me at the way Sion's accent so seamlessly matches Máthair's. The familiarity throws me off balance.

Sion is intent on the wood grain of the tabletop. "Pardon, Colleen. Acting the ass."

My eyes rest on the crown of his head. There's a single spot near the center where all those curls originate. Maybe I will give him a chance. The only thing he needs to do to legitimize the apology is raise his head and meet my gaze.

He doesn't.

The closest I get is an unfocused sideways glance. Not so *Dear Irish Boy* after all.

"I am sorry, Eala. I hope we can be easier with each other." There's a flicker more green than brown as he peeks through his lashes at my chin, but he's up and heading toward the bar before I say a word.

Uneasiness fills my stomach, and I can't take another bite. Eala sounds too comfortable on Sion Loho's lips.

Colleen's evil eye at Sion's retreating back could set a stone on fire. "If that creeper bothers you again, La, I'll clunk him in the head with a splintery shillelagh."

I nearly spit out my water with a laugh. "Splintery shillelagh? Are you channeling one of Máthair's Faerie stories?"

Charlie trails a finger along the side of Colleen's face. "You know, it's not unheard of for pub owners in Ireland to also be undertakers. One stop shopping for you, Flutter, murder and burial." He extracts a small paperback book from a pocket and thumps it on the table.

365 Things to Know About Ireland.

I squirm on the bench. It's going to be an ugly trip with Colleen plotting Sion's death the whole time. "We're stuck with him."

"Maybe Sion's got it right. We can tolerate anything with an assist from a twig of Irish whiskey," says Charlie, eyebrows dancing.

My appetite reasserts itself. I pick at the last of my potatoes, uncovering the ones with the thickest crusts of burned butter and herbs. "Maybe we can get a group discount on twig therapy."

A commotion at the bar cuts our chat short.

The rotund Irishman who chatted up Jeremy at the bar must be the "Ole Robbie" Sion referred to earlier. The man shoves Sion in the direction of a makeshift stage in the corner of the pub. "Up there with you, Sionny. Give the Yanks one of your stories."

Jeremy leaps off his stool to block Sion's path to the stage. Creases between his professorial eyebrows are lines of boiling tar. "Our itinerary calls for an authentic storyteller."

Robbie waves off Olk. "Sionny here is from down the way. He's got more stories under those curls than a cow's got milk at daybreak."

Before Jeremy's second offensive, Sion whispers to the pub owner who claps him on the back. I swear Sion's gaze fans over me as he fades toward the snug at the far end of the bar.

Máthair told me her late husband asked for her hand in a snug, the bitty room tucked away in the corner of a pub. He couldn't do it in the pub proper since in her day, it wasn't cool for women to stand and drink at the bar. How many fathers bargained their Irish lasses to husbands over a pint in a similar small private room?

A voice booms from the corner, sending waves of jollity over the crowd. Robbie's tone is a delicious butterscotch brandy to warm the insides. The owner sheds his publican apron to reveal a round belly forever destined to separate the buttons on his vest from their buttonholes.

My jeans press tight against my full belly as I wiggle my cell from a pocket to check our schedule. Sure enough, *Storyteller Robert Corrigan* is listed right after *authentic Irish breakfast*.

Robbie sweeps a hand across the benches of students. "*Dia duit*. That's how we say hello in Irish. Let's hear ya." He cups a hand around one ear.

As if singing the chorus of a song where not everyone bothered to memorize the lyrics, the room *Dia duits* him back.

Our storyteller drops his head into his hands. "Saint Patrick will send every snake back to Ireland with a greetin' like that. Give it another go. Dee-ah-hoich."

The second attempt is far from native. Hopefully, it's good enough to keep serpents off the island.

After pulling up a stool, Robert Corrigan points a finger at us. "It's not all leprechauns and pots of gold. Irish stories are dipped in darkness, but they do open a window into who we are, our wit, mystery, and dreams." His eyes dart to Sion and then back to the group.

Sion leans against the wall, arms crossed, his stare locked on the storyteller. Behind him, above forest green wainscoting, an oval of missing plaster reveals a brick wall nearly the same color as the undertones in his hair.

I'm jealous. I was raised on these stories too, but Sion gets to spend his life hearing them told and retold. All I have left are memories of cold winter nights and firelight from the hearth tickling the walls of our living room as my grandmother shared tales of magic salmon and the cost of bargaining with Faeries. Her stories eased me into dream flashes as flames took on shapes of characters to bring her narratives to life.

The audience erupts in laughter as our host dips his head, shooting a warning look across the room. "And that's why you never ask a cat a question. He might answer, and then your fortune is no better than curdled cream."

Charlie straddles the bench to gather Colleen in his arms. They ooze sweetness. For her sake, I hope the lightning bolt between them ignites passion instead of a scorch.

Robbie continues to toy with his audience. "Famines, war, invasion. Ireland's had its blows and bruises. Stories are the tie keeping us bound to this land with the promise—when we're at our most desperate, *Tír na nÓg* will answer."

A profound longing for Máthair slams a fist to my heart. Is there a window in *Tír na nÓg* where she can look out to see me?

I'm here like you asked, grandmother. I've come to your Ireland.

The story shifts to the somber tones of a prayer, recapturing my attention. "And a swan shall rise above the crest of the sea from the west, *Tír na nÓg's* messenger, beating mighty wings to chase shadow from the land of trapped souls."

Gentle breath warming my ear makes me jump. "Country folk here put great store into these myths." I'd been so inside the story, I missed Sion sidling back beside me. "Robbie's got the gift, doesn't he?"

I want to push him away and run, not from fear or dislike, but because his accent, his way of speaking, is too close to home. The timbre and the cadence of old-fashioned phrasing in his voice is so like Máthair's, I hunger for it. Dripped in darkness indeed.

When I glance across the table for an assist, Colleen and Charlie have vanished. I twist in my seat, scanning the pub for them.

"They've gone to give the snug a go."

I see two silhouettes melting into one behind the frosted glass of the snug. That explains Sion's reapproach.

"Robbie's gearin' up, love." Sion taps my shoulder, withdrawing his hand so quickly, it seems like it burns him to touch me. "Now the ole *seanchaí* will be serving tales of the Irish supernatural."

I start at the familiar word for storyteller. Máthair claimed it was her duty to be my *seanchaí* and teach me the lore of the Irish folk she swore I belonged to.

"He'll be asking for a Faerie shilling as payment for his yarns."

I turn my head a fraction to drink in more of Sion's accent. "Faerie shilling?"

His squarish hand with its stubby fingers helps itself to a piece of bacon off my plate. He gestures with the breakfast meat before popping it into his mouth while he whispers a story involving a coin gifted from a Faerie to a human that always returns to the mortal's pocket after being spent. Robert Corrigan tackles the same topic from the stage, but it's Sion's voice swirling around me. My eyes drift half-closed. I want to pull his words closer, tuck them inside my coat and savor the pool of comfort their sound brings me.

Find me.

An image of Máthair's ring bobs on the current of Sion's story. Maybe it's not a single thing or person I'm looking for but pieces of what I've lost with her absence. Could the melody of this man's words be one of them? If only there were a way to separate the voice from its owner.

When I don't respond, he nudges a shoulder against mine. "Do you believe me?"

I shrug.

"I'm guessing the way you push your lips out is not asking for a kiss."

My face heats from tepid to volcanic as an image of dotting a kiss on Sion's lips flashes through my mind uninvited. I address the table. "Believe a magic coin keeps popping back into your pocket? I give that the same credibility rating as a leprechaun's kettle of gold."

I can tell by his grunt he's put distance between us. The withdrawal of his voice and its warmth opens an unexpected hollow in the center of my chest. I'm struck with the odd feeling I've disappointed Sion for the second time in two days. First, for my refusal to climb Blarney Castle, and now for dissing his Faerie story. I hate that it leaves a bitter taste on my tongue. This guy is nothing to me, and I'm no more to him than an Amerrrrican with an ample ass who refused to climb a stone staircase and won't believe in shilling regeneration. I hear him muttering as he scratches the tabletop. The few words I pick out are not very generous, and it hits me that moments ago, I was actually enjoying the thaw between us.

When a leg slides next to mine on the bench, I nearly jump. Whipping around, I prepare to free Colleen's hands from around Sion's neck. Instead, I'm face-to-face with a fat braid trailing down one of our first-year grad student's back.

Daisy Kelly looks between Sion and me. "I hope I'm not interrupting, Ella." She rapidly fans the air in front of her mouth and giggles. "Sorry, I mean Owlie? I'm not used to your new name, Professor."

"Eala," says Sion with a derisive noise I'm rapidly learning is his equivalent of Máthair's, *For the sake of all that is holy.*

Daisy swivels to face Sion, ignoring his correction. "I'm Daisy. You're the local expert, right? Your name's Shahhhhhn?"

Before I realize what I'm doing, I release my own version of Sion's grunt. The scowl on his face will be a beaut after Daisy's slaughter of his name, but when I sneak a look, he's smiling like an *amadán*, steadily meeting her gaze. My self-worth drops to sub-basement level. He's never met my eyes. All I rate from him is frustration, forced apologies, and his damn mesmerizing voice.

"Sion Loho. Local Irishman at your service."

For fuck's sake, he might as well bow and kiss her hand. Since when did he become a ball of charm?

"I love the way you say Oirishman."

I swing my feet to the outside of the bench, giving the impression I'm riveted on Robert Corrigan and his stories.

Daisy slides away from me, which means she's closing in on Sion. "I've been sent over here on a mission. What's a Sidey hog?"

"Och!" says Sion loud enough to earn a few shushes. "Don't let Robbie be hearin' you butcher the name of his pub." The teasing in his voice makes me want to scream. For us, he downgrades the pub to a soup kitchen, but for Ms. Kelly's sake, it regains its quaint drinking establishment status.

"Shee-hogue's the way you'd say it." Sion's voice gets even more flirty as he stretches out the translation. "Lep-re-chaun." My breakfast sours in my gut. So, he can be nice. It's me who activates his thorns.

I loosen my scarf to release the heat building up on the back of my neck. I apologized for the crack I made yesterday, but apparently that's not enough to rate his kindness. It's as if he keeps testing me, and when I fail, he takes it personally.

What is wrong with me? I don't give a Sheehogue's ass if Snarly O'Nasty wants to ignore me and hook up with Daisy. They're both adults. Surely Olk vetted him before allowing Sion to join our study trip. Disappointment knocks despite my attempts to bat it away. If he stops talking to me, then I won't get to hear any more of his stories or echoes of Máthair in his voice that smooth the jagged edges of the ache of missing her.

"Leprechaun is so much cuter than Sheehogue," says Daisy.

The irrational bitter undercurrent of being robbed of Sion's attention snaps my restraint. "I'm sure we agree cute is what matters most in life." My hand flies to my mouth, but my comment sputters through the air like a balloon with a hole in it.

Sion gives a low hum. "Not a philosophy I'm familiar with, Mistress Eala. Socrates, is it?"

I'm too mortified by my outburst to properly gauge if Sion's tone is amused or mocking. So much for a thumbs-up eval from Daisy.

"And if I've one bit of advice for the lot of you," Robert Corrigan calls from the stage. "It's not to rush your days. Enjoy each one like the jewel it is."

I'm sure as hell rushing my day away from making a bigger fool of myself in front of Sion. I grab my purse and make a beeline for the toilets. Behind me, Daisy loud-whispers to her Irish conquest. No doubt I'm the subject matter and it's not complementary. She'll tell him about the flap I caused last quarter, insisting my lecture be moved from a top story classroom to the ground floor after I had an embarrassing vertigo episode. Sion will counter with my cowardice at Blarney Castle. I'm so happy my fear of heights supplies them with material to bond over.

Why, out of all the decent people in Ireland, does Sion Loho and his voice connect me with the wish on my grandmother's ring?

Find me.

What have I found, and how do I get rid of it?

CHAPTER 6
THE DOLL

Jeremy leads our group past a giant oak near the ruins of the old gate lodge at Charleville Castle. Thick branches sprout from blackened smudges on the truck and reach parallel to the ground, ending in twisted wooden fingers.

"The King Oak," he announces, nodding in deference to the old tree, "is believed to be the herald of doom. Each time lightning struck the tree, a member of the family living in the castle perished."

The gargantuan tree poised at the edge of Charleville Forest looks fully capable of housing otherworldly tenants bearing curses. I'm stationed by the side of good Professor Olk to create a unified visual impact while yielding the stage to his narrative. I startle with an undignified squeal when Charlie sneaks up behind me as the group disperses for the trek to the castle proper.

"Prepare yourself, Eala." He wields his Ireland book like a magician's silks. "We're heading into one of the most haunted places on Earth." He swirls around me. "Ectoplasmic presences await you on the castle staircase."

Colleen commandeers his book as we cross the threshold into Charleville Forest and reads. "...in the midst of the most ancient primordial oak woods." She peers over the top. "Beware. This is the haunting ground of Ireland's druids." Lowering the book, she smiles. "Right up your alley, La."

The wood is a tangle of trees, underbrush, and lacey clumps of white flowers. The canopy of leaves overhead is so thick, sunlight only passes through in green droplets. Next to the path, a fallen trunk is coated with velvety moss and festooned with runs of ivy sprouting between split wood grain.

I walk backward and flip my scarf at them. "If you start singing *Ghostbusters* again, I will disown you both. We're not out clubbing on Halloween."

My threat eggs Charlie on. He busts out twitchy shoulders to a solo of *Monster Mash*. Colleen adds her shimmy to his choreography.

I shake my head. "Confirmation that the two of you should form a Halloween classics cover band."

Jeremy's voice cuts through their distraction. I move closer to enjoy the traveling lecture. His passion on the subject of castles brings its own brand of magic.

"When the current owners first came to Charleville Castle, it was engulfed in a tangle of brambles and briars. Think Sleeping Beauty's Castle pre-princely kiss."

As we round the bend, a neo-Gothic beauty with towers and crenellations reveals itself. The sight of the grand edifice makes it easy to buy into a fairy tale. This place isn't beat up like Blarney Castle. Thick stone walls wear a scumble of grays sprinkled with peppery flecks. The castle's two mismatched towers rise into a powder blue sky. The pair are fashioned like chess pieces, one the queen and the other her king. A knight in full armor chasing a dragon would fit right in here.

The dreamy quality of Jeremy Olk's voice drifts like mist over the group as the great glass windows above Charleville Castle's front entrance sparkle in the sun. On either side of the door are what appear to be crosses cut into the stone itself.

Daisy Kelly's voice intrudes on my wonder. She hangs all over Sion, babbling. "That show with psychics and paranormal investigators who swear Charleville is infested with spirits. Absurd of course."

The smile sitting on his face as he indulges her ranting congeals breakfast into a lump at the bottom of my stomach. I turn away, agitated at myself for letting their prattle bother me.

The sun disappears behind a cloud, sending morning into faux twilight. The gauzy feel of shifting reality settles around me. Figures lose their edges, melting into shapeless gray smudges. There's a muffled roar from the stone lion next to the path. Up ahead, slate-colored fog seeps from between the hewn rocks of the castle as I stumble into the familiar haze of a dream flash. The fortress shifts from the home of princesses to the domain of original Grimm's fairy tales with eye gouging and horse heads nailed over doorways. Only one figure maintains its definition in my altered world—Sion.

Breezes scratch their way through the surrounding oaks, moaning, *"Pierce. Tear. Rip."* The crosses beside the castle door reveal themselves to be arrow loops as a feathered shaft zips through the murk toward Sion's skull. Around him, bursts of firelight the size of my thumb incinerate the arrow before it catches him.

Clouds pass by the sun, stealing my dream flash with them. Charleville Castle resumes its romantic visage. A calico cat rubs against my leg, and I bite my lip to chase away the dark edges of my living dream.

An arrow to Sion's head?

I scoff. Harsh punishment from my subconscious for the crime of being a smart ass and going full flirt with Daisy. I'm waxing way too overdramatic about this stray dog tagging along on our trip after one story and his alluring voice. Who needs a local "expert" anyway when we have the eloquence of Jeremy Olk? I hang back to let Sion and Daisy get ahead of me, allotting exactly two minutes to get over myself.

The whine of a saw is so out of place, it's almost comical. A couple of guys carry armloads of boards around the far corner of the castle. If not for the tool belts, I'd mistake them as part of our group.

Jeremy's hand on my shoulder startles me. I flush, hoping he doesn't notice. I'd like that hand to slide down my arm until our fingers twine.

He slashes the air with his free arm, brandishing an invisible sword. "I'd love to have been the knight who vanquished legions of thorns to bring this castle back into the light."

I'm not the only one here with a fertile imagination. Oh, the things a pair of active imaginations might concoct after a night at the pub. What am I thinking? Hooking up with Jeremy on the trip isn't professional. Maybe when we're in Kennard Park, and I'm the department's newest tenure-track professor…Even if, fortune forbid, I'm still an adjunct, professorial romance is my turn on.

Jeremy nods to the far right of the castle where sawhorses are set up next to a couple of pickup trucks. "Those folks are a team of volunteers working on restoration." His gaze climbs the castle wall. "How marvelous to use your hands and bring the past to life."

His reverie is interrupted by a woman with a clipboard calling our names near the entrance. With a wink, he's off to connect with our hostess, Samantha. I follow and introduce myself to the woman dressed in a black cotton shift with green and gold Celtic knots embroidered around the neckline.

"Professors, your group is very welcome to Charleville Castle," she says with a sweep of her arm, inviting us in.

Jeremy and I cross the threshold. I wonder if his friends call him Jerry or Jer. The rest of our party follows us, a line of baby ducks waddling after their mother.

The moment I step into the castle, a wave of freezing air hits me. Sion and the students shuffle past me, unaffected by the drop in temperature. It feels as if I've been turned inside out and dipped in a tub of ice. I shiver, teeth chattering. The sensation of invisible eyes watching me from dark corners makes the chill even worse. I wrap the scarf tighter around my neck and shove both hands in the pockets of my navy pea coat. Zero relief. It's so cold, I'm surprised puffs of my breath aren't hanging in the air.

"La, are you okay?" Colleen crooks an arm around my elbow. "You're shaking."

Sion whips around to stare. His gaze hovers between my chin and neck. Why won't the ass look me in the eye? It's getting creepy.

I lean into Colleen's warmth. "Aren't you freezing?"

She narrows her eyes. "It's warmer in here than outside."

As we take a few steps deeper into the castle to the foot of the main staircase, the arctic blast disappears with ear-popping speed. "I must have walked through a draft."

Colleen rubs my arms. "I hope the chills don't mean you're getting sick."

Samantha waves a hand along the stairs. "Up you go." A coal black cat weaves between her feet, nearly tripping her. "I'll not feed you beast, even if you are the devil." She nudges the cat out of the way and grins at us. "Any strange noises you hear—cats."

Framed in an archway on the second floor, History Buff Olk gestures with a flourish at the ceiling inside the double doors. As soon as Colleen, Charlie, and I join him in the long room, I see what the fuss is about. The expanse above us could be a wedding cake covered in lace. A pattern of huge upside-down cones flows the length of the room. Scallops and floral details radiate from the center of each point. I'm sure if I could reach the ceiling, I'd come away with a huge dollop of ivory buttercream frosting on my finger.

Jeremy, Jerry, or Jer Olk's tone shifts from admiring to giddy. "The fan vault design creates an acoustical environment that's pure heaven." He practically skips halfway down the length of the room. "Do you hear?" he says in a low voice that reaches my ears as if he were standing next to me. "No amplification necessary. I've picked this room to introduce you to the ghosts of Charleville Castle."

Colleen's previous moniker of Professor Adorbs does fit him nicely.

As we gather round, I notice Sion peel away from the group and head to the far end of the room where a quartet of musicians is setting up on a makeshift stage that's far from historically accurate. They greet him with embraces and slaps on the back.

I check my schedule, *Folk music at Charleville Castle*. Another tour joins us in the room, gravitating to the band as Jeremy starts in on a ghost story. Light knifes through the window, giving his cheekbones and chin a bladelike quality, his little boy look from the plane gone. He's pulled off his glasses, waving them through the air for emphasis.

Before he can finish his story, the wail of a violin drowns him out. Pipes join in and rollicking Irish music fills the ballroom. The volunteers, a few still in tool belts, stream through the door to enjoy the show.

Jeremy isn't happy his storytelling is cut short as music trumps ghost tales. He scratches the stubble on his chin, humming a rhythm that does not match the song bouncing around the fan-vaulted chamber. I move closer, planning to lean shoulder-to-shoulder with him and whisper encouragement that his lecture is postponed not overshadowed, but stop dead when a familiar voice joins the melody.

Sion.

Our trip add-on sings from the stage. His voice as gorgeous and rich as a salted caramel truffle fills the room. Even though he's twenty feet away, I hear him as clearly as if he were crooning softly in my ear.

Only to me.

So lovely.

"Put off that mask of burning gold
with emerald eyes.
'O no, my dear, you make so bold
To find if hearts be wild and wise,
And yet not cold."

I know these words. It's not a song, or at least it didn't start out that way. It's a poem by Yeats. Máthair adored Yeats. His words were as much a part of our home as my grandmother's quilts. Which one is this? Mask of burning gold? *The Mask*—That's it. Burning gold like the tiny ring around the green in Máthair's eyes.

I'm not alone in being drawn to Sion's voice. There isn't a single sound in the room apart from the music and the singer.

"I would but find what's there to find,
Love or deceit.
It was the mask engaged your mind,
And after set your heart to beat,
Not what's behind."

We're all prisoners to Yeats and Sion Loho. Their grip is silky, yet unrelenting. I'm afraid to move, as if a single blink of my eye or step will break the spell.

"But lest you are my enemy,
I must enquire.
Oh no, my dear, let all that be;

What matter, so there is but fire
In you, in me."

Even though the musicians have stopped playing, the notes refuse to die. They linger in the tracery above us before sliding into reluctant silence. No one applauds at the end of the song. Sion's head lowers in reverence to the essence of magic he's sent to every corner of the room.

The crack of Olk's hands coming together is the lightning that spoils a sunset. There's a stitch of disappointment in my chest. I want to continue to float in a song, weaving Máthair's spirit into every note.

Jeremy wears a look of pure disgust. This time, the chill in my blood isn't from a weird pocket of cold air. His expression leaves no wiggle room for misinterpretation. Jeremy Olk detests Sion Loho.

The room turns battlefield as Sion stares pointedly at Jeremy while the group launches into the intro of their next song. When Sion joins in, his voice spirals through the room until it collides with me on a single word.

Eala.

Sion sings my name. Our gazes lock across the room as his voice grows more challenging. *"An Eala Bán."*

The white swan.

Eala.

Sion sings a song with the name that now belongs to me. A name that sounds as if it belongs on his lips. Emotions and memories smash and collide with one another. Máthair. Ella O'Dwyer. My greenhouse in the sky.

All gone.

With every eye focused on the musicians, no one, not even Jeremy, notices me rush from the room and away from the beauty and memories in Sion's voice. The words of the song about a man pursuing his swan trail after me.

I am being pursued by the ghost of a life lost to me. Pursued in the way Sion's lovely voice reminds me of Máthair's, reducing me to a colossal brew of sadness, confusion, and the uncertainty of my life if I don't land the tenure-track position. Adjuncts live a term-to-term life, hoping to snag a class or two each quarter with no guarantee. I crave permanence.

Visitors to the castle have been drawn to the music. I'm alone in the dim upstairs hall with no one to ask if I'm okay. How can I be okay? There's no such thing as okay anymore. Where's my simple? My small? My safe? A few weeks ago, I thought a stupid DNA test would give me a foundation. Now, I'm thousands of miles across the sea with a new name, floundering in a future with crepe paper guideposts.

I come to an open door. I'll escape inside this room until my misery sloshes its way back to some measure of composure.

To my surprise, the room boasts a grand wooden stairway curving up several stories. The wall beside it is ornately carved. A padded rope between the wall and banister warns me not to climb, so I drop onto the bottom step. Each spindle supporting the sweeping handrail forms a mini-Gothic arch. Steps rise to a landing draped in shadow. I hug the closest spindle and hum one of Máthair's lullabies in an attempt to stave off this feeling of breaking into fractals.

If I lose the job, how can I go on at Kennard Park and face the humiliation of rejection? Maybe I should stay here in Ireland. There are plenty of small towns to mimic the security of Kennard Park. Celtic studies here is simply living. Did my grandmother intend Ireland to be my new reality? Does this island, instead of the one I was raised on, hold claim to my identity?

Teacht orm.

A high, squeaky voice breaks my concentration. Its Irish accent is as light as the draft curling up the staircase. "Did you lose your dolly too?" A little girl, no more than eight, skips down the last few stairs and ducks under the rope to sit beside me. Her hair is smoothed straight against her head until it melts into chocolate ringlets falling over lace-covered shoulders. She's dressed in what Máthair would call "Sunday best." Smudges of dust on the front of her skirt hint she's been into mischief, climbing stairs where she doesn't belong.

"No. My dolls are at home." I flash on the boxes in the apartment storage locker that holds my past life. Inside one is my rag doll, Molly, that Máthair made from my favorite baby blanket. I'd snuggled with her every night since kindergarten. I wish Miss Molly were with me so I could bury my face in her yellow plaid dress and suss out my life.

The girl rests her chin on chubby fists, a colossal pout twists rosebud lips into an adorable circle. "My dolly fell down the stairs. I can't find her."

I'm tempted to use my teacher voice and say that's what you get for poking around by yourself, but instead, I walk to the doorway, doing a quick scan for frantic parents. No one seems to be on the hunt for a stray kid. "Where are your grownups?"

When the girl flings her arm toward the music, ringlets bounce. "I want my dolly."

I stand and offer my hand before she can dart away. "How about I help you find her, and then I'll take you to your parents?"

She jumps up and dances from foot to foot before taking my hand. Her fingers are skinny and insubstantial. I can barely grasp them. With her other hand, she points under the stairs. "There she is."

A doll is sprawled behind the curve of the bottom step. Its curly hair and dress match the girl's. Painted lips on a delicate porcelain face smile at me. Dolly is one lucky gal surviving a plummet over the banister intact.

As I stoop to retrieve the toy, the girl bolts out the door. "Wait, honey."

By the time I give chase, she's history. Thank goodness I'm wrangling grad students and not kidlets. The girl probably found another hiding place to finish soiling her frilly dress. I turn to set Dolly on the step before I go report the wild child to our guide, Samantha.

"You call me rude, at least I didn't run out on a fellow's perform—"

Sion startles me so badly; I grab my heart to keep it from bursting through my jacket. His approaching footsteps had been as silent as dust motes floating in the shaft of light cutting in from the window.

Instead of finishing his reprimand for my less than graceful exit at the height of his solo, Sion Loho stands dumbstruck, gaping open-mouthed at the doll in my hand. When I follow his stare to see what's flipping him out, my knees give way, and I drop hard onto the bottom step.

In my hand, a jagged circle of broken porcelain is all that's left of the doll's face.

CHAPTER 7
THE FAERIE RING

Colleen tugs so hard on my sleeve as we trudge up the grassy hillside, I nearly lose my footing. "What did it feel like when the ghost girl walked through you?"

Charlie jumps in. "Was her voice like...oooooo lady help me find my doll?"

"You're supposed to be a scholar, Charlie." Curse, Sion Loho. I'm sure he's blurted his ridiculous ghost story to every person on the tour. The ass is supposed to be our local expert not the resident bullshitter. "I did not see the ghost of Little Harriett. It was a kid causing her parents grief."

"Is this the girl you saw?" Charlie shoves *365 Things to Know About Ireland* in my face to show me a portrait of Little Harriet. Smacking the book away doesn't deter him as he reads. "*At a midsummer party in 1861, Harriett, youngest daughter of the third Earl of Charleville, fell from the top of a stairway to her death. This added a heartbreaking link to the chain of untimely deaths in the Howard-Bury family. Is Charleville Castle cursed? Decide for yourself.*"

Charlie's sporting the brown tweed flat cap Colleen begged him to buy in Rowan Bend. The stiff brim shades his eyebrows. I have an urge to toss him a couple of coppers for a newspaper hot off the press.

Colleen taps Little Harriet's picture. "Today, she haunts the castle with her new friend, Eala."

Exasperated, I power past them up the steep hill on the way to the campsite. Truthfully, I'm hiding a bone-deep fright. The photo confirms the girl I saw in her frilly frock and ringlets at Charleville Castle could play Little Harriett in the movie.

I attempt to train wisps of hair out of my eyes as I follow a line of fence posts made from skinny tree trunks. Rusting strands of barbed wire loop from the top of one off-kilter post to the next. A stone's throw away, loosely woven sheets of metal fencing separate rolling fields into sections. A determined cow or sheep would not consider the flimsy excuse for a fence alongside me as a challenge, but it certainly adds character to the landscape.

I nearly turn an ankle misjudging one clot of the wild grasses that spread across spongy ground. Off to my right, a battered silver pickup bounces along a lane parallel to the fence. Our travel backpacks get a free ride to the campsite. I don't mind the hike. The air is crisp with the perfect amount of moisture to make my skin happy.

Colleen catches up, dancing backward in front of me. "Professor Jeremy says we're having a Beltane bonfire tonight."

"Beltane's four days away."

She waves a dismissive hand. "We're pre-celebrating since we'll be in Dublin on the actual night."

Charlie grabs Colleen's hand. "Hey Flutter, let's call fire spirits to yon Faerie hill." They hurry up the last bit of slope.

Together, the two are such a charm generator, I expect matching sparkle trails to burst from their asses.

A pair of women grad students from the Midwest catch up to me. "Professor O'Dwyer, were you purposefully looking for the ghost of Little Harriett or did she find you?" asks the one with a messy bun in a puffer jacket.

"Please, call me Eala, and I'd rather answer your questions about the *Daoine Sidhe* and their blood magic than a ridiculous ghost rumor."

The two look chastened. "Sorry to bother you," says the one who questioned me.

Apparently, my tone comes off as less than friendly. "No, it's fine. I'm a jet-lagged grump."

Messy bun manages a forced smile. "Yeah, long day. See you at the bonfire."

I attempt a breezy, happy face. "It should be fun."

They pick up speed to pass me. So much for my stab at scoring a new friend every hour. I'll make nice with that pair later to salvage a decent eval from them at tour's end.

As I reach the crest of the rise, a circle of megalithic stones looms before the fading sun like crooked black teeth. Some slabs are as tall and wide as a door. Others are thinner, leaning at wonky angles. Stubby boulders round out Charlie's yon Faerie hill.

My feet root in soft ground. The current of students heading for the hilltop breaks around me as I stare at the circle. Máthair had great reverence for standing stones and any other remnant of druid mystery. I twist the ring on my finger and face my second stone circle in two days.

"They're a sham."

I jump at Sion's voice behind me. Does he get off on making me flinch?

When he moves next to me, I lower my voice. "I don't appreciate you spinning crap about what happened to me at Charleville Castle." His loose lips especially stung since Sion was the one who sat next to me on the steps, listening to me babble about the kid and the broken doll until Jeremy came looking for me.

He lays a hand on my sleeve. "I'd not do such a thing to you."

There's an earnestness in his expression that makes me want to believe him. "Who's doing it then?"

He nods up the hill. "The one feeking your friend every chance he gets."

"Whoa. They're not—" I stop abruptly and have to grab his arm to keep from tripping.

His other arm slips around my back, and I appreciate the firmness of his grip steadying me. "Feeking...kissing."

I relax. "It sounded a bit too close to...never mind." A bit too close to what they'll probably be doing before the end of the trip. I don't pull away. "So Charlie's the blabber?"

"None other."

We linger in the half embrace. I lift my chin, willing him to raise his sunglasses so I can get another glimpse of those captivating eyes. Sadly, those eyes are trained on the hilltop.

"Sorry to say there's no magic, ley line, or Faerie path in these parts. Bobby Corrigan and good Farmer McKean hauled those stones here for tourist groups. That's the truth of it." He chuckles as my eyes widen. "Did I smash your plan of passin' through a stone to fall into the burly arms of a kilted medieval Irish clansman?"

I snort and ease away from him. "Yes. Exactly what I planned, right after I pop a Faerie shilling into my pocket and tuck the ghost girl in with a bedtime story."

Stripes of persimmon and flame from the dying daylight reflect off Sion's sunglasses. It reminds me of an abstract painting at the Met. He's alone. No Daisy Kelly attached to his hip. He limps past me but stops, turning back when I don't follow.

"Is this where I leave you?" The corners of his lips sneak up. The resulting dimples distract me from answering as he backtracks to where I stand. "Corrigan and McKean started a right lucrative tour group racket," he says, scratching his neck where the bottom of his floppy curls swish against skin. Sion spreads his arms wide. "Authentic Irish Breakfast, pub storytelling, and a bonfire night in a magic stone circle. Och, don't get more Irish than that." He checks to make sure his hair is covering the tips of his ears as he gazes at the stones. "Brilliant."

One of Máthair's stories pops into my head. A farmer insisted on building his house on a path used by the Faeries. Nearby neighbors warned him not to build there, but he ignored them. The first night in the new house, he woke to a hundred tiny teeth gnawing at the wooden frame holding up the roof. Before the moon rose, the farmer was buried under the shambles of thatch and splinters from his chewed-down house. He took the hint and skedaddled. The next morning, a circle of sunbeams broke through the clouds to land on a nearby hill. The farmer followed the light and built his new farmhouse in that very spot, this time off the Faerie path. The Good People, or Fair Folk as Máthair called the Faeries, never bothered him again.

"To the stones with you, Eala," says Sion and sets off again. "I'll shoo off any Cluricaunes lurking here abouts."

The vision of him in a slap fight with the icky version of a leprechaun almost makes me laugh. I fight the urge to run ahead and adjust my pace to his limp. He's being pleasant, so I return the favor. I prefer this Sion. "If a stumpy little tree man with a bad attitude jumps out at me, I'll let you play hero."

Like I've flipped a switch, Sion's sharp edges reappear. "If it's a hero you're looking for, best adjust your expectations." With a grumble, he stuffs hands in pockets and walks away.

I frown, watching him practically stomp off and wonder what the hell I said this time to curdle his mood.

Our group gathers at the far end of the stone circle. Not far beyond the flat ground of our campsite is another rise with a line of trees broken by a trailhead leading into the woods. In the distance, a haunted tree if ever I saw one marks the edge of the forest. Its trunk looks like a collection of knuckle bones glued onto a cylinder. There's a human-sized triangle crevice at its base plugged with a boulder.

The sky shifts to slate gray, holding off night a few moments longer. At the bottom of the hill, the lights of Rowan Bend glow liquid amber.

Jeremy Olk stands in front of the tallest stone addressing the group. The low crackle of the fake Beltane bonfire sends his shadow flickering across the granite surface. His features soften into the boyish contours I glimpsed on the plane. It's nice to have this version of him back instead of the grouch from Charleville Castle.

I join Colleen and Charlie, but Sion hangs at the outskirts of the group, scratching his neck as he listens to the presentation.

"Beltane means bright fire," says Olk to the group. "It heralds the onset of the light half of the Celtic year." He gestures to a pile of cardboard boxes next to the base of a rock shaped like an oversized gravestone. "We've got hawthorn, garlands, berries, and—" He reaches into the closest open box to pull out a strand of Christmas lights. "Illumination."

Coils of orange extension cords lay on the ground beside the boxes. I didn't expect living rough to include a power source.

The stone decorating contest confirms Sion's point about this venue catering to tourists. Real standing stones don't need twinkle lights. Early Beltane and fru fru as Máthair calls gaudy décor, on a Faerie ring, fake or not, could be asking for trouble.

The scholar's eyes sparkle. "We'll dance like druids in the firelight." His excitement would be contagious if the specter of my grandmother shaking her head over the potential irreverence of this situation didn't hound me. "The Veil is thin near Beltane, my friends." Olk's voice gets very quiet. "Who knows what might pass through the barrier between worlds to join our festivities?"

He believes. I see it in his eyes. The thought is as potent as a slap in the face. Like Máthair, this man's life is devoted to the past. He accepts the truth hidden in the stories, darkness, the power of the unseen, and the fantastic. Jeremy may put a nonchalant spin on it, but such beliefs are the foundation of one's being. It certainly was for my grandmother. I imagine invisible tendrils of Olk essence reaching down through moss to nest within the soul of the land. It's land that makes the people. This land produced Jeremy Olk's kin, Máthair, and possibly me.

I imagine sitting in front of a cozier fire with him, his voice sliding over my skin to leave a trail of goosebumps for him to kiss away.

A memory of Máthair's voice floats over me. *"Faith is to believe what we do not see, and the reward of this faith is to see what we believe."*

"Saint Augustine," I whisper in the direction of the forest and bow my head for a moment, giving quiet thanks to the man and his words that meant so much to my grandmother.

Warmth spreads through me. Not from the fire but from surety I am on the path to find what Martha O'Dwyer, my Máthair, wanted me to.

Olk's fervor competes with the rising bonfire for intensity. He leans conspiratorially toward his audience and pitches his voice lower. "Stay within the stones. Don't let the keen of a Banshee lure you to the woods."

From the shadow between the stones farthest from our storyteller's pulpit, Sion's grunt leaks into the night. Luckily Jeremy misses it, or Sion might be bidding his tenuous spot as the local talent goodbye.

Farmer McKean joins Olk to point out the mound of sleeping bags and pads for our use under the stars. "Watch for foxes. They'll bark and nip at ya but not cause harm unless you're mallet-headed enough to corner 'em.

Never forget their red coats are the color of the devil hisself." There's a girly squeal from someone not too keen on foxes or devils. "The fiends sneak out of the woods to steal any food ya got stashed in your packs." He sweeps an arm at the road. "We've got safe boxes in the back of the truck to stow your goodies for the night." My stash of peanut power bars doesn't seem likely fox fare, so I keep them in my pack.

Charlie and Colleen settle sleeping bags at the edge of the general throng. Loneliness prickles my insides. I'm happy for Colleen. By all appearances and compatible hyperactivity, Charlie could very well be her soulmate.

"Here La," calls Colleen and motions to an empty space between her and the next closest camper. My brief pity party escapes with the embers leaping out of the now substantial bonfire. Máthair would say the tiny bursts are souls on their way to the afterlife. I watch one cinder fighting to stay lit as it climbs as high as the treetops. Sadness hits me when it loses its battle and turns to ash.

I grab a sleeping bag and pad from the pile and give both a discreet sniff, hoping Farmer McKean is conscientious about his laundering between tour groups. Thank goodness, I catch a whiff of flowers instead of the previous occupant's sweat. Laying my bag in the vicinity of Colleen's, I feel like an intruder being this close to where my best friend will likely be doing more than sleeping tonight. Maybe I should find a spot closer to Jeremy.

Once the outdoor dorm is established a safe distance from the bonfire, frenzy ensues as the group digs into the boxes of decorations. I hang back to bear witness to the melee. The poor unenchanted stones take on the guise of a post-holiday sale aisle at Gerald's Hardware in Hell's Kitchen, Máthair's favorite place to buy gardening supplies.

Next to foxproof boxes in the bed of the truck, a boom box held together with silver duct tape comes alive with Irish folk music. Really awful attempts at step dancing break out around the bonfire while others writhe and circle in the American version of druid partying. Firelight and smoke add surreal brushstrokes to the dancers.

I glance around for Sion to enjoy his inevitable disgust for this sham of a Beltane soiree. Maybe he's using the frivolity as an opportunity to clock behind-the-stones time with Daisy Kelly. I spot her weaving through the crowd on the hunt too, but neither of us achieves success. Sion's probably slipped back to The Sheehogue to replenish his supply of whisky-soaked twigs.

"I'm glad you ditched the creeper," says Colleen as she squeezes my shoulders. "Dance with me, La." She drags me into the circle of bodies worshipping the fire.

I indulge her by busting out a few steps of the jig Máthair and I used to do in silly moments. "No, Colleen. Heel, cross in front, toe." I demonstrate and soon we're jigging so fine, the Faeries could learn a thing or two from a pair of Irish American women.

It's fun until too many people take notice. I ease away from the main circle and let Colleen, our fearless trip planner, take center stage. The fire sets her auburn streaks ablaze as she laughs and dances. My friend is the May Queen, a Beltane princess who showers her audience with pure delight. A Faerie spirit indeed.

In my PhD dissertation, I'd mentioned myths are truths subjugated to untruths to keep people from being scared to death of what their world is truly made of. Do I believe myths and stories are constructs of reality or reality itself? I convinced Sion easily enough that I thought the supernatural was a load of dung, but St. Augustine and his unseen also tug at my heart. Layers real and unreal, myth and truth, seen and unseen, dance through my head.

The surreal sense of a dream flash weaves its cocoon around me. The night is coated with the sheen of my imagination. A Pooka, the coal black demon horse with eyes of burning sulphur, rips the fence apart with its teeth to burst into the stone circle. Instead of bewitching a victim to ride upon its back only to be thrown to a neck-breaking end, the Pooka bows before Colleen. She caresses its tangled mane into a sleek wave and gallops her conquest into the clouds, their shadow crossing a full moon.

Realization that the true waxing moon in the sky no more than three quarters full coupled with fatigue from the jam-packed day chases away my vision of myth personified. This phase of nature's night light is calming. Máthair always credited waxing in a moon cycle with clarity of intention or goals.

Find me.

I'm looking, Grandmother.

My body shivers as I slip away to the sleeping bags outside the reach of the bonfire. No one calls me back. It's so strange a thing as mighty as a bonfire has a finite end to its influence. Two steps closer and I'd return to its warmth, but here, beyond the sphere of illumination, chill is master. With distance, the dancers' silhouettes are primal spirits. I understand how a real Beltane bonfire inspires prophecy and convinces even the greatest skeptic Cluricaunes, Pookas, and Banshees do lurk in shadows.

At the moment, if a Banshee felt inclined to lend me her wool cape, I'd take it as long as she kept her wailing to herself. I wish I had a thermos of hot tea inside my pack instead of a half-drunk water bottle, but it'll do. Jigging works up a thirst. My eyes adjust from blazing firelight to darkness, and I find my nest.

When I reach for my backpack, it appears to wiggle away. I'm about to chalk up the phenomenon to the wavering of distant fire when the cutest little fox pokes its head over the top of my pack. Every ounce of its preciousness disappears when the damn beast digs back in and comes out with my cloth bag of peanut bars in its mouth.

"Hey, you. Drop it." There are long stretches between meals on this trip, and damn if I'll surrender my snacks without a fight. I probably shouldn't confront a wild animal, but it's not any bigger than a poodle. The critter's face wears neither fear nor shock but satisfaction. The red-coated fiend turns tail and trots toward the woods. Damn fox isn't afraid. It could be one of the squirrels in Central Park who've figured the cuter they are, the more goodies they score.

I'm not sacrificing my peanut bars to an oversized cat. If I can spook it before it gets too far, hopefully it'll drop my bag. I kick at the ground around my sleeping bag, hoping to find a rock or clump of sod to throw at it. Nothing. I grab a flashlight from the outside pocket of my pack. As long as I avoid getting close enough for the wee bastard to bite me, game on. With the mighty beacon from my double A battery flashlight and a war cry, I take off at a run after the furry nuisance.

CHAPTER 8
THE FOX

I pursue the bugger through the small field beyond the stones. Thin trees pop up on either side of a path more fit for cows than hikers as we near the forest proper. The knuckle oak I noticed earlier squats next to a pair of rowan trees whose high branches touch, framing an entrance to the woods. The fox slows, twisting a pointy muzzle in my direction to check if I'm still following.

"Oh, I'm coming for you, devil!" I call out and fly forward in an attempt to spook it into dropping my peanut bars.

No such luck. It flicks a fluffy tail until it stands straight and then lopes between the rowan trees.

I skid to a stop at the threshold of the forest. My panting has more to do with nerves at the thought of going into the woods than being winded. Not far off, the bonfire blazes. This is a risk. The very thing I spend my life avoiding.

The first star pierces the mist above me. These woods are on Farmer McKean's land. They must be safe, or fear of liability would keep him from encouraging campers near its borders.

"Damn you, fox." If I keep sight of the bonfire's glow, I'm still within screaming distance. Twin columns of trees I recognize as yews from a photograph in Máthair's greenhouse border the path beyond the rowan gateway. Their branches intermingle like pairs of dancing lovers to weave a woody latticework ceiling. A trunk near the entrance wears clumps of lichen and moss giving it two eyes, a nose, and a mouth. Any moment, the tree face will ask the password to enter the forest. To my relief, it keeps still as I pick my way along the path.

My heart skitters when fox eyes gleam in the darkness. They float a good four feet off the ground. "Holy crap." My brain gives my heart permission to resume normal function when I realize the critter isn't levitating. It climbed something blocking the path, a boulder or fallen tree.

I luck out and find a decent sized rock near my foot. "Drop my peanut bars!" I holler and pitch the stone. It clunks against the fox's perch just beneath its paws. With a *yip,* my nemesis opens its mouth and drops the bag. I charge forward in case devil fox has any notion of reclaiming its ill-gotten booty.

When I stoop to retrieve my bag, a wave of lightheadedness makes me pitch forward. Thankfully, my hands and not my face hit a stone cylinder, the obstacle leaning across the path. I rest my forehead against its cool surface. I need to eat.

Around me the forest is still. Almost too still for comfort. There's no scuffling of critters or birds. It's pleasantly warm and the delicate haze lingering among the trees gives me the sensation of floating.

My fingernail catches on a crack in the stone. Not a crack. I point the flashlight to reveal a series of deliberate markings on the leaning cylinder. "Wow." I run a finger along the grooves. They're familiar slashes from the ancient Ogham alphabet I've seen so often in texts. Druid's work. Farmer McKean missed the boat by not dragging this beauty into his fake circle. Here's one leaning stone that might actually house old magic.

I laugh, disturbing the peace of the sleeping wood, and smack my palm against the stone. "You're as fake as the rest of this tourist trap, eh fellow?" I picture Farmer McKean out here with his chisel, scribing druid curses copied from a book into the stone to scare impressionable tourists and travel groups. "I hope you're up for garland and twinkle lights."

The leaning stone is rooted far enough into the ground to render it climbworthy. I tuck my flashlight into a pocket and choose a spot high enough on the perch to swing my legs and still be within jumping distance to the path. The solitude of the woods and a peanut bar are the perfect combo for mellow.

Lovely scents of lemongrass and spearmint as comforting as one of Máthair's healing teas float around me. She insisted herbs and faith fix everything. I'm as calm as if I'd downed a cup of her meadowsweet tea with plenty of honey. Here I sit alone in a forest after chasing a wild fox, and there isn't a drop of anxiety dribbling in my veins. Strange but nice.

I swallow the last of my snack, stuff the wrapper in my pocket, and recline on the stone. An invisible current, not a breeze exactly, flows around me. Druids believed in tree magic. Am I sensing the energy of oak, yew, and rowan? Through a gap in my leafy ceiling, I see a thousand stars. Who needs ancient magic? There's a tapestry of dreams above me. I raise one arm, close my eyes, and feel the kiss of starlight on each fingertip.

"Eala."

The voice jars me. Abruptly, I teeter to the side and slip off the stone. For a breath, time feels suspended. When I realize I can't get my feet under me in time to break the fall, my cry of panic rivals a harbinger of death.

Arms taut with corded muscle trap me against a soft padded jacket. In a panic, I grab a fistful of material. Outside my closed eyes, the world tilts and spins.

"Please stop screaming like the devil's on your tail."

My eyes snap open. For the first time, Sion Loho's striking green eyes stare directly into mine.

"Are you hurt, love?"

For a long moment, we clutch one another, each locked in place by the other's wide-eyed stare. I barely know this man, yet I feel protected in his arms. He's first to relax his hold. My weight shifts, and I slip. Before I can get my feet under me, I drop hard onto my backside. "Ouch."

"Sorry." He reaches for me, but I hold up a hand to stop him and stand on my own.

"What are you doing here?" Embarrassment heats my face as I realize the logical reason guys duck into the woods from a campsite. It's all I can do to keep from checking that he had time to button his jeans.

"I heard someone raising the dead and came running."

"I was yelling at a—" I'm not going to admit I was idiot enough to chase a fox into the forest. "Never mind."

A shaft of moonlight crosses his face. My heart pounds to the point of pain. Glassy eyes, not the hazel I noticed before but closer to the color of my grandmother's greenhouse, watch me. As if alive, a thin band of gold grows and shrinks around Sion's irises. His eyes were pretty before but now they hold a piercing beauty. I whisper, "You're looking at me."

His eyes narrow, staring even deeper into mine, then his gaze quickly darts away. Foul-tempered Sion appears. "I'm surprised you had a mind to notice."

Fouler-tempered me snaps back. "It's hard to miss when someone never bothers to look you in the eye." I jab two fingers at his face. "Why look now when everything I say or do seems to chap your ass?" He ruined my beautiful moment of woodsy solitude. I'd never have fallen off the leaning stone if he hadn't shouted my name, ambushing me for the second time in as many days.

A creepy feeling washes over me. How did he get so close without me hearing him? I scrabble backward, hyperaware of how vulnerable I am. "Are you following me?"

"Technically, you followed me."

I back away, keeping him in sight. "I had no idea you were here."

He moves toward me with one hand outstretched as if I'm a horse ready to rear and stomp him. "Eala, wait."

I point a finger. "Stay right there. I'll find my way to the bonfire." I nearly trip on a stone. Ammunition. I scoop it up. "If you try to follow me, I'll throw this at your head."

To my surprise. Sion drops cross-legged onto the path, hands on his knees. The tightness in my chest eases. He's anything but threatening hunkered down in the dirt. "I won't be moving from this spot 'til you give permission. Please don't go until you hear me out."

"Don't bother with another one of your apologies. We can't talk for more than five minutes before I piss you off, and I don't care." Even as I say the words, guilt boils in my stomach. I'm not outright mean to people, but I've never felt judged the way Sion seems to constantly judge me. "I think it's best if you keep your distance for the rest of the tour." I cut him off when he tries to speak. "Don't talk." I want to yell *stay* at him like he's one of the dogs Colleen is constantly fostering, but he keeps his word and doesn't move.

When he hangs his head, springy curls shadow his face. His voice is gentle, almost pleading. "I can make no promise to stay away from you."

His words spin through the air and then around my body like warm wind. I almost amend my suggestion of separation remembering his patience after I saw the ghost girl and his other short-lived stabs at friendliness. Sion Loho is making me crazy. I honestly believe he intends to be decent, but we're baking soda and vinegar. Our conversations always erupt into a mess.

"Yes, you can."

Sion pounds the dirt with one fist and then shakes both at the sky while he mutters, "Damn himself for cursing me with you."

"Himself who, and now I'm a curse?"

His impatience with me explodes as his eyes flash to mine. Damn, it was better when he didn't look directly at me. His stare burns like an accidental glance at the sun. I swear tiny bursts of light swarm behind him in the trees.

I whirl and stomp toward the edge of the forest but falter. Nothing is familiar. I've come farther into the wood than I meant to. Fucking fox. There's no sign of the bonfire. Off the path, the trees are denser than I remember. Any assist from the moon fades, so I reach for my flashlight. It chooses this moment to die. Fumbling, I dump the batteries and switch their positions to eke out enough light to find my way to the campsite. No luck.

"Eala, please wait. I swear I'll not do you harm." Sion's up and getting too close given the wave of vulnerability washing through me.

I slip off the path to hide behind a thick trunk while I reassess his threat level.

A silvery patina covers the wood. One thin splash of moonlight allows me to see him clearly as he strides along the path. What in the name of my grandmother's dandelion tea? Sion is not limping anymore. It's not my breath I worry will give me away, it's my heart doing an impression of a kettledrum. His gait is confident with the grace of an athlete in top condition.

He drops nearby and resumes his cross-legged vigil. At least it doesn't appear he plans to tear through the underbrush and drag me out.

"I'm gonna say my peace. If you run, I'll not follow, but I'm asking for the courtesy of your ear." He inhales slowly, and I swear the wood turns blacker. Not frightening tar black, a satiny black with just enough sheen to make out the form of trees and the man sitting on the ground. It's eerie the way his voice lands a direct hit on my ears the way the fan vault ceiling manipulated sound in Charleville Castle.

He grunts. "Och. I thought you'd be easier to deal with."

I should be more wary than curious about his cryptic statements. I'm stuck in the unknown with no one but a stranger bursting with anger issues. Should be, but oddly, I'm not. Even in our scene reminiscent of a slasher movie, Sion's voice draws me in the way it did at The Sheehogue. The sensation of his arms holding me, grounding me to the earth as I fell off the stone returns in a rush. If he intended to do something awful to me, he had every chance, but he didn't.

"Truth is, I need you, Eala Duir. And it takes a chunk out of me to say that." His huff is aimed at himself, not me. Cocky Sion recedes. "You've been sent as my last chance. I've got a task put before me I've failed at more times than a hen's got feathers."

Sent to him? This guy didn't exist for me until yesterday.

He exhales. "I'll feed you truth in small drabs."

I peek a little further around the tree. He's furiously scratching at his neck curls.

"Maddest notions first," says Sion.

Curiosity throws a net over me. I'm locked in place, hanging on his every word.

"I said you followed me into the wood because you did. I'm him who stole your food bag."

It takes all my willpower not to run out and cuff him on the ear the way Máthair used to do when she'd catch me in a whopper. Mad is right. He actually expects me to believe he's a thieving fox with a hankering for peanut bars.

"My name isn't Sion. Well 'tis, but if I be truth telling, it's Sionnach."

His accent thickens as his phrasing dips into a time warp. A lifetime of an ear tuned to Irish folk tales recognizes his tone. He's telling me a story.

Sionnach does mean fox. I suppress what threatens to be a doozy of a snort.

"I'm such a grumpy bastard because I need you to be doing and believing in things you wipe away like you're dusting crumbs off the front of your coat."

"Like what?" I slap a hand over my mouth and slink behind a different tree as if that'll throw him off.

His head turns smack dab to face me. "Refusing to climb a tower. Pissing all over things you don't see in front of your face." He appears to be addressing himself more than me. "Pissing all over things you *do* see in front of your face like the ghost girl."

I think back to the two of us sitting on the steps of Charleville Castle. It hits me now that due to being shaken to my core, what I interpreted as supportive was Sion coaxing me to admit I'd experienced something outside the bounds of ordinary.

Sion's signature disgust infects the forest. He blows a breath into the night and continues to grumble. "My mother always said faith is to believe what we do not see, and the reward of that faith is to see what we believe." The grumble upgrades to a growl. "It'll take the heavens to open and rain fire to get cynical Eala Duir to believe anything save what she can poke with a stick."

A tear trickles down my cheek. Even with all his critical glory, Máthair's favorite quote from St. Augustine has the beauty of a ballad coming from Sion Loho's lips.

Sionnach Loho.

A fox?

I step out from behind the tree to face the echo of my grandmother in this strange man.

"Say it again."

Despite the darkness, Sion's eyes are full of light. "The heavens'll have to rain fire before—"

"No. What your mother said—St. Augustine's words."

At the mention of St. Augustine, his expression softens. "Faith is to believe—" I close my eyes and speak the rest of the words with him. Our voices twine together, becoming the notes of a song.

In the silence of the wood, my gaze finds Sion's. All around us, the bursts of light I thought I'd imagined dance up tree trunks to settle twinkling in branches. A surge of moonshine brightens the forest. The gold band in Sion's eyes twinkles like a ring of starlight.

The beginnings of a shift in reality make me anticipate the familiar hum of a dream flash, but I'm not whisked into a fantasy. The sting of my fingernails digging into my palms tells me I'm not imagining this. I stare at the tiny sparks around us and then down at Sionnach. "What's happening?"

Sion reaches to grasp my hands. The quickness of his movement causes me to pull away.

"You have my oath, I'll not hurt you." He leaves his palms upturned, inviting.

Around us, the little bursts intensify, diving inside trunks, branches, leaves, rocks, and grasses until everything in the woods glows with unearthly beauty.

"What—" The question dies on my lips as I stare, mesmerized by the lights.

Slowly, I touch my palms to his and our lifelines meet. "Welcome to the Veil." His head swivels to take in the living forest. Those curls shift between the spicy rust of a fox's coat to a smoky pumpkin color.

I involuntarily squeeze his hands. "The Veil?" He's kidding. This can't be the space between reality and the realm of magic from Máthair's stories. "No."

"'Tis."

The lemongrass and spearmint fragrance blossoms around us. I close my eyes and breathe deeply. "The scent. It started back at the leaning stone."

"You smell soap bubbles?"

"Soap bubbles?"

"Aye." Sion uses the term unironically, unlike Charlie's attempts to sound Irish. "The soapy smell is the proof I count on to know I've crossed into the Veil." He raises his nose and sniffs. "Clean and fine."

"It's lemongrass and spearmint."

Wrinkling his nose, Sion drops my hands. "Strange." He pivots, sweeping his arm in an arc. "Can you see the Veil Sprites?"

"Sprites? Those tiny sparkles inside the trees?"

He nods, and an undercurrent of awe colors his voice. "You do see." Sion sniffs again. "Lemongrass, huh?"

"And spearmint." How can this odd moment be anything but a dream flash? It's unlike any I've ever felt before. I never speak in them. I observe. I experience. Pressing a fist to my lips, I try to make sense out of the nonsensical. This is too lucid. Too real.

It's not a dream.

The moment my mind decides to accept my situation as reality, a warm tickling sensation wakes inside me like tiny butterfly wings alight with flames. There's no burn or pain. It's an adrenaline rush of sparks.

I grab my stomach. "Something is happening to me."

Sion's eager smile raises my temperature even higher than my internal lightning bugs.

"Flicks of heat?"

I nod.

"I knew it." He runs a finger up my arm, lingering at the pulse point on my wrist, and smiles. "The Veil Sprites have taken you in. Or rather, you've taken them in."

Veil Sprites? I take a step back and stare at the man so unfazed by all things weird. "Who are you?"

"Sionnach Loho at your service." He sweeps into a bow. His tone is warmer, more genuine than the way he used the same line on Daisy at breakfast.

Disorientation mingles with an overwhelming sense of belonging. I'm thoroughly confused, my voice shaky. "What are you?"

"*Fánaí*, same as you."

My teeth grind into my lower lip. I understand the Irish word perfectly. Too perfectly. The usual flipping through virtual vocabulary cards in my head isn't necessary. Tiny vibrations of alarm waver in my stomach.

Real?

Unreal?

Where am I on that continuum?

"Foe-nee," he repeats with more patience than I'd ever give him credit for being capable of.

"*Fánaí*, wanderer, I get it." I rest my hands on either side of my head. "Why do I get it?"

Sion gently lowers my hands. I snatch his wrist, copying his earlier gesture and press my finger to his pulse. A steady rhythm thrums beneath my touch.

He's real. His heart beats.

"You're a product of the Veil same as me, Eala. We *fánaí* can walk between the worlds. Here to there. Now to then."

I break contact. "A product?"

He waves his hands through the air as if erasing his last statement. "I'm not dandy with words. *Child of the Veil* is a better way of it."

I bite my tongue—hard, using the technique that's pulled me from oncoming vivid daydreams in the past. It doesn't work. Doubt is a thunderhead, rising from my toes through my body to fill my chest. "This is too bizarre. I don't get it. I-I thought for a moment I might, but—"

I back away. The dancing prickles of heat beneath my skin pulse. The glow of Veil Sprites in the woods dims around us as if sensing my waning belief.

Sion's brow creases. His words are strangled. "Hold on to it all, Eala. Hold fast."

"Take me to the bonfire." The fluttering inside me slows. The pins and needles pain like circulation returning to a limb replaces it. I shake my arms to rid myself of the sensation.

Without a word, Sion snatches my hand and marches us toward an opening in the trees. I'm so grateful to be returning to a place where the world makes sense, I don't fight him. Oddly, there's confidence in his grip I don't mind. In moments, we pass the leaning stone. How could I have been near the campsite and not seen the bonfire painting an orange wash across the sky? He doesn't drop my hand until we're free of the wood.

Sion points to the sky. "See the moon." Rings of light radiate in concentric circles around a completely full moon. It's then I notice that far away is a familiar colorful shimmer like the edge of my dream flashes.

What the hell?

I stare nonplussed at the transient sky. Where has the three-quarter moon gone?

He addresses my confusion before I can voice it. "Moon's always full in the Veil. Provides the energy for travel."

I whip my gaze down the hill where the bonfire belongs.

It's not there.

We're in a small clearing with forest extending over hills in every direction. Shit. This is not the wood I chased a fox into. My eyes shoot to the moon, the one that held a different phase before I entered this forest.

A shiver skitters through me. I point in the direction where Colleen, Charlie, and Jeremy Olk should be. "Where did they go?"

"They went nowhere. It's us who did the traveling." He drops his gaze. "When you climbed the stone, and I caught you from the fall, we passed through the curtain of the Veil to this place."

I point to the trees. "But I saw the same leaning stone?"

He shakes his head. "Not the same one. Many Veil forests are marked with such stones."

The more I look around, the stranger the landscape becomes. Huge trees with multiple curving trunks twist high into the night. There's no movement to the air. No night wind. The full moon illuminates clouds that seem frozen in the sky. Ambient sound is nonexistent in this stalled reality. Our voices are the single break in the silence.

I should be raging at him. What he's done is nothing short of a bizarre abduction. I close my eyes for a long moment, but there's no fear in my gut.

"Where are we, Sion?"

He lowers himself onto the damp grass, back against a tree trunk. He beckons me to join him. I go as far as the large flat stone in front of him and sit.

"Are you ready for more drabs of truth?"

"No drabs—everything." There must be an explanation aside from the fact we exist in a fantastical dimension where only Sion, me, and what did he call them, Veil Sprites, have presence?

The moment I think of the Veil Sprites, warmth prickles inside me. With inexplicable certainty, I know they create the heat.

A flurry of questions blows through my mind like the beginning of a winter snowfall. "Why aren't you limping? What do you mean we traveled? Who's *himself* you were talking about, and what curse?"

Sion's eyes glaze as he fiddles with his hair. With minimal thought, he blurts, "Himself is Finnbheara, the one who sent you to me." My silence causes him to lean closer. "Finnbheara, High King of the Connacht Fae, the Good People."

"I know who he is. How does he know who I am?"

He thrusts a hand inside his jacket sleeve and madly scratches. "He makes it his business to know."

My throat is so dry, I barely eke out words. "You're a Faerie."

He rubs a hand across his mouth, shaking his head. "No. I'm as human as you, but also a Veil guide, a wanderer as I said before and you're meant to be my—" His gaze catches the moon as if the word he seeks might be etched across its surface. One finger rises in the air. "Partner." Suddenly, he kneels in front of me. "Have you ever been awake, but the world around you changes? Things happen that ought not to be happening surrounded by a wee shimmer of color?"

My dream flashes.

I nod.

"It's the Veil showing itself to you. You've been dipping a toe into it your whole life." He spreads his arms. "Tell me, love, are you frightened? Does this feel wrong?"

Can this be true? Were the fantastic images within a prismatic shell that I've seen as long as I can remember this Veil playing with my mind?

Oddly, I'm not frightened. Inklings of alarm melt away. Fingers clutch my grandmother's charm hanging around my neck. Is the absence of fear the strength it promised?

Confusion pecks harder at my brain. Here with Sion, I haven't felt this at home in my skin since the last day Máthair and I worked together in the greenhouse. I search for sense in the strangeness, but it's out of reach.

"Not wrong exactly—different." I study his face and those eyes that see me now. "I can't find the words yet, but it doesn't feel wrong. *You* don't feel wrong." I tap a finger on the back of his hand. "Why don't you feel wrong when all you've done since we met is make me want to smack you?"

He stiffens on the defensive. "It's you's been taxing me since you walked into the Druid's Cave with your wobbly courage." Sion's shoulders collapse, and he stares at the ground instead of me. "I was sure Finnbheara chose a weakling to help me, a fraud to mock my failures."

Slowly, his chin rises, and those green glass eyes capture me in their gaze. "When you spoke with the ghost girl, my faith caught fire. I began to believe the Veil called the right one home." He grabs my upper arms, breath hot across my face. "Eala, as I said, there was no little girl at Charleville Castle. No missing parents. 'Twas a spirit who recognized you have the sight."

His hold grounds me as each new shard of mystery threatens to break me apart. "Sight?"

"What's invisible to others is visible to you. A gift from Finnbheara."

"Finnbheara's gift was to show me the spirit of a dead kid?"

"No. He showed you the girl's virtue. Purity. You answered with kindness, not fear."

"What does purity or her virtue have to do with a lost—" Words die as I think of her and the doll's shattered face. Anomalies of time. Wisps of memory. A soul lingering.

He speaks carefully. "That's part of the bigger story—"

I cut him off. "You saw her too."

"You and me, love. We're the ones who see."

My fingers slide into my hair as the girl, the doll, the staircase float through my mind. The odd sensation of her present yet insubstantial hand. Memories of silence instead of the clicking of a child's dress shoes on the floor as she ran off.

"Holy sh…" I take in the sky, the landscape, the man in front of me, and the sparks of energy coursing through my body in a wild current. I'm part of this, whatever it is, whether I want to be or not. "So, you're right about the girl?"

He nods. "And the Veil." His hands slide down my arms, then lightly touch my waist. I'm tempted to lean into him. "Have you come home, Eala Duir?"

At the bonfire, any notion of being close to an embrace with Sion Loho would strike me at best as unnerving. Here in what he identifies as the Veil, if I let myself believe that is where we are, I ache for the reassurance of his arms. This prickly man has become my anchor in reality turned inside out.

I start to laugh like a crazy person. My body convulses as if it's shedding a skin of skepticism. "If I believe in the ghost girl, I'm supposed to accept you're a peanut bar stealing fox?"

His teeth shine, quicksilver in the moonlight. "That I am."

"Show me."

He blows out a long, slow breath, his gaze locked on mine, but doesn't object. Fog puffs in a column around him then settles to reveal a familiar thieving scoundrel. The fox lets go a yip I swear sounds like, "See." Before I manage a pair of blinks, distortion twists the air, and Sion is back.

I swallow wrong and start to choke. He pats my back as I sputter. "Bizarre. Completely bizarre."

Sion rakes fingernails up and down his chest under his shirt. I catch a glimpse of flat, toned stomach muscles. "The damn change itches like I've been doused in a shower of starving ants."

I fan a hand along the length of his body. "But, how—?"

He stoops to scratch his shins. "Something Finnbheara dropped in my toolbox." With a grunt, he straightens. "I don't have much call to use it." Sion watches me. "It served me well enough tonight." His eyes widen as he continues to stare into mine. "Will you give me an answer now, Eala *bán*? Does the Veil feel like home to you?"

"Well, Sionnach, I wouldn't call it home but here—" I sweep an arm across the landscape. "Is definitely nowhere I've ever been before." Not a dream flash imposed over the mundane—a separate reality.

Sion's mouth quirks into the bare beginning of a smile, his prelude to celebrate a victory he's reticent to claim completely.

Before I return his smile, the world wobbles as a surge passes through me. It's not heat, sound, or wind. I sense it in every cell. Matching my internal sensation, ripples cross the sky overhead, but the clouds don't move. When the unseen pulse reaches my inner ear, my balance shatters, and I tip backward.

Sion catches me. "Felt that, didja?"

I hum an answer deep in my throat. With him, I'm not alone in a membrane between worlds, this Veil.

His eyes are bright. "That was you."

"I didn't do anything."

He runs a hand up my spine to grip the back of my neck. Heat builds where his fingertips touch skin. "Your mind called to the Veil, and it answered." Our faces are inches apart with matching looks of intensity.

His touch, his breath, those green glass eyes mix together in my senses, sparking feelings I'm not prepared for.

When I pull back, Sion's face flushes as russet as fox fur. Judging by the heat crawling up my neck, I'm doing the same.

I tilt my head to gaze at the treetops. It's all true. Sion can turn into a fox. The Veil is a conduit to a parallel reality. Stories are not just stories.

He shoots me a look that begins as a question, but then shifts to genuine concern. "Dancing with the Veil feels a bit like losing your mind until you get used to it."

A fluff of hair falls over my eyes. Sion traps it between his fingers, rolling it back and forth for a moment, studying it. "As pure white as a swan." He tucks it behind my ear, and I shiver. "Are you losing yours?"

I fiddle with my scarf. "Considering it." An upward glance reveals no change in the clouds. Gray construction paper collages hang in a static starry sky.

Is Sion seriously asking me to dabble in whatever Veil traveling is? Why? What if I've encountered a trickster from folklore, name-dropping a king of *Tír na nÓg*? How many tales have I studied where mortals have fallen into a similar trap?

As if sensing my doubt, he asks, "Do you know what the center of a Celtic star stands for?"

A five-pointed Celtic star hung on the wall above Máthair's bed. In its center was a circle of emerald chips that caught the light of the rising sun. Every morning, she'd touch each point of the star one at a time and tell me, *"These five points are for the senses we understand."* Then she'd kiss her fingertip and rest it lightly in the middle. *"This is for what we believe."*

"My grandmother said it was the crossover."

His look is as intense as the bizarre energy emanating from my heart like the circles that surround a rock dropped in a pond. "Aye. Where humanity meets Sidhe, Otherworld." He covers my hand with his. "Here. The Veil is part of that."

Memories of Máthair smiling, laughing, and holding me in her arms fill me with a presence so strong, I expect her to step from behind one of the tangled trees at the edge of the forest.

Find me.

"Are we in *Tír na nÓg?*" Is this what my grandmother meant? If I find the Veil and the gates of *Tír na nÓg*, will I find her?

Impatient Sion Loho reappears and shoots to his feet. "What did I just tell you?" He bats curls off his forehead. "We're in the Veil. Do you need further tutorials?"

Disappointment knocks the wind out of me. The eerie lack of movement in our surroundings, except for the tangible but invisible current of who knows what, gives me a chill. Not *Tír na nÓg*. I haven't found my grandmother, but if insanity hasn't taken me round the bend and stolen my ability to reason, then Sion, a wanderer, this Veil guide, may be a link to her.

"If you want—" I flick a finger between us. "To continue on any level, you need to stop being ridiculously short-tempered while I attempt to understand what's going on here."

Sion hangs his head and fusses with the tips of ears threatening to bust through his mop of hair. A way of counting to ten, I suppose. Or hiding ears ending in points. Is it Faeries, Elves, or both with pointed ears?

I stand. "And if I ask you a question, I expect an acid-free answer."

He raises his face, kisses two fingers on his right hand, and lays them over his heart.

The air around me thickens and pushes at my body. I teeter and rub a hand across my forehead to rid myself of the floaty sensation. My first thought is *this would be such a lovely dream.* Faeries, the Veil, Sprites, Sion changing into a fox—Máthair would relish every bit of what's happening.

When my gaze meets Sion's, my hope for a lovely dream shatters. We're not in Farmer McKean's cozy wood. I traveled to this place via the fodder of legends. The supposition of my dissertation leaps to the forefront of my mind. *Myths are truths subjugated to untruths to keep people from being scared of what their world is truly made of.*

I need to sleep. I need to process. I need to decide what to do with this massive dose of weird. "Okay then, let's go back to the campsite."

Alarm flashes across Sion's face. "Back? No. We've got to get crackin.'"

CHAPTER 9
THE TOWER

S ion strides to the edge of the forest. When I don't follow, he waves an arm. "Crackin'. Moving. Come on, love."

I set my hands to my hips. "First, stop calling me *love*. Second, I'm not crackin' anywhere except to the bonfire."

He circles back and attempts to seize my hand. "We've got to do our work while they sleep."

"They?"

Muscles pulse in his throat. "The bunch at the campsite."

I wipe hands down the sides of my face. "No more unintelligible fragments." I try to mentally smooth the tension knots beading along my spine. "You call me your partner and now want to drag me off to do heaven knows what away from the people I know and am responsible for?" I raise a finger. "I assume we're crackin' to do whatever you claim Finnbheara accuses you of failing at?" I ball my hands into fists. "Do you get how insane all this sounds?"

His own fists bounce against muscular thighs. I'm privy to the wrestling match going on in his head through the narrowing and widening of his eyes. He stills, green glass fixing on me with such determination, I raise my foot to step away from him.

Quick as one of the flashes of light I saw in the forest, Sion scoops me off my feet and into his arms. Before I can scream or smack him, glass-like sheets harden around and above us, forming a space akin to a giant elevator car. Moonlight splits through the barriers, revealing every color of the visible spectrum. I gasp, recognizing them as solid versions of my dream flash boundaries. I peer down to see his feet resting on something I've never seen in my visions, a carpet of spheres the size of gumballs that glow in soft electric turquoise and violet.

The beauty of shimmering colors momentarily douses the indignation of being plucked off my feet. "What is this?"

Instead of answering, because it's the thing he doesn't do with anything resembling clarity, Sion Loho walks straight through one of the prismatic walls.

"Look there." He points below us as he sets me on my feet.

The electric gumballs conform to the soles of my feet like memory foam sneakers. When I glance down past the small island of jewel tone spheres holding us, my heart accelerates from trot to gallop. We're hovering at least fifty feet in the air.

I can't draw a full breath. Alternating between gasps and gulps, I fight to keep from passing out. We're too high. There's nothing between me and the bodies in sleeping bags near the smoldering mass that was once the bonfire.

I bury my face into Sion's jacket and grab fistfuls of his padded sleeves. I don't care what he is or what he's doing. If I'm up here a moment longer, my heart will burst.

"Down," is all I manage. The roar in my ears from absolute panic renders me deaf, mute, blind, and utterly useless to save myself.

Sion coos in Irish and gently turns my face to show me our feet are back on solid ground. We stand in the shadows outside the stone circle.

I release my death grip on him. "Don't ever do that to me again." I drop my face into my hands. "You know damn well I can't do heights."

He raises my chin with his thumb, his stare boring into mine. "I swear to you, Eala Duir. You'll never fall when you're with me."

Untainted sincerity is a fresh and welcome note in his repertoire on this unbelievable night with rainbow walls and men who turn into small mammals.

A faint shimmer wavers between us and the peaceful campsite. "No one seems very concerned I've disappeared."

Sion juts his chin to where Colleen and Charlie snuggle against one another. My own sleeping bag is not empty. "They've no notion you're gone."

"What the—is that a shell of my body or something equally disturbing?" Images of spirits rising free of their human forms race through my mind. Did Sion and the Veil separate my body from my soul? I clutch my arm, relieved to find it solid. I'm not an astral projection here, but what am I down there?

Sion stands so close behind me, I feel his chest rumble with a quiet laugh. "It's your backpack I've stuffed in there."

This is all true. We're travelling between worlds, dimensions, realities.

He takes my hand.

Flash.

We're back in the prism chamber engulfed in streaks of rainbow light.

Flash.

We pass through a different wall.

Now, we're at the edge of yet a third forest. Not the one by the campsite and not the Veil forest we first traveled to. Trees rise behind us in a semi-circle, blocking the land beyond from our sight. In front of us is a grassy hill spotted with caps of embedded granite slabs.

Sion points to a stone tower not fifty paces away. "There's no slow going with this. Take a breath and give me a chance to tell you all."

Black fissures run through decaying stones of what once might have been the single turret of a larger castle. At its foot amidst sprouting grasses rests a pile of rubble reminiscent of a cairn or burial mound. The tower perches on a low, sheer cliff. The river below hisses discontent as its current crashes against hulking boulders. Spumes of brilliant white spray upward.

Before I can make sense of our location, I double over. A wave of nausea racks my body, and I clutch my stomach. I'm going to be sick.

Sion rubs my back. "Shh. Whisht. Sorry, I pulled you through too fast. You'll get used to Veil travel. I swear it."

I strive for calm so I don't vomit. "What have you done to me?"

"No more than a wee bit of crossing through the Veil."

Truth hits, a fist to my already tender innards. I'm powerless against Sion and his intentions. He lured me into his Veil forest and will smash us through fantastical walls to wherever he chooses. I need to slow this insanity and get clearer answers.

"Stop everything. Turning into a fox. Yanking me through dimensions without giving me a say."

"Can't risk stopping."

He takes a step back when I charge him. I keep advancing until the distance between our noses is too close to measure.

"Risk what Sion? What?" My last word cracks through the air like a cat-of-nine-tails. "Stop shoving disjointed puzzle pieces at me. What's the big picture here?"

My *partner* takes half a step back, rubbing a finger under his bottom lip. "I've never had to explain—" His gaze climbs the tower, locking onto a window near the top. When he speaks, his voice is cracked and tinny. "Ever heard a cry in the dark you convinced yourself was a night bird or the wind itself?"

I shrug, unwilling to admit how often I've heard strange cries in the city or the park. Breeze trickles through loose strands of my hair. The mossy smells of water-logged stones and dirt fill the air. The current world isn't stuck the way the Veil forest appeared. Sounds, smells, and sensations that surround us are active, alive. Clouds cross a full moon, not a three-quarter one.

Is this place the Veil too? There's no wavering sheen in the sky or glowing spheres on the ground.

A wail of profound sorrow rends the air. I dig fingers into his sleeve. "What the hell?"

"The *why* we can't stop." The melancholy softening his features matches the air of misery dropping around us like a silken drape. "The reason I need you, Eala." He raises his hand, palm up to the tower. Harmonies of lamentation flow from the single high window. "Up there's the soulfall. They're calling to us."

Soulfall?

I search my memories of Máthair's stories, but the word is new to me.

Whatever it is, I'm grateful for Sion's fingers twining through mine. I hope St. Augustine was on the right track with blind trust. I still only half accept I'm moving through a strange reality holding hands with a curly-haired enigma. This is exactly the situation that usually I'd run from, not embrace.

We trudge over grass-covered mounds, skirting rocks until we're next to the foot of the tower. Below saw-toothed crenellations, the dark opening of a window brightens with candlelight. To my horror, the silhouette of a child, a girl, hovers at the edge of the sill.

I wave my arms and shout. "Back up, kid." Negligent parents are about to pay the ultimate price. "Someone pull her in!" With both hands, I shove Sion toward the opening at the base of the tower where a door has long since rotted away. "Get her away from the window. Run." My eyes fall to the collection of boulders spiking out of the river. Demon jaws lick watery lips in anticipation.

Sion doesn't move.

Fear twists my throat. "Please." I don't know if I'm talking to Sion, or fate, or God. Anyone who will listen and keep this tiny being from falling. I can't look at her anymore and turn away from the window.

Sion swivels my body to face the tower, crisscrossing his arms around me to lock my back against his chest. "Watch."

I thrash with every ounce of my adrenaline-charged hysteria. "What are you doing to me?"

In the next second, the child steps from the sill into mid-air. I want to hide my eyes, but I'm paralyzed. The shadow that lives in my heart, fear of heights, wraps bands of ice around my body, riveting me to this spot, to this sight, to violence. It whispers to me.

See what happens when you climb.

Sion rests his chin on my shoulder, rasping words into my ear. "It's not as it seems. You'll understand if you don't turn away. I promise."

The little one's dress billows around her, a parachute opening to the wind. She glides slowly downward, a strand of lace on a breeze. Moonlight peeks around the tower, illuminating her balletic descent.

Black vines of terror crawl up my body.

Sion holds me tighter. "Isn't it lovely how she floats?"

Her delicate fall brings her level with us. Details become clear: the doll hugged in tiny arms, ringlets of her hair, a Sunday-best dress.

"It's the girl from Charleville Castle."

Sion hums confirmation.

Little Harriett's gaze finds mine, and her face breaks into a smile. When the tip of her shiny black shoe touches the highest boulder that juts mercilessly out of the frothing water, she bursts into a million fireflies. Gravity has no dominion over the child. Her light flutters upward, tracing the path of a moonbeam and then dissipates into the sky to become pinpoints of stardust.

"Purity," Sion breathes into my ear. "Her fulfillment is your doing, Eala." I shudder in his arms. "You set her on the path to peace."

Inside my heart, there's a flicker. It moves through my chest and then out to every part of my body as if the girl's fireflies are inside me instead of reaching for the moon.

Sion shudders when a woman steps onto the window ledge. The awful shrieking from the tower window is a needle of ice scraping my bones.

"You're seeing souls falling, not flesh and bone." His chin bores deep into the muscle of my shoulder. "Tortured spirits waiting for—"

The woman leans out the window until the sky claims her body. She slides on an invisible plank toward the roiling white soup. Skirts flaps around her. The figure is all in gray tones, blurry and indistinguishable. When she meets the boulder, no sparks rise into the night. An explosion of sludge, blacker than ink, splatters over the surface of the rock.

I twist enough to duck my head into the hollow of Sion's shoulder, letting loose a keen of my own.

He wraps steadfast arms more tightly around me as his voice attempts to soothe. "Not flesh. Not bone. Shadow. Spirit. Soul."

I find the courage to raise my eyes to the tower and watch three more wraiths step into oblivion and end as viscous misery dripping into the river.

Sion drones in a monotone, repeating the same words over and over as the souls are destroyed. "Purity. Mercy. Humanity. Humility. Diligence. Sacrifice. Compassion."

The weight of the soulfall's despair infuses my blood. I slide from

Sion's arms to collapse into a heap on the spongy ground, unable to watch any longer. After a time, the wailing from above stops. A pillow of damp grass revives me. I push up with my arms.

Sion isn't here.

How could he force me to watch the decimation of souls and then abandon me? Máthair's warning of Faerie paths and crossing wits with powers too great to understand falls like a weight across my shoulders.

The weight turns out to be Sion's peacock blue jacket. He's moved a few feet away, giving me space. Sionnach, the fox-man, hugs his knees to his chest as he burrows against the curve of a dense bush.

I pull his jacket tight around me. "Where did you go?"

"Not far." His green glass eyes stare at the tower. Buttery candlelight no longer wavers in the window. It's a black smudge against gray stones.

Sion's expression breaks my heart. Sadness wraps in layers across his face like a shroud. He's stretched as thin as dough for a delicate pastry and bruised from being dredged through depths of unnamed despair.

I slide close enough to wrap his jacket around both our shoulders. He fits himself against my side and pulls his knees in tighter. "It's them I've failed."

"I don't understand. Why did everyone but the little girl—" I have no sensitive term for a soul turning to rancid goo and splattering all over a rock. "Where did she go?"

"Heaven, I suspect." His eyes glaze as he stares into the wood across the river. "They each yearn to go to the place where light calls them." He tilts his head but doesn't make eye contact. A hollow opens in my middle. I don't want to go back to Sion Loho keeping his green gaze with its golden circle away from me. This force that has begun to connect us is confusing, but not something I'm ready to let go of. "It's a question of faith. Heaven for most, especially Catholics like me. *Tír na nÓg* for others."

The gravity of his words roots me to the earth like the half-buried stones surrounding us. "Those places are real?"

To my relief, his reassuring gaze finds mine once again. "I hope so."

"Why am I here, Sion?"

He nods to the tower. "For them. For me. I told you this was my last chance. Theirs too. It's my job to do what needs to be done to guide them out of the soulfall and up to the light. If I don't free their spirits by Beltane, they'll be trapped in this soulfall forever."

"Do what needs to be done?" I drop my head onto my knees. "Why do you think I can do anything?"

His arm slides around my back, pressing us closer together. A series of noises pop and skid in his throat as he searches for words. "Because you already have. You saved the girl. I lost count of how many times I've tried to find her key, and you found it on the first go."

"Key?"

"An artifact from their lives that reminds and reconnects a soul with the virtue they've lost. Seven souls in a soulfall. Seven lost virtues, one for each. Purity. Mercy. Humanity. Humility. Diligence. Sacrifice. Compassion. Artifacts are the keys to help them move beyond this passage of misery they're trapped in."

My lifetime of Catholicism gives me a shot at decoding. "Purgatory?"

Sion's derisive grunt joins the conversation. "Wandering through purgatory seems a might better than dropping from a tower to break onto rocks."

Thoughts braid and unbraid themselves in my head, trying to connect the scant bits of information Sion offers and make sense of them. Lessons from religious ed. class shove their way to the front of the line. "You were chanting the seven virtues as they fell."

"Virtues that need restoring, like I said. If a person dies with all seven virtues intact, you'll not be finding them in a soulfall."

Frustration grinds my molars against one another. "You've done a fair job convincing me to change my stance on the supernatural, but—" I raise a finger when he tries to interrupt. "Where exactly do I fit in with dimension-travelling foxes, girl ghosts, prism walls, moons that change phase on the same night, and shades of people falling from a tower?"

Sion starts giving off waves of heat as he gets excited. "You're clever. It's their keys you'll be helping me find. The way you did with the doll." He leaps to his feet, shrugs back into his jacket, then holds out a hand.

I take it, and he pulls me up. "The doll was lying there. I didn't do anything."

He rests his hands on my shoulders. All this touching, this closeness to a man I barely know, would usually put my defenses on high alert, but not with Sion. If anything, I find myself drawn to him the way people sharing a secret forge a bond.

"But you did. You saw it and the child's need for it." Sion blows a puff of air that riffles his bangs. "It was so simple."

"Simple?"

He touches a finger to my crinkled nose and smiles. "I miss things right in front of my nose."

"How could that little girl have a tainted virtue to restore?"

His eyes rake the field of stars. "Children are the essence of purity."

"Then why hadn't she—" I spin my hands, searching for the right word.

"Passed on." He lays one hand on the back of his neck, shielding it from the tickling curls. "Her death was an anomaly. It never should have happened. 'Twas a fracture in time." He levels his gaze at me. "The fear to pass on, a hiccup in a faith she wasn't mature enough to fully embrace, tainted her purity and stuck her in the castle. Whatever she saw ahead was more than a wee lass could bear."

I imagine Little Harriet skipping from room to room in Charleville Castle, her eternal playground. Familiar but empty. A place devoid of the comfort family and hugs provide. The internal prickles of heat I felt before reignite. Maybe these Veil Sprites in my body are personal truth detectors, signaling I'm on the right track.

"Hugging a doll can be a powerful comfort to a kid." My eyes climb the tower to the high window. "There's your simple. The doll she'd lost in the fall gave Harriett the courage to take the next step. She wasn't alone."

Sion's voice is as gentle as two leaves rubbing in a night breeze. "Aye." His seismic mood shift strikes again when he grabs both my hands. "You're my perspective. After all the time I've been trying to free the souls, I can't see simple anymore like you can." He snorts. "As if I ever gave simple value in the first place." He leans in and kisses my cheek. Warm, full lips chase the chill from my skin. "That's why you've been sent to me. Ole Finnbheara don't keep his arse on the throne for nothing."

Tír na nÓg. Finnbheara. Sionnach Loho. Beltane. The Veil. Máthair's stories aren't so fanciful and far-fetched anymore.

"Eala, step lively." Sion is halfway to the tower. "Up the stairs with you so you can hear Mrs. Kennedy's story. She's the next soul. It's the virtue of mercy that's gone amiss with the woman." He gives a jaunty hop and twirl. "We've got a generous slice of time before dawn to find her artifact."

Stairs? Shit! He expects me to climb to a chamber filled with unrelenting death and those horrible wails. My eyes lock on the window.

"I can't go up there."

Sion whirls around. "Don't be daft. You're not going to fall. We've got but four days until Beltane. No time to tarry."

"Why Beltane?"

"I'm given from the equinox until the fire festival when the year passes from dark to light to free the souls."

The year. He's referring to the Celtic year. In the moonlight, I see a ruddy flush cross his cheeks as I stand my ground.

He flings an arm at the tower. "You've got to hear them speak their peace to figure out the artifact we need to restore their lost virtue, the keys to their redemption."

I cross my arms to hide my shaking. "You go listen, and then tell me what they say."

He stomps a mushy mud clod, splattering droplets of mud on his jeans. I steel myself for a class-A Sion Loho rant. Instead of anger, desperation hardens the angles of his jaw. "Do you not see? That's why you've come. I've listened to their stories over and over again and failed. Fate only gives a feller so many chances, and I'm on my last one. Take a risk, Eala. For the souls not yourself. Let their stories tell you what I can't hear."

I want to help. Even though I only comprehend a tiny fraction of what he's telling me, I believe something essential is going on here. Hollowness begins to spread through my chest. He may be pursuing the wrong person for help.

What if there are windows or arrow loops on the stairs? I'll be able to see as the ground falls farther and farther below me. A wave of dizziness hits hard, and I close my eyes to keep the world from spinning. In less than ten steps, I'll crumble into a ball. I whisper, "If climbing a tower is what I have to do, then you're mistaken. I'm not the partner you need."

Sion grips my shoulders. I'm surprised how fast it steadies me, and I open my eyes. Moonlight turns his eyelashes the color of an orange tabby cat.

His voice reflects the anguish on his face. "All I'm asking is for you to take a single step with me. If you can bear that one, then take another."

It hits me I've been reading his judgmental attitude toward me all wrong. His grit and growl are not entirely a reaction to my deficiencies. It's fear for the fate of these souls.

I lay a hand on one of his. "I'm so sorry. I'll never make it to the top." Now it's me who can't look him in the eye. "I'll wait for you here, then you can tell me exactly what Mrs. Kennedy says."

Sion sputters and paces, intermittently shooting me looks ranging from frustration to rage to despair. Finally, he turns his back on me and disappears into the door-shaped shadow at the bottom of the tower.

CHAPTER 10
THE BARGAIN

I take refuge on a cluster of stones. After twisting my riotously uncooperative hair into an approximation of a bun, I lean back and count stars until the whirlwind left behind by Sionnach Loho downgrades to an intermittent breeze.

He won't leave me. He's promised as much, thank goodness. I need him to stay away long enough for me to decide if I can handle an eternity-bending responsibility. How many attempts has he made to break this chain of agony?

I trail fingertips across my forehead. Of course, I want to help him and the souls. Imagining these poor people crashing into sludge over and over is enough to make me want to lie in the wet grass and never get up again. The enormity of such a task should make my heart heavy, but a sense of wonder begins to crack my shell.

I've moved through the Veil.

It's real. Afterlives are real. Ghosts are real. Finnbheara, a Fae king, is real. Whatever Sion claims to be, a Veil guide, is real. How can I continue to doubt the validity of these strange things after what he's shown me tonight? I don't feel crazy. The Veil Sprites dance within me, flashing quick reassurance my thinking is correct. Of course, it is. In my studies, I've immersed myself in Celtic spirituality. The strands of belief: nature and community, equality of men and women, and imagination as the key to understanding both mankind and deity, meshed so well with my grandmother's philosophies I never had cause to doubt them.

"You told me to remember ancestors and the past. I will, Máthair. I'll remember you for the rest of my life and—" I glance at the tower window still as black as ink. "Whatever comes after." I twist my grandmother's ring on my finger. Heaven. *Tír na nÓg.* Nirvana. Even Valhalla where Thor will battle Loki as long as there is consciousness to imagine such epic struggles.

A steady wind meanders through the forest, raising whispers between the trees. "I promise to work in harmony with the natural world, Grandmother." Just as her greenhouse spoke to her in the unvoiced song of living things.

A shiver runs through me as the third strand of my promise comes to mind. "I'll keep an open mind to the connection between the spirit realm and reality." Tonight, I've seen damn convincing evidence of that bond.

A flicker from above catches my eye. After some respite, the light in the tower window returns. The silhouette of the first woman in the soulfall stands poised on the edge of oblivion. Her cry shakes the night, and again she plunges onto the waiting teeth of river rocks.

I try to watch and understand my place in the redemption of these souls, but I hide my face long before the end. Their song of sorrow permeates my own soul. Guilty relief fills me when the night is still again. How does Sion stand to be in a room enmeshed in helplessness as each of his charges chases their spiritual tails time and time again?

"Did you watch it all?" I startle when Sionnach appears next to me. He's sure got stealth, whether man or fox.

I shake my head. "I couldn't. It's too much to handle."

His shoulders droop. "That'll do for now, but I'll need you to be seeing it through to the last soon enough." Sion gazes up at the tower. "As I said, next is Alaina Kennedy. "Her boy, Matthew, went missing, and she refuses to move on until she knows if he's dead or alive. We need to grant her the mercy of knowing."

I pop off the rock. "That's an easy one." I root in my pocket for my phone. "I'm sure we can find him online." While waiting for my screen to power up, I get down to business. "Where does Matthew Kennedy live?"

The beginning of a smirk on Sion's face annoys me. Where's the humor in a mother searching for her missing kid?

"Leap Castle in Roscrea."

I shake my phone. It refuses to wake even though I charged the battery on the bus from Charleville. At least my hours of pouring over the map of our itinerary with Colleen pay off. "Hey, that's not far from here." It hits me that I'm not exactly sure where here is. "From the campsite in Rowan Bend." I tap the cell screen, hoping it'll coax a faster wake-up, and then knock a fist against my forehead. As if there'd be cell reception in the Veil. "How long ago did he go missing?"

"Sometime in the early 1500s."

My arm drops the useless phone to my side. Even if it did revive, I can't Google a five-hundred-year-old missing person. "You're not serious."

"Swear on my ma's life."

Goosebumps pebble my skin as yet another truth slams into me. "By Veil travel—you mean time travel?"

"I do."

I rub my arms. "Can't we deal with ghosts in the present like Little Harriett?"

Sion inhales very slowly and times his exhale to match. "Every soul's story sends us down a different path."

These soul paths are more akin to Alice's rabbit hole.

"Matthew worked as a serving lad at Leap Castle for the O'Carrolls. He'd boarded there since he was thirteen but managed a visit to his ma and da every few months." Sion fiddles with his curls. "There was a poor winter when traveling would have been too much for the lad, but come the spring and then summer, Matthew did not show at home."

Okay, I can do this. Listen to Sion tell the soul's story and ask what he's already done to find the artifacts. Hopefully, I'll help point him in the right direction. My analytical PhD brain clicks on. "Did his parents go looking for him? Or try to write?"

"Aye, but no help for it from the O'Carrolls." Sion snorts. "They're not what you'd call a hospitable clan." He rubs his lips together. "I've found those that've heard of the lad at Leap Castle, but never laid eyes on Matthew himself. Not a soul knows aught of what became of him."

This story of an absent loved one is too close to home and my sudden loss of Máthair. No wrinkled cheek for me to kiss. Just a packet from a lawyer and a ring with a vague message to find her.

Sion drops to one knee. "Eala, I'm begging you. Come with me to see and hear what I can't."

A rush of frigid air has me longing for Sion's jacket. "Wait. No." I flap my arms for him to stand. "Don't ask me to go back in time with you."

He stands and grabs my waist. "It's the only way."

I drop my head. "Impossible." The risk of stepping through the Veil to barely post-medieval Ireland makes my head spin. I'm glad Sion has me in an iron grip or else I might sink into the damp ground.

A flash of Sion snatching me into his arms again to whisk me through time without my permission snaps me on guard. Flattening both palms against his chest, I push him away. "I'm not going with you."

The corners of Sion's lips curl into sharp commas. "Well, ain't that grand the way you can step away from those who you see are needing you?"

"I'll still help." I put more distance between us to avoid being forced through time. "You go and gather all the intel you can. Pop back here, I'll help you make sense of it, then you can return and grab the artifact."

Sion shakes fists at the sky. "It's on my own I've been failing them." Tears make his eyes shine.

It isn't possible to feel any crappier. This man is trying to save souls, but he's asking more than I can give. We're at a standoff. His pleading slams into my complete and utter incapability of surviving in a world that's already relegated to the crispy pages of a history book. I wouldn't begin to know what to say, how to act, or keep myself from being identified as wrong. For the love of sanity, back then, they torched people for being odd.

When I was six, a rabbit shot out of the bushes onto the path of Central Park where Máthair and I were making our way to the carousel. It froze, black eyes stretched wide, taking in what must have appeared as two giants ready to stomp it. The rabbit dropped dead. Right there. One second it was hopping in search of munchies, and the next, bunny was stone cold past tense in the middle of the path.

I'm that rabbit. Not strong or brave enough to pop into the sixteenth century and chat up the locals without dropping dead from fright.

The variety of noises coming from Sion are quite extraordinary: trills, growls, clicks, and all matter of rumbles. He bends both arms, pulling them into his chest and sets his chin atop fists, the cherry on an ice cream sundae. Bending his knees, he drops into a crouch. His display, so like an exotic bird warning off predators, works well. I have no desire to go near him.

He rakes the hair straight off his face. Sion's forehead catches the bluish tint of moonlight. "If you go with me, I'll help you find what you're looking for."

I've seen Sion Loho angry, wry, sarcastic, mean, frustrated, desperate, witty, earnest, almost sweet, impatient but never pathetic. He has as many facets as a cut gemstone. Turn him to the light and there's no telling which surface will pick up a reflection. It's brutal to face this stripped raw Sion, especially when it's my cowardice that broke him.

"I'm sorry. I wish I could meet things head on without a second thought, but I can't. The most I can do is try to help you unravel what you find. Figure out the key for each of the souls."

"You're not hearing me." Sion's hand pinches the finger with Máthair's ring. "If you go with me, I'll help you find *her*."

Find me.

I barely have enough breath to speak. "My grandmother?" Is it possible? Can Sion, the *fánaí*, take me to Máthair?

"It's sacred rules we'll be breaking if I help you try to contact her, but I'll do it in trade for you traveling with me."

My thoughts tumble. Can I handle this if it means seeing my grandmother again?

I grip the charm around my neck. For Máthair, I'll find courage. The possibility to see her again is worth any risk Sion asks of me. My thumb rubs the symbol cut into the metal disc. I'll find strength, no matter how deep it's buried in my bones.

"If you swear you'll keep that promise, then I will take a single step with you." I cover Máthair's ring with my hand. If traveling with Sion is horrible, I'll never do it again. He'll still owe me his part of the deal. "You'll help me find my grandmother." I'll even endure madness once for her.

Sion peeks at me through his lashes.

"What?"

"I'm asking for more than a single step. I need you by my side for all the souls before we set out to find your gran. There's no time to spare for sidestepping."

I want to pound his shoulders with my fists and demand an escape clause, and then my heartbeat quickens, remembering the tormented cry of the souls.

He crosses his arms, knuckles glowing as white as the moon. "You've got to understand. In four days, we win or we lose." Sion flings an arm at the tower. "They win or lose. I'll not be bargaining any more with their eternity."

On his face is the raw truth of the matter. This is more than life or death for the spirits trapped in the soulfall. It's their forever. In a crazy twisting reality, I'm connected to them.

"What if I say the wrong thing? What if I give us away?"

His smile downgrades the tempest raging in my chest to a squall. "I won't let you. I'll keep harm from touching you."

"Is that a promise you can keep?"

"Swear on my ma's soul." He offers me his hand.

I take it. This is madness, but at the core of what shouldn't be, I feel a sense of responsibility. Sion wasn't looking for a random teammate. For reasons I don't yet understand, Finnbheara designated me to be part of this. I'd be lying if I didn't admit that buried deep in serious apprehension, my scholarly interest is piqued. "Alright, Sionnach, I'll go to Leap Castle with you."

I'm really doing this—traveling through time. My heart stutters. I can't believe it. Somehow, I know Máthair would.

We dip inside the tree line and stop at a trio of stunning white trunks that begin from the same plot of earth, curve away from one another before bending back to an invisible center. Tiny green triangles climb the bark in an unnatural motif. Sion reaches between two of the trunks and produces an overstuffed canvas laundry bag. He dumps the contents at my feet and rifles through it. "A few skirts, an apron, and a *leine* ought to do you fine."

"Lay-nya? Oh, you mean like an under tunic?"

"Aye, Professor." He's already pulling off his shirt. The dips and planes of his chest are as well-defined as any athlete with a neat patch of russet hair filling the space between his pecs. His limp hasn't compromised a more-than-decent physique. I've only been involved with underfed bookworm types. What would it be like to explore those muscles with fingertips and kisses? He's quite pleasant to look or semi-gawk at, which is what I'm doing.

"Hey, what did happen to your limp?"

Sion searches through the pile and pulls out a long muslin shirt. *"Leine,"* he says, tossing it in my direction before diving back into the collection.

"Limp?"

"It's a wicked-twisted story."

I bark a laugh, surprising myself. "What isn't with you?"

"Promise I'll whisper it in that sweet ear of yours during one of Olk's long-winded speeches." How strange to think Sion and I will once again sit on a tour bus with normal people. He wrestles a larger version of the *leine* from the tangle of fabric and drops it over his head. The garment falls to his knees, and he wrestles with the fly of his jeans. I'm about to suggest privacy when he drops his jeans and pulls on a pair of breeches, giving me a glimpse of boxer briefs and sleek muscled calves. A surge of heat having nothing to do with my Veil Sprites pools low in my belly. What is this man doing to me with his mesmerizing voice and fine body? I give my head a curt shake.

Jeremy Olk is my type.

"Interesting fact," he says, waggling his eyebrows. "They didn't wear underthings where we're going."

"Lucky we're not staying long then." I carry my armful of period clothing behind a screen of bushes to dress. As I put on my Halloween costume of multilayered skirts, apron, vest, and cap, I call to him over the greenery. "Are you sure these clothes are period accurate enough for us to fit in?"

"Peasant fashion doesn't change much. We'll not be noticed."

I have no choice but to assume he's right. Clothing, apart from ceremonial garb, is not an area I'd paid much attention to as I leaned more into the spiritual and intellectual arms of Celtic studies instead of Pagan runway fashion.

I separate rumpled fabric. Interesting that Sion has women's clothing mixed in his cosplay. Perhaps I'll get another whispered story to explain the skirts in his collection during our next history lecture. The impression of a mystery girl in these clothes isn't one I can let go. "So, I'm not the first fair lassie to travel with you?"

"You are."

I snap one of the skirts, smoothing it so I can shimmy into it.

"I've known you'd be coming for a long while. I wanted to be ready."

I tie the back of the skirt as unease tightens my chest. "How long?"

Evading the question, Sion exhales loud enough to send a small breath cloud into the chilly air.

I narrow my eyes. "Another wicked-twisted story?"

He chuckles. "That it is."

Add *I've known you'd be coming for a long while* to my growing list of talking points with Sion.

When I emerge from my leafy dressing room, a fine Irish peasant waits. He's donned boots and holds a pair of cloth slippers out to me. I use his shoulder for balance and slip them on.

He fiddles with the ties of my skirt, and then holds me at arm's length for analysis. "Grand." He winks. "Even without stockings."

Damn it, why does Sion talking about stockings conjure an image of strong hands running up my legs to remove—? For goodness' sake, Eala, get a grip. I pretend to be occupied with straightening my outfit. Do Veil forests hold an aphrodisiac component he's failed to mention?

As I watch Sion expertly adjust his clothes, I stare at him. "How long have you been trying to fix the soulfall?"

He gives his vest a final tug and stares at me too long before he answers. "If I tell you, I need your word you won't run off."

Oh, shit. Here comes another avalanche of weird.

Sion grins. "You might say this isn't my first parade."

"Rodeo."

"Eh?"

"The saying is: It's not my first rodeo."

"Rodeo. Grand." He rearranges the leaves on the path with his toe, stalling. "As I've said, my days to serve are limited from Éostre to Beltane every year."

I'm not sure I want him to answer, but I ask anyway. "How many times have you had these days?"

"Closing in on two hundred."

I back into a tree trunk and cling to it to keep from falling.

He reaches a hand toward me but to his credit, holds his ground. "Honestly, it's less than three years over time if you do the calculating of possible days." He gives me a guilty smile. "It's no time at all if you divvy that up between devoting time to each soul's artifact."

My chest is so tight, I barely draw breath. Even though he doesn't look a day past thirty, Sion is saying he's over two hundred years old. How can he exist in the same lifetime as me as if he belongs here?

He takes a step closer. "Ask only what you need to. Time will have its way with us soon enough."

"How do you fit in and seem as normal as you do?"

"Short way is, I've got maybe forty days every year to catch up on the world." He blows air out his lips with a low whistle. "It's not a hard deal. One year to the next ain't much different." He lifts his chin like he's measuring the moon. "I reckon all this hasn't had adequate time to settle in your noggin, but we'd best be off."

He's right. My noggin is full to bursting. If I'm accepting the Veil and time travel, I guess Sion's bizarre existence is just one more part of the package to buy into.

"We'll talk again on it. I promise," he says, shifting his weight from foot to foot. "Can we be off then?"

Sion is so casual. I'm freaked out in equal parts to his calm. Have I lost my mind? What will it take to trade overwhelmed for being rooted in the now and stay safe? I should make Sion take me back to the circle of fake standing stones with their garlands and twinkle lights and let my grandmother rest in peace.

My chest tightens. What if Máthair is in a soulfall? Is she waiting for a Veil guide to find her key to pass into *Tír na nÓg*? I've got to find her. If my grandmother is cracking over a giant boulder in a different parade of doomed souls, maybe Sion and I can save her as well.

I lay a hand on Sion's. The contact sends a pleasant hum up my arm. "Are there other soulfalls?" He nods. "Will you go fix another if we get everything right with this one?"

My partner in our escapade wears a mask of weariness. "I'm not meaning to dodge your questions, love." A hand rests over his heart. He pauses as if counting the beats. "But I'm begging for a deferment until after we deal with Master Matthew."

Given the extremely loud ticking clock of a single Celtic day that I'm now aware of, I tamp down the urge to argue for now. "Okay." As soon as we return to my reality, I'm going to pin him to the ground until I get answers. The image of Sion's body pinned beneath mine ignites a burn across my cheeks as well as regions lower in my body.

His eyes twinkle, and my blush intensifies, mortified at the notion this strange man may be able to slip into my very thoughts. Sharing and Sion are not two words that fit companionably side-by-side so I'm in the dark as to how far his otherwordly reach may be. Given my last mental image, I'm not going to bring up the question right now.

"Ready?" he asks.

How can anyone be ready for backspacing five hundred years? I fight another onslaught of nerves. I'm doing this for the souls and the hope Sion can help me find Máthair. My heart aches with loss as fresh and violent as the day I lost her. If there is a chance to make sure she's found peace, I can't fritter it away because I'm scared shitless. "Not even a little."

He wraps an arm around my waist. "I won't be leaving your side, Eala *bán*. You have my word."

I thread an arm around his back, needing to cement myself to him. "And you promise we'll find my grandmother if I go with you?"

His muscles turn to granite against my arm. "I'll do my best to see it done."

I want to ask why he's so tense about his half of the promise. Is he bound to a Celtic afterlife rule book? In this place of soulfalls and Faerie kings, how can contacting Máthair's spirit be that big a taboo?

I hear Sion murmur before the prism walls fracture light around us. The barriers are gauzier than before. We glide through streaks of color. The rainbow box turns into a passageway. Far off I hear a chime, and then a sweet, sustained note. A violin, the music of my dream flashes. A second note rides beside it in gorgeous harmony. And then, in a breath, it all disappears.

CHAPTER II

THE ELEMENTAL

The light of the full moon nearly blinds me seconds before a wave of nausea and dizziness makes my legs buckle. Sion half carries me into a grove of trees, gently lowering me to the ground. I drop my head to my knees that are trapped beneath layers of skirt. His thumb kneads the back of my neck until the movement soothes the shudders wracking my body.

Closing my eyes helps as the world decelerates beneath me. "You said using the Veil would get easier."

"I'll teach you the proper way to cross when we've got more time before us."

I hate to break it to him, but once we're done with tonight's riddle, he's bound to his half of our promises to help me find Máthair. I'll use that as leverage if I have to before busting through time again. I'll still do my part. He can go collect clues on his own. I'll help the soulfall by doing the figuring out from my side of reality.

A loud roar and then strains of music from pipes, fiddles, and drums sound on the far side of a cluster of trees. Party time 1500s style. I reach for Sion's hand, desperate not to be separated from him. "Let's get this over with."

What I judge to be a block down a curved road, an old-fashioned tower house rises in front of the setting moon. Not old-fashioned yet, I remind myself. Very trendy for our current now.

Rivers of fast-moving, gray-black clouds stream above the boxy castle. The visual creep factor of this haunted-looking place contrasts with the firelight dancing inside and sounds of merriment pouring from arrow loops and windows. There's even singing coming from a group of men manning the rooftop. It's five hundred years ago, but trees are still trees, the grass beneath us still grass, people still sing. Maybe tonight won't be as insane as I expect.

"Big doin's at Leap," I say. Sion's face is a mask of serious, so I temper my lighthearted tone. "What do we do?"

"Shh," he warns, and then whispers close to my ear. "Wait for backup and then go in." We tuck deeper into the trees.

Am I in a cop show? What's sixteenth century backup? A cartload of armor and broadswords?

The backup arrives, and my blood freezes. A ghoulish figure materializes in front of us. The smell of dust, dung, and food left too long in the pantry fills the air. Sion's hand parks itself over my mouth in time to stifle my scream.

"Och, I told you to be slow about it, Pwyll."

A skeletal face with eye cavities large enough to fit my fist through and a perfectly round hole where a nose should be hovers in silence. A full set of yellow teeth outlined with brown decay are set in the thing's bony jaw. It flashes a perpetual grimace. Actually, more of a clench.

Sion slides his hand away from my lips. "Pwyll, this is Eala."

The head, neck, and shoulders of Sion's gruesome apparition nod ever so slightly in my direction. If I can call it a nod. The whole entity tilts forward in one hunk, individual pieces not moving independently. I swallow the ball of fear in my throat before it explodes into full terror. Underneath the collage of gasps, sobs, and trembles I'm trying to hide, I sense a low thrum in the air around us.

Holy shit, the bones are attempting to communicate.

Sion waves a hand at Skeletor. "Eala, Pwyll."

I bob my head at the Pwyll thing. "Hello?" I'm talking to a skeleton with no moving parts who smells of moldy cheese. I ache to return to the campsite. This is too out there. I thought we'd be mixing with ale drinking clansmen, not an ancient set of animated bones. I was prepared to pretend I'm at an uber-realistic Renaissance Fair but not stuck in a crypt.

"Pwyll's a bit of a timeless celebrity in these parts."

I manage a shaky smile. "Oh?"

"The ole druid's decided to hang around the place for a century or ten."

The thrum gets louder, its pitch rising and falling. I think Pwyll the druid might be laughing.

Sion bumps my shoulder with his. "This boyo is still around in your time."

My time. Not Sion's time. Another question for my ever-growing list. When the moon frees itself from the cloud stream, the whole of Pwyll becomes clear. He's skeleton from skull to toe bones. Not a *Día de los Muertos* dancing collection of bones. He's wedged into a very narrow coffin that comes to a point just above his head.

"Folks hereabouts call him *The Elemental.*" Sion wiggles his fingers as his voice wavers in a cheesy horror movie cadence Pwyll appears to appreciate.

"You understand him?"

Pwyll gives me another ghost bob, as if I'd asked him about being able to understand Sion. I close my eyes for a long moment and think of Máthair. She'd probably be clapping her hands or dancing with the ancient druid, maybe exchanging spiritual uses for herbs. Weird worked for my grandmother. If enduring oddities allows me to see her, I'll suck it up and power through the disturbing.

"He's helped me as best he could all the times I've tried before."

"But you never found the boy—Matthew?"

Pwyll's thrum turns into a wail that momentarily silences the singing on the roof. We duck deeper into the shadows until the chorus above us fires up again.

"Take your ease, man. She didn't mean it as a judgement. It's me failing not you."

Pissing off a druid ghost seems like a bad idea. "I'm sorry, Pwyll. This is all very new to me."

The thrum of their eerie sonic chat rises and falls along with Sion's head tilting. As quickly as he appeared, Pwyll vanishes. I semi-collapse against Sion.

He threads his arm through the crook of my elbow. "You're doing well."

It's hard to believe him when all I want to do is vaporize like Pwyll and get the hell out of here.

"We'll go in by way of the kitchen and hunt for the lad." Sion leads me through the trees and down a slope toward a door that opens to the lower floors of the tower house. "Once I have proof Matthew is here, Pwyll can help lead us to him."

I appreciate the way he holds my hand, firm and protective.

Jeremy Olk is my type.

Jeremy would be dancing a jig to be here with us.

Smells of onion and roasting meat make my stomach growl as we slip into a cavernous room. Apparently, a peanut bar doesn't keep you full with a five-hundred-year gap in play. Iron circles packed with candles hang on chains from the ceiling. Their flickering light trickles downward to merge with the crackle of fire roaring and spitting in a hearth as tall as me. We stand in a symphony of flames both tiny and ferocious. At least a dozen people work at loading platters of meat or tend to bubbling cauldrons of what I assume are stews and soups.

I cover my nose with the back of my hand. One awful smell permeates the kitchen above the rest. People. They reek of sweat, flatulence, and body odor potent enough to wipe out an entire town in one whiff. My eyes water, and the bustling kitchen blurs as Sion drags me through an archway.

I dig in my heels in at the bottom of a stone spiral stair. "What are you doing? I can't go up."

He clamps his hands on my hips and hoists me onto the steps in front of him. "It's only one floor. I'll keep you away from windows."

Before I can protest further, there are complaints behind us from a serving man juggling pewter pitchers.

Sion hustles me up the stairs. They twist and wind in a tight spiral, making navigation a chore that demands my full attention. The width of the steps is uneven, and I trip in a constant rhythm. Without Sion propelling me upward, I'd be falling and crawling instead of climbing.

Above us, the sounds of a gathering grow louder. Before we reach the source, Sion tugs me through an archway off the stairwell into a space that serves as a compact antechamber to a larger room. There's a glowing niche in the wall with something stretched in front of what must be candles. The light is gentle and warm. It reminds me of the luminaires I used to make for Halloween parties. Curious, I poke the fabric stretched across a wooden frame in front of the niche.

"Sheep stomach," says Sion, and chuckles when I yank my finger away. A few feet past us is an archway into a room lit solely by moonlight. Under a desk near the window, a barely audible mewling sound reaches us.

"Kitten?" I ask.

Sion shakes his head. "Child, I reckon. Hiding from the mayhem."

A flurry of servants streams up the steps, heading toward the festivity. Sion is a runner poised on the block, ready to sprint after them. He ducks his head back into the stairwell but doesn't resume the climb. Fear tightens his features.

"What's wron—"

Instead of answering, he guides me backward against the wall, locks an arm around my waist, and presses his mouth hard against mine. Fingers tangle in my hair, holding me captive. His lips grind with a pressure sure to bruise. I struggle to wrench my hands free and push him off, but I'm trapped. No matter what fleeting thoughts of appreciation I might have entertained at the sight of his bare sculpted chest, I didn't ask to be jumped. His thighs secure my own against the wall, giving me no chance to knee him.

He shudders at my struggle and tries to whisper something that sounds like an apology against my lips. The kiss shifts from surprise bombardment into tenderness. His mouth brushes gently over mine with the barest hint of desire. Instead of pinning me forcefully against stone, he eases up, molding his body to mine. My initial anger shifts into curiosity. Our position and the heat rising between us aren't entirely unwelcome.

The length of his body touching mine suggests interesting possibilities. But why now?

Before I can examine the sensation any closer and decide what returning the kiss might start, a deep bass more bear than human rumbles throughout our nook. "What sport's here?"

Sion spins so his back secures me against the wall. He bows his head. Over his shoulder, I see a hulking shape lumber close. The man's black beard and equally black mane tangle together like a pelt. A lecherous smile reveals broken yellow teeth. Leather and furs crisscross the giant's frame. He's no serving man. The three of us crowd the small space.

A slab of a hand covers Sion's shoulder, and he's thrust against the archway. "I'll have a quick go first, lad, and then I'll leave her good and ready for you."

A bear would probably smell better than this pervert. The man's shadow covers me. Fingers with crusted black fingernails clamp around my breast.

Quick as the fox he is, Sion reinserts himself between the beast and me. "I'll thank you to take hands off my wife."

"Your wife, is she?"

Sion raises my hand with Máthair's ring. "She is."

A huge roar from above vibrates through the stone walls of the castle, drawing the goon's attention. He leers at me. "I've got more willing hens to pluck than the likes of you." Without another glance at us, he pounds up the stairs.

I'm shaking so badly; Sion has to support me as we stumble through the arch into the dark room. We slide out of sight behind a chair and drop to the floor.

"Are ya all right, Eala? Oh, God." Sion smooths the hair from my face and pats my arms, searching for broken bones. When I gingerly touch my swollen lips with the tip of a finger, he flinches.

My voice quavers. "I'm not supposed to get hurt."

He hangs his head. "No, you're not. It was reckless of me to fly up the stairs so. I couldn't think what to do but claim you as mine." His hands slide along the sides of my face, thumbs tenderly caress my cheeks. "I swear, from here on, you'll be treated as the rare gem you are." Sion rests his forehead against mine. "Forgive me. I beg you."

"I want to go back to the campsite."

He pulls away, conflict screwing up his face. If we leave without finding Matthew, Mrs. Kennedy's soul will repeat her fate against unforgiving boulders in an endless loop. Sion will add another failure to his scorecard. He said he only had until Beltane, and there are souls besides Alaina Kennedy to free.

Sion stands, bringing me with him. His features are stone. "We'll go back."

"Wherever you be going, will ya take me?" The voice from under the desk makes us both jump. A boy no more than eight- or nine-years old crawls out to stand before us. Thick chocolate waves frame a gaunt face. His eyes catch enough light to reveal desperate hope. He's dressed in the garb of a serving lad. My heart breaks a little for Sion. This kid is too young to be Matthew Kennedy.

"Your masters will beat you for leaving," says Sion matter-of-factly.

"If I stay, I'll be dead."

Sion kneels in front of the boy. "And who'll be killing you?"

He's so kind and easy with the kid. It's a side of him that coaxes awake a soft spot in my heart.

The boy gestures to the stairwell. "They kept some of us aside. Said we'd serve the wine to the McMahons during the feast."

I stand behind Sion and address the boy. "Isn't it your job, honey?"

This close, I see how badly the kid shakes.

"I heard soldiers talking. The wine is poisoned. The O'Carrolls will be killing the McMahons to keep from paying them for the fighting."

"Damn me," Sion whispers and looks up. "The Bloody Chapel." His grip on my arm promises another bruise as he drags me toward the stairs. "I've lost my bearing and brought you on a cursed night. We've got to get out of the castle, NOW!"

When the boy doesn't follow, I wave him on. "Come with us."

Sion hisses in my ear. "I've got no claim on his soul. If we help him, we might miss Matthew."

"We'll send him into the woods, tell him to run."

"Fine."

"Wait." I kneel next to the boy. "Do you know Matthew Kennedy?"

He speaks between sobs. "Aye. Mattie's another they pulled aside to serve the wine."

I smooth a strand of hair out of his eyes. "I need you to do something for me. Get outside, then run as fast as you can into the trees. Don't stop until you get to a place with kind people. Understand?"

He nods, and I drop a kiss on the top of his head.

It's horrible to leave the little guy, but we fly down the stairs. Sion asks every servant we pass on our way if they know Matthew's whereabouts, careful not to mention poisoned wine.

The sword of terrible truth pierces me. I can get hurt here. Slip ups have the potential to be fatal. Sion lied to me. His protection has limitations. If that brute in the hallway decided to rape me, what could Sion do once he was knocked out cold?

I'm not cut out for this.

We burst through the kitchen door and strike for the tree line. Ducking behind the widest trunk, Sion peeks around to make sure we weren't followed. I'm panting so hard my chest aches and it's not easing up. How much fear can a heart take before it splits?

I give a tiny shriek when Pwyll materializes, separating Sion and me.

"A wee lad spoke the name. Proof. Matthew Kennedy is here. Can you now find him?"

Pwyll doesn't nod or disappear. He floats in the open space between trees and castle, humming.

Sion snatches my hand. "Come on, then."

What choice do I have but to follow a thousand-year-old druid and a two-hundred-year-old Veil guide? I can't knock on the castle door and ask for directions to the twenty-first century on the night a room full of soldiers is set to be poisoned instead of paid. Or any night, for that matter.

Pwyll leads us to the corner of the castle. We scrabble backward in time to keep from plunging over the edge of the cliff the castle perches on. Below us, a countryside dusted in moonlight spreads to the edge of sight. The peaceful lowing of a cow drifts up the hillside, a disconnect from the bloody history about to be made inside the walls of Leap Castle.

Pwyll turns and weaves, leaning with his coffin from side to side, drawing an invisible path in the air. At least invisible to me. He goes one way and then backtracks, curving, twining. I gulp a mouthful of air when he glides straight through the stone wall of the castle and then back out. It's mad. How will we ever get to Matthew in time if we're supposed to follow this Elemental's maze?

I shake Sion's sleeve and jerk my chin at the castle. "If we go out in the open, they'll see us?"

"Whisht!" He lays a finger against my kiss-swollen lips. "It's nearly finished."

"What?"

Sion strokes a finger through the air. "He's spiral walking. Pwyll's drawing a Triskele. It's a Celtic spiral pattern for the three-layered nature of the human soul. Where it ends will point to young Matthew."

Sure enough, a pattern glows so faintly, it looks like brush strokes of moon beam and shadow. Suddenly, the commotion from above changes timbre. Instead of cheers and singing, hideous strangling noises and cries of pain run down the castle walls. Clanking of metal on metal punctuates unbearable sounds of torment. The dirge of the soulfall was the worst nightmare soundtrack I'd ever experienced until now. This is hell's symphony.

Sion and I hold one another, heads bowed onto each other's shoulders until silence replaces the death rattle of a hundred spirits. Pwyll moans, stretching his design back around to the front of the castle where he inclines the top point of his coffin to the right of the wooden front door.

"Steal my soul," says Sion. "The *oubliette*."

Rhythmic thuds come from the other side of the wall where the tip of Pwyll's spiral leads us. Muffled shrieks of pain reverberate through my skin.

Sion follows the fading glow of the Triskele toward the main door. Before we reach it, he points to a cart near the corner of Leap Castle. "Hide there. I won't be but a minute."

I wrap both arms around one of his. He can't leave me alone. "Where are you going? You can't go in. They'll take you."

The door is open a crack. Nobody stands near it. There's no sound from the main floor. Faint firelight is all that filters through the slit between wood and stone. Sion peels my hands off his arm, leaning in to whisper, "In the corner of this room, on the other side of the wall, is the *oubliette*."

He reads the horror in my expression and continues. "You know of the hidden shafts for putting things you don't want anyone else to find." Sion lays his palm gently on the side of my face. "You don't want to be seeing what's there now. Stay out of sight."

Without warning, there's a wisp of mist and Sion seems to collapse. A fox trots to the wooden door, nosing it aside enough to squeeze through. Okay, Sion's fox morphing business can come in handy. Down the path from the castle, the low conversation of guards rolls through the trees. I'm not staying put to slam into any more drunken, ham-handed rapists.

Careful to hug walls and shadow, I make my way to peek through the door inside the darkened room holding Leap Castle's chamber of secrets. The space is deserted save the dwindling light of a neglected fire and the rumble of men's voices spilling down the stairs. My stomach knots, imagining the bastards above me clinking tankards and congratulating themselves on mass murder.

As I slide into the room, I find the stuff of madness. Pwyll hovers near the corner to the right of the door where plaster and stone shift between transparent and opaque. Either the druid or Sion eroded the substance of the wall to reveal a macabre sculpture of bodies. A tower of limbs overextends and twists. Heads face backward, dolls put together wrong.

I lift a hunk of skirt and shove it into my mouth to muffle a scream as a new body drops from the Bloody Chapel above onto the heap. The metallic stench of blood, Pwyll's decay, and general foulness nearly overwhelm me. I breathe into my apron to dilute what I can.

Sion's strained voice reaches me through the darkness. "Is there anything I can say to your ma so she knows I've found you? A song she sung? A story?"

Stuttering moans answer. Through the fading wall, I find Sion wedged in beside the carnage.

"Come on, lad. It's for your ma. Give me something."

My fingers tremble with an urge to slap Sion's insensitive face.

He's found Matthew Kennedy.

If the boy is on this pile of death, time has run out to find any key, that necessary proof to bless his mother with the mercy of knowing her son's fate.

What happens now? Can't Sion come back earlier on this night and save the boys doomed to serve the poisoned wine who will be killed to ensure their silence? He should let Matthew die in peace now and then return instead of badgering him like a criminal.

A sob rises in the dark. I can't tell if it's Sion, Matthew, or a different victim crossing from life to death in the pile.

"I want to save your ma. Do ya understand?" It's Sion who weeps. His cries slice my own soul. If I'm supposed to be the one to help him free the soulfall, I won't succeed by hiding.

Clutching my skirt, I step through the shimmering wall and press next to Sion in a corner of the narrow shaft. The deathscape is a thousand times worse up close. Bodies twitch in the stack. Gasps sound from under corpses. The flickering light animates forms, thick black snakes writhing and sliding in an overcrowded nest.

I slip between Matthew and Sion, who grasps my arms to turn me away, but I've already seen. The body of Matthew Kennedy, a slender teen with delicate features akin to an antique porcelain doll, arches over the evil wooden spike piercing his body.

I don't understand how he can still be alive. Is the Veil sustaining him long enough for Sion to find the key to his mother's redemption? I'm forced to shift a body out of the way to lay a hand on Matthew's cheek. Death presses in around me. It's suffocating in the cramped shaft that can't be more than five or six feet square. The insubstantial give of the transforming wall is the only reason Sion and I can maneuver at all. Even so, he wraps his body around mine to fit into the tiny space.

Will the proof we've found Matthew be enough of an artifact to release his mother's soul? Máthair's ring glints in yellow flickers. I check Matthew's fingers for a ring. Harriet needed her doll. What does Alaina Kennedy need?

I brush a lock of hair from the dying boy's eyes. "What can we take to your ma to remember you?"

Sion sputters. "He's got no more words."

With painstaking slowness, Matthew bobs his chin twice to his chest. I run a hand over his vest. A button? A pin? What does he want me to find? In a final effort, he lolls his head to one side, and I see a thin leather cord around his neck. As gently as possible, I slip my finger beneath it, tracing its length until I find the knot holding it in place. It isn't hard to work free. A simple silver cross with worn etchings across its surface dangles on the cord.

Sion makes the sign of the cross, touching his forehead, then three points on his chest. Matthew's mouth purses so slightly if I wasn't staring at his face, I'd miss it. I hold the silver jewelry to his lips for a final kiss. A moment later, he's gone.

With a featherlight touch, I close his eyelids. "May angels sing you home, dear one."

CHAPTER 12
THE MORNING LIGHT

S ion and I stumble out of the Veil passage like drunkards misjudging the height of a curb.

Our less than graceful travel pummels my insides. I take a series of deep breaths to stave off nausea and force myself to look up.

"Go." I push Sion toward the soulfall tower. He disappears between mossy stones. The cry of souls, fingernails scraping concrete, resonates to the roots of my teeth.

"St. Augustine, let Sion make it before she jumps." I can't bear to watch Alaina Kennedy's soul drowning in her gray loop of sorrow once more when we've brought the key to end it. We found her Matthew, and she deserves peace.

Alaina's figure fills the arched window. The silhouette of her clothing against tangerine firelight is strikingly period now that I know her context in time. Her woeful song drifts down over the grass. I clasp my hands and hold them to the sky. "Please, let Sion reach her."

She steps into the air, but this time, instead of flinging her arms wide, hands press to her lips. Moonlight bounces off the river, catching the silver of Matthew's cross as she kisses it. The precious piece of metal shines like a beacon. With a slight turn of head, Alaina faces me. She reaches out a hand as if asking to grasp mine before she bursts into a million raindrops of fire.

I collapse onto the damp ground. We've done it. Victory sweeps the last of my nausea away. Alaina Kennedy's virtue of mercy is restored. A mother is blessed with knowing her son waits for her in heaven.

A cry of misery with enough power to banish clouds from the sky blasts from the tower, a reminder Alaina is but a single spirit freed from this labyrinth of torment. I curl onto my side to avoid watching the remaining souls pound onto rocks. Nothing, not even my arms wrapped over my ears, shields me from the sound of their grim endings.

When silence returns, I release my senses from shutdown and become aware of someone lying close.

Sion

He's next to me not quite touching. How has he endured listening to the soulfall without going mad for—

I shudder.

Two—hundred—years.

Is it because he's actually dead? The heat radiating off his body says otherwise. Sion isn't in any ghost or spirit form I know of. He's as real as I am. People see and touch him.

Whatever this man is, we now share a bond of purpose.

He gently eases me onto my side and spoons his body around me. A muscular arm slides over my shoulder until his hand finds mine. We hold tight with the need we share—to be close. For reassurance? Banishment of fear?

The pulse in his wrist thumps against my skin.

Not-a-Faerie.

Not-a-ghost.

Sion is a *fánai*, wanderer, Veil guide. St. Augustine pushed me to the limits in the unseen belief department, but I can't discount what the last few hours have shown me. I've stepped beyond the fantastic.

Sion's voice is as tight as his grip. "I couldn't send her on without you, my blessed Eala. The merciless unknowing over the fate of her son would have consumed her soul forever." He abruptly shifts onto his back, not letting go of my hand. I hear the *thump thump thump* as he pounds his chest with his free hand. "I'm reckless and blind."

I squeeze our joined hands. "If it weren't for you and Pwyll, Alaina Kennedy would not be saved. You've done the groundwork. I merely sharpened your focus."

"The lad's last letter to his folks arrived after the bloody chapel murders. Stories of the O'Carroll's treachery and malice have always driven me to avoid that particular night. The thought of experiencing the agony of so many souls ripped from life was more than I could bear. My cowardice nearly cost Alaina Kennedy her eternity." He stares at the moon.

"Did the timing of the letter lead you to believe he survived the murders?"

He nods.

My heart aches for Sion, Matthew, and Alaina. "All the time you spent looking—he was already gone." I roll onto my side to face him, tugging at his shoulder until he turns toward me. Carefully, I gather him close until there's no space between us as he trembles. My heartbeat reteaches his how to beat at a steady pace.

Our lips are inches apart. Lips that kissed once. Will they kiss again?

"Thank you, my Eala *bán*." He pinches one of my flyaway strands of hair, sliding his fingers all the way to the end before he hands it off to the breeze. "'Twas your presence with me in the Veil steering us to the right time."

The gravity of a crossroads moment presses down on me. If I want to end the continuation of this bizarre trek, the time is now before I'm in any deeper. I took that first step with him and saved Alaina. It's well within my rights of our bargain to demand we search for Máthair, and then I'll never travel into danger again.

The Veil Sprites inside me rage with disapproval, sending tiny shocks against my bones. How strange to be a part of the stories I teach of the *Daoine Sidhe* and Finnbheara, King of the Connacht Fae, known for his penchant for mortal women and enigmatic trickery. There's a wonder and a horror to it. Even though escape is tempting, the idea of turning my back on Sion and the souls steals my breath.

He stares at my mouth. "When you push your lips out, are you pouting or checking the way of the wind?" Sion braces himself on an elbow, separating our bodies ever so slightly.

I fight the urge to throw my leg over his hip and pull him back to me.

His smirky smile returns. "I hope it's blowing favorably in my direction."

I gaze into his vibrant eyes as languid want settles over me, longing for those wanderer's lips to meet mine again. "Heading that way." I'm acutely aware of our proximity to each other and the possibilities it presents. My hand slides up the side of his face, learning the softness of skin beneath the stubble. I lean in to dot a kiss on his cheek and linger, wondering if I should cross the small distance to the lips I've just begun to know.

I remember listening to a colleague describe the overwhelming need to make love with her husband after they walked away from a terrible car accident. Is that what I'm feeling for Sion right now—survivor's passion?

A hundred simultaneous surges of heat flash through my body. It's so intense, I cry out. Damn the Veil Sprites. I can't tell if my new internal passengers were vehemently in favor or opposed to the idea of a kiss.

Sion clutches my shoulder. "Are you all right, love?"

I lay a hand over my heart. "How do I get the Veil Sprites to take it down a notch?"

He laughs. "They aren't a bit shy over sharing their opinions."

I decide to interpret their message as a rush for saving Alaina Kennedy. Their fiery presence flows inside me like a pool of molten goodness.

I nudge Sion. "Are they inside you?"

He scoffs. "I need no reminder that I'm well acquainted with the Veil."

I may not fully comprehend the power of what I'm meant to do, but I do know I'm not ready to abandon it. Not ready to abandon Sionnach Loho.

Above us, clouds stretch into a feathery dome. Two distinct streaks of light travel side by side along their lower edge. I read the sky as a sign of encouragement, which opens a floodgate inside me, and I'm suddenly ravenous to understand this new part of me, this calling. There won't be much time for questions before the soulfall begins again, and I need to cocoon inside my arms.

"Are we in the Veil now?"

"A part of it."

Weariness in his voice and knowledge of where it came from sparks more tenderness toward him. When he drops onto his back again, I nestle my head into the crook of his shoulder. He's stiff with surprise at our initial contact, but soon his tension eases, giving me a softer pillow.

"More please."

He groans softly without conviction.

"Man of few words doesn't cut it with me anymore, partner."

Sion chuckles. "I suppose not."

"The tower? The souls? Where are we?" I point to the shifting clouds. "It isn't frozen here, the way it was when you first took me inside the Veil."

"This is a waiting place."

I nudge him to continue.

"The Veil creates these pockets like, ah, annexes."

"For soulfalls?"

Sion sits up, carrying me with him. He flattens his hand and then bends his thumb and pinkie over his palm so three fingers stick up. "Put your fist in the middle of my hand."

I rest my fist over his curled fingers. "Your fist is the Veil. Think of it as a hub. We can either pass through it, or what do you Amerrrricans say? 'Hang out,' inside it."

"Oh, like we did in the forest of glowing balls."

Sion spits out a laugh. "The Veil might not take kindly to being called the forest of glowing balls."

I laugh with him. While Sion continues my Veil lesson, I take a closer look at him. One eye is slightly larger than the other, but they're so round and cute it doesn't matter. In moonlight, their green is the color of blown glass. The curls and waves of his hair are scattered with russet and gold, fall leaves not fully turned.

For him, is our cuddle here in the grass born only of a shared victory and survival? I can't deny the pull I feel toward him. No matter how appealing I find his touch, Sion hasn't given any sign of personal interest in me beyond my usefulness of problem solving. Then again, there was that kiss against the castle wall. I know he initiated it to protect me, but then it shifted into something more intimate—more confusing. So much has happened tonight, my emotions are in freefall. Rational thinking, my old friend, suggests we aren't meant to kindle a Colleen and Charlie spark. Sion and I are business partners of a sort with a cosmic deadline.

Jeremy Olk is the right match for me.

Interesting how very little the steady, academic Jeremy has come to mind on this strange evening.

Sion smirks. "We'll leave off the balls and call it the place that smells of lemongrass and spearmint."

"And soap bubbles to you."

"Besides moving through the Veil itself, we're offered three destinations we can travel to." He wiggles his index finger. "Anywhere we intend to be in the present." Switching to his middle finger, he says, "Other times and places." His ring finger waves up and down like it's doing squats. "Soulfalls."

"No zips into the future or other planets?"

"The whole of history don't satisfy yaaaaa—" Sion's last word stretches into a groan. He smacks a hand to his chest. Pain splatters across his face, and he chokes out his words. "We've got to go. Break day is coming fast."

In the distance, a thin gray line sketching the horizon widens.

I put my hand over his. "What's wrong?"

The moment our fingers touch, a painful jolt rockets through my chest, knocking me back onto my side. The Veil cinches around us like a giant elastic band, swallowing our yelps of pain into its wavering prism.

Moments later, we're flat out underneath the leaning stone, clutching our chests and panting for breath. Sion's skin is gray.

Dawn birdsong erupts around us. The flashlight I dropped rests on the path nearby. We're back in the forest where I unwittingly chased a fox and shattered my reality. He drags himself next to me, laying one hand on my heart and one on his own. Every heartbeat is agony as it presses against the pressure of his palm. I try to speak but only manage a drawn-out moan.

The Veil has decided to kill me, and judging from his condition, Sion too. For a second, I wonder what celestial rule we broke to earn a death sentence after saving Alaina Kennedy's soul. I close my eyes. Is it an afterlife for me or a soulfall? I wish I'd had a chance to say goodbye to Colleen.

Instead of dying faithfully by my side in our skewed version of Romeo and Juliet, Sion starts to sing. My heart warms beneath his palm. Vibrations from his voice wave over my skin. Moments later, I'm calm.

Sion slides an arm around my shoulders. "Are you all the way back from the Veil?" A slight pink rises under his cheekbones, replacing his near-corpse gray tint.

"Are you?"

"Aye. In the nick."

Satisfied we've both side-stepped death's welcome mat, I round on him. "What the hell was that?"

His face flushes the same chili powder color as his hair. "Me being a gobshite." He stares past me into the forest. "Seems I'll be spending a good portion of our time together apologizing to you."

"Cut the puzzle talk and explain." The ample sleeve of my *leine* makes a nice handkerchief to wipe the sweat from my forehead. "I'd prefer to avoid future cardiac arrest."

"I'm with you there." He shakes his head, freeing the curls sweat-plastered to his temples. "We overstayed our time." I windmill my hands for him to continue. He frets and pops his lips. "Traveling is like this. The Veil answers to a Celtic day, sundown to sundown. That's when we travel. Here a single night passes. The hours don't match exactly."

I want to pull his hair and not let go until he gets to the point. "What—almost—killed—us?"

"A hundred thousand heart beats are the limit we're allowed to travel during a single Celtic day."

I press a fist to my lips. "How in the world are we supposed to keep track of heartbeats?"

"It's your typical number of heartbeats in a day. As long as we finish wandering before what's dawn to us, there's no bother with counting."

I use the stone to stand and fluff my skirts. "That's a huge need to know, Sion. You're ridiculously stingy with vital information."

He dusts off his britches. "I'll write you a manual."

I groan in frustration at the immense lack of information I'm getting from him. "Your manual better include a chapter on me not getting killed while we bop around time." I lock hands to hips. "You lied when you said I was safe when we travel. What about the caveman on the stairwell? Some gamble, flashing my grandmother's ring, *husband*!"

"I didn't lie. You were fine. I'd a called the Veil to pull us out if the milk turned sour."

I give his shoulder a light backhanded smack and find it wildly satisfying. "That is what you should have led with."

Instead of fighting back, he bows to me. "Forgive me, *wife*." He tilts his head. "Are we done bickering?"

I defy anyone not to smile at the sparkle in those green glass eyes. "For now."

He gives his chest a good scratch. "It's the blazing time as a fox that fooled my reckoning."

Sion stretches an arm over his shoulder, aiming for the center of his back but can't quite reach.

I move around him. "I'll get it."

He almost purrs as I vanquish his itch. My hands long to sneak up the inside of his shirt to relish the warmth of bare skin. This overwhelming need to touch him is baffling. Less than a day ago, I wanted Sion out of my life. That was before we bent time and saved a soul. "What does your freaky fox trick have to do with keeping track of time?"

"A fox's heartbeat is a gallop to our trot. Drains the heartbeat quota much faster." He grunts. "Finnbheara's gifts always come with give and take. Mostly take."

I lay a palm over my heart, checking, and am relieved to feel it calm and steady. "I didn't turn into a fox. What screwed my quota?"

Sion's lip crinkles. "You're tied to me, love." He looks over my shoulder, eyes calculating. "I'll not gamble using the fox again this close to Beltane."

I shudder as the memory of the *oubliette* washes over me. "Was it you or Pwyll who allowed us to walk through walls?"

He kicks a stone. "Me. That particular effort stole heartbeats as well. Thank grace we made it back at all with me being so reckless." His gaze meets mine, and he winks. "Another chapter for the manual."

I blow a stream of air, sending hair dancing around my face and wish there really was a manual.

"Good, on we go." He reaches into his pocket and produces three tiny, interconnected metal rings. "These belong to a laddie who squired for Strongbow. Chainmail is what you'd call cutting edge technology in the grand ole twelfth century."

Oh, for the love of reason—the twelfth century! There's a slice of yore I'm not anxious to leap into. I take the rings from him and lay them on my palm. "Strongbow."

There's a low rumble in his chest. For a moment, I expect him to roar like the king of the forest. "The feller who brought the English shitestorm to Ireland."

My finger stops tracing the shape of the chainmail, indignant that Sion feels the need to mansplain Strongbow to a Celtic studies adjunct professor. "I'm well aware of who Richard de Clare is." I quickly get over my pissy moment. "Wait. If you've already got the artifact, why is Strongbow's squire still in the soulfall?"

Sion threads his pinky through one of the rings and twirls them. "We've got the key alright, but it hasn't completed the work to restore the virtue. The squire stole this chainmail from his master. The lad figured he'd make a pretty penny selling it, owing to Strongbow's fame."

"Is that what screwed up the squire's virtue?"

"Led to it. Once the young fool had the chainmail, he deserted his lord to make his own fortune. Not so noble." Sion lays the rings in the flat of his palm. "Didn't go well. The lad was mightily overcome with shame for betraying a man who'd been nothing but good to him, and he went barking mad. Roamed the countryside, begging and searching for Strongbow to return the mail rings." Sion grunts. "Pity and the waste of a life. I'm positive Sir Greatness never missed these wee pieces at all."

"I don't get it." I rub my nose against my shoulder, trying to work out our next case. "He's a thief. What virtue fixes that?"

"It's not the thieving. He repented. Even confessed to a priest." Sion picks at the curls over his ears. "He lost himself, his humanity." His eyes widen expectantly. "If we return the chainmail to Strongbow, we'll grant the squire's soul a clean slate. His humanity can work its way back in."

No doubt my *partner* is ready to dive into our next adventure, but I'm still not entirely sure my heart isn't going to explode. I touch my forehead to the frigid leaning stone and use it as an ice pack for my throbbing head. "I may need more recovery time than the day before my next sucker punch from the Veil." After our vacay into the sixteenth century, I'm not eager to set the time machine back any farther.

The memory of Little Harriett tugs at me. "Do we have to hand the chainmail to Strongbow in his time? What if he's a ghost skipping around the Irish countryside?"

Sion leans next to me with his back against the stone. Both eyes wobble while he contemplates my question.

I wrack my brain for Strongbow details. Where might said ghost be floating through walls? The baggy sleeve of my *leine* snags on one of the slashes in the stone. Shit, we're still in our period garb. "We've got to change and rejoin to the group. Colleen will freak if she realizes I'm gone."

Sion squints at the sun rising through the forest portal. "Aye."

"Let's brainstorm on the bus to Dublin."

He flashes me a smile that turns my knees to putty. Who am I? One kiss plus post soul-saving cuddles and I'm into him?

"Aye, we will." With a wink, he moves a few feet along the path and then zips off into the forest. "Over here."

Stepping into shadows, I watch him reach into the middle of the same trio of white trunks where he retrieved the clothing bundle before our jaunt to Leap Castle.

"Didn't we leave your bag..." I search the immediate area. The tree with the clothes was at the edge of a forest, and now it's in the middle of one?

Sion strips the sixteenth century to his ankles. I turn my back, but not before I treat myself to another peek at the expanse of his freckly sculpted chest with its center of foxy fur. "We did. The tree follows me when I travel. You might say tree energy and leaning stones give Veil travel a grand boost."

I drop my head back. There's so much of this that's normal to Sion and beyond unbelievable to me. Will my thoughts ever stop furiously spinning?

"I considered trying to keep a family of hedgehogs for company in there." He rattles on while my modern-day clothes sail over me and into the dirt at my feet. "The white poplar is a sacred tree you know. These green triangles in the bark form a pattern saying it's mine so no other guides try to use her. Some call this the tree of life, *Eadha*, and claim her roots go down past our world to the other."

I slip behind a wider trunk to change back into jeans and a sweater. Máthair's scarf is balled up in one of the sleeves. I smile at a fleeting image of Sion and my grandmother chatting over Irish breakfast tea in the kitchen of our New York apartment about hedgehogs and sacred trees. She'd like him despite all the riddles.

"I call her Alfie." Sion pats the trunk. "As in Al—find your sorry arse, Sionnach, no matter where you fly off to."

It's strange to accept that this merry, laughing version of my new partner is the same snarly chancer I met in the Blarney Castle Druid's Cave less than two days ago.

Two days.

The intensity of our time together makes it feel like two years. I toss my serving wench costume to him. He jams it into the canvas bag, which he deposits in the space between Alfie's slender white trunks. I make a mental note to zip into a Tesco market and buy dryer sheets for the clothes sack, hopefully cutting back a smidge of sixteenth or whatever century odor.

Sion offers his hand, and I take it. Yesterday, he was off-putting, but this morning, walking hand in hand feels as natural as if we've been doing it forever. I press my lips together. He is a form of forever. My forever companion who sends souls to the light.

"We did something good tonight." His thumb slides across the back of my hand. "Something very good, and I thank you for it."

We.

Sionnach and Eala.

The fox man and the swan gal.

Together, we gave a spirit her peace. The rising sun on my skin and the heat from Sion's hand are as soothing as a warm bath. We're about to crest the last rise before the downslope to the standing stones when Charlie nearly plows into us at a dead run.

His face is as red as the streaks bobbing over the horizon. He clutches my arm, forcing himself between Sion and me.

"Shit, Eala, I said he wasn't a bad guy." Charlie jerks his chin at Sion. "Which doesn't translate to mysteriously disappear with him."

Charlie's grip sends the feeling of being trapped through me. I pat the hand attached to my arm. "I'm fine. You can let go."

The crown of Colleen's auburn head rises above the curve of the hill. "La!" she calls out, covering the distance between us in less than one of my hundred-thousand heartbeats.

Colleen collides with me in a full throttle hug. "When I found your backpack in an ice-cold sleeping bag, I imagined at least five abduction scenarios."

"I'm cutting off your obsession with true crime documentaries," I say, holding her at arm's length.

"You'll be letting too many Faerie stories roll about in your head," adds Sion.

His words drip with sarcasm. With the snap of a finger, unappealing Sion is back. I have the urge to thump his chest with the back of my hand and tell him to shush. Thoughts tangle in my head. Do I suggest Sion and I cozied up to one another last night? We may not be a couple in the Colleen sense of the word, but we're partners in purpose. What will play with our audience without seeming sketchy or unbelievable? My muscles stiffen as the stink of a double standard rises from dewy ground. It's cool for Colleen and Charlie to fall for each other in a minute and a half but not us?

Colleen lays the back of her hand against my cheek. "You're freezing."

When Sion moves back to my side, Charlie takes a menacing step toward him, eyes blazing. A jagged fork of lightning collides with the tallest tree in the wood. A wave of ozone hits a moment later.

Colleen cries out in surprise as a slate gray swirl of clouds spins in the sky above the forest only to be burst apart by a gust of wind.

Sion nods in the direction of the whirlwind and lightning strike.

"Impressive. Have the ear of Taranis do you, Charlie?" he says with his signature smirk.

Is Sion kidding about the Celtic sky god, or is he baiting Charlie? Heaven knows what I might find if I peel back Sion's insider knowledge of the universe any further.

Sion chuckles. "You Yanks aren't used to our fickle Irish weather."

Charlie doesn't laugh. His face wears an acid look.

Since we've been caught leaving the woods holding hands, the cozying up scenario makes the most sense. Easing away from Colleen, I tuck against Sion's side. As if this is completely natural for us, he wraps an arm around me.

"You guys can relax. Sion and I—we're good."

Colleen's mouth forms a series of small, medium, and large Os then studies us skeptically. I can practically hear *this guy instead of Jeremy Olk* screaming through her thoughts.

Charlie shares a look with Colleen. "Really?"

"Reeeeeely," says Sion, imitating Charlie before kissing my cheek. He shoots Charlie a smug look of triumph. "You needn't concern yourself with Eala's well-being on my behalf, mate."

I pinch Sion's side to stop his—what did he call it at Blarney Castle—acting the maggot. He jumps, and then retaliates, burying his nose in my hair to nip my earlobe in a very foxlike way. Damn, I like it.

I take two oversized steps toward the campsite, pulling him along with me. "So, on to breakfast before we get stuck in the rain?" For a second, I wonder where my bag of peanut bars ended up.

Sion kisses my hand. The feel of his damp lips against my skin does crazy things to my core that has nothing to do with the Veil Sprites who seem to have switched off for now. I'll question Sion about their supernatural schedule when we're alone. I lean to murmur in his ear. "Keep pushing her buttons, fox man, and Colleen will hit you with a rock."

He snorts, and then calls over his shoulder to Colleen and Charlie. "Truth be told, I've fallen hard for an Amerrrrican woman. I can't keep my hands off her." His voice shifts, sliding through the air, honey running down a spoon. "And to think my fool mouth almost ruined my chances."

He gazes at me the way fairy tale princes drink in princesses after saving them from dragons.

My knees go wobbly. If this is a performance, Sion is a damn good actor. A brazen ray of morning sun smacks aside the clouds and sets the coppery undertones of Sion's hair ablaze. The color is a gorgeous contrast to his peacock jacket.

Colleen interrupts my appreciation of Sion's curls. "I've never seen you smitten this fast, La."

"I could say the same for you," I nod toward Charlie.

Colleen stares at me. "Since when are your eyes super green?" Her lip crinkles into a scowl.

At her comment, Sion gives my hand a bone-crushing squeeze. A glance at his face tells me something is off, but he recovers in an instant, flashing me another mushy smile. "As emerald as morning dew on the grass."

What is he talking about? My eyes are as far from emerald as dew is from sand. They do go greener if I'm wearing green, but aside from that, they're closer to dove gray with a sprig of mint.

Colleen's gaze assesses Sion from cowlick to sneaker. She leans close to whisper to me. "Are you going to tell me the words on your ring mean, *find him?*"

"We'll talk later," I whisper back.

Charlie's eyes narrow. "So you two are a thing?"

A thing. That may be the best description of us yet. At the same time, Sion and I both say, "Yeah."

"As new a thing as you two," I say, shooting Sion my version of an adoring smile that somehow feels real. "We stayed up all night besting each other with Irish folktales. Kindred spirits you might say."

Sion trains a strand of hair behind my ear while staring into my eyes. "This lovely one's rendition of Deirdre's story 'twas wondrous."

Even though he must be doing it for Colleen and Charlie's benefit, I can't look away.

"When Eala told the part of the story when the fir that grew from the grave of Deirdre on one side of the loch reached..." Sion raises his arm, fingers stretching wide. "...And then the way the other tree across the water rose from the grave of her one true love, Naois..."

I lift my hand and thread my fingers through his. His voice trails off as we float in each other's gaze. How have I become bound to someone so completely in a single Celtic day? A man devoid of a single drop of the stability and comfort I crave.

I finish Deirdre's tale I know well from Máthair's telling. "The two branches unite in a knot in the sky above the water—forever."

Desire to kiss Sion pools in my chest. As if reading my thoughts, he leans in. My heart races. Charlie kills the moment by grunting and pawing a mound of grass like he's trying to bore a hole to the center of the Earth.

"Uh...ah...well...shite," he stammers, sticking to his attempts at Irish lingo. "I might have, ah—"

Colleen rubs his arm. "Are you okay, C?

He pats her hand. "Uh, huh, C."

Their cute factor spikes high enough to rival Veil travel nausea.

Charlie flings an arm at the woods. "When I came here to take a piss, I heard you guys and—"

I don't realize I'm squishing the bones of Sion's fingers together until he gives my hand a shake. I frantically replay our woodland conversation. Did Charlie hear any of our talk about heart attacks, soul saving, or Veil travel?

Sion's thumb gives my hand a series of taps as if he's sending me a coded message to let him do the talking. He shoots me a suggestive smile. "Eala tells Faerie stories with high-volume enthusiasm."

Obviously, a master at thinking on his feet, I imagine Sion has faced more precarious pickles than convincing Charlie nothing otherworldly went down in Farmer McKean's woods.

Charlie holds up both hands as if preparing to ward off a punch. "What I'm trying to say is—I mentioned to Professor Olk you guys went off together."

I drop Sion's hand and take a step away from him. "You did what?"

When the four of us turn toward the stones, my eyes lock on a figure streaking across the campsite in our direction.

Charlie tucks in his lower lip, voice curt. "You brought Olk's reaction on yourselves. If you'd given us warning about your sneaky rendezvous—"

Last night, Jeremy Olk checked every box in my dream man scenario. Sion checks none of them, yet here I am with a gut full of tumbling emotions for this character that could star in one of Máthair's folktales. On top of that, I certainly wasn't prepared to announce I'm part of an insta-couple, but the bizarre circumstances of our partnership obliterates any subtle reveal of our togetherness.

Sion catches sight of the approaching ground level Olk storm at the same time I do. "Damn," he mutters. "Feller's wearing a pair of boss eyes for both of us."

"Don't say anything to make things worse," I hiss, half-expecting the current mood of Kennard Park U's newest professor to trigger more lightning.

We meet Jeremy halfway to the campsite. He throws a protective arm around my shoulders. Sion plays it smart instead of confrontational and gives us space.

Jeremy cups the side of my face. "Are you all right, Eala?" Before I get a word in, he launches a venomous stare at Sion. "You, Loho, are no longer welcome with our tour. I don't know what you pulled to separate Eala from the rest of us—"

"You've not got the right picture here, sir," says Sion in the tone of a lion tamer who dropped his whip and dearly hopes not to become dinner.

"I don't care to hear any more from *you*." Olk spits out *you* in a condescending and hateful way. My temperature rises. How dare he? This *you* dedicates his existence to a cause outside Jeremy Olk's realm of mortal comprehension. As fast as my stress level rose to nervous meltdown at the prospect of facing Jeremy, it now drops to cold disdain for his rudeness to Sion.

I hold up my hands. "Let's all take a breath here. There's been a misunderstanding."

Sion can't leave. There are a handful of days before Beltane. Without easy proximity, what will happen to our partnership and the soulfall? By his own admission, Sion has failed and failed again. Little Harriet and Alaina Kennedy can't be our only successes.

A warning pings in my head. Sion said this was his last chance to save the souls, but he hasn't told me why. I burn with the need to know. Is his forever in peril? What is the consequence of a Veil guide's ultimate failure?

Colleen looks from me to Olk to Sion and for once doesn't step into the center of a maelstrom. It's me alone who holds any hope of preventing Sion's banishment.

I step away from Jeremy. "There's no problem here."

The four stare at me.

"I asked Sion to show me the wood." I face Olk and lift my ring finger. "You speak Irish, right? See *Teacht orm.*"

His eyes focus on the ring. "Find me?"

"It was my grandmother's ring. I came on the trip because I believe she wanted me to find her Ireland. The one where beauty grows easily from this earth." I reach to pluck a handful of grass and raise my palm. Blades fly in the pre-storm breeze. "The one where trees, like the ones in that wood, are sacred." I nod to Sion. "I asked him to take me to the trees. I didn't want to go alone. Since he lives nearby, I figured he'd be the best person to show me."

Colleen chews on her lip. "It's true Eala has no sense of direction."

I'm a little thrown by her support. I thought she'd heave Sion under the bus and encourage me back in Jeremy's direction.

My new colleague frowns while scratching his morning stubble.

"It's my enthusiasm to share the place that kept Eala from letting you know we were going off," says Sion, playing the contrite card. "I truly meant to have her back by the time the lot of you woke."

I jump in before Jeremy unleashes any more *you* comments. "Sion, you don't need to cover for me. I'm the one who rushed us deeper into the forest." Deeper is right. I'm neck deep in potentially losing a good recommendation from Jeremy.

I don't know Olk at all. Is he so pissed because he has a thing for me? Is he petty enough to down talk me to the powers that be at Kennard Park if he thinks I took up with Sion instead of him?

The good professor takes a few steps away from us and stares off into the distance. His shoulders rise and fall in measured rhythm like he's prepping for one of the Tai Chi routines I've watched groups do in Central Park. The energy pouring off him is anything but centered. The longer he stays silent, the tighter my muscles lock.

Colleen looks back and forth between Sion and me. She raises her eyebrows in an *are you going to tell Jeremy about the two of you* question. I shake my head. I'm not prepared for this to come down to a choice between Sion and the tour. I need to help him with the souls, but I also can't wipe the university from my future.

I want to curl against one of the standing stones and hide my head under Máthair's brandied melon scarf to think. New realities. Old realities. Where is my place in the world? I catch Sion's eye. He gives me an encouraging nod as one corner of his lip rises. In that moment, I know I'm not alone no matter which way the Olk wind blows.

"Fine." Jeremy Olk's voice cracks the delicate veneer of morning. "Please note that news of a missing colleague is not my preferred wake up call."

Sion's fingers twitch at his side, and for a terrible moment, I'm afraid he's going to throw a mock salute. "Apologies."

Olk turns to me without acknowledging Sion. "Eala," he says, gesturing for me to walk next to him as we head toward the fake stone circle. "You must excuse my passion." He brushes a hand across my lower back. "I take my trip lead responsibilities quite seriously." Lowering his voice, he leans closer. "Let's chat about your pending position at Kennard Park."

He knows something. Yesterday, I would have been excited. Today, I'm nervous where this *chat* might be headed. What does he know?

Jeremy's demeanor shifts to friendly. "I happen to own a copy of your book."

My eyes widen in surprise. I did publish my dissertation to up my ante as an academician, but I've never had anyone tell me they'd actually bought it.

He casts his gaze down, a tiny smile playing on his mouth as if he's enjoying a private joke. "Your fascination and appreciation of Celtic folklore reminds me—" He pulls off his glasses and waves them in my direction. "Of me."

In a blink, my safe little tomorrow, in a college town, with a small life, welcomes me back. Will fate and the Veil allow me to return to that dream? Maybe my attraction to Sionnach is a biproduct of our shared responsibility to the souls? Are these feelings born of a moment in time and nothing more?

Jeremy skips over the top of a sunken boulder. "Have you ever thought of teaching a summer session at Trinity College while spending more time doing further research in this glorious land? I'm happy to introduce you to my connections."

A summer? Does that mean he believes I'll be ensconced in the tenure-track position at Kennard Park U. for the regular school year alongside him?

My gaze meets his. I never noticed how much the whites of his eyes show when he looks sideways. It's a little creepy. His pupils are the size of a pinhead.

I steal a glance over my shoulder at Sion. His shoulders slump as he limps behind us, rubbing his eyes. My exhaustion echoes his with the force of a full body slam. He looks up as if I called his name, and we exchange half-smiles.

The campsite is nearly deserted. Students hike down the hill to Rowan Bend for another Robert Corrigan authentic Irish breakfast complete with Irish traditional music. Farmer McKean throws sleeping bags and boxes of décor into the back of his truck. When the good farmer catches sight of us, he waves his arms and hollers for Olk.

Jeremy pushes his glasses up his nose. "Excuse me, will you?" When I nod, he squeezes my shoulder. "To be continued."

As the good professor walks away, Colleen sidles next to me. "To be continued. Sounds like he's still an option, the better option."

"Excuse me! You just asked if I think Sion may be the *find me* on my ring."

"Or is it Professor Olk?"

I shoot her a *drop it* look. "Or neither. Stop over-analyzing."

She shrugs. "Beware the fling that ruins the dream."

Out of the corner of my eye, I notice Sion giving Jeremy a wide berth as he takes a few limping steps down the hill, pausing to look back at me.

The limp.

So many questions. Last night at Leap Castle, he was as spry as a prancing Colleen.

Charlie hands over my travel backpack. "Is she going with us, Flutter?"

I thread my arms through the straps while he holds it. "Where else would I be going? Dublin or bust."

Colleen throws her arms around Charlie and plants a juicy kiss on his lips before turning back to me. I wonder how cozy their night got.

"Charlie, my knight in shining armor, has volunteered to brave a stick shift and the left side of the road to drive to my grandmother's house in Wexford."

I settle my pack as we leave the circle of powerless megaliths without any Faerie mishaps. "I can't ditch my tour responsibilities in Dublin." That would clinch a thumbs down from Olk.

Charlie whips the itinerary onto his cell screen. He's as organized as Colleen. "Museums in the morning and then free choice afternoon/evening."

Free choice nap in a nice Dublin hotel sounds perfect, especially if I'm going to spend my night chasing down a legendary English noble with Sion.

"You remember my grandma, Shanna, from the time she came for Christmas when we were in junior high?" says Colleen.

"I do. She's a kick."

"So, you'll come?" She holds her hands to me, imploring. "My grandmother won't approve of me driving around Ireland alone with a guy I just met. She's old school—safety in numbers."

Charlie gives her an open-mouthed stab at acting affronted that ends in an equally open-mouthed kiss. When their PDA times out, Colleen turns to me. "Well?"

My gaze drifts to Sion. Sunlight bypasses the outer layer of his chestnut hair to fire up hidden cantaloupe curls. It's beautiful. He catches me watching him and smiles, bobbing his head in invitation to join him.

I shrug at Colleen, nodding at Sion. "Sorry. I'm booked. I'll catch up with you at breakfast."

Her narrowed gaze makes it clear this discussion is not over.

I give her an *everything is dandy* smile and take a step toward Sion.

Suddenly, the hillside seems to jolt into a steeper angle. My stomach lurches as insanely harsh heartbeats steal my breath. Clouds and grass slowly smear together into a greenish gray blur. Arms, legs, spine seem to melt as I go down.

The last thing I remember are raindrops tickling my face before Sion catches me in his arms.

CHAPTER 13
THE CHAT

I dip in and out of consciousness. Moments of clarity begin to brighten then float away.

Sion carrying me down the hill, his warm cheek pressed to my cold one.
Colleen's worried voice repeating my name over and over.
Sion pressing a hand to my heart and singing.
Jeremy calling for a doctor.
The security of being tucked against Sion's solid chest.
Charlie promising Colleen I'm going to be alright.
Sion's lips pressed to my forehead.
Sion
Colleen
Jeremy
Charlie
Sion
Sion
Sion

A hand strokes my hair as Sion's soothing voice pokes through my flipbook awareness. "Drink a bit more, love."

I'm aware of being supported as a water bottle tips to my mouth. I cover the hands holding it and attempt to chug the cool liquid. My throat feels coated in sand.

Sion eases the bottle from my lips. "Slow a bit. Robbie's got loads more." He resumes gently sliding his fingers through my hair. I lean into his touch like a contented cat.

I'd love nothing more than to close my eyes and drift back to sleep, but Colleen's voice pulls me in the opposite direction. She crouches nearby, rubbing my arm above the blanket that covers me. "Hi. Welcome back."

I blink at the painfully bright room, focusing on her face. "Hi." My voice is raw and rusty.

"How do you feel, La?"

I'm propped up against Sion, lying on a sofa in a living room under a soft blanket or two. The combo of his body heat and layers of plaid wool make for a very toasty cocoon. Across the room, Charlie perches on an armchair near a blazing fireplace.

I burrow closer to Sion and his soothing warmth. "Snug." My stomach gurgles too loudly to be ignored.

Colleen looks relieved. "Ready for food?"

"If there's coffee involved."

"Absolutely," she agrees and leaves the room with a quick backward glance at Sion. I know that look. She hasn't decided what to make of him. I get it. Her brain is still processing how I could connect myself to Sion when he's miles outside every bullet point on my ideal man checklist. I wish I could share real details with her. If anyone could help me make sense of this rapid-fire attraction to him, it's Colleen.

I pep up a bit and claim the water bottle for another slug. "Where are we?"

Sion pulls the blanket tighter under my chin. "You're in Robbie's flat, above the pub."

I bunch a fistful of blanket. "And I'm here, why? What happened?"

I feel Sion breathe in and out as if steadying himself. "The short of it is, you keeled over." A battle of how much more to add plays across his face. Adrenaline fires up in my chest. His unease suggests whatever took me down may be connected to our nocturnal travels, but this is definitely not the time to over-share.

A tall, sandy-haired man by the window who I didn't notice at first approaches, picking up the thread of the question. "From what your friends said, too much cold, not enough food, a bit of dehydration, and to throw out a highly medical term—wicked jet lag happened to you." He pats me on the shoulder. "I'm Dr. Murphy...David." He reaches for my wrist. "May I?"

Sion doesn't make any move to relinquish me as Dr. David checks my vitals.

Charlie raises a mug with a curl of steam rising into the air. "You were bound for a colossal face-plant and classy roll down the slope if Sion hadn't caught you."

I swear to you, Eala Duir. You'll never fall when you're with me.

Sion deserves credit for sticking to his word. I need to shake the fog from my brain. The aroma of Charlie's coffee calls to me. I hope Colleen is on her way with mine.

I nudge Sion. "Thanks for the save."

His eyes twinkle as he gives me a squeeze. "Always."

"The good news, Ms. Duir, is that nothing looks twisted, sprained, or broken," says Dr. David. "No signs of concussion either. Any pain?"

"Just the embarrassment of..." I jerk my chin at Charlie. "Almost colossally face-planting in front of an audience." I feel the rumble of laughter in Sion's chest.

"Take it easy. Eat, drink, squeeze in a nap, and you should be up and full crackin' in a few hours." With a friendly wink, Dr. David leaves the room, squeezing past Jeremy who holds a tray piled with enough food for the entire tour group.

"Breakfast," Jeremy announces.

Colleen follows with a blessed mug of caffeinated elixir. "Too much cream and not enough sugar, just the way you like it."

Jeremy sets a heaping plate of bacon, potatoes, tomatoes, and black pudding on the coffee table, then digs my hand out from under the blanket. "You're looking better, sweetheart. Your splendid rosy glow is back."

Sion goes rigid at *sweetheart* and glares at Jeremy's hand on mine. Before he says anything to escalate the tension between them, I pipe up.

"Thanks for the food, Jeremy." With Sion's help and minimal maneuvering, I sit up and accept the coffee while he maintains hip-to-hip contact. Grabbing a piece of black pudding, I smile at my visitors. "I'm sorry for worrying you all." My next thought kills the luxury of a leisurely breakfast. "What time is it? Shit, we've got to load the bus if we're going to make the Dublin activities."

Sion's arm clamps more securely around my back, making it clear he isn't keen on me going anywhere.

Colleen checks her watch. "It's fine as long as we hop to it soon. Our crew downstairs is finishing breakfast. We'll leave in a few, make the drive, check into the Dublin hotel to freshen up, and still make our itinerary in plenty of time."

Sion's gaze bores into mine with a *follow my lead* look. "Eala, do you think a bus ride is the best idea? The train is a much smoother go. After you've finished breakfast, gotten out of these damp clothes, and had a shower to warm your bones, I'll see you up to Dublin." He leans his forehead against mine in a gesture more intimate than a single night together swapping stories warrants. "We'll stop off first to get you snacks since you've lost your bag of bars."

Message received. We need some alone time for whatever he's not sharing with the group.

I pat his cheek then face our folks. "Good idea. I guess one of those thieving foxes stole my peanut bars." I dig my fingers into Sion's thigh under the blanket. "And I'm still a little wobbly. A shower would help me reset if Robbie doesn't mind the intrusion."

"Naw, he says to stay as long as you like." Sion nods at our audience. "I'm sure you'd all agree it's easier to sleep on a train than a rattling bus. Lulls you like a babe." He winks at me. "Train's faster too. Even if we leave a spell after the bus, we won't be far behind the meetup at the other end."

Not one of our three travelling companions looks happy about Sion separating me from the herd. It's clear he doesn't have a single fan among them.

I take another bite of black pudding and wave it for emphasis. "I'm not going to allow the tour schedule to go off the rails because I didn't take care of myself. It took a lot of wrangling to arrange the lecture with the professor at Trinity College, right Jeremy?" I sink against Sion, feigning more fatigue than I feel. "I'd rather stay a smidge longer before heading up to Dublin." I fake a laugh. "No need for a repeat keel over."

Colleen switches her focus from Sion to Jeremy, clearly conflicted between leaving me and her duty of keeping the tour on schedule.

I motion her over. When she's near, I pull her by the scarf down to couch level and kiss the top of her head. "I'll be brilliant, love." I throw as much Irish accent as I can muster especially exaggerating the *love*. It does the trick and my bestie smiles.

"You have my word I'll deliver Eala to Dublin without a scratch," says Sion.

Jeremy aims a stormy expression at him. "I'm more than happy to linger and take the train with you, *Professor* Duir."

His acid tone makes me flinch. Emphasizing the title we share is a none too subtle claim of superiority over Sion's resident local expert status. Olk doesn't even bother to make minimal effort to mask his rude contempt for Sion. I wish he'd back off.

Colleen steps in front of Jeremy. "Oh, no. You can't stay. I've got to have at least one Kennard Park faculty on that bus."

Professor Olk regains his composure. "Of course. If you're sure, Eala." His gaze flashes over Sion but softens when it lands on me, awaiting my response. Next to me, Sion's body temperature rises as he fights to stay civil. What will it take for the two of them to call a truce?

I summon my breeziest smile. "I am. It gives me time to enjoy Robbie's authentic Irish breakfast part two."

Jeremy exhales loud enough for the whole room to hear. He shakes his cell at me. "Keep us posted."

I wiggle my hand at him as if I'm holding my phone. "I promise to text you and Colleen when we leave Robbie's, and once we're on the train with our Dublin ETA. Are we good?"

After a hug from Colleen and another that goes on a beat too long from Jeremy, the trio heads back downstairs. Charlie is the only one who leaves the room with unhunched shoulders.

As soon as they're gone, I reluctantly scoot out of Sion's protective custody. "Well, partner, your close personal attention convinced our audience we're definitely into each other despite our rocky public start. A little hanging out at Charleville castle and a single sneaky night telling stories in the woods...I think we've redefined whirlwind romance."

Sion's face flames as he pops up off the couch. I hit a nerve. I'm just not sure which one.

He paces in a lap around me. "You should know, it's been longer than that for me."

I stare at him. "Longer than what?" My stomach performs an unpleasant twist.

His shoe paws the carpet. "The time here in Ireland."

I'm gripped in the all too familiar feeling of Sion knowing scads more than he communicates.

There's serious curl scratching while he blows out three slow breaths. "I haven't told you all, but will you accept my word that it's not because I'm lying or deliberately keeping you blinded? There's a world to say and—"

A rush of anger, or maybe the infusion of coffee, prompts me to cut him off. "You don't trust me to handle it even after I've survived the boatload of weird you've dumped on me already?" I smack the couch cushion. "Time travel, the soulfall, Pwyll, the *oubliette*—hello? And again...what the hell do you mean by it's been longer than our time in Ireland?"

Sion stands behind an armchair, fingernails digging into its back. "I told you Finnbheara intended you to be by my side for this final go at the soulfall."

I twirl my hand, signaling him to keep going.

"To understand who you'd be..." His words drift off as he struggles with the rest of the explanation. He punches the chair's headrest. "I've seen..."

His evasiveness sets off a dull ache at the base of my neck. "Spit it out, Sion."

He wilts, closing his eyes as if he's afraid to meet my gaze. "Finnbheara showed you to me."

I press a hand to my racing heart. "What does that mean? Did you spy on me in New York?"

His eyes pop open. "No, it's not like that." He rubs his forehead and then looks back at me. "Himself offered me visions."

An image of Sion sitting next to a fairy king, watching blurry videos of my life streams through my mind. "Of what exactly?"

The tension in Sion's features relax, and a shy smile plays upon his lips. He leaves the barricade of the armchair to sit on the coffee table facing me. "You helping tend a garden. A kind smile for a troubled soul. Spinning tales before your class. Grand appreciation for trees in a great park shedding their summer green for wondrous gold."

"Was anyone else in the visions?" The concept of these intrusions unsettles me. I don't like the idea of anyone I care about being pulled into this morass of the soulfall and time travel.

His voice is quiet and gentle. "Only you, love. Only you." He meets my gaze, his own inscrutable as he waits for my response. When I don't answer right away, he continues. "Those moments showed me your enthusiasm, a generous heart, kindness. I..." He trails off.

The look in his eyes mirrors the same pull that's been simmering inside me.

"Eala." He takes my hands in his. "I need you to know if I could ask for one thing apart from ending the soulfall, it would be to spend easy days with you without unforgiving time hanging over our heads. I want to learn more of your beautiful heart."

This earnest, soft-spoken version of Sion is my favorite one yet. My frustration with him and the creepy notion he's magically spied on me begins to ebb. Visions, seeings, and premonitions are all elements of the folklore my scholarly life is steeped in. If I continue to embrace the truth that I'm currently rooted in parallel realities, it's not far-fetched to be tangled up with the intangible.

In a neck-cracking change of mood, Sion drops into a crouch next to me, pressing his body against my legs. Words spill from him like a dam burst. "When you toppled on the hillside, my chest near tore in two. Fear I'd caused you harm shook my bones. Fool that I am, I convinced myself you were fine when we came from the woods." He's now hugging my knees. "I should have kept a closer watch. Travelling once in a night when you've never done so before is hard enough and here, I ripped you through the Veil half a dozen times." Sion drops his head onto my lap. "It's a gift from above that I didn't kill you."

Both his voice and body shake. It's my turn to comfort him. I stroke his russet curls, thoroughly enjoying their soft silkiness. This intimacy is not for the benefit of our friends. Could it be this brash and unpredictable man is catching feelings for me the way I am for him? I decide to wait. He's said he wants to know me better. Good advice. That goes both ways.

I tilt his chin so he's looking up at me. "I'd wish for more easy days with you as well—to help me get to know you better."

His eyes shine with relief. He plops down next to me on the couch and stabs the biggest piece of roasted potato with a fork. "We may not have days, but we have now. Ask away."

I take another gulp of coffee. "Given our situation, I suppose I'll have to look at time differently." Leaning my head back, I stare at Robbie's white ceiling. "I've had two regular plus one Celtic day with you versus you watching me for a lifetime. Not exactly a balanced investment."

"No, but you'll catch up."

I turn my head to look at him and am rewarded with an expression of interest I'd like to see repeated more often from Mr. Sionnach Loho. Catching up could be a very interesting prospect.

Even though I still have scads of questions about the soulfall and where our travels may take us, I resolve to appreciate these moments of pause. To be honest, I'm not certain I'm ready for the hard truth of his answers. "Tell me about your family."

A crease forms between his brows. He wrestles with the question. After helping himself to my coffee, he leans back. "There was only Ma, Da, and me. No brothers or sisters." He grins. "Lots of responsibility on one lad to make them proud." His gaze drifts and after a tiny shake of his head, he keeps talking. "I helped Da work the sheep and what crops our small farm could manage. Ma was a wonder with herbs. We'd take what little we grew to market and got by. There's a peace to working the land I loved until…" He trails off then shrugs.

I'm tempted to make a comment about his farm-bred muscles. So in his lifetime, Sion had been steady and hard-working, the qualities I'd always admired in academic types. Maybe under all his impatience and obfuscation, I sensed that about him. Does a soul call to another soul even when the mind hasn't caught up or yet approved?

I munch on a tomato. "I don't have any siblings either. I'm adopted. It was just my grandmother and me. She was a gifted gardener like your mother." Thinking about the perfect tomatoes Máthair grew makes it hard to swallow. I grab the water bottle. "She died a few months ago. I'm still dealing with it."

When I look back at Sion, I catch the sheen of tears in his eyes. His parents are lost to time. We both breathe into the moment, appreciating and accepting the bond of individual sorrows. We do share common ground apart from our celestial purpose—singularly focused lives, his with the land, mine with my research and teaching.

My academic interest flares. Here I have a man that's experienced two centuries of history, not to mention otherworldly responsibilities. I may never have this opportunity to probe again. "Who taught you how to Veil travel?"

Sion huffs. "One of Finnbheara's lackeys. It was more of a shove than a lesson." A look of guilt plays across his face. "Och, I suppose I've done the same to you."

"Not gonna argue with you there."

He looks exhausted. I'm not the only one who could use the downtime of the train ride. I decide not to pry any more for now. It's satisfying that our night of Veil travel erased his initial disappointment in my abilities to help him with the soulfall. I'm accepted and possibly more. It's a place to start. Whether my pull to Sion is survivor passion or the rush of a shared goal, the next few days might provide more clarity or at least give me space to examine my feelings—and his— more closely.

I pat his knee. "So, our budding relationship—how do we play it? Besides the fact we've apparently been married since the 1500s."

He rubs his nose. "We keep playing it. Your people thinking we're together will make it easier to travel."

Back to business. "Not much at sweet talking are you, *husband?*"

Sion takes my hand and kisses it. "Not so. Ms. Duir, would you do me the honor of a proper date?"

His lips against my skin send pinpoints of warmth flowing through me. "What do you have in mind?" The memory of our first kiss, at least the preferable second half of it, sets off pulsing heat low in my belly. I suppose it may be the only one I ever get from Sion unless we're performing for the benefit of others.

Sion locks his hands behind those sweet curls. "Hmm? What do you say to a train ride to Dublin?"

I clasp my hands to my heart. "How did you know that's always been my dream date?"

We both laugh.

Sion grips my leg above the knee. "See, I've just learned more about you."

"Without a vision." His expression goes from relaxed to pinched. I regret spoiling the mood, but in the spirit of getting to know one another better, there is one last thing I need to be truthful about. "Last night you admitted concern that Finnbheara sent you a weakling."

He looks stricken. "I wish I'd kept that bit to myself."

I lay my hand on his chest, enjoying the contour of those farmer muscles. "You're not entirely wrong. Will you help me be stronger?"

He takes my hand and thumps it over his heart. "Swear by my hundred thousand heartbeats, I will." Too soon he breaks contact, reaching into his pocket to extricate Strongbow's chainmail. He dangles the three rings between us. "Now, how shall we go with these?"

CHAPTER 14
THE KING OF LEINSTER

olleen and I stare at Daniel Maclise's massive painting *The Marriage of Strongbow and Aoife* in the National Gallery of Ireland while we wait for the rest of our group to assemble. One of the docents in the gallery provides a full dose of Strongbow. Armed with a new set of corroborating details on the guy, I'm even more convinced it's a crime against nature the man's poor squire is condemned to a soulfall for stealing from a self-aggrandizing English *amadán*.

Colleen pitches her voice low so as not to disturb the docent. "Remind me not to hire this Maclise guy to do my wedding portrait."

"Good call." The painting is a disturbing tangle of depression. Writhing bodies of the defeated and tortured Irish surround the happy couple of Strongbow and his Irish princess bride, Aoife. The cruel groom smashes a Celtic cross under his boot. Ugh, what a devil.

Jeremy Olk arrives with postgrads in tow. Caught up in his professorial glory, he usurps the docent's narrative. Even though the woman backs off graciously, his rudeness bothers me. After all, we're guests in her domain. This isn't a part of Jeremy I'm a fan of. His sarcastic response at Charleville Castle after Sion's beautiful solo was off-putting, as was the condescending *you* he leveled at him this morning. I'm tempted to intervene, playing it off as if Jeremy was unaware of his slight to the docent. Since I may be treading a fine line for Jeremy's approval after my defection to the train with Sion, I keep quiet.

"Henry the Second, who was none too fond of Strongbow," says Jeremy with a dramatic lip press and narrowing of the eyes. "Killed two birds with one stone when he sent the knight off to Ireland. The king rid himself of Strongbow on home turf and gained a man on the inside to *tame* the unruly Irish." He waggles a finger at the painting. "The knight married Aoife, the King of Leinster's daughter, in a move to gain personal clout and power, but King Henry kept a firm hold on Strongbow's leash, opening the door for England to grind the native Irish under its boots. Hello Anglo-Norman invasion."

"And a decent brand of hard cider," quips one of the grad students, earning a laugh.

Strongbow—definite jerk. The man doesn't deserve to be the namesake of a decent cider.

Charlie squeezes between Colleen and me, flapping his book. "Strongbow was one ballsy dude. Made the deal to proclaim himself King of Leinster once his father-in-law, the actual king, died."

I snort. "Newsflash for Strongbow: You don't get to consider yourself Irish if you're still in a bromance with the King of England."

Colleen frowns at the painting. "I know I should appreciate the historic value here, but I need something with sunshine and puppies." She scrolls on her tablet. "When did I schedule free time to start?"

"After the cathedral tour." I check my phone. Damn, Sion's been gone nearly two hours since he and I left the hotel to meet the group at the museum. On the train ride to Dublin before Sion and I both fell into an exhausted sleep snuggled up against one another, I Googled Strongbow's tomb and discovered it was in Christ Church Cathedral, the next stop on our itinerary. In the few moments before I joined Sion for our well-earned nap, a wistful thought floated through my mind. What if I had met this complicated man without Veil traveling and the soulfall in the mix? How would that have played out?

In an attempt to smooth any festering resentment Jeremy may still have from this morning, I clocked quality time with him on our stroll over here. We dished about the Celtic studies faculty at Kennard Park with me supplying insider info on the quirks and idiosyncrasies of our esteemed colleagues. To my relief, the casual chat appeared to reset the sunny side of Olk's disposition.

Sion and I had agreed that in Dublin, he would duck out to slip the chainmail into Strongbow's tomb inside the cathedral to test our theory of redemption for the squire being possible without a Veil jump. To avoid antagonizing Jeremy with my additional separation from the group, Sion insisted on going alone. If fulfilling the squire's quest works in real time, that's one less gut-twisting hop through history for us. With the Beltane clock ticking, we need to devote every moment during the three remaining Celtic days to free the last trio of souls.

I scan the cliques of postgrads who are blissfully independent, giving me more freedom. Jeremy's post lecture Q&A about the historic painting sates their curiosities and they scatter to their preferred galleries. Earlier, I made sure my presence was obvious as we worked our way through highlights of the museum. I felt useful, fielding the odd query about folk tales and druids, leaving out my date night with Pwyll. I even regained the good graces of the pair of students I'd potentially alienated on the trek to the campsite by oohing and aahing over their gorgeous woolen sweater purchases from the mill where the group nipped in for a coffee stop on the way to Dublin.

I stare at my watch as if it has the power to answer my burning question.

Where is Sion?

He should have rejoined us by now. Despite the cool gallery, my face heats like I'm back in the sweltering Leap Castle kitchen on murder night. It's essential to our plan for him to use his Finnbheara-gifted talent of transforming solid into not-so-solid in order to slip the chainmail into Strongbow's stone effigy.

Fear sizzles through me. What if that particular skill affects his heartbeats in real time? Images of walking into Christ Church Cathedral to find Sion slumped on the floor intensifies the flush on my cheeks until the front of my neck reddens like a bad sunburn.

Charlie stands, hero-worshipping Olk's every word as they move to the next painting. A less mesmerized Colleen threads her arm through my elbow. She's hit her art history limit and sashays us across the polished wood floor of the gallery. "Since Sion is making himself scarce, and you're taking a pass on Shanna's, will our gallant professor earn your free time favors?"

"Sion'll catch up any minute." I lean in. "He thought avoiding Jeremy for a few hours was the wise choice after this morning."

Colleen frowns at me as Jeremy and Charlie join us. "Ladies," says our team leader. "Change of plans." He taps his cell phone. "There's been a fire at Christ Church Cathedral."

Colleen madly taps her tablet screen to confirm.

My heart thuds so loudly, I expect the three of them to stare at my chest. "Fire?" Shit, did Sion's attempt to return the chainmail to Strongbow's tomb end in catastrophe?

Jeremy waves a hand. "A small flare they put out quickly, but the cathedral is closed for the rest of the day." He zeroes in on me, smiling. Tiny crinkle lines lift the corners of his eyes.

Kennard Park's newest Celtic studies professor is undeniably handsome. Some of the warmth I first felt for him begins to ease its way back in. Sion is the wildcard in my life. Jeremy is a much steadier option, a smarter option. It would be so convenient if I felt the level of spark for him like I do for Sion.

"Since we're free, I'm off to Trinity College to connect with a colleague. I'd love for you to meet him, Eala. If you'd care to join me, I believe you'll find his passion on the subject of Celtic lore engaging."

Colleen slips her tablet into her crossbody bag. "Sounds right up your alley."

I know her heart is in the right place. She's dead on that Jeremy makes sense for me. It's not that I possess zero interest, but until after Beltane, there's no time to devote to him. Right now, Sion is my priority. "Thanks, but I've, ah got to—"

Sweat pools at my hairline as I continue to perseverate on the fire. Was Sion hurt? Did the flare up originate at Strongbow's tomb? I dig fingernails into my palm. Mr. Veil Guide has no cell phone. I've got no way to contact him. We're buying him a burner phone as soon as we can break away from the group.

Colleen reads my panic with lifted brows. "Eala and I need to make a girl stop." Charlie waves us off, pouncing on Jeremy with questions about Georgian architecture while Colleen and I head down the length of the gallery.

As soon as we're out of earshot, she lays the back of her hand across my forehead, checking for fever. Instead, she encounters an unappealing reservoir of sweat and wipes her hand on my sleeve. "You're not in great shape." She hands me a water bottle from her bag. "Hydrate. Do you want to head back to the hotel?"

I unscrew the top and take a long drink. "No, I'm almost back up to speed." I scan up and down the gallery. No Sion. "I want to check the museum's archives for some folklore illustrations I've been trying to track down."

She eyes me skeptically.

"You're welcome to come with," I say, knowing that's a solid no for her. "I'll text when I'm done."

Charlie nips any further questioning by calling her over.

I take advantage of the opening to head toward the exit, bent on making my way to the cathedral when a familiar figure leans out from behind a pedestal topped with a marble bust.

"Eala." Sion's voice is low as he keeps to the shadows.

I rush to his side, grabbing him by the shoulders. "Shit—a fire." I'm relieved when a quick once over doesn't reveal any burns or singes. "Please tell me it didn't have anything to do with you and Strongbow's tomb."

He guides me past a pair of sweeping staircases into the next gallery, clinging to me and panting. I'll bet he sprinted the mile between the cathedral and here. "I can't be sure."

I pull him closer to keep nearby patrons from overhearing us. "Was it the artifact? Did it flare or ignite when you pushed it through the stone lid?"

We stare intently into each other's eyes. He leads me to a deserted nook away from the nearest docent. We drop onto a white platform with a *Do Not Sit* sign under a painting called *View of the Devil's Glen*. The dark subject matter of the art does nothing to relieve my rising trepidation.

"I had no chance to return it." He lays the metal rings on my palm.

The longer I stare at them, the shakier I feel. "Why not?"

"Fixing things isn't always as easy as 'twas with the Kennedys." He fiddles with the zipper on his jacket. "Problems do crop up."

He thought our jaunt to Leap Castle was easy? Blood pounds in my temples. "Problems? As in fires?"

He rests a hand on my thigh. "I sat in a chair next to Himself's tomb and waited 'til no one but me was close. When I touched the mail to the likeness of Strongbow, flames started down the row of chairs next to me. The fire put me off what I meant to do."

"If you were the only one near the effigy, who started the fire?"

Sion's battle whether to tell me or not rages across his face. I grip the hand on my leg. I'm overwhelmed by a need to touch him. Our contact sets off pleasant currents across my skin. A definite closeness is building, but there's more than a semantic difference between accomplishing something side-by-side versus hand-in-hand. Which is it for him?

I bounce a fist off the top of his thigh. "Sionnach, you can't call me your partner and then pick and choose what to tell and what to hide."

The light aimed at the painting above us hits the side of his face, sharpening his features. He pulls a twig from the snap pocket on the front of his jacket and madly chews it. A whiff of whiskey tickles my nose while I stare him down, waiting for a response.

Finally, he wheezes in a loud breath. "In the past, there's been, ah… complications. A thing that blocks me from getting a key or bringing it back to the soul."

I shiver at the implication. "A thing? As in enemy?" It never occurred to me there would be resistance to this soul-saving business. The desolate cave in the center of *View of the Devil's Glen* catches my eye and darker parts of my Catholic upbringing start demons and exorcisms parading through my head.

"Oh, love," he pulls me to his chest and wraps arms around me.

The way our hearts gallop together, I fear we won't have our full allotment of a hundred thousand heartbeats the next time we cross the Veil.

He slides a palm against my cheek. "I've turned your bones to ice."

Peering into my face, he speaks soft and gentle as if to croon my fear away. "It's not enemies such as wicked demon horses I'm speaking of." Sion plays with a strand of my hair. "When sin rubs against the virtues we're working to put right, there's bound to be friction."

"Friction? From where? From what?" I pull out of his grasp. "Be specific for fuck's sake."

He rakes fingers through his curls. "I dunno. Fate. Destiny. Powers we're not privy to."

St. Augustine's quote about the unseen takes on sinister shadings. I hold my hands together creating one giant fist. "How do we fight invisible friction that wants us to fail?"

Sion swallows my hands with his. His touch thaws the ice crystals seeping across my skin. "With faith, my white swan, faith."

I drop my chin to my chest.

Faith.

A tattered remnant of faith brought me to Ireland to follow Máthair's wish. Instead of a payoff for my faith, I've landed in a rapidly dwindling hourglass to save souls.

Faith is not my friend.

"You can't dole out false promises about keeping me safe, Sion, when tombs are burning, and I barely missed being manhandled by a medieval rapist when we searched for Matthew Kennedy. This Finnbheara mission of yours is more than solving virtuous riddles."

He shifts uneasily on the platform. "I may have underplayed the risks a bit."

"Clearly."

His grip on my hands tightens. "Truth—Yes, I've held back, done everything in my power not to scare you off. I'm glad of it because now you're with me." Those green glass eyes stare me down. "I'd never have found the cross to take to Mrs. Kennedy. That was you seeing things fresh." He stares at the ceiling. "I've been stuck in my ways of trying to fix it for too long. Without you, I might as well stop trying and take my punishment."

I stare at our joined hands. I'm not a risk taker in the first place, and now he's introducing a massive danger factor.

"Your punishment?"

"Och, be deaf to my foolish choice of words. I beg you."

The all too familiar sense of my equilibrium going to hell begins to drift over me.

Punishments.

Danger.

An attack of vertigo hits me on this platform that's not more than two feet off the ground. "Oh, shit." I grasp Sion's arm for balance.

He hugs me to his chest. A strong hand strokes my back. His touch ignites warm eddies that permeate my body, driving away the crawling sensation of panic.

I cling to him. "How are you doing this? I've never been able to pull out of an episode so quickly." Memories of his singing to calm my racing heart after the Veil nearly did us in this morning wraps around me. He may not be a Faerie, but the man definitely has something of magic in his touch, his voice.

Sion separates us just enough to touch his forehead to mine—his voice a whisper. "I promised, I'd never let you fall, neither from heights nor from fear." Sion lifts my chin and touches the tip of his pinkie to the tear lingering in the corner of my eye. "We're meant to do this, me and you."

My heart swells, pushing doubt farther from my center to make way for a surge of feelings for Sion.

We're meant to do this...

I believe him. I made a commitment to a journey the moment I agreed to go to Leap Castle and find Matthew Kennedy with a man who falls Finnbheara only knows where on the human spectrum. Little Harriett and Alaina Kennedy rising to the stars must be my talismans for courage.

I lay my head on Sion's shoulder. It feels so right, natural. "I know."

"So," he gives our still joined hands a shake, blowing past the tenderness of the moment. "Tonight, we'll go to Dunamase to pay Strongbow and Aoife a visit. We'll sniff around for a chance to return the bugger's wee rings of steel."

And back to business. It seems every time I almost muster up the courage to pry into his feelings for me, he steers our ship back to the task at hand. "Dunamase?"

"Himself's castle." Sion blows a stream of air. "I've tried to convince Pwyll to travel, but ole rattle bones will have none of it."

I sit up. "A druid on the team would be handy." It was scary enough to go as far back as the sixteenth century to Leap Castle. Picturing a jaunt to the Rock of Dunamase in the even more barbaric twelfth century threatens to turn my guts to mush. Visions of the stacked bodies in the wedding painting add to the potential liquefaction of my bones. I've got until sunset to convert my watery core into bravery. At least before we travel tonight, I'll have time to scour the Internet to brush up on details of life in the 1100s.

"Wait." I tap a finger to my lip, conjuring the memory of Sion's kiss last night at Leap Castle. A piece of Olk's Strongbow lecture plays through my head, connecting with my mental catalogue of facts. "The cathedral is a bust, but rumors say there may be another tomb where Strongbow ended up."

"There's a claim the old boyo's final rest is on the grounds of old Fern's Cathedral down Wexford way, but Christ Church is where a betting man puts his money."

"Wexford?"

"Aye."

"If I can get us to Fern's to check out this other potential burial site before the start of the Celtic Day, will you at least try to put the chainmail in whatever grave might be there before we Veil travel to Dunamase?"

Sion drops his head back and grumbles.

I lay both hands on his cheeks and return his head to the upright position so he has no choice but to look me in the eye. "Will you?"

He closes his eyes for a long moment and then groans. "All right, Swan. I suppose it's worth a go if you can get us there without wasting heartbeats." A crease rises and falls like a wave from beneath one of his brows, dipping across the bridge of his nose until it completes a final curve under the opposite brow.

"I'll do my best, Fox." We're close enough than even a semi-lean from either of us will bring our lips together. The thought sets off a simmering pool of desire below my navel.

Even though Jeremy is a good option, it's Sion my body responds too.

He claims he isn't a Faerie, but my urge to kiss him feels dangerously close to tales of Good Folk mischief. I should pull away before I kiss him and possibly add complications between us and our already complex partnership, but I don't. Neither does he.

Our faces are close enough for breaths to mingle. "Colleen and Charlie are driving to Wexford to visit her grandmother. She invited me. You come with. We'll borrow their rental car and hit Fern's Cathedral."

Sion's mouth parts a fraction. His eyes catch the flick of my tongue dampening my lower lip.

"Ahem." Colleen stands at the corner of the nook, arms crossed. She frowns at the *Do Not Sit* sign. "Good, you didn't make it to the archives yet. Jeremy is asking for you."

I break contact with Sion and shoot off the platform like an ant on a skillet.

One thing is clear. If both Sion and I want to stay in Jeremy's good graces and avoid drawing attention to our nocturnal travels, we can't be caught almost kissing in a private niche when I'm on the Kennard Park University tour clock. Wrenching my phone from a pocket, I toss it to Sion. "Call Colleen's contact in five minutes. I'll fill you in. My lock code is *harp*."

Colleen hustles me into the center of the gallery. I skid to a stop and dart back to Sion. "You do know how to use a cell phone, right?"

Sion barks a laugh and nods. Top of our agenda—grabbing him a phone.

"He doesn't have a phone?" The thorns in her voice are sharp. We're a few yards from colliding with Jeremy and Charlie.

My mind is on the request I have seconds to blurt out. "Sion would like to come with us to your grandma's." A feeling of surety makes me stand straighter. Yes, this is a solid plan. Down in Wexford, we'll be out of Olk's range of scrutiny.

Colleen *humphs*. "So, you're a no-go with Jeremy and Trinity?"

"For now," I say, tossing her a bone.

Colleen's eyes become slits. "And suddenly you want to go to Wexford and bring Sion."

"I'd like to."

Colleen points a finger at me. "I think we need to talk."

Nothing pleasant ever follows that statement. "Absolutely." I agree quickly so I don't appear any shadier than she's already picking up on. Before we get closer to Jeremy, I whisper to her. "I think it's best if you don't mention Sion in front of Jeremy."

Her eyes bounce from right to left several times in rapid succession in a decision-making dance. Before she shares whether her spinner landed on *okay* or *no way*, we reach Jeremy.

"Ah, you found her," he says, flashing me an expression of warmth that should give me a little thrill. Only a sense of relief that I'm still on Jeremy's good side buzzes through me.

I drum up an answering smile. "Fell into a wander, taking everything in."

"Not all those who wander are lost," says Jeremy, quoting vintage Tolkien. "Are we on for Trinity College then?"

An errant thought of the two of us sitting in front of a fire, sipping tea, and discussing *Lord of the Rings* strikes me. Maybe I am leaving the Jeremy door open wider than I thought.

"Eala decided to go with Charlie and me to my grandmother's place in Enniscorthy," says Colleen.

I pray Jeremy doesn't hear the disapproval in her tone and ask for follow-up questions.

"That is Trinity's loss." He gazes out the window. "The Book of Kells and the Long Room in the old library are not to be missed." Jeremy lays a hand on my shoulder. "Are you sure I can't lure you away?"

"Not today. Maybe we can squeeze in a rain check before we leave Dublin. I don't want to miss the chance to visit Colleen's grandmother or the renowned Enniscorthy fish and chips."

He grins. "A worthy quest."

Colleen darts a look between us. "Charlie's grabbing the rental then meeting us at the hotel." A thumbnail finds its way between her teeth. Thank goodness Jeremy doesn't know her very well. Nail biting is the dead giveaway she's stressed.

Jeremy gives my upper arm a gentle squeeze then steps back. "Then I bid you safe travels and *bon appetite*. We'll reconvene in the hotel lobby at ten tomorrow morning," he says. His gaze lingers on me as he removes his glasses to clean them. "Perhaps we'll find time tomorrow to chat." There's no missing his eagerness at the possibility as he waves round frames at us. "If I'm not mistaken, Enniscorthy is not far from Fern's Cathedral. The site holds quite a slice of history if you have time to pop in."

His mention of Fern's Cathedral makes my smile falter. Of all the places to bring up—Faerie mischief indeed. I sink my teeth into my bottom lip. Or is this a sign from Otherworld that we're on the right track and Fern's is where the chainmail belongs? If so, then at least the *turn your body inside out* sensation of Veil travel can be devoted to the next spirit in the soulfall. I send a wish to whoever is listening that Sion's prior knowledge and my insight might allow us to check off artifacts for everyone in the soulfall tonight. If we succeed, further Veil travel won't be necessary.

Colleen waves me over to a bench facing tall windows overlooking an atrium. "Please tell me you are aware Jeremy is into you."

"I don't know if I'd go that far. He's very friendly and collegial."

She pinches the bridge of her nose. "Can I be honest with you?"

"I expect nothing less."

"I can't shake the feeling Sion is a misstep. I get you want to honor Martha's *find me* message."

I shake my head. "I never said Sion was connected to Máthair's ring." I didn't say it, but Sion promising to help me *find her* is feeling less and less like a coincidence.

Colleen waves her hands. "And I totally understand you're in a vulnerable place with your future in flux waiting to hear about the professorship, but clocking sexy time with the first Irish accent you meet isn't going to make your life easier."

"Colleen, you're misreading the situation."

"Am I?"

She knows me too well. It would be impossible for her not to see I've got feelings for Sion. Colleen is worried that my good decision making is broken. She sees Sion as an irresponsible fling and figures Jeremy could be an anchor for my life adrift. Colleen and I have always watched out for one another. That's what we do, and overly cautious me is acting way out of character by attaching so quickly to Sion.

Colleen presses fingertips to the corners of her eyes. "Another thing, I can't shake the feeling I'm being left out of the loop since you met Mr. Irish Guy."

I run a hand along her arm, grateful when she doesn't shake me off. "I swear you're not. I'm not keeping anything important from you." The lie burns my throat. She read me right. I'm keeping monumental secrets from her but not the ones she imagines. Colleen wears her feelings a hundred layers closer to the surface than I do.

She points at the reflection of my eyes in the window. "Weren't we going to do the contact eye color thing together?"

My breath catches when eyes shining like the glass of my grandmother's greenhouse stare back at me. Even stranger is the tiny bright band of gold around the iris, a Faerie ring reflecting a yellow moon. I'm looking at a dead-on replica of Sion's eyes. Did he do this to me? Is my new eye color some twisted, possessive brand?

There's no feasible explanation for the change in my eye color so I go with the one she already believes. "We did. I needed a distraction so I went for it." For a fleeting moment, I consider caving and confiding every detail about Sion, the Veil, the soulfall tower. A series of tiny painful stings erupt inside me as Veil Sprites weigh in on the decision.

Ah, they do follow me into real time and just wait for their moments. Another need-to-know Sion blew off. I do trust Colleen. It would relieve some of the stress to have an objective third party. Then I think about Sion's confession of danger. I could never put her in harm's way.

I grab the hem of her sweater when she starts to turn away. "Look, there will be plenty of time to get to know Jeremy at home. Sion is...I—I find him intriguing." I thread an arm around her back. "You held me together after I lost Máthair and a hundred other times." I flip through every file in my brain trying to choose words that will calm her. "You're right. The whole *find me* thing with Máthair's ring is messing with my mind. It's taken over. Maybe the message refers to Sion or Jeremy or something completely different. Whatever it might be, I have to allow for all potential options. But I promise, I won't let anything come between you and me."

"Oh, La." She throws her arms around my neck. "I love you."

"I love you too." I hug her back. "Colleen, Sion is a good guy."

"We don't know him." She tugs at her hair.

"You'll get to know him better on the Wexford trip."

She rubs her lips together. "He was very sweet this morning."

"And has excellent catching reflexes." We share a laugh. I nudge the spotlight off me. "So you and Charlie?"

She sighs the high note of an aria. "Oh La, it's like a Fourth of July sparkler goes off inside me whenever I touch him." She levels her gaze at me. "I know we clicked fast, but I have a gut feeling he's going to be important in my life." Her face pinks like a ballet slipper. "We're dying for some alone time." She scoffs. "That won't happen at my grandmother's."

It worked. She's backing off of Sion.

Colleen nudges my shoulder. "You okay with being short one roomie when we get to the hotel tomorrow night?" She leans back on her hands. "Did I tell you we FaceTimed Charlie's parents? He was dying to introduce me."

"Wow."

Her gaze drifts over the greenery in the atrium. "He's against my usual type. That must mean something, right?"

"Absolutely." Here's my opening. "Will you give Sion a chance? For me?"

Realization strikes me like the blast of frigid air on a New York City winter day. I want Colleen to like Sion.

I can't deny the connection between Sion and me has the earmarks of fate. It's not only our shared goals binding us together. I'm drawn to his heart, the one that sang alongside my own for one hundred thousand beats in a Celtic day. The commitment he's pledged to the spirits in the soulfall surrounds me with the light of a person so selfless, so determined to do good. Despite his crusty edges and questionable patience, I want to be with him, touch him, walk our path together.

Colleen is right to worry. Sion is farther from safe than I've ever dared travel before. My version of her chest sparklers warns there may be no turning back if I continue the way I'm headed. Up until Sion, I'd be collapsing with fear to fall into a life too big to handle, but with him, I'm holding it together.

Colleen blows a breath that makes her bangs dance. "Watch. Shanna will be enchanted with Sion and think Charlie is a goof."

I pat her knee. "Charlie is kind of a goof, but so are you."

Colleen raises her hands in surrender. "Guilty."

Our trip to Wexford is on. One more hurdle behind me to keep tonight's Veil traveling from becoming crazy difficult or worst-case scenario—impossible. With time ticking away, that can't happen.

Colleen's phone trills. "Look, you're calling me." She hands me her cell. "Do me a favor, La. Make the guy get a phone."

CHAPTER 15

THE BREACH

S ion fakes sleep during the drive down to an adorable coastal village and our rendezvous with Granny O'Halloran. I'm grateful he opted for the snooze ruse instead of butting heads with my friend and her new man during the nearly two-hour trip.

Colleen's grandma treats us to drop-dead delicious fish and chips with a side of mushy peas. After buttering up Granny O. with compliments and mutual admiration for her favorite Bishop's Water Irish Whiskey, Sion and I head off on our own. It takes roughly fifteen minutes of his driving to ruin the afterglow of a yummy meal.

I long to be back at Fitzpatrick's Inn with its whitewashed cinder block walls and red door, taking in the gorgeous Irish sea. Better yet, lazing on a dune surrounded by the salty tang of ocean air while I digest culinary bliss. Instead, I grip the edge of my seat while Sion whips the small rental along questionably paved backroads.

"When did you learn to drive?"

He grins. "Before I bought my first cell phone."

I wonder how long before cell phones were invented, or phones for that matter, it was since Sion was born. Why isn't he sharing more personal bits about his life? I wonder if it's because I'm not asking.

Sion slides his hands along the sides of the steering wheel. "With his mad display of peacock feathers, I had my doubts Charlie would surrender the car keys."

Maybe I nudged Colleen partway over to Sion's camp, but the fire in Charlie's eyes says he believes this rogue lured then ravished me in the woods. "You sure won Colleen's grandma over with whiskey talk and your story about visiting dear Uncle Finnegan." I cock my head to one side. "Do you even have an Uncle Finnegan?"

Sion pops his lips. "Can't take all the credit. It was this car that did the trick, not my Uncle Finn."

I smile, recalling the skepticism in Granny O'Halloran's eyes as she sized up Charlie and then the well-worn car. "We're lucky Colleen's grandma insisted they take her car to visit Glendalough."

His lip quirks. "Glendalough and the Wicklow mountains are grand. The round tower and the whole of the Monastic City are a sight to see." He sighs with pleasure. "You don't need Veil travel to sense the past there." He glances over at me. "I'm sorry to make you miss it."

I shake my head. "Miss it for now. Take me there another time."

He raises an eyebrow. "Hanging around for a bit, are you?"

"If things go south back home with my job, I might consider becoming a volunteer at Charleville Castle and lingering in Ireland for a while." The unspoken question is: Will Sion be here with me?

His smile fades, and he makes a low sound in his throat.

"What? You don't think I'll do it?"

His voice is quiet. "I think you'll do as you do. I'd like to be around to see it."

I press a hand against the sharp pain in my chest. I'm blathering about a future Sion may have no part in. He saves the souls and moves on, or— No, I can't let my imagination run wild on dark speculation about what may become of him if we fail.

We trade the seacoast for a palette of green. Growing up in New York City, I never appreciated the phrase *rolling hills*. Here, the land undulates under a blanket of grasses, donning crowns of gold where the sun catches the crest of a hill. Bands of rich cobalt sky house congregations of clouds so dense I could jump from one to the other. It's almost too much, the enormity of land and sky without the gray specter of buildings to obscure the view.

My world grows larger every minute. I'm a pendulum swinging between missing the comfort I created in my slice of a huge city or the security of a small college town for awe at the vastness of this land whose beauty holds me on the verge of weeping.

I can't tell if the silence I created between Sion and me is relaxed or tense. Judging from the hyper-focus he has on the road; tense takes the lead. I kick myself for thickening the air when my time with Sionnach, a man whose essence calls to me, is so limited.

I begin to wonder if I'm romanticizing this thing between us too much. Despite my growing affection, is our connection at the same level for him?

Sion points at a textbook Gothic revival church. "We're here."

A handful of vehicles park by a sign for St. Aedan's Church. "This isn't it."

He nods to a set of ruins behind the building. "It was." Only a few people stroll through the old graveyard. According to the sign, there are no services today. We can snoop at will.

Wind whips hair across my eyes. I do my best to grab it into a ponytail, knowing the futility. As long as we're outside, it'll surround my face in a wispy mane of cotton.

"Didja find where to start looking for our friend?"

Unfortunately, what I did find on my quickie Internet search was that Strongbow being interred here is likely hearsay. I haven't broken the news to Sion to buy myself poking around time while I muster the nerve for tonight's Veil jump.

My voice quavers. "Let's try inside first."

We start up the long, carpeted aisle that's flanked on either side by rows of reddish-brown pews. Ahead, a huge, pointed arch frames an altar backed with a trio of floor to ceiling windows. Afternoon light passes through the stained-glass images on the center strip, spilling color onto the altar.

Suddenly, Sion grabs my arm and drags me toward the nave. "Up there." His voice bounces off the walls, disrupting the reverence the space deserves.

Tucked in a corner is the stone effigy of a man draped in robes with arms crossed over his chest. The figure lies in a gothic-shaped coffin that reminds me of Pwyll's. Sion is already on his knees grasping the edge to find a way to move the slab top.

My heart drops when I read the plaque on the side of the tomb. I grip Sion's shoulder. "Stop."

He throws himself into his effort. "Open, you fecking box."

"This isn't Strongbow." The muscles beneath my fingers go as hard as the stone effigy. "It's an old bishop of Fern's."

Sion releases the lid and sits hard on the ground. He rests his forehead against the tomb. After a few heavy breaths, he raises his face to the stained glass. "I'm willing to push my body and mind past their limits, do what it takes, but why is it always so damnably hard?" Without another word, he walks down the aisle and out of the church. A sense of failure clings to me like a stalled storm cloud, black and filled with the unspent rage of thunder and lightning.

A sickening wave of understanding makes my stomach clutch. This despair, the utter feeling of uselessness, is what Sion has dealt with since he was given the stewardship of the soulfall. It's not the cut of knives or spears, but an unbearable weight that cannot be shed.

Have I hurt him by playing on the trust he has in my help, bringing him here, and offering misguided hope? Worse, did I waste some of the precious little time we have to succeed? A chilling thought follows. If we do fail, will I lose any chance for Sion to help me find Máthair?

Teacht Orm.

I run through the doors after him. At first, I'm afraid he escaped into the Veil, but then I catch sight of his peacock jacket as he limps through the graveyard in the direction of the original cathedral's ruins. I'm about to call his name when his voice floats to me on the quickening breeze.

"Peace to you McCloud. Peace to you Keatons."

He's addressing the headstones, taking care to accurately bless a single inhabitant or the family beneath the grass. Máthair called this grave walking. We'd visited the Sleepy Hollow Cemetery on a trip to New England when I was ten, and she'd done what Sion is doing now.

"There may be none left who remember these souls, Ella, so we will."

Clumps of purple flowers sprout here and there between markers. Lavender. Máthair called lavender the great healer of restlessness. She devoted an entire corner of the greenhouse to different species of lavender. Whenever she was agitated or worried, she'd drag a stool over and sit with her eyes closed, breathing in the scent until calm returned. I suppose there couldn't be a better plant to occupy a space where restless souls may be searching for peace beneath the sod.

Sion's put significant distance between us as he reaches a craggy wall of stone.

"Sion, wait." He doesn't face me but goes no further until I catch up. "The tomb inside. I misled you. I'm so sorry. I didn't find any proof online Strongbow was here. I went along with the rumor about this being a possible burial site."

He raises a hand to silence me. "And you didn't think to tell me you'd come up empty?"

I turn away, upset with myself that I've disappointed him. For once, I'm grateful my hair has a will of its own since it shields me from the look on his face.

He drops his head into his hands. "I'm so weary of it all."

Afternoon light fades and shadows stretch across the ground. I spot a squat rectangular gravestone by itself not far from the side of the church. The image from the Internet search comes to me along with a name whose significance is on the tip of my tongue.

"Remind me. Who is Diarmait MacMurrough?"

Sion's voice is rough and strained like it was when he spoke to me before I knew his truth. The way he spoke to a woman who frustrated and annoyed him. "Not the King of Leinster we're after. Diarmait is Strongbow's father-in-law."

A low thrum pulses through my body, waking the Veil Sprites. "Give me the chainmail."

He grunts in the all too familiar sound I never wanted to be directed at me again and smacks the metal rings into my hand. His gruffness feels like a dismissal.

The chainmail is warm from being in his pocket. I close my fingers around it, climb over the ruins, and cross the short expanse to MacMurrough's grave marker. No grass covers the large, flat gray surface. In the center, a rectangular stone sits on its end atop a granite slab. There are Celtic markings on the gravestone. As I stand on the edge of the grassy fringe, the rings grow hotter in my hand, but when I move next to the marker itself, they cool.

Sion parks himself on a broken headstone not far away, watching. Huge oak trees loom along the west side of the graveyard, hurrying the darkness that begins a Celtic day.

I close my eyes and wander over gray slate. The chainmail changes temperature like it's playing a kid's game of warmer or colder to find a hidden object. When I turn to the west, a faint blue line inside my closed eyelids etches the outline of a gravestone lying on its side. *20 April 1176* hovers above the image instead of being carved into the stone. The chainmail suddenly burns my hand, and I drop it into the grass with a cry.

Sion is by my side before the pain ebbs, eyes stretched wide. "What happened to you?"

I croak an answer. "He is here. Strongbow." Sometimes rumors can trace their roots to truth. "His grave is a stone on its side. I—I could picture it. The top corners are chipped away, and moss covers most of the markings."

Sion's eyes flare even larger, and he crosses himself. "*Faix!* Faith, love, you've had a seeing."

I walk toward a copse of trees in the far corner of the graveyard, calling to him over my shoulder. "I dropped the chainmail. Find it, then help me look for that stone."

He drops onto the grass, skimming it with his hands. "Got it."

Racing the dwindling light, I tear between graves, hunting for the one from my vision. Headstones rise from the grass, some straight others leaning, but none is a match for the one I seek.

I don't check on Sion until I've reached the edge of the markers, hoping to find him waving arms in triumph. He stares back at me with the same hope. Over the dead, we both wither with defeat.

I turn away, unable to face the mirror image of my failure. The wind sings its shrill whistle through the trees. Branches sway and leaves flutter, adding a dusting of sound to the air. Below the closest oak, the wind's symphony parts a wild tangle of grass, and I see it. The surface of a stone the size of a suitcase juts out of the greenery in a nondescript lump.

I run toward it, shouting Sion's name. When I reach the grave, I drop to my knees in the soggy ground. My fingernails claw at the moss that obscures its carvings. They're unreadable. I close my eyes and trace the grooves with my fingers. *20 April 1176* shines behind my eyelids.

A whistling through my head might be the wind or the whine of my thoughts. I rip up handfuls of grass and dig into the moist dirt, deeper and deeper until I catch the lowest edge of the buried stone. When I slide my hand underneath, a shock runs through me.

My sight blurs into an image of the soulfall tower. In the high window stands a familiar silhouette, one I believed to be the hunched figure of an old man, waiting for us to supplant his sin with virtue. Now I recognize the form as a young man swathed in robes similar to the ones worn by the effigy in the church. His garment is in tatters, waving and tangling around his body. The soulfall readies itself as the Celtic Day is set to arrive.

My hands burrow deeper into the soil, and the figure in my vision stands straighter. Knowing burns in my heart.

Strongbow sleeps beneath my fingertips.

As my touch grows closer, so does redemption for the squire who fractured his soul with the guilt and shame of betraying the man he pledged to serve.

I lie on my stomach, arm in the earth nearly to my shoulder.

Sion's voice is frantic. "Eala, is it a seeing?" He tries to pull me away.

I resist. "Give me the chainmail." My outstretched arm wears a sleeve of earth.

He presses the three rings into my palm, closes my fingers around them, and kisses my gritty knuckles.

I plunge the chainmail into the earth, sliding it deep beneath the stone.

As soon as my fingers no longer touch the metal rings, silence snaps around me. I slump, resting my head on the gravestone.

Sion gently frees my arm from the grave. He gathers me to his chest, stroking my hair.

I'm completely at peace for a few brief moments until a need to be sure I've succeeded squeezes my chest. I barely breathe the words, "Soulfall tower. Can we travel from here?"

"From anywhere." He scans the graveyard to see if anyone is watching, then cocoons himself around me. There's a waver in the air and then the violent tug of the Veil. Traveling with my body encased by Sion's is like rolling together down a grassy hill instead of being slivered and reassembled.

We arrive near the base of the tower. The river hisses and spits from the opposite side of the boulder we lean against. Saffron flickers of light from the tower window dance across stone. The uppermost curve of the full moon peers over clouds. Keening from the soulfall thickens the air around me. My lungs ache with the effort to breathe.

I force myself to look at the window, but the squire from my mindscape doesn't stand on the ledge. The silhouette of a portly man dressed in a suit steps out into the night only to be destroyed by the river's teeth. We've missed the beginning of the soulfall.

I burrow into Sion's chest. "Can you tell? Did we free the squire?" The glow from the tower window slides through the mist, creating a pool of illumination around us on the riverbank. I leave muddy handprints along Sion's sleeve.

"No telling if his turn passed before or after we returned the mail. We've got to wait for the soulfall to begin again."

Melting out of Sion's embrace, I curl onto my side, covering my ears to wait for the spirits to finish their ghastly parade until we can watch the squire test his fate.

Sion speaks in a low, soothing voice. "I know it's much to ask, but as I said, soon you'll be needing to watch the end of the soulfall, *anamchara.*"

The word is strange to me, but I'm too consumed with blocking out the piercing melancholy of the soulfall to ask what it means. I yearn for the blessed silence between repetitions of the souls' tests of fate. A tendril of wind skates across the river and finds me with its icy touch, proving Sion is no longer there to shelter me.

I hate that he leaves. It's another hint my deepest feelings will go unanswered by him. If my weakness didn't disappoint him, would he cradle me in his arms? Kiss me? Even if my affections are one-sided, he must know his presence is the only support to make the woeful song of spirits bearable.

Didn't finding Strongbow's grave atone for my inability to watch the souls yet to be saved? I refuse to get used to the soulfall. I need it to sear my own spirit. This palpable torment motivates my commitment to end it. Why can't he appreciate that? I pull tighter into myself. I'm too drained from what Sion called a *seeing* to engage him in an argument even if he had stayed with me.

Finally, the cries of the dead take their pause. I rise, brushing dirt from my arm and sleeve.

Sion walks up the slope from the river, shaking droplets from wet hair. Has he grown such a thick skin he can ignore the souls' laments to splash water on his face? I wish there were time before the soulfall starts again to do the same, but the pause is all too brief. The moon shakes free of its cover, bathing the scene with a silvery touch.

Soon enough, the low whine that precedes the moan of spirits rides the wind. Candlelight spills down the side of the tower, setting moss and stone aglow. I raise my eyes to the window.

The squire stands tall, arms extended to the sky.

Instead of plummeting from the ledge, the night eases him from the tower. I hear the snap of his robes and the sound of muffled bells. The moment his foot meets rock, the sky blazes with fireflies that twirl in an elongated helix, stretching from the river until they cross the face of the moon.

I reach toward the twisting lines, shining with the virtue of his humanity restored. "Godspeed. Peace be with you." As the last stream of light clears the moon, I find my feet and bolt for the woods. I'm elated one more soul is on the bright side of their journey, but there are more still caught on the spikes of torment. Confirming Sion's opinion of my weakness, I refuse to stay here in the open where my own soul absorbs their boundless misery.

Once I find shelter under the trees, the sound of the soulfall is muffled but not extinguished. I want to leave. Go to Enniscorthy and spend a normal evening with Colleen, Charlie, and Granny O'Halloran before we chase down the next soul's virtue.

I cup my hands and call out. "Sion."

No answer.

"I want to go back. Now."

If he's callous enough to wash in the river during the soulfall, he can damn well take me through the Veil without waiting for the end of the cycle. I scan the wood for a white poplar with green triangles on its bark, his Veil guide's tree. Maybe, if I find Alfie…That first night, Sion claimed I'd caused a ripple in the Veil. Does that mean I don't need him to travel?

Silence comes more quickly than I expect. It makes sense. The soulfall is half of what it was. When I turn in the direction of the tower, I see Sion, painted steel blue with moonlight, waiting in an opening between the trees. He's as still as the trunks flanking him.

When I take a step toward him, he falls to his knees. Any thought of traveling alone disappears as I run to him. He throws both arms around my waist, burying his head against me. His body trembles violently enough to shake mine.

I drop over him as gently as a coverlet, arms tight around his neck, face buried in curls. He doesn't act like a man who can't wait to see the end of me. The scent of lemongrass and spearmint surround us as we hold one another.

Sion is first to speak. His voice cracks. "So much time squandered in failure. How can I be forgiven for the hell I've wrapped tight around the souls?"

"Shh." My fingers find a path through his ringlets. "We're not failing now."

As he stands, his body slides against mine. The contact ignites a slow burn across my skin. I want those strong hands tracing every one of my curves. When he tilts his face to me, instead of matching the desire that surely smolders in mine, his eyes glisten with the last of his tears.

"You're a wonder, my swan. I will not doubt or question you again." He lays a fist over his heart. "My service is yours."

I shake my head. "You have to question me. I don't know what I'm doing."

He cradles my face in his hands, kissing my temple as the heat between us intensifies. "Maybe this doesn't." A finger trails down my neck, across my collarbone until reaching my pounding heart. "But this does."

It takes all my willpower not to smash my body to his and confirm how perfectly we fit together.

"You're gifted with true sight, Eala *bán*. You see between worlds. The ghost girl knew it and so did Strongbow. His soul called to you."

I rub fingers over my eyes. "What if the seeing was a one-time deal? I may not be able to do it again."

He kisses my hair. "You will. All you need to do is wrap your heart around what's shown to you, like your shadow stories in the fire."

My eyes widen. Whenever Máthair told me tales of Faeries and heroes, I'd imagine the scene as a shadow puppet play in the flames of our fireplace. I hold him at arm's length, our potential moment of passion dissipating. "How do you know about that?"

Sion lowers his gaze, lips crinkling. "I sent them to you."

It's suddenly hard to draw a breath. "You what?"

He peeks at me through lashes. "If I confess all to you now, we'll lose time. Will you take my promise that I will tell you everything before the end?"

The Veil Sprites within me flair in harmony with their kin in the Veil forest treetops as the soulfall dirge begins again, ripping my focus from shadow puppets and confessions. I cover my ears. "It's getting worse."

"Desperation rises the closer we get to Beltane."

Behind Sion, a shocking blue flash nearly blinds me. The smell of burning metal supplants the Veil fragrances filling the air moments before. Throughout the forest, Veil Sprites wink out.

The flash thins into a path of tiny, bright blue flames, etching Sion's outline in the air.

I point. "Look."

The sketch of cool fire disappears with a *pop* as he turns. Sion takes a defensive stance, pulling me against his side. His eyes rake our surroundings. "Tell me."

"It was—strange, frightening as if something drew your shape with a purple-blue fire pen." Glancing at the space where the bizarre phenomenon happened, I notice a Sion-shaped distortion still hangs in the air like heat waves off asphalt in summer. "See, part of it is still there."

As soon as Sion's gaze locks onto the spot, he sweeps me into his arms, and we punch through the Veil. The travel is frenetic and unforgiving. His back slams against the side of the rental car as we fall into reality and onto the grit of the car park.

I wipe gravel from my palms. "What the hell?"

He tosses me into the passenger seat. I barely pull my legs in before he slams the door and vaults straight over the hood of the car.

Once in the driver's seat, his face glows as white as the car's paint job except for two bright spots of scarlet on his cheeks. He turns wild eyes on me. "We're being followed."

CHAPTER 16
THE LIMP

S ion stands a discreet distance away while I relinquish my entire
fish lunch in front of a pair of mules. The indelicacy of our hasty
Veil travel compounded with teeth grinding fear and staring out
the rear window for malevolent Faeries on the hunt did my stomach in.
Both animals poke their heads over the fence and sniff. They nod in
unison, and then one unleashes an ear-splitting *hee-haw* to voice
disapproval at my soiling of their roadside.

With a napkin rescued from my small day pack, I wipe my face.
"Finished," I say, returning to the car.

Sion hands me one of the water bottles Granny O'Halloran made us
take on the trip. His tense gaze fixes on the road we've just come down.

"Anything?" I ask, squinting off in the distance.

He shakes his head.

"Who's following us?"

Sion shrugs, but I've studied his face enough by now to know the
blank look he shifts into is forced. Certainty he's keeping something from
me sets off a stress headache. I've also learned I can only press him so far.
If he were willing to share whatever's swimming under those ringlets, he
would have.

I opt for easier questions to draw him out slowly. "Where are we?"

"About fifteen minutes from Enniscorthy."

My woozy self leans against the side of the car. "Good. We can regroup at Granny O'Halloran's place."

Sion moves beside me, copying my position against the car. He raises a hand to measure the last slice of lavender daylight sinking into the west.

"Sionnach?"

He runs a hand through curls. I expect them to tinkle like bells.

Faerie bells.

The longer I'm with him, the greater the need to dig into the volumes of weird he's keeping from me.

He lightly bumps my shoulder with his. "I do like you calling me by my proper name."

So, we're back to misdirection. What happened to the promise he made after my *seeing* to be more transparent and not doubt me? Perhaps in the mind of my fox, promises made in moments of extreme emotion are subject to retraction.

And a fox he is. I'd chuckle if I weren't as wobbly on the inside as the legs deciding whether or not to hold me upright. His trickery and sly methods of getting his way are as much a part of him as the strands of paprika hair hidden under their chestnut cowl. I miss the unleashed fire of his real locks that shows itself in the Veil. Despite our potentially dangerous situation, I smile at the thought that Sion's shifting hair color matches the fickle nature of his personality.

I take in miles of stone fences, fields, and trees as night descends and the clock of a Celtic day starts ticking in earnest. Across the landscape, trees catch the wind in a to and fro dance. There's wildness in this land, untamed and volatile, full of the unknown.

Like Sionnach.

An urge to capture him, this place, the Veil, and the soulfall in a poem or story seizes me. I haven't cracked my journal since we landed, and doubt I'll get the chance while souls depend on me—on us. Our situation with the souls is ripe for poetry. Emotions and realities not overtly stated but rather shared with a scarcity of words digging into the heart—the enormity of our purpose. I'll call the piece *A Hundred Thousand Heartbeats*.

I wait Sion out a few more moments. When he offers nothing, I take the lead. "If we're being followed in the Veil, we won't use it. No traveling. We'll restore the rest of the virtues in the present. It worked with Little Harriet and Strongbow's squire."

Sionnach works his jaw. "Can't risk depending on that. We've only got three Celtic days left before Beltane."

I roll my head to face him and deliver my sarcasm A-game complete with Irish accent. "Ignore the nasty in there, Eala. We'll outrun it and be grand."

He stops moving his jaw but stays silent.

Above, a single early star shines so bright, at first, I assume it's an airplane until it doesn't move. "You need to trust me. Tell me who or what you think is after us."

He paws the pebbles on the side of the road, earning another scolding *hee-haw* from the mules. "Dunno. Could be another wanderer overlapped our path."

"I don't believe you."

He levels his gaze at me and then smacks the side of the car. "The flash you saw by the soulfall tower is connected with the fire in Dublin."

My legs lose the battle to hold me up. Opening the passenger door, I drop sideways onto the seat, feet dangling over the roadside grasses. "How do you know?"

I watch his Adam's apple bob as he swallows hard. "It must be. Neither was working in our favor."

He won't meet my gaze. Damn it. He's withholding. My voice is raspy with fear. "If you're right, tell me how we protect ourselves from whatever is blocking us."

His face is drawn so tight, creases and wrinkles break out across his forehead and from the corners of his mouth. "If we're spooked and tentative and avoid the Veil, the soulfall doesn't stand a chance."

I rub my eyes, attempting to downgrade my freaked-out status to rational. Too much is at stake to devolve into a whimpering mess. "Then we figure how to travel on the down low." I tap the dashboard. I'm a planner. The stability of where my next step will be in life keeps me afloat, which is one reason not knowing my professorial future is making me crazy. "Let's act differently than this opponent expects. Save souls out of order, zig zag our way around, no predictable destinations."

I rub my nose against my shoulder. New York City/Kennard Park Ella would avoid danger, dive under her quilt, and wait for Beltane to pass. Ireland Eala is turning into quite a different creature.

"We'll go back to Shanna's house. Throw off whatever's tailing us by being around people as we plan our next move. Hopefully, it won't want an audience. Then we'll sneak away to travel."

His face flushes as ruddy as his Veil curls, and he sucks in a rattling breath.

My stomach flip-flops, sensing before my brain I'm not going to like what he's about to say. "Sionnach?"

He moves to stand in front of me. "While you were havin' a gawk at the roadside, I called Colleen and told her we're staying the night with Uncle Finn in Ballywater." As if he senses my desire to kick him, he presses his legs against mine. "We can't waste any part of a night, *anamchara*." He rolls his shoulders. "Truth be told, I'm as wrecked as you. A place to rest my head is calling, but time is a rare bitch."

Anamchara.

There's that word again. It probably means simpleton, person I can bamboozle with my charm to do my bidding. "What is an *anamchara*?"

Even in the scant dome light of the car, blush colors Sion's face and neck. His bottom lip crinkles as his gaze slowly finds mine. "It means soulmate."

The blush is catching. My own face heats.

Soulmate.

Time pauses as we appreciate the stillness, the sweetness of the moment fixed on one another. The word drifts into my heart and finds a place there. The Veil Sprites flow rather than dance through my spirit.

Soulmate.

A hopeful look replaces his shy one as he steps between my knees to reach me, tracing the side of my face with a fingertip. "Okay?"

I nod and smile, relishing this tenderness. Sion drops a soft kiss on my forehead and I long for more. He pats my legs, encouraging them back inside the car then closes my door and moves around the front of the car with the jerky gait of his limp.

My dear romantic Colleen has been on a life quest to find her soulmate. Did I stumble upon mine by walking into a cave in the Blarney Castle Rock Close? Graduating from partners to soulmates is quite a leap, but since we are in the business of saving souls, it fits like a second skin. My face still tingles where he touched me with fingertip and lips.

Anamchara.

The Veil Sprites dust my insides with their little fires.

I watch from the corner of my eye as he slides behind the wheel. Is he pondering the same question I am? Have we indeed moved from side-by-side to hand-in-hand? I flex my fingers, remembering the feel of mine joined with his.

He starts the car and pulls onto the road. "It's an apt term for my pal in the soul-saving business, doncha think?"

Pal?

What the hell. My heart shrinks a couple of sizes, and a bubble of embarrassment encircles me. I'm an idiot. This man is focused on his otherworldly quest, not me. I'm nothing more than a useful tool to him. Hand-in-hand my ass.

"Sure."

When he sneaks a glance at me, I look away so he can't catch the misinterpretation of *anamchara* flashing across my face. Message received, we're in the soul-saving *business*. Sion's words confirm he feels nothing special between us aside from mutual goals. I'm a pal, a buddy, a chum. He doesn't think of us as a couple in the romantic sense. We're business partners.

I rub my lips together, conjuring our kiss at Leap Castle. No, I can't count that as a kiss. It was a device to serve a purpose. All the cuddles in Robbie's flat were part of our act for my friends.

He pats the steering wheel. "We'll meet Alfie, my *fánaí* tree, in a wee wood outside of Enniscorthy. In the morning, we'll get back to Colleen and Charlie in time to make Dublin by Olk's witching hour." Under his breath, he grumbles, "Never trust a man with round glasses."

Disappointment keeps sloshing over me in waves. Beltane will come.

Sion and I will part ways. Visions of growing roots here fade as I force the picture of Kennard Park University and the small, tidy life it offers into my head.

I press a hand to my stomach as Sion tears up the road like we're in a damn rocket instead of a compact car. "You swore I'd get used to crossing the Veil, but it makes me really sick."

Sion pats the hair over his ears. "That's my fault." He smiles at me. "I'll be fixing it right soon."

Long, smoldering questions in my brain flare, flaming with a need for resolution. Since Sionnach's defined our partnership in corporate terms, and we may or may not be in fucking danger, I'm not holding back. "Why wouldn't you look me in the eye before the night in the forest?" My voice is sharp.

He squirms. "I promised myself I'd avoid such contact until I got you into the Veil. I knew once I looked into your eyes, it'd be hard to stop." His smile is so sweet, I taste it on my tongue, but sugar quickly turns to salt.

I don't want Sion to sense any trace of my naïve hope he might see me as more than a sidekick so I keep talking. "Did the Veil change my eyes?"

He nods. "You've got the mark of a wanderer, green with the gold band."

Every drop of blood pools in my feet. Máthair's eyes were like Sion's. Did she travel too? I stare at the roof. Surely, she would have told me, at least dropped breadcrumbs in a story for me to follow.

I spin the silver band on my finger. Could this be the breadcrumb?

"You've lost your color again, love. Do you need me to pull off?"

I shake my head. "Why don't you limp in the Veil?"

His foot stutters on the gas and the car lurches, jerking my neck to the side. Sion's face assumes a not-so-pretty shade of purple as he holds his breath.

"As we say in America, suck it up. You owe me explanations."

"I do." He slows our trajectory from the speed of light to a steady clip. "Well?"

After a long, deep breath, he speaks. "In the times we've traveled back to, my limp hasn't happened yet."

I'm sure in Sionnach's mind, that's an answer, or as close as he ever gets to one without prodding. If I can count on anything, it's his stinginess with information. Before I beg St. Patrick himself for patience, Sionnach continues.

"I took a musket ball to the knee."

My insides crumble. Not bullet—musket ball. Truths about Sionnach continue to explode in my face like spray from an incoming wave. I'm still digesting the fact that he's been around in some form for two hundred years.

"I left Ma and Da to make money in Dublin city. I told you our farm was small, an enterprise that eventually stopped putting enough food on the table." His grunt bounces around the car. "Guess I was born a fool and stayed a fool."

I find my voice. "Why a fool?"

"A lad my age who 'seeks his fortune'—" He frowns as he exaggerates the phrase.

From the light of the dashboard, I watch his knuckles whiten on the wheel.

"Either turns soldier or spy." He bites his bottom lip. "Both get shot at."

"You were a spy?" What other choice would a fox make? Goosebumps rise across my skin. "When?"

"Just after my twenty-eighth birthday."

"Sionnach!"

His mouth curls into a rueful smile. "Och. You'll not be letting anything pass, eh?"

"Nope."

He runs a hand through his hair. "Good. Keeping secrets is a mouthful of dry biscuit you can't swallow."

I cross my arms. "Swallow."

He treats me to an exaggerated gulp. "Ever heard of a shite called Cornwallis?"

"Of course, our Revolutionary War nemesis."

"The very one."

"As in surrendered at Yorktown?"

He chuckles. "Forgot I've a scholar on my hands."

I have no clue how to react. My stomach is crumpled paper. Sion is referring to the late 1700s. How am I ever going to wrap my head around him being alive so long ago?

"So, you know the tosser came here after leaving America with his tail between his legs to smash anything Catholic for his nutter of a king?" His eyes slide in my direction for a second, and then he keeps going. "Being a good Catholic sort myself, I worked as the eyes for a certain Father Colm. He trained priests under the nose of the English. He'd do a bit of schooling for the candidates hisself, then the good father smuggled his lads off to Spain to finish. They'd return as full priests dedicated to preserve the faith in Ireland."

We traveled back to the 1500s to find Matthew Kennedy. Before Sion was born. Before he became a spy for this Father Colm, and before he was shot. Therefore, no limp. Despite pieces of the timeline making sense, it doesn't even scratch the surface to explain who or what is driving the car.

"But you don't limp at the soulfall tower or in the Veil forest by the leaning stone."

He fiddles with the curls over his ears, avoiding my stare. "The Veil is generous with making a person whole when they're inside its influence."

My throat turns so dry, words come out in a raw croak. "What are you, Sionnach?" I wave my hands in the air between us to head off his stock answer. "And don't tell me a Veil guide or time traveler."

He stares ahead as minutes tick by and then eases the car onto the side of the road so he can face me. "I'm a man who is both young and old, charged with responsibility." When I open my mouth to comment, he lays three fingers across my lips. "And you are a woman sent to reverse my failures and heal time."

Slowly, his fingers slide downward, separating my bottom lip from my top before he draws a line under my chin to the hollow at the base of my neck. My body is the foam at the top of a receding wave. "Favor me with a thing, Eala."

"Hmm?"

"Ask me no more questions about myself."

I will my body to solidify and guide his hand away from my throat. "Fine, but the topic of danger in the Veil is not off limits."

He rubs a knuckle over his chin, saying nothing.

I sputter in disbelief. How can he lay all of this on me and then cut me off? "I'm sorry if questions make you uncomfortable, but please remember it's you that dragged me into an insane situation. Did you expect I'd just smile and do whatever you tell me?" I growl. "Do you begin to fathom how much my mind is scrambled?"

He looks utterly wretched. "If we succeed, I'll take you to the Hill of Tara and answer everything you care to ask, but now, you're getting far too close to what I cannot say."

I press fists into my thighs. "This isn't fair. I'm supposed to heal time and be blind to the big picture? And you won't even come clean about what awful thing might be trying to stop us."

My trust in Sionnach Loho thins to a thread's width. I'm so done with his merry chase. His avoidance of truths and the sting of soulmate being relegated to buddy status drive me to strike at him. He called himself a fool. Well, that makes a pair of us. I'm a fool for beginning to believe he might have caught feelings for me. "You realize I'm not doing any of this for you. It's for the souls and to see my grandmother."

Sionnach's chest sinks like he's been slugged. That hurt him and hurt him good. The verbal blow ricochets off him to me, and I'm equally breathless. I don't do mean well. The truth is, I'm lashing out at someone with the noblest of intentions because I ache for him to feel for me the way I do for him.

Wherever Máthair is, I sense her watching me with a mix of sadness and regret at my petty emotional attack on Sion. I stare out the window. It's not his fault I want him. Why shouldn't he act like he cares? He believes I've been sent by Finnbheara, King of the Connacht Faeries, to help him throw open the gates of forever. Of course, he holds me close and makes promises.

Anamchara doesn't mean to him what I want it to, but despite my anger, I do believe he values me. It's damn hard to appreciate that when he doles out information to suit himself, discounting what I need to be an equal partner in our sanity-challenging journey. I want to be the compassionate person my grandmother would be proud of by sticking to my commitment to help the souls.

Sionnach Loho's evasions don't make that easy.

CHAPTER 17
THE KISS

S ion squeezes the car behind a line of oak trees. I can only imagine the upheaval if an abandoned rental in Charlie's name is found by the roadside, and we're nowhere in sight. That'll cement our reputation for indulging a sex-in-the-forest fetish.

As we trek through the woods toward his traveling tree, Sionnach delivers a monologue bordering on babble with minutiae about the next soul. After my crack that I'm doing this for Máthair and not him, he's working overtime to placate me with what he thinks I want —information.

I try to pay attention. My mind is bent, but I can't allow it to snap. The first step in surviving our partnership is to bury any feelings I have for Sionnach. I stumble, imagining him instantly aging hundreds of years and blowing away like dust the way *Oisín* did in the old tale when he left *Tír na nÓg* to return to the real world. I mutter to myself. "In real time, he's my age—exactly. Is twenty-eight some numerological mythical key?"

Sion surpasses myth. He's my reality. The words don't do anything to help me forget I'm walking around with a potentially long dead Irish guy.

Stringy light loops through the treetops, turning Sionnach's face an unfortunate corpse blue as we find Alfie, the *fánaí* tree. I look away to shore up my nerve. Then I remember Sion's touch, his embrace, his heartbeats. The man digging through centuries of clothing between the trunks of a white poplar is anything but dead. If he were, one hundred thousand heartbeats wouldn't matter.

I grit my teeth. With my one-way emotions, partner I can deal with, but if he calls me his soulmate again, I'll insist he stop.

Sionnach spins his arms in circles between us. "I'm hoping this will go fast. The artifact is simple. It's your finesse needed to help the Earl of Rosse accept the significance behind his artifact." He tosses me a long white apron from his Mary Poppins-like bottomless satchel of period garb. "I've not convinced him."

The tight-fitting Victorian maid's uniform is scratchy against my skin. I slip my head through the neck of a floor-length white apron, and Sionnach ducks behind me to tie it. His equally solemn uniform with tails, stiff white collar, and double row of brass buttons is flattering enough to raise a sparking tease from my Veil Sprites. We're set to step into a public television drama loaded with curtsies and "yes ma'ams."

"I'm right giddy for you to see the Leviathan telescope at Birr Castle. Once we send the Earl on the way to his stars, I'll treat you to such a sight."

He lingers behind me. His breath loosens strands of my hair from under my lacey cap so they dance across the skin of my neck. I close my eyes, weary of trying to deny how much I enjoy the sensation of him. I press teeth into my bottom lip. As tempting as he is, if I give in to this want and Sion just uses me to blow off sexual steam, I'll be wrecked.

Or will it be a sweet memory of a man who once called me his soulmate?

Ach.

To tame my misplaced libido, behind my eyelids, I conjure the silhouette I've witnessed of the chubby man in a finely cut suit filling the window frame of the tower I've learned is the Earl of Rosse. He's next in line now that Strongbow's squire has been freed from the soulfall.

"Sion—" I pause, doubtless we're both aware I've gone back to the short version of his name. "If someone wants to screw with us in the Veil, I think it's a necessary strategy to mix up the order of the souls we visit."

He lays a hand on my shoulder, fingers gripping harder than necessary.

"It's a fine notion but skipping around won't keep the friction off us." I feel the rumble of a groan through his fingertips. "Fate knows, I've given that a go."

I want to press the point we should give it another go but embrace the futility. Sion will dig in as hard as a standing stone in a Faerie circle. I lift my gaze to the horizon. "Which virtue is the Earl of Rosse missing?"

"Humility."

Sionnach is still close enough that heat from his *h* slides down my neck to the top of my spine. The sensation of my core tightening into a coil renders me silent. I don't want to want him like this, damn it, but heaven help me, I do.

"He built the finest telescope the world had seen; a monstrous thing called the Leviathan. It showed him galaxies outside this one. Beyond amazing."

The Veil Sprites and I are hyperaware of how close his body is. I should put distance between us, but I can't force myself to move away. My voice finds its way out. "That's a huge accomplishment. Doesn't he deserve to puff up without being condemned to a soulfall for lack of humility?"

"The earl never got credit for seeing so far into the heavens. A feller named Lowell earned the lion's share of praise for eyeballing firmaments outside the Milky Way."

I hold as still as the oaks around me, afraid if I don't, Sionnach will break our tenuous contact. I may have no future with him, but I will collect these moments together and keep them like Veil Sprites twinkling in my heart. I understand the pull between us is absolutely necessary for the soulfall, even if it's clear he intends to keep it side-by-side, not hand-in-hand.

Does each beat of a broken heart still count as one whole?

I fuss with the ruffles on the apron's twisted straps and focus on our next target. "And the earl's bitterness landed him in a soulfall?" This guy must have been the ultimate poor sport.

"'Twas his right loud huff from beyond the grave, his hauntings. Bad fortune's been known to befall folks poking around his Leviathan."

I pinch a ruffle between my fingers. "Wait. He was already dead when Lowell glory-hogged the credit? How can a dead guy lose his virtue?"

Sionnach chews on his lip. "Rosse's spirit refused to leave the Leviathan. The way Little Harriett was stuck at Charleville Castle. Virtue can be lost because of what's in the heart of a soul who lingers, not only what leaves the lips during a lifetime."

I'm glad for the wool servant's uniform when a chill runs through me at the revelation. A soul who hasn't achieved their ultimate destination can be condemned to a soulfall via post-death thoughts? This is intense afterlife shit.

"I've tried to convince the earl's spirit that joy is in the accomplishment itself, not recognition, but he won't break ties with his creation."

"Wait. If he haunts the telescope, we can connect with him in real time."

"That would be grand if we could predict when he might honor us with a visit. Most of his hauntings cluster around *Samhain*, but they're irregular. Too big a gamble." He shakes his head. "The best guarantee is to go back to a time just after his natural end when his humility breathed its last."

I slide the last of my rogue strands under the cap. "All righty then. Let's do this." Sionnach laughs, and I swivel to face him. "What?"

He copies my accent. "Let's do this." Fanning a hand up and down my uniform, he laughs even harder. "The phrasing don't exactly match the wrapper."

I laugh with him. There's no crime in enjoying the time I have with Sionnach Loho as long as I keep my lapse in emotional judgment in check.

"Are you ready, love?"

I drop my face into my hands, dreading the Veil crossing. "I'm useless. It's on you to do all the work, yank us through the Veil and keep an eye out for trouble. I'll be concentrating on not puking on your butler shoes."

"Stay here." There's a ripple in the air, and Sion disappears.

Before my mouth forms words of protest, he's back. "Where—"

"I had to check if it's safe inside."

"Is it?"

"Nothing but rainbows." With the grace of a dancer, he twirls me to face the forest and then presses my back against his chest.

The position does not help my resolve to stay rooted in buddy status.

"We're going to Veil cross right this time. Close your eyes." He trails his fingers from my right shoulder, down my arm, until he lifts my hand. Slowly, he draws circles in the air with our joined hands. "Keep the touch light. Gentle. Call the Veil to your mind. Stroke its surface. Coax it to let you in. See it as the wall of a bubble. Push too hard and you'll break it, but wonder at it, and you'll find a thousand colors of ribbon twisted together."

A delicate scent of soap bubbles tickles my nose. Sion's soap bubbles. Beneath my fingertips, I feel a thin membrane like an expanded balloon. It reacts to my touch, curving and giving way as I slide my finger across the Veil wall.

Sionnach's chin rests in the joint between my shoulder and neck as he whispers. "Give over. Don't fight. Let your feet leave the ground. The Veil will hold you."

I gasp as the solid earth beneath my feet disappears, but there's no fear. My vertigo, my terror of high places, doesn't take over. Strains of violins layer note over note sweet enough to lull a babe into peaceful sleep. It's enchanting like so many of my dream flashes, or as I understand them now, those glimpses of the Veil and its possibilities. Sion told me I'd been connected to the mystical edge between worlds my whole life.

I believe him.

His free arm wraps around my body, locking me tighter against him. He promised never to let me fall. In this moment, I trust that. We sway and I relax.

"The Veil knows you, Eala Duir. You belong to it."

Soft, damp lips move against my neck as he speaks. Millions of bubbles the size of pearls bob inside me. The sensation of floating is intoxicating. I'm as feathery as my hair, drifting through the Veil.

"Open your eyes, Swan."

All around us, a membrane as delicate as a wall of burnt sugar wavers and shimmers. The formidable glass walls that defined the Veil on my earlier travels now ripple like silk curtains. Veil Sprites dive and spin around us. Barely perceptible iridescent streaks waver through their light.

Our feet rest on the carpet of the shining turquoise and violet orbs I saw the first time Sion took me through the Veil. This time, I feel no disorientation, only joy.

I lean my cheek against his. "It's beautiful." Our lips are so close, we share breath. His arm stays locked around me. I spin as delicately as a leaf on a breeze until our bodies are face-to-face. I twine my arms around his neck, leaning into him until I'm aware of every button on his coat pressing against my dress. His hands slide around my waist until they meet at the small of my back.

The Veil is ours. We ride a mystical Celtic breeze through time and place. Sionnach the fox is right. We belong to the Veil and it to us. Who I am. Who he is. The parents I never knew. None of that matters.

Find me.

The Veil called me to Ireland, to this man who is both young and old.

Side-by-side be damned. I thread my hands into Sion's galaxy of curls and pull his mouth to mine. The moment our lips touch, Veil Sprites pierce our bodies in cataclysmic delight. Passion moves us into a rhythm, banishing any question of trust. The kiss deepens and deepens until we are Veil Sprites, illuminating darkness by splitting white light into a spectral glow. Spirit becomes magic, the visceral—incandescent, joy our truth.

And then a violent jolt clunks my temple against Sion's collarbone with a *crack*. Mud soaks into my skirt as we settle into soggy ground.

I start to unleash every curse I've ever heard in English and Irish when Sion hoists me out of the grass and muck onto a slope peppered with stones. One of his arms stays firmly looped around my waist. As soon as I stop struggling, he points upward.

Across an expanse of ragged lawn, stretching toward the clouds is indeed a leviathan. The structure looks like a disjointed castle. Walls studded with towers that must be fifty or sixty feet high reach into the night. Crazy tall ladders climb to elevated walkways or stairs. Jutting from the center is a tube wide enough to drive the rental car through or for a man to discover galaxies outside the Milky Way.

"Up there's where we'll find the earl."

The river in the woods behind us muffles Sion's words. "On the left platform."

I recognize the figure from the soulfall. The Third Earl of Rosse, master of Birr Castle, leans on an arched wooden rail curved liked a crooked finger, staring at stars that stretch from horizon to horizon. The round glasses on the edge of his nose remind me of Jeremy Olk's.

My head swims from traveling. Not with the nausea of the passing but from a kiss that replaces my bones with soft warm clay. I'm glad we're off our feet because I'm not ready to stand.

Sionnach continues to stare at the earl, ignoring me. Dread, colder than the mushy earth, comes a calling. Was our kiss in the Veil crossing real, or a dream flash? I kissed Sionnach without hesitation or doubt. Did the Veil show me an image of my wish, or did it happen?

I have an urgent need to put distance between Sionnach and me. What if he read my mind while we travelled and saw me kissing him? Not exactly the definition of a platonic partnership.

When I begin to slide away from him, something sharp slices my calf. "Ouch." I grab the object. Victorian era mud in an open wound is a recipe for a horrid infection.

He plucks the hand-sized shard of dull copper from my hand. "Fast work finding the artifact, my darlin' girl." He leans in, lips claiming mine in a maddingly possessive way. I greedily answer his passion with my own. Our kiss lasts long enough to ignite a steady pulse of need between my thighs. Teeth capture my lower lip in a promise of more before he breaks the kiss.

Not a dream. Not a wish. A kiss. Oh, if only we had one night to ourselves without souls to save.

Relief floods my previously bubble-filled veins. What happened in the Veil wasn't simply a manifestation of my desire. It was real, and good sense help me; I want it to happen again.

Sion brushes my nose with his. "I've been wishing to claim your sweet lips since I first laid eyes on the spirted woman in the Druid's Cave."

I press my mouth back to his and whisper. "I didn't think you wanted this between us."

"Then you'd be thinking wrong." He pulls my body against his as we kiss slowly. I open my lips and his tongue slides against mine, driving all thoughts of the earl out of my head until I shiver with cold. Sion eases me away. "I much prefer this, but on we must go."

He's right of course. Excitement and adrenaline waltz together in my chest. I know exactly how I want to spend tomorrow in real time, and it isn't on a tour of Dublin Castle. I raise the shard in my hand. "This is the key to the earl's virtue?" I use my skirt to wipe goo off the bit of metal and then attend to my cut.

Sionnach lifts the artifact to catch moonlight. "Our friend shattered a lot of metal trying to make a mirror for his beastie of a telescope. The earl finally figgered the reflecting piece had to cool slow-like for weeks on end. He baked the final product in an oven massive enough to roast an ogre. Genius."

Wind through my wet skirt and separation from Sion's body make me uncomfortably cold. I scoot closer to him. "How will broken metal restore humility?"

Sion surges to his feet and holds out a hand to pull me up. "Let's meet with the good man, and you give that a go."

CHAPTER 18
THE FIRE

"Hold up." I study the earl as he gazes at the moon. I don't see a soul in turmoil. "Catch me up. What have you said before to try to convince him to let go of the need for recognition?"

"What haven't I said? I've fought with the man. Laid out the pros and cons. Tried to scare the stuffing out of him by painting a grim picture of eternal misery." Sion waves a dismissive hand at the telescope. "For a stretch of fifty years, I squandered all my time on him alone and there he stands, the stubborn bugger."

"He's a dreamer."

"Eh?"

"A dreamer." I gently take hold of Sion's chin and tilt it toward the stars. "A universe of answers waits up there. He's asking the questions."

Sion presses his lips together so tightly they nearly disappear. "And I've been bullying him to reclaim his virtue."

"Be gentle with him. The same way you just brought me through the Veil."

Moonlight catches a twinkle in his eye. "Don't be expecting me to kiss the man." His full lips meet mine in a soft peck.

Through puddles and patches of mud, we cross the grass to the base of a gigantic ladder. Sion's limp makes the slushy ground hard for him to navigate. I mentally calculate. We're in Victorian times, American Civil War times. After the date he'd been shot.

He tucks the metal piece in a pocket and starts to climb.

My muscles lock before I set foot on the lowest rung. "I can't."

"Tuck up your skirt." He resumes his climb but stops, shoulders drooping.

Tendrils of his disappointment writhe through the air and stab me like knife points. "I'm sorry."

He speaks through clenched teeth without turning. "Eala, I need you up there with me. If I misstep again, it could cost us a Celtic day. If I start to go rough on him, pinch me."

The world spins at the mere thought of climbing to the top of the Leviathan. Suddenly, arms lock around me.

Sionnach flings me over his shoulder, and in seconds we're climbing. "Close your eyes. I won't drop you."

Damn, he's strong. Fear pounds in my chest as I wonder about his climbing stability with the limp. I feel muscles bulge in the arm around me as he goes higher. I cling to him as best I can without hampering his movements while I press my face into the back of his coat between those broad shoulders.

We reach a platform at the top of the stairs, and he sets me on my feet to climb the final few steep steps to the high walkway where the earl stands. I thread my arm through his, knowing I'll need an anchor once my mind registers the truth of how high we are. The heady sense of dread never comes. Sion's touch, his nearness, keeps my fear at bay.

The figure sharing the wooden span with us wheels in our direction. The Earl of Rosse stands before us, his head of lumpy curls cocked to one side. "Ho there."

Sionnach sticks out a hand to the earl. "Sion Loho, sir. We've met before." He tactfully leaves out the number and nature of their encounters.

The baffled earl takes Sion's hand and then nods to his uniform. "You are not in my employ."

"No, but I've brought a thing for you." Sion offers the piece of mirror to the earl.

The man recoils as if he's been shown a rattlesnake. "Who are you to mock me with reminders of my inadequacy?"

Sionnach stiffens. "I'm no bog trotter, man. This is to help you move on."

Given his snippy tone, I pinch him as he requested and take over. "I promise, that's not what he's trying to do, sir," I say, drawing a startled look from the earl.

Sionnach steps aside with a half-bow and sweeps his hand in my direction. "May I present my companion, Miss Eala Duir, from America."

"William Parsons at your service, miss."

When the earl executes a bow, Sionnach passes his hand right through the man's head, confirming for my benefit that William Parsons is a ghost like Little Harriet.

Sionnach breathes deeply before continuing. "We're here to celebrate your success. This wee bit of mirror is no sign of failure. 'Tis a jewel in your crown of perseverance."

My stomach twists as I follow the earl's gaze to the bog below. Parsons leans on the rail. "How is it not failure when one's accomplishments are passed over?"

Sionnach flings a hand upward. "You saw the moons of Saturn, man. With your own eyes. You looked toward heaven and found much. What do accolades matter when you've glimpsed such things?"

The words Sionnach spoke before we traveled here flash through my head so I repeat them. "Joy is in the accomplishment itself, not recognition."

"Aye, sir," says Sionnach. "Did you not sense the presence of something bigger than yourself when you pierced the curtain of the firmament to see whirlpools of stardust?"

The earl's ghost stares at the moon. "It was grasping the hand of God."

Sionnach bumps shoulders with the soul, which results in his body going halfway through the earl's. "After such grace, credit for a thing is small indeed."

I reach for Sion's hand and twine my fingers through his. There is poetry in him.

The ghost of William Parsons, the third Earl of Rosse, reaches a hand to the sky. His finger paints images he alone sees. "Here," he says, and then uses a different part of the sky for his canvas. "And here." He drops his hand. "They called to me as if longing to be hidden no more." He sweeps a hand through the darkness. "And they were not."

Sionnach's voice is reverent. "'Twas you that listened. You woke them. If you hadn't, they might never have called to another. Who names them is no great matter."

Creases in the earl's forehead relax. His form becomes more solid. It's hard to imagine this gentle soul haunting visitors at his Leviathan telescope.

My fox's hand trembles within mine as he looks questioningly at me. I nod toward Parsons and smile.

He gestures as if to lay a hand on the earl's sleeve. "Are you ready to join your stars, sir?"

The ghost's eyes glisten as they travel over the Leviathan.

A farewell.

With a sigh, he turns back to Sion and raises the broken piece of mirror in salute. "Just so, young sir. Just so."

Before me, the spirit of a newly humbled man shines with an aura of gold. The light surrounding Parsons splits into lines that crisscross in front of him, a screen woven with golden thread. After a bow to Sionnach, the Earl of Rosse, shimmering with the glow of virtue restored, disappears with a contented sigh and delicate *pop*.

Wind blows through trees loud enough to mimic surf crashing to shore. With the moon over his shoulder, my partner turns and gathers me in his arms. He pulls the cap from my head, combing fingers through my hair until it's free to catch the breeze. "Feathers of a swan," he whispers, and then buries his nose past my feathers to kiss the tender skin behind my ear.

I tilt my head, exposing the length of my neck to his lips. "We need to go to the soulfall tower."

His breath warms my neck more than Máthair's brandied melon scarf ever did. "Is there doubt in your heart he's passed on?" He pulls back, waiting for my answer.

I shake my head. "None. You do a damn fine gentle."

"Thanks to you, *anamchara*."

I picture William Parsons turning into sparkles that spin to the stars, joining those souls whose virtues are restored. I've been given such a gift, glimpsing the essence of spirits en route to eternity, but where does the journey take them? Sionnach asked Parsons if he was ready to join the stars.

"After the souls—" I twirl a finger at the moon. "Where do they go?"

Sionnach huffs, aiming for exasperation, but the corner of his lip twitches into a smile.

"I only agreed not to ask questions about you," I say, giving him a playful nudge.

He settles me against him, laying his head on my shoulder. We sway back and forth in a slow dance. Part of me wants to pester him for the answer, but the rest aches to do whatever is necessary for more kisses.

"There's a stop between this world and the next. Picture a road." His fingers slowly slide down my spine until he presses just above my tailbone. "Here's the bit when a soul parts from the living." He bounces one finger higher and higher, gently poking until he stops in the center of my back. "The next place is what you might call spiritual triage to check if the soul does indeed have all their virtue intact. If they do—" Fingertips walk up my spine to the base of my neck where he draws what could be a Celtic spiral against my skin. "Up you pass to the eternity matching one's beliefs."

Sionnach unbuttons the top few buttons on my dress. His lips repeat the Celtic pattern on the hollow of my throat. I teeter on the edge of abandoning my quest for further details but manage enough breath to ask, "And if a virtue is missing?"

Tension crackles through him, and I'm embracing a pillar of granite.

"Soulfall." He threads fingers inside his stiff white collar to rip it from his neck and stuffs it in a pocket.

I unbutton his jacket and ease it off his shoulders. He hums approval and sheds his vest as well, draping both over the railing.

Sliding my hands up his chest and over his shoulders, I knead his muscles until they shift from stone back to flesh.

He rests his forehead against mine. "Does your well of questions ever run dry, love?"

This isn't my first dance with intimacy but with Sion, there's a pull, a surprising sweetness wholly new to me. My body understands the language his is speaking, one of longing—of lost objects being found. I don't question or overthink. I let us happen. Has the Veil or Finnbheara's machinations guided me to Sionnach Loho? Maybe there is something to the *anamchara* business after all.

Sion undoes another button of my dress, sliding the black wool off one shoulder. His lips brush my skin, and our dance resumes. The heat of his mouth momentarily scrambles my attention from the soul journey and spiritual triage. I force myself to refocus. Instead of a vision of Saint Peter at the pearly gates, I picture Jeremy Olk standing at a lectern in a classic New England college classroom with fall leaves splashing oranges and yellows outside the windows. He's got two enormous stamps—one dripping with red ink that says *REJECT* and the other doused in silver with the word *ONWARD*. People line up holding passports to receive Jeremy's yay or nay. Heaven's Gate might not be pearly and golden after all.

My vision is so absurd, I giggle.

Sionnach stops swaying to hold me at arm's length, one eyebrow raised. "A soul's journey sets you to laughing?"

I sober quickly as the soulfall comes to mind. "Sorry. I mentally stalled on the judgement piece."

His tiger curls bob as he rubs a hand under his nose. "I 'spose you being in the thick with me, 'tis your right to hear truths." Treating me to a saucy smile, he tugs my dress back into place. "Limiting my distractions while I elaborate."

We settle on a wide bench topped with several well-worn damask cushions probably pilfered from a grand salon in Birr castle. I picture the earl dragging them up the Leviathan ladder for comfort as he spent countless nights drifting off to sleep, gazing at his beloved heavens. I run my tongue over my lips. "Just momentarily."

"Aye to that." Sion sighs, gazing pointedly at my mouth. "When souls rise instead of—" He makes a motion with his hands to indicate the splatter and drip of souls we haven't yet freed. "They return to the judgment place." His eyes shine with longing. "The Glade of Chimes."

As usual, he doesn't give me enough. "Glade, as in forest?"

His storyteller cadence clicks in. "It's a bit of a clearing in the middle of a forest of sacred oaks, yews, and rowans so old there's no telling when they first greeted the sun. Some branches stretch out of sight while others trail along the ground." He wiggles his fingers. "Like a tangle of wooden octopi."

Duir, my real last name means oak. I am the branches he's describing. Parts of me reach toward the sun and the moon, to powers that surround me, defying understanding. I'm also the gnarled and twisted limbs of sorrow from losing my grandmother, too heavy to rise above the ground.

"At the edge of the trees is a lake. The water's not what you'd call blue exactly. It's got a thin layer of crystal over teal-colored waters. The surface shines like diamonds." He takes in a deep breath. "When a soul arrives at the glade, they reach into the water three times and are gifted three rods of silver. Spirits dwell in the trees. One of them will beckon, and the soul hangs the chimes on the branch of their tree. The spirit within bark and leaf will play the three notes of your soulsong on the chimes."

A memory stirs deep inside me. Máthair used to hum a tune I'd never heard anywhere else. I swear she called it her soulsong.

"Once you sing the sacred tune designed for your soul and no other, the places beyond—" He sweeps an arm across the stars. "Hear you calling and bring you home."

"All souls pass through the Glade of Chimes?" I can picture Máthair, dipping her hand into the gemstone lake and lifting her three chimes from its depths. Her soulsong must be beautiful, full of love and faith, and her hopes for me—all things that cannot die. I miss her desperately.

His expression darkens. "All souls enter. Not all earn their song."

The enormity of the soulfall presses against my body, squeezing to the point of pain. "We must free them."

"Aye. Every soul deserves their song." He stares at the moon. "I've told you this is my last chance to end the soulfall in my care. If I fail again, the Glade of Chimes will be my penance."

"Penance?"

His chest rises and falls. "Himself will banish me there." A smile wilts on his lips. "My last name Loho means yew. I'll become a yew tree spirit in the glade, writing soulsongs but never passing to the perfect place myself."

"Souls with tainted virtue become tree spirits in the glade?"

"No. Most are condemned to soulfalls." His lips twist. "I'm what you might call a special case."

I want to pry for more detail, but the melancholy in his voice prevents me. When we've freed the souls, I'll ask more. With every step closer I get to him, Sionnach is a bigger mystery. Why is this his last chance to save the souls in his charge? Forever is a long time. Why put a limit on helping people find a virtue they've lost? There must be a reason he's not destined for a soulfall. Surely a place that sounds as wonderfully magical as the Glade of Chimes isn't a punishment. The biggest *why* buzzing in my mind is his belief I was sent to him. He's so convinced, but I'm not. I can't deny our connection, but was it really designed and not discovered?

We sit in silence, listening to the shush of wind and calls of night birds. My inquiries definitely doused his passion. I need it back. It's time for my well of questions to run dry.

"Thank you for telling me." I drop light kisses along his jaw, pausing shy of his lips.

Sionnach cups my face in his hands. "A marvel you are to me, Eala *bán*." He draws me in and taps his lips lightly against mine, questioning. I run a hand up his thigh to the crease where leg meets body. The tip of his tongue approves as it glides along my lips. Do I taste of spearmint and lemongrass? I close my eyes, and we kiss as if we have a million heartbeats to spare.

We break and breathe. "Sion, is there time for—?"

Birr Castle glows in the distance, an enchanted palace without curses or sorrow. Sionnach eases me down onto the bench, his body melting against mine.

He whispers in my ear, lips grazing skin. "Do you trust we've sent the earl on?"

My fingers dig into the well-defined muscles of his back I've been curious to explore. "I do."

"As do I. We needn't travel to the soulfall tower to confirm. Shall we steal a few heartbeats just for us, love?"

I steal those heartbeats along with his lovely full mouth as I move my tongue against his, asking for more. He answers, tasting, exploring, claiming. From the forest, birds and animals chirrup and trill approval, their song growing louder to echo our enthusiasm.

I undo his shirt buttons. He moans softly when I trace a finger through the thick, silky tuft of hair on his chest. Moving lower, I learn the dip and rise of his stomach muscles. Feeling bold, I continue down along the V starting at his hip bone until I brush the back of my hand along the hard length straining against the front of his pants.

Deftly maneuvering onto his back, Sion pulls me to lie on top of him. Fingers trickle up my neck into my hair. I raise my chin until his lips find the pulse in my throat and linger. Despite being high on the Leviathan's rampart, far out of my safe zone, I've never felt more grounded, more connected to the earth. This dear Irish boy is my safe zone now.

I feel Sion's heartbeats quicken as he grows harder against me. Encouraged, I crush my mouth back to his, stroking his tongue with mine. Three times. Each pass slower than the one before. Three notes of a promise.

His self-control breaks. Lip-bruising kisses turn savage as if at any moment we'll be torn apart, and tonight is our only chance to drink in each other's passion. When I scrape my teeth over his tongue, he groans as his hands find their way under my skirt to grab my ass. As soon as he does, he stills, as if he's gone too far.

I run my hands down his arms across every farm-built muscle to encourage him. "Yes, more." I want this. I want him.

To further prove my intention and permission, I slide my knees to either side of his hips and arrange myself on the cushions to straddle him until my hot center settles over his cock. His fingers dig into my hips as wonderfully garbled words flow out of him. Moving slowly, I rock against him, adding more pressure with each pass. Our combined pleasure builds higher and higher during this monumental shift in our partnership until our desire is bold enough to split the moon.

With a cry, he has me off the bench on my back against the hard boards of the platform. Even though his strong arms lowered me with care, I'm thankful for the thick wool of the dress. As fast as a late afternoon whirlwind capturing a pile of leaves, he jerks his pants to his thighs then rucks up my skirts. His knee splits my legs apart as he rips my panties off. He looms above me, fumbling with cock in hand ready to drive it inside me.

I flatten my hand against his bare chest and fail to suppress a giggle at his eagerness. "Whoa there, mate." His eyes widen as I twine my fingers through the thickest patch of hair between his pecs and hold tight. "I know we're in a bit of a rush but…"

The look of confusion on his face makes me pause, and then something hits me. Maybe he doesn't realize he's skipping some very nice steps here. I cup his cheek with my free hand. "You've done this before, I mean back…in your lifetime?" I can't imagine he had time for sex in the scant span of days he's had between Éostre and Beltane to save souls.

He starts to move away, but I hold him in place. "Wait."

"It's a man's sweetest dream for a woman to laugh at his cock."

Before the delay takes him out of the mood. I move my hand from his chest to wrap my fingers around his still eager member. "I'm not laughing at your cock, Sion. It's quite grand." Slowly, I begin to run my palm along his hot, silky skin. "Answer my question."

"Aye," he groans, eyes fluttering as I stroke him. "I've had a go at a rut and burst in my past."

This time my laugh is explosive. I gently release him to sit up. "A rut and a burst? It's a woman's sweetest dream to hear sex described like clearing a drain."

He shrugs one shoulder, joining me in laughter as he sits back. "That evens us up then. My hilarious cock and your shunning of a lovely rut."

I lay my hands on his shoulders and bring him in for a slow kiss as we sit facing one another. My tongue caresses his until I sense the heat reigniting between us. Moving my lips to his ear, I take his lobe in my teeth for a moment before whispering, "You've had sex, but have you ever made love to a woman before?"

His voice is breathy. "I need a bit more clarity here."

"Watch me." I stand and shuck my apron. Button-by-button, I rid myself of the woolen Victorian prison, shoes, and bra until I'm naked in the moonlight. As my hands roam my body, brushing up my sides and across my chest, Sion's gaze is riveted on me. He lets out a breathy hum as I enjoy the heavy feel of my breasts, dropping my head back with a loud sigh. He doesn't move from his seat on the planks, pants clumped at his knees, dick at full staff.

I spread my dress on the wooden platform like a blanket, bending to give him an eyeful of my ass and enjoy the variety of sounds coming from him. No need for either of us to get splinters in uncomfortable locations. I motion for him to straighten his legs and kick off his shoes so I can take hold of black pants and briefs to slide them off. All the while, staring into his eyes.

"Come sit in front of me."

He scoots onto our impromptu blanket, bracing his back against the bench. I settle on my knees in front of him to take his hands and guide them to my breasts.

"Have you ever taken the time to enjoy the fullness of a woman's desire for you to grow beneath your touch?" I teach his hands to squeeze and massage in a way I enjoy. He's a fast learner and his attentions send me arching back and gasping for breath.

"This is pleasing to you?"

"Do you feel my body speaking to your touch?"

His eyes widen as I press my breasts more firmly against his hands. "You're so lovely, Eala."

"Satisfy your curiosity, Sionnach. Watch how my body responds. I'll tell you if you're too rough."

His caresses become more powerful. As his rough palms slide over my hardened nipples, my breathing quickens with desire.

I lean forward and brace my hands on either side of his neck. "Now taste me, Fox." I pull his mouth to one nipple. "First with your tongue then take me deep in your mouth. Watch how I grow for you."

He follows my instructions. As my nubs plump, he adds foxy nips to his ministrations. A heated wire snaps between my breasts and core. I stroke his cheekbones and temples with my fingertips as his explorations grow hungrier.

I'm dangerously close to my own burst. My core is spiraled into a devastating knot. Determined to hold on as long as possible to give Sion the full experience of bringing a woman to orgasm, I ease his shoulders back.

He sits up straight, clasping the indent of my waist in his hands. "Did I harm you, love?"

"Absolutely the opposite, my fox." A sweet look of anticipation knits his brows as he waits for my next command. "Kiss your way down my body." Leaning back on my elbows, I offer myself to him.

"With pleasure." His green glass eyes reflect the moon in twin pinpoints of brightness. Desire deepens his voice to a syrupy richness.

Rough hands continue to worship my breasts as his kisses dip lower and lower. He avoids the apex of my legs, kissing and licking the inside of one thigh then the other. I writhe with pleasure and the pain of holding back. I can't be the patient teacher any longer. "Now here." Clutching handfuls of those wonderful curls, I guide his mouth to my slickness. He lets out a sweet cry of surprise.

"Taste how my body longs for you, Sionnach. Have you ever paused to savor a lover's want?"

He grunts a negative while his lips dive deep and his tongue takes its fill of me. He lifts his head for a moment to smile. "You've grown brilliantly ripe under my kisses." As soon as he finishes the compliment, he's back at it with even more enthusiasm, finding new places to visit that make my need for him cross the line into desperation.

Inside me, a thousand dots of heat from the Veil Sprites escalate until I can't bear it a moment longer. My orgasm smashes into Sion's kisses. I raise my hips to offer him his fill of me. He greedily laps my desire, humming with pleasure. As I slowly shudder, returning to a measure of sanity, he kisses his way up my body, pausing his travels long enough to give my nipples each a deep suck before he reaches my mouth.

He speaks against my lips. "I hope I'm doing right by you, because you're driving me to brilliant madness."

I kiss him hungrily. "Too very right."

The corded muscles of his arms quiver as I hold tight to them, worried I may roll off the platform in my ecstasy. I'm impressed the man who was so ready to take me with minimal preamble has held back. I slide one hand down his side and across his hip until I grasp his ready shaft. The heat and pulse against my palm nearly undo me a second time. Moving slowly, I learn every delicious contour of his cock. The desire to taste him falls to second place behind my urge to welcome him inside me.

He raises himself above me. "As much as I appreciate the making love lessons, and I do…"

His breath is ragged and damn sexy. I wish we had the whole night for lessons.

"…I must have you now, my swan, or lose my mind."

This time I take charge of the guiding, circling his tip around my thirsty opening until I finally press him inside me. Raising my hips, I invite him to go deeper.

He braces himself above me, stroking my hair as he slides his length in carefully, testing our fit. His slow pace nearly kills me.

"Make love to me, Sionnach." When I cross my legs over his back and drive my hips into his, he moans.

"You've made a beautiful path for me by being as wet as the tears running down my face."

I'm moved by the glistening tracks across his cheeks. As his thrusts grow more urgent, I ride stroke for stoke with him. A word plays through my mind.

Anamchara…anamchara.

At Sion's release, I see the shimmering walls of the Veil wink to life for a moment around us and then melt away as he finishes. A sweet little wheeze plays through his breath as the pulses inside me diminish. He begins to roll off me, but I hold him in place.

His voice is a growly purr. "I thank you, love, for taking my seed so…"

I give his ass a tiny slap. "Enthusiastically?"

"I can settle on that."

Laying a finger beneath his chin, I raise it until we stare into each other's eyes. "Do you understand the difference now between your 'rut' and making love?"

"Aye, oh aye." He gathers me in his arms. "I've the notion there's even more to it."

I kiss his collarbone. "So—much—more." My lips brush the side of his neck. "Sionnach?"

"Yes, love."

"Don't you dare ever try to 'rut' with me again." He startles against me. "Only make love with me."

He dips his head to give my nipple a quick lick then a playful pinch. "You have my word."

We lay together, descending from the wonder of it all. My head rests on his chest as he hums melodies in my ear, his fingers tapping their soothing rhythm on my back. Making love with this man surpasses satisfying. It's enchanting. My selfish heart wants to squander the night here in his arms, but we'd both regret our weakness. I want to ask him if there is any version of the future where we can stay together but hold back. For now, I don't want to know. After the last soul is saved, I will bring it up.

If he's still with me.

If not, I'll have my answer.

For a fleeting moment, I worry about our recklessness. I'm on the pill, so pregnancy is not an issue. I calm myself by deciding Sion's waltz with being human and the eons of time since he's been with a woman seriously decreases his chance of passing anything else unwanted to me.

Pressure builds in my chest. Whether from lingering passion or the progression of the Celtic day, I can't tell. Sionnach draws in a quick breath and presses an ear to my breast above my heart. He looks confused for a moment and too worried for my liking.

"We'd best be going. The closer we get to Beltane, the harder it is to judge time. We've enough left of our day to push on to the next soul." He sits and pulls me onto his lap, kissing his way along my cheekbone until he stops at my nose. "Your wee nub is as round and sweet as a Faerie kiss."

Máthair would like him, I know it. And now that he's stopped holding back his feelings for me, I just might be starting to love him.

We stand. He dons his rumpled shirt, slipping into the vest and jacket while I dress in my Victorian layers. His eyes slide from my lips down the length of me as he dresses. For a charged moment, my body begins to respond in a counterproductive way given our tasks at hand and time limitation.

"No need to change clothing before we cross to meet the next soul." I'm barely listening. It's all I can do not to shove him back onto the deck.

Taking my hand, he raises my arm to the moonlight. My cuff is pushed halfway up my forearm. He touches my freckles one at a time. "Drops of gold across glorious marble skin."

Sionnach captures my gaze with his as he slips my sleeve into place. I steal a light kiss on a tiny mole the color of caramel above the arch of his left eyebrow to confirm it tastes as sweet as it looks.

His hands glide over my hips to the small of my back. Slowly, he brings our bodies together. The Veil Sprites, my internal keepers of the Celtic clock, begin to flap in protest. Our kiss is liquid fire, flowing between us until our lips fall away from one another, and we recall how to breathe.

I want to shed my clothes and stand naked with Sionnach in the moonlight. I want to see him and him to see me with nothing separating our spirits. I want to feel his heartbeat against my bare breast and deepen the connection between us.

It can't be this night. Making love does not stop time. There are souls in our care, and they must come first.

Wordlessly, he threads his fingers through mine and leads me to the eyepiece of the Leviathan telescope. I close one eye and peer in. The moon is close enough to hold in my hand.

Sionnach strokes my hair and sings. "Greeting to you, gem of the night! Beauty of the skies, gem of the night! Mother of the stars, gem of the night! Foster-child of the sun, gem of the night! Majesty of the stars, gem of the night!"

At the end of this Celtic folk prayer that I've heard my grandmother whisper every month to the full moon, me the swan, and he the fox, float on druids' breezes into the arms of the Veil.

Shrill screams of Veil Sprites pierce the air around us. Darting in a mad frenzy as if trying to escape the passage, the Sprites sting in panic wherever their light touches my skin. The walls of the Veil shift between prism glass and membrane, unable to hold either form. Beneath our feet, turquoise and violet orbs deflate and spill out through cracks opening across the floor.

A ghastly howl no earthly creature is capable of rises between the transforming walls just out of sight. Sionnach whirls toward the sound, shoving me behind him. With a sickening rip, holes burn and gape in the Veil walls around us like wax paper ignited by the purple-blue flame of a torch. Heat sears across my face intense enough to singe flesh.

"Run!" Sionnach yanks my arm as we sprint down the tunnel of the decaying Veil. A roar grows louder behind us. Flames crackle from every direction. Licks of heat slap our legs, bodies, hair.

I push beyond my capabilities, and with a burst of speed, we gain enough distance from the oncoming thunder to dive through a yet unspoiled section of the Veil. Our bodies tumble onto a patch of dewy grass, colliding with bone-crushing force.

We scramble away from the flickering walls. Sion insinuates himself between me and a tunnel of fire spinning in the air. A shadow manifests from the inferno, rising as tall as a tree and as wide as a country road. It flounders behind the last lingering barrier of the Veil. Around us, an evil wind shrieks to block all other sounds of the night.

The figure continues to grow as it looms higher. Mystical walls entrap it in a cocoon, but still the thing expands, stretching the Veil with it.

This is no dream flash. My blood sings a warning that whatever I'm seeing is deadly. A man swathed in heavy robes with a cap on his head stretches an accusing finger in our direction.

Sionnach's voice is as thin as a blade of grass. "Forgive me, Father."

Forgive? This ugliness can't be the lost spirit of some random priest, demanding forgiveness or trying to cross to a better place.

It's a hunter.

Thrumming vibrations course through my body, warning me we are its prey.

The shape reminds me of the statue of a Puritan man in front of the Witch Trials Museum we visited when Máthair took me to Salem, Massachusetts. The somber statue shook me to the core with its malevolent vibe, the same way this shadow does now. I seize Sion's arm to keep him from being consumed by the swirling gray mist pumping from the evil before us.

I attempt to drag him into a huge vertical gouge that stretches up the trunk of a ragged oak, bent on getting out of sight. "Come on, Sionnach." He's nearly as unmovable as the tree. Flickers of purple-blue fire from the ruined Veil reflect off his green glass eyes.

Before we reach the cover of the wood, the shadow shatters the last fragile pane of Veil glass. The thing flows purposefully toward us. Sionnach snaps out of his trance and scrabbles backwards, dragging me with him.

An arm draped in a fluttering sleeve hangs in the air, ink suspended in oil. It telescopes longer until the tip of our pursuer's finger touches Sionnach's chest at the heart. Screams erupt simultaneously from Sionnach and the monster, fragmenting every cloud in the sky into pieces the size of cotton balls. Even the moon dims and bobbles as a shock wave passes over it.

The hunter dissipates in a gust of wind, and Sionnach falls limp in my arms.

CHAPTER 19
THE DRUID

It takes a few tries before I find the thready pulse in Sionnach's neck. I press my lips to his hair and rock him. After smoothing away curls, I give his cheek a gentle slap in the hope of reviving him. My rag doll doesn't respond. Fear courses through my veins. He can't leave me.

In desperation, I push his lips apart with mine and whisper his name over and over to send my breath into him. Slowly, his mouth moves against mine. Those beautiful green glass eyes flutter open then flare.

He sits too quickly and falls back against me. "Something's wrong."

"We're way past wrong." I place a soft kiss on his forehead. "That shadow nearly killed you."

He splays one hand over his heart and the other over mine. Both pound with strength to rival summertime thunder. As he assesses the balance of our heartbeats, I'm tempted to stretch one of his cherry ringlets then watch it spring back.

With a grunt, Sionnach drops his hands, pointing at our real-time waxing moon. "We've enough heartbeats to spare. Break day is far off."

"Where's this Veil countdown clock you see and I don't?"

He collapses onto the grass and pulls me into the hollow of his shoulder. "Lie with me a moment." He hums the same song he did that first night we overstayed our time in the Veil. Vibrations in his chest buzz softly against my cheek, and my heart steadies.

He pushes to his feet, bringing me along. With a slight bobble, we're up and stalking toward the now familiar white poplar at the edge of the woods where we left the car. I can't believe his *fánaí* tree stayed with us amid a Veil wildfire with a freaky shadow demon on our tail. Sionnach runs his finger over a line of char on one of Alfie's trunks.

I tap a row of dark green triangles. "Why is that nasty thing wrecking the Veil to chase us?"

He rips off his jacket. "Get changed. We're staying in the present for a spell."

I grab his arm. "What in the name of sanity just happened to you?"

Sion pauses and then curves his hands around my waist. "Swear on Alfie's bark, I don't know." He crosses himself. "I've never seen such hellfire in my traveling."

"The shadow, the man in robes who hurt you, you called him *Father?*"

Sion's hands cover his heart. "Truth of it, he had the look of Father Colm I told you about."

With the robes and cap, the shadow did match the childhood imaginings of what a priest enraged by my sins might turn into on the other side of the confessional screen. "You said you worked for Father Colm. Maybe he's not hunting us. It could be a warning."

Sion makes a low hum in his throat.

I'm afraid to ask the next question. "Is the Veil gone?"

Steady hands cup my face. "No. It can't be undone. The power that created it has no equal. Since we're close to a feast day, it's at its thinnest, most vulnerable." He kisses the end of my nose. "It's but a wee stretch that's roasted."

"A wee stretch!" A thought smacks me in the ribs, and I put my hand on his. "Sionnach, the fire at Strongbow's tomb—were those flames the same purple-blue color?"

He scratches at his hair. "Started as such then went orange."

"Do you think this thing can stop us?"

He rips off my apron and then continues stripping himself. "I told you before, I won't let anything stop me."

A crawly sensation runs across my chest. "But it did stop you." I hug myself. "I was terrified you wouldn't wake up."

He sets his jaw. "I did, and now we've caught sight of what's after us."

"That doesn't mean we can fight it."

Sionnach's eyes glow. "I'm at the end of my chances to put all the virtues back to rights. I'll fight what I must."

"And you expect me to do the same?"

He gives a curt nod.

I turn from him to change into my clothes. Finnbheara didn't think the whole mess through when he picked me. Run and hide are what I bring to this, not fight. I know Sionnach well enough to accept the futility of arguing with him when he's worked up. I'll wait for my moment to make the point that I'm fully incapable of fighting evil shadows.

I call to him through Alfie's branches. "What now?"

"Pwyll. I'm hoping the boyo has insight for us about the shadow."

I point a shaky finger to the grass where we tumbled back to reality. "I'm not going into the Veil with that thing hanging around."

He pulls on his jacket. "I wouldn't let you. We're driving."

"Driving?"

"I told ya, Pwyll never left Leap Castle."

Tossing my shoes into the car, I slide into the passenger seat. My skin ripples as I envision a Pwyll encounter in my time. "Isn't Leap hours away?"

"Not the way I'll be driving." Sion jumps behind the wheel.

"We've got to meet Charlie and Colleen in time to get to Dublin by morning." I don't want to jeopardize my shaky standing with Jeremy Olk by appearing to shirk my tour responsibilities with another tardy arrival.

I try to sleep on the drive while Sion mumbles to himself. Shards of dread and helplessness clank together in my brain, keeping me awake. I run a finger across my bottom lip still puffy from the more positive aspects of the past few hours.

Reaching over, I slide a tentative hand under the curls at Sionnach's neck. Warm skin covers muscles bunched like braided stone. He utters a tiny sound of pleasure as my thumb maneuvers over a particularly ornery knot.

"Do Faeries believe in hell?"

His muscles snap to attention so quickly, I wouldn't be surprised if my thumb bruises.

"I told you, I'm not a Faerie."

When I move to withdraw my hand, he covers it with his, encouraging me to continue.

"So noted, but you said a certain king sent me to you. I figured you might have insider info on the subject."

He pulls my hand to his lips. "You want to know about hell and Faeries?" He turns my palm up and kisses it. "Fine."

The tingle from his lips starts at my palm and shoots quickly to parts better left untingled given our strict timetable.

"The Fair Folk believe in dark places but not your fire and brimstone from Sunday sermons." He twines his fingers through mine and rests our hands on his thigh. "Why you askin'?"

I give his leg a squeeze. "I'm trying to make sense of the Father Colm hell beast. Why would the real soul of Father Colm want to hurt you?"

Sionnach sits straighter in the seat. Dashboard lights reflect off the sheen of his unshed tears. "The man I knew would rather burn for eternity than lay a finger on another."

My gut says he's not coming clean about everything. "You asked him for forgiveness."

"What else would you have me do with a priest pointing a finger at my heart?"

I crush his fingers between mine. "Don't keep truths from me."

His eyes flash. "I can't swear it was Father Colm, so talking of him gets us nowhere."

I chew my lip. "Is it possible when the Veil burned, it allowed inmates of hell to bust out?" I can't imagine the monster was from anywhere else.

He scratches the cleft in his chin with a thumbnail. "Let's put the notion to Pwyll."

"Can I ask you something else?"

Sionnach bounces our joined hands against his knee. "Someone save my sanity." He exhales with a groan. "Fine. Send your bucket back down the well if you must."

"My grandmother? Where do you think she might be?"

He stiffens. "When we finish."

The longing for Máthair expands inside me. "What if we don't finish?"

He releases my hand and grips the wheel. "My life is a pile of promises with cracks and ruined edges. I'm trying to sweep that away to see if there's any part of me still worth a speck of value under the rubble."

His hand clamps my thigh. There's raw power in his grip. He's not hurting me. It's as if he's holding on to keep from falling.

"If I think of failure or broken promises, I'll lose the bit of courage still lingering in my bones. Movin' ahead is my only way." His hand darts around my back and, with a jerk, he pulls me closer. "I'm begging you to understand why I can't talk of such things."

The all too familiar niggle he's parceling out rations instead of real information nags at me, but I'm too weary to battle. Instead, I lean in and kiss his cheek. "I do."

His face breaks into a smile as we close in on Leap Castle.

The first sign something's off is the clog of cars stuffed into every driveway on the road near the castle. It's two o'clock in the morning. Any event should be buttoned down for the night and the place deserted.

We reach the old gate lodge. I brace for impact as Sionnach screeches into the scant space between a news van and a Garda car that looks far too small for the rental. I wonder how many time-bending visits it took him to master driving.

Beyond the trees, the top of the castle is bathed in a shock of light. The short road to the entrance swarms with a sea of onlookers, buzzing like an agitated wasp's nest. I feel as if I'm home in Times Square where electronic billboards turn night into day.

With a death grip on each other's fingers, we weave through the crowd. The underlying pulse of this place sets my teeth on edge. Too many people. Too much friction.

The castle's triple gothic arched front entrance is familiar even though in the present, pock marks and cracks mar its stony surface. Before it, the press interviews a cluster of priests decked out in vestments as grand as an Easter sunrise mass. Angry voices and waving signs rise from the crowd.

The Elemental Curses You!
Bring back our ghost.
Druids welcome here.

Cliques with opposing viewpoints pack in around the press, jamming the circular drive between castle and surrounding stone walls with bodies. They raise hands to the skies, chanting to their chosen deity.

Sionnach crushes my hand to paste. Sweat mashes curls to his forehead. The shadows under his brow remind me of Pwyll's bottomless eye cavities. He snatches the upper arm of the closest reporter and spins the man none to gently toward us. "Why's the place as mad as a box of frogs?"

"The Fathers," he nods at the group of priests. "They've gone and exorcised the Elemental. All hell is breaking loose because of it." He jerks a thumb off to the side. "You've got ghost hunters over there, cursing the priests." The man distances himself from Sion and points to another group of people on their knees. "And that lot's trying to call the ghostly feller back." He moves away, keeping a wary eye on us, not sure which throng of zealots we belong to.

I grew up with priests as objects of comfort and guidance. The collective intensity on the faces of this brethren with their billowing sleeves raised to the heavens is damn terrifying. Poor harmless Pwyll.

Sionnach's eyes roll back in his head, and for a moment I think he's going to pass out. I pull his face to mine so he can hear me over the rumble of the crowd. "Look at me."

The panic in his voice lights a fire of the same flavor in my gut. "I can't hear Pwyll."

I tug on his sleeve. "Let's head for the trees and call him from there."

Sion nods, a furious haze of ringlets frame his face. We slam our way between lights, priests, protestors, and dumbstruck participants in this media circus to run for a cluster of trees at the side of the castle. After squeezing through the place where a waterfall of broken stone pieces offers an opening in the wall, we make our way to the spot near the edge of the cliff where we rendezvoused with Pwyll five hundred years in the past. Sion cuts a path in the wet ground, pacing back and forth. Fragments of the otherworldly language he and Pwyll spoke hang unanswered in the air.

I get out of his way and lean against the ropy trunk of a tree. Lights from the front of the castle bounce off the clouds to wake the fox red of Sionnach's hair. He's a walking torch, threatening to ignite every branch and leaf he passes.

I tuck my hands inside my sleeves and grip the fabric. I'm not certain the Catholic prayers I grew up on hold any weight with druid spirits, but I give it a shot. If it's true—if Pwyll has been exorcised—does that mean he was a demon? Druids do have the rep of human sacrifices on their scorecard. I push the thought away. A demon would never lead us to Matthew Kennedy to send his mother's soul to heaven. Pwyll is one of many threads weaving between now, then, the Veil, and who knows how many dimensions not comprehensible to my limited human mind.

Sion drops his hands to his knees. His body shakes, and I hear the quiet sound of weeping. I rush to his side, throwing an arm around his shoulders.

"I can't hear him. I don't see him. There's a terrible chasm opened around the castle, and he's fallen into it." He buries his head against my shoulder. "He's gone, Eala. Gone."

Feeling helpless, I stroke his hair. "He might be hiding." Voices rise in a hymn of salvation. "I'd run from this crazy bunch too."

"I've been in the thick of mess and danger too often to miss the stink of it." Sionnach drops to hands and knees, crawling around the base of an oak while he pats the ground. A choked sob bursts through his bared teeth as he holds a splintered section of board.

A shattered coffin lies in the grass. The last identifiable piece left intact is its pointed gothic top. My body collapses against the tree. "Oh, Pwyll."

Sionnach's skin turns dark chocolate in the shadows. Crouching like a feral cat, his head whips side-to-side in search of prey. Spittle flies as a snarl rips from his mouth. "Something foul ripped Pwyll out of existence." He surges to his feet with one hand reared back, fingers folded into a fist. For an ugly moment, his stance suggests the blow is intended for me. Before I can force my legs to move, Sion's knuckles collide against the woody trunk with a loud *crack*.

At impact, shards of bark as sharp as knife points fly at me. I cry out as one digs into the side of my neck before it falls to the ground. Blood covers the fingers I press to the sting. Sion doesn't react to my distress. He's oblivious to anything but fury. His shoulder smacks hard against mine as he muscles past, hunting for an invisible foe. I use the tree to keep from being knocked down by his rampage.

Just beneath my hand, fluid spurts from the wood where Sion struck the blow. It drips down the trunk, disappearing and reappearing through crags in the bark as a metallic tang fills the air. The moon clears the tower of Leap Castle, revealing a crimson line of liquid as viscous as blood. What the fuck is this? A tree spouting blood screams of darker forces Sionnach's kept from me.

He is in no state for me to ask. The fox circles in front of me. Half his speech is in a language I can't follow. The other half is pure rage. "A thing vile and evil. That fiend in the Veil." He shakes a bloody fist at the sky. "Damn you to hell."

I back away from the bleeding tree and the ferocity burning in his eyes. My Sionnach is gone. This being before me has transformed into a primal entity. He's energy condensed to the killing point of a sword. Prism glass walls of the Veil blink into existence around him. "I'll chase the bastard down."

I've given my all to be brave, to serve something greater than myself, and possibly even started to fall in love, but this tree-punching version of crazed Sionnach rips jagged gashes in my thin layer of confidence. How can I follow violence personified, this conflagration of wrath unleashed, into a Veil consumed by fire with a creature lurking inside that might be responsible for wiping an ancient druid spirit from the world? Sion knows this shocking, dangerous facet of himself exists and has hidden it from me until now. No wonder he detests my endless questions that may lead to revelations of his murkier truths. I'm barreling full speed to the place where every risk I've ever taken ends up—in fear and the feeling the world waits to swallow me.

The raw truth of the man before me, a being not quite human, obviously capable of violent rage, burns my heart to ash. I can't find the Sionnach I just made love with inside this raving creature. He's the biggest risk I've ever taken. From him, I'll fall the farthest and land in a bloody heap.

Unless I run.

I tear past trees, through the opening in the wall, and back to the chaos brewing at the doors of Leap Castle. The crowd buffets and shoves me behind the row of reporters with their lights blazing. Through the tangle of bodies, my eyes catch the movement of a shadow seeping upward along the castle wall. It spreads, tendrils stretch like limbs of an ancient tree as the figure grows toward the moon. Outlines sharpen and the wavering essence takes human form.

I stare into the collection of holy men, trying to define the image as a macabre distortion of one of the priests created by the lights of the news teams.

I can't.

The tangle of vestments on the ground blend into a multicolored tapestry as the fathers collect into a singular body with no one form distinguishable from the others blocking the light. The source of the shadow remains elusive as its darkness flows higher and higher, overtaking one Gothic window and the next until it swallows both front towers and the row of crenellations joining them.

The shadow splits to become two men. One dark angel cradles the wilted form of a second in his arms. A jolt in my gut tells me I'm watching a death. I frantically check the people around me, but no one else watches the shadow play.

The horrifying spectacle expands past two dimensions into a disturbingly lifelike three. The fallen man disappears as the inky arm of the other reaches through the night. Its outstretched finger draws closer and closer to where I stand. This time, I'm the target of the unnamed assailant. I pivot, exploding through the crowd before the malevolent touch finds me the way it did Sionnach outside the Veil forest.

My scream garners no attention. It's just one more voice crying to the night in thanks or recrimination for Pwyll's demise.

Elbowing aside anyone in my way, I head toward the outermost layer of the crowd, praying Sion left the keys in the car. Once I reach the lane between castle and gate lodge, I break into a sprint. A figure jumps out to block my path, and I plow straight into the rock-solid chest I left ranting like a madman in the forest. Sionnach locks his arms around me.

I thrash and try to escape. "Let go of me. I'll scream for the Garda."

"Whisht. Whisht." Despite my slapping and twisting, he manages to maneuver us to the car, yammering in my ear the whole time. "I'm sorry, Eala, love. I lost my wits back there."

I'll never fight my way out of his grasp. He's too strong. Too fast. I go boneless in his arms, and he nearly drops me.

Using the break in his grip, I stumble backward. "Lost your wits! The man I thought I knew disappeared. Did you even register I got stabbed in the neck from your tree punch? For a moment it looked like your fist was headed for me?"

He reaches for me. "No...I'd never—"

"I can't...keep—I'm done with travelling and that freak in the Veil. I want to be safe again." Tears blur my vision. I wipe and wipe, but the world doesn't become any clearer. Sadness makes my soul ache, but I can't stay with Sionnach. Not after the frightful specter he became in the woods and the risks he refuses to acknowledge. How can I trust that version of him won't turn on me next time? My heart aches. Leaving him means I forfeit any chance of seeing Máthair again. Wherever *teacht orm* was supposed to lead me will forever be a mystery.

"*Anamchara*—"

I point a finger at him. "Never call me that again." I shake my fists. "You're no better off than me. No matter what you say, the Veil's ruined." I'm shaking so hard that I nearly bite my tongue. "I can't save anyone. You've made a terrible mistake. Your Faerie king didn't send me. I'm no one."

He lunges, attempting to throw his arms around me.

I flatten my palms against the front of his jacket and push him away. "Go. Leave me alone."

He raises both hands. "I can't. It's you who saved them, not me. You're the one with pure sight."

"Stop trying to manipulate me." I stab a finger into the dark. "Go finish the last two souls on your own. I want no part of whatever that literally bleeding tree is or what you became in the woods." Backing away slowly, praying he doesn't follow, I whisper. "I can't trust you anymore. You and all your omissions and dark secrets terrify me." My escape is cut short when the sensation of falling shoves against my chest. I drop to my knees, lowering my head to the ground while the world spins and spins.

The crash of Sion's fists against the roof of the rental car snaps me out of the spiral.

"I keep things from you to protect you. I swore I'd tell you everything when we finished." He redirects the blows to his temples. "If there were any chance to do this on my own, I'd leave you be."

Bending, he digs fingers into my upper arms and lifts me to my feet before I can get away. "You're hurting me."

He doesn't relax his grip. "Harriett, the wee girl at Charleville, it never occurred to me to connect with her ghost in the present. I've been travelling back to the day of her death and done nothing to pull her from the soulfall. And Alaina Kennedy, my own fear kept me from the very night holding the answers I needed to save her. Even there, I thought seeing the corpse of her boy would bring her the mercy of knowing his fate, but you knew it had to be a link between mother and son to send her to the light." Sionnach's long, straight nose nearly touches mine. "I've shaken that piece of mirror at the Earl of Rosse more times than a rooster calls the sun, and never managed to speak words to free him until you were next to me."

His hands switch to the sides of my face, thumbs pressing into the skin beneath my jaw. I don't want him to touch me, but I'm afraid resisting might reignite the frenzy I witnessed in the woods. The hum of energy beneath the pads of his fingers sends shocks through me. Sionnach is a man poised on the brink of irreversible desperation, capable of ruthlessness to get what he needs. Where's my guarantee that I won't be hurt or worse in this near madness?

His breath reeks of whiskey, and I see a pair of thin brown wood splinters beneath the corner of his lip. He chewed one of his spiked twigs while he left Pwyll's coffin to come after me.

Sionnach's forehead touches mine. "Stars could shift in the heavens for a thousand years, and I'd never seek Strongbow at the edge of Fern's graveyard."

To my relief, these words expend the last of his fervor, and he breaks contact. "It's a terrible task to lay at your feet." He rakes fingers through his hair. "Yes, there is danger. The Veil is breached. We don't know what's running loose, but I'm still begging you to stay with me 'til the end."

This hard-won admission of danger from him tips my decision closer to leaving despite the damn pull I feel toward him that's impossible to erase. "I can't." I step away from him. "I'm not the person you think I'm supposed to be."

Away from his touch, the night's bitter cold brushes my skin. Our beautiful evening at the Leviathan telescope fades. Crystals of ice form around memories of kisses and lovemaking. I can't believe it was only persuasion or insurance I'd stay by his side to finish his quest. I truly thought our passion was shared. Am I a fool? His attention is a potent strategy. Draw the vulnerable woman close. Kiss me as if he were the one seeking love.

I give my head one strong shake to rid myself of the thought. I know in my soul neither of us gave false kisses under that glorious moon.

A roar rises from the crowd, and I half-expect a mob of peasants waving pitchforks to march down the road singing of their victory in ridding the world of the Elemental. A sense of the horrible Veil shadow passes through me, and I focus on the pale oval of Sion's face.

I'm finished, but I won't withhold information from him the way he chronically does from me. I can't bear the thought of harm coming to him. "It's here—the thing that touched you from inside the Veil. You've got to leave too."

The way he whips his head frantically, taking in the trees, the road, the sky, stokes my fear of being chased. "Where did you see him?"

"I saw the shadows of two men against the front of the castle. One died in the other's arms and then vanished. The one left tried to touch me."

To my horror, the undulating walls of the Veil boil up around us. I leap farther away from Sion. "I won't travel. And you shouldn't enter your time-warp highway this close to the vision I just saw." As swiftly as they appeared, the walls dissipate.

Sion reaches out a hand as if to catch the fading shimmer. Incredulity infuses his whisper. He stares at me. "You sent it away."

The sensation of a trillion bubbles popping inside me makes the ground feel as if it's rising and falling. Sion grabs my arm to steady me. He's the only life raft in an angry sea.

He holds fast, desperation in his voice. "Eala, you are the person I know you to be."

I yank my arm free. "And who is that?"

He raises his palms. "The reins of my runaway intentions."

"You are a ruthless jerk obsessed with your own failure. What about my life? My soul?"

"Your soul," his voice falters, "is the most precious thing in the world to me. Do you not know it?"

For once, I hear the simple purity of truth in his words, a single chime in a silent forest. It's jarring. "How could I possibly know you feel that way?"

His shoulders stoop like an old man's. The fire of his drive has gone out. He won't fight or force me anymore. I hold power over what comes next.

His face is oddly peaceful and damn it, full of hope. I am the stasis in his turmoil. Chewing my lip, I grasp at swirling thoughts to arrange them in some sort of order. The soulfall is dwindling because of me, but the fact does not erase my fear and disgust Sion has no qualms over dragging me into potential disaster and possible death.

"Two souls left, love. Stay with me, please. The Veil will not fail us."

I'm a doll whose stuffing has been removed. Veil Sprites, each no larger than the point of a sharpened pencil, link through the marrow of my bones, radiating heat, begging me not to abandon them.

Two more souls. I find the moon in its place midway across the sky. The Celtic day waits. Can we finish before dawn? My urge for self-preservation collides with Sprites, souls, and feelings for Sion that still smolder inside me despite his terrifying transformation in the forest. I'm more convinced than ever before this is madness.

I never speak the word *yes*, but the walls of the Veil undulate around me, questioning. My heart expands and contracts as its magic brushes my skin. With a shock, I realize I'm calling it. I close my eyes and reach out. Its walls curve beneath my fingers.

It's the Veil that convinces me not to run. Two more souls and our task will be finished. I must believe there is a life waiting for me afterward. One I don't want cursed with haunting regret.

I call the Veil and allow it to wrap me in its ethereal cocoon. Shafts of prismatic light cross before me as their energy wafts through me. This passage between time and place answers to me now.

Sionnach's control is done. I choose to finish our task so the failure haunting his soul will not tarnish mine.

Reaching for the ancient power surrounding me, I search for any specter of evil approaching. Nothing dark stirs nearby. Sionnach's presence is near me but not touching. I do not resist as he steers us toward the next artifact. The music of the Veil, faraway strains of a violin, draws a long single melancholy note that echoes in my heart.

CHAPTER 20
THE VICTIM

I lift the skirts of my Victorian maid's uniform to move faster. Luckily, Alfie's stash had a spare apron to cover the mud stains from the bog at Birr Castle. Sion rushes along Clonskeagh Road in Dublin toward the home of Sir Arthur Vicars. Not the Dublin where I'll meet the travel group tomorrow, but well past midnight in Dublin of the early 1900s.

My heeled shoes click against stone as Sion waits for me to catch up. I avoid his eyes. Keeping as much distance from him as possible is more than a priority now. It's survival. I tell myself over and over that he is the ass from the Rock Close at Blarney Castle and the ranting nutcase from the aftermath of Pwyll's exorcism, not my Sionnach, my fox.

He's danger.

Sion moves to lay a hand on my arm but thinks better of it. "This'll be simple, splat, done, I promise."

Nothing in my association with Sion Loho has been simple, splat, done. My skin prickles from our series of peek and sneak Veil jumps to confuse the shadow menace.

"My gut always told me Sir Arthur's key, his artifact, is literally a key." He gestures at a house near the end of the row. "Feller was custodian of the Irish Crown Jewels. Someone lifted the bitty spare key he kept at his house and stole the treasure. Vicars took the fall." He stretches a cinnamon curl. It does spring back the way I imagined. "He spent the rest of his life howling his innocence to the moon, even in his will."

Quick calculations in my head glare with a piece that doesn't fit. "But Vicars was alive just over a hundred years ago. You said you've been trying to end the soulfall for two hundred years."

Sion studies the ground. "We needed the man to represent the last missing virtue and complete the soulfall."

"You're telling me soulfalls can grow?" My eyes widen. "How can they ever be fixed if they're open-ended?" I crush the skirt in my fists. "Are more souls going to just pop in?"

Again, Sion reaches for me then retreats. "No. I swear. Once the soulfall counts every virtue, it's set."

"So, you've had less time for Vicars than the others?"

He nods. "I thought he'd be simple to turn around."

It feels too straightforward. If saving Vicars is as simple as a real key, Sion could have solved this mystery a hundred times over. "How do you know his soul is telling the truth?"

"We're meant to restore his diligence." A shudder runs through me when he says *we're*. We are not a *we* anymore. I'm only here to nudge the remaining pieces of the souls' puzzles into place. Not take Sion's hand and walk into the first rays of dawn.

"His virtue cracked after living so many years under a cloud of false accusation. His words said innocent, but the number of folks doubting him burned his faith to ash. His spirit gave up the fight. Diligence to believe he'd be exonerated of the crime left his heart even though his voice kept at it."

"If he recorded his innocence in his will, where's your proof he gave up?" The words are barely out of my mouth before I realize the answer and whisper, "The soulfall." Vicars wouldn't be there if he kept faith his innocence would be believed.

Sion grimaces.

"Did you try giving his soul the artifact?"

"Of course."

I want to scream. Why in the name of reason does he think the literal key is going to work this time if it didn't before? My brain wearies from sorting out his messes.

Sion's gaze wanders. "It's got to be my timing that's off. We'll pinch the spare key ourselves before anyone else does. The jewels won't be stolen and Vicars not accused. The man will die without a stain on his name."

He darts forward, backtracking when he realizes I'm not by his side. My mind pings with warning. "You're changing history."

His face clenches.

"Are you allowed to alter the truth of what happened in the past to restore a virtue?"

Irritation blooms in his eyes. We've barely spoken since we hopscotched our way through the Veil to get here.

He lifts his arms to the smoke gray clouds overhead. "History is the villain here."

I rub my nose against scratchy wool. His plan is impulsive, without substance, a kiss to heal a broken arm. I trail behind as he heads for Arthur Vicars's house.

The sense of wrongness hits us at the same time, and we both stop. Ahead, lights blaze from a single house on the row.

Sion motions for me to tuck against the nearest wall. He slinks ahead to a pool of darkness straight across the road from the house where the spill of light doesn't touch him, a fox on the job—a spy.

I pull the shawl I grabbed from the wardrobe bag tight around my shoulders and follow him.

Through the open door, we watch a crowd, including Dublin police, swarm the front room of Vicars's house. Off to the side, a woman sits in a chair, head in hands, weeping.

I tug on Sion's sleeve. "Do you see Arthur Vicars?"

He shakes his head, strides across the street to the open front door, and raps on it. An annoyed looking policeman greets him. "What's the noise?" says Sion. "I'm from across the way."

In a voice too low for me to hear, the man grumbles a string of words at Sion and shuts the door in his face. Wisps of dread swirl around me like static air before a storm.

Sion stands frozen for a few moments and then limps along the street in a zig-zag path as if he's dead drunk.

I hurry to where he collapses against a lamppost. "What's happened?"

"Arthur Vicars is dead."

"Dead?" I twist my apron into a knot. "We jumped to the wrong year. You said that nasty shadow might throw the Veil clock off." The thought of risking any more time in that mystical passageway to hit our mark isn't a happy one. I press the heel of my hand against my heart. With all the hopping around we've done tonight, we can't have an abundance of heartbeats left.

Sion's voice is strained. "We've come to the right time. I heard talk in the house. The jewels were taken tonight. Arthur Vicars was shot by soldiers even as he denied the deed."

I press my tongue to the roof of my mouth, thinking. "He's not supposed to die tonight."

He fixes boiling green glass eyes on me. "Someone beat us here and made a mess of the past. Changed time."

I bite my tongue to keep from reminding him that's exactly what he intended to do.

His hands ball into fists. "Vicars wasn't shot for the theft on this night. He lived on for years swearing his innocence until his diligence finally turned to dust."

My hands shake. "Are you saying the shadow creep came for Vicars? Why?"

Sion's features harden. "To ensure my failure."

Thorns puncture the narrative of poor impulsive Sion Loho who was never able to match all the artifacts to restore virtues. "Damn you. This history twisting has happened before, hasn't it?"

He freezes, betraying nothing.

I grab handfuls of his jacket and shake. "It's not the first time you've been chased or truths have been altered."

He rips out of my grasp and slams a fist hard into the palm of his hand. "Of course not. Do you think me such a fool as to fail for two hundred years without opposition?"

Sion's secrets crash into my gut. I double over, shawl slipping from my shoulders to puddle on the ground next to me.

Sion shows his teeth and snarls. "Enemies never look the same. We'll go into the Veil and hunt the bastard down. This one will not bring me to my knees. With you at my side, we've the wits to undo it."

The Veil walls thunder to the earth with a shuddering *boom*. When Sion reaches to pull me in with him, I squeeze my eyes and send the Veil off. I know I've succeeded from the string of curses he unleashes.

"Fuck's sake, Eala. For once, quit playing the weakling and stand with me."

"Stand by your omissions? Your manipulations." I kick the shawl at him. "You expect me to stand shoulder-to-shoulder with you and fight a shadow?" I take two steps back to keep from slapping his face. When he tries to follow, I hold up a hand to stop him. "I'm done being dragged into God knows what." I call the Veil. A fragile sheen rains around me. This time, Sion sends it off.

"Let me say my peace."

"How can I believe a single word out of you?"

He steps away. "I've known you all your life, Eala. Watched you. Tried to speak to you through visions." Sion bends his knees as if he's ready to spring and then slaps a hand to his thigh. "I was convinced if I found a way to tap into your sight without calling you to my side, answers for each soul would be clear to me without you. I'd leave you be." He steeples his hands, pressing them to his mouth. "More of my blind arrogance."

My legs start to numb. "Visions?

"Shadow stories in your fireplace. Animals coming alive on the carousel. Colors of spring blossoming in snow and ice."

It's my turn to grab the lamppost for balance. He's talking about my dream flashes like the one I had at the Central Park carousel right before I came to Ireland. The walls of the Veil so like the far edges of my visions. Sion used the Veil to control all those times when a gray world shifted into a riot of color behind my eyelids as vibrant as the page from a child's storybook.

My lips move. Barely a whisper escapes. "Shadows in the fire?"

He nods. "Do you remember when you were a wee thing and the birds called you into the sky?"

I stare wide-eyed. How can he know about the day Máthair saved me from flying off the rooftop during the dream flash that incited my lifelong fear of heights?

He hangs his head. "'Twas reckless calling to you then, and I'm sorry for it."

The explanation should register as ludicrous. A bird version of Sionnach Loho calling the child, Ella O'Dwyer, into the skies above Manhattan. But I've seen too much in the past few days to dismiss it.

I press fingers to my temples. "You've always been in my head?" Anger forms a knot behind my breastbone. I push off the post and shake my fist. "You almost killed me that day."

His eyes dart back and forth. Damn him. He's still editing what to say and what to keep from me.

"You weren't ready to come to me then. She told me so, but I called you anyway." He bounces in time with his agitation. "I do curse myself for making it so you can't look down on the world without being overtaken by a fear that rips the heart of you clean out."

She told me so.

She.

My breath catches in my throat. "Who? Who told you I wasn't ready? And ready for what?"

His face contorts as secrets flutter beneath his skin like the swarm of moths around the light of the lamppost. "For this." He sweeps a hand between us. "To fight for the souls."

Fight, not save. It's been a battle all along, not a safe and cozy mystery with a trail of quizzical clues. A battle that's waited for me to join for how long—my whole life?

My voice is the edge of a knife. "Who told you I wasn't ready?"

The alarm in his eyes is answer enough. Only one person in my life could tell this Veil guide, this version of a human being whether or not I was ready to stand by his side.

My grandmother.

Suddenly, Sion's innumerable deceits pale next to Máthair's.

I must see her. Now. The Veil will help me. The moment the magical passageway enters my thoughts, the street is obscured once again with its filmy presence, wavering around both of us in a massive sphere. "You know where my grandmother is."

"I do." For once he doesn't dance around the truth.

I want to scream and land my fists against his chest until ribs crack. How could he be so cruel, using my grandmother as bait all this time to keep me by his side? He said he'd help me find her, not that he knew damn well where she was.

Nothing, not my future with Sion, danger, or even the fate of the soulfall will stand between Máthair and me now. She owes me truth and answers. "Take me to my grandmother."

The corners of Sion's mouth droop, as the light in his green glass eyes dulls. "Once I do, there's little chance you'll again stand the sight of me." He doesn't try to talk me out of it but extends his hand. When it's clear I have no intention of taking it, he drops it to his side. "We've got to pass through the Veil quickly." He shoots a wary eye around. "Before the priest knows we've gone in."

My breath catches. So, he is sure it's Father Colm turned vengeful priest, who erased Pwyll, and tracks us on our quest to end the soulfall. By his own admission, Sion's been pursued and thwarted before. That's how he knows what's after him. The dark spaces holding the volumes of what Sion isn't telling me could blot out the stars. What truly happened between this priest and him to threaten the very substance of the space between worlds?

I don't care right now. One pinpoint of light calls to me across time, and every part of me aches to seek it out.

Teacht orm.

Find me.

Clasping my fingers around Máthair's charm, I pray there are enough heartbeats left in the Celtic day to confront her.

CHAPTER 21
THE TRUTH

I'm not lingering inside the familiar passageway we usually travel through. Instead, the thin membrane of the Veil conforms to my shape like an opaque body suit. I stretch my arms and take a tentative step. The casing doesn't limit my movement but obscures all details of the massive shapes towering above and around me. I seem to be in the midst of a conclave of giants that neither speak nor move.

Tentatively, I whisper, not eager to disrupt the quiet. "Sion?"

Outside my elastic prison, a gentle chime of bells repeats a phrase of music again and again. A voice as pure as a new blanket of snow echoes the succession of three notes—once and then silence.

"Sion? Are you here?"

My sheath falls away. The scene before me stops my breath. Gnarled feet of my imagined giants are roots as thick as my body. They twist and flow to form a U-shaped curve around a small meadow of clover that appears to be made of silk instead of leaf.

Rising from this river of roots, trees mimicking the shape of oak, rowan, and yew surround me. Yet here, their trunks are a pastiche of wood in shades closer to dark gold than brown. Bark and branches are infused with chips of glass that sparkle and reflect light from a crystal sun, hanging unnaturally low in the sky above me.

"Sion, where are you?"

Layered strands of glittering bark twist upward, encasing each trunk until they join to weave a canopy just below the gemstone sun. From there, branches split into a thousand lines and cascade to the ground behind the trunks like the flowing hair of a goddess.

I can't see past the maze of branch works. Any space between shines with a brilliant white flame. Instead of leaves, millions of tiny silver tubes as thin as pencils hang from the trees. They sway in dainty arcs but make no sound.

Frustration causes me to abandon delicacy, and I raise my voice. "Sion!"

The half-circle of trees ends at a lake with bobbing currents of azure and cyan. Clover spills to the water's edge on a shore no wider than four or five yards. Frosting the surface of the lake is a barely perceptible diamond-like film.

Glittering trees, silver tubes hanging from branches, a lake wearing a coat of precious stone—

Awe softens my tone. "Is this the Glade of Chimes?"

Sion's description is as inadequate as a child's first sketch. I lay hands over my heart, realizing the music a few moments ago must have been a soul singing its song to enter eternity.

"Yes." Sion sits on a stone nearly buried beneath the roots of a tree. His perch is no ordinary stone. It's a deep amber color with veins of teal and chocolate chasing over a surface polished to a mirror finish. It reminds me of the precious stones lying on black velvet cloth in the Metropolitan Museum of Art's gift shop in Manhattan.

"Where is my grandmother?"

He steps over a root positioned like a leg casually crossed over a knee. Sion stops in front of the tree closest to the lake. In front of him are the crooked slats of a wooden door wedged between two giant bulges of bark strands covered in glittering emerald moss.

"Is she in there?" I hurry across the clearing to him.

"Go stand by the water, Eala."

I start to protest, but who knows what the rules of this place might be? Keeping an eye on Sion, I make my way to where lake glass meets clover.

Pinpoints of dazzling silver light reflect off the surface. If I reach into these crystalline waters, will I withdraw the chimes of my soulsong?

Sion knocks three times on the door and steps back.

"Whose time has come?" The voice from within is a whisper wrapped in an echo, but I know it.

My grandmother is here.

Before I cry out to her, the voice comes again. "Sionnach?"

"Aye, Máthair."

My wonderstruck awareness takes a sharp turn toward bitterness. How dare he use the Irish name for mother? I call my grandmother Máthair because that's what she is to me, more mother than grandmother.

Light suffused with a river of Veil Sprites bursts from between the slats of the door, and my grandmother's voice winds through the glade. "Is it done then, *Mac*?" The light flares, and Máthair speaks again, her tone flat. "You're not alone."

For a moment, the only sound in the glade is a pair of heartbeats, mine and Sion's. The light behind the door fades. A keening to shatter bone fills the glade. Sion drops to his knees, palms against the door.

"I'm so sorry, Ma. I had to bring her here. She's fixing on leaving me before it's done."

A gust of wind blows my hair into a snarl. The tree door slams open, knocking Sion backward and striking the trunk with a teeth-jarring *crack*. Silver mist in the shape of a sideways cyclone streams through the opening. It spirals around my body, sensing me. From within its grasp, I recognize the sensation of my grandmother's embrace.

"Eala. My dear, dear one."

There's no substance to the energy around me. I close my eyes and remember her smile. "Máthair, your ring said to find you. I came here to Ireland." I spill the words I've ached to say again since the day I lost her. "I love you."

The mist releases me. "Forgive me, my precious swan, *a stór*. Forgive me." The fluttering cloud rises above the lake and then plunges into its depths.

"Máthair, no! Don't leave me." I move too quickly. My feet tangle, but Sion catches me.

"She's moved beneath the lake glass so you can see her," he says and guides me to a large flat stone overhanging the water.

A spectrum of grays bleeds across the top of the rock, dabs of paint on an already water-soaked paper. The surface is as smooth and polished as the stone outside Máthair's tree. I sit near the edge, aware of Sion hovering close by.

After a slight hesitation, he drops down next to me without touching. "There." He points a few yards in front of us.

My grandmother's face, the one I've missed to the point of agony, ebbs in the currents beneath the lake's crystal topcoat. Her gaze fixes on me, and I meet her eyes. "You left me with so many questions. My real name—"

Her focus switches to Sion, whose cheeks flame the color of his burnt orange hair. "Did my son not tell you?"

My heart thuds. "Your son?" *Mac.* She called him *mac.* Irish for son. The enormity of what I don't understand explodes through my body, and I almost pitch forward into the lake.

There's an angry exchange in Irish between my grandmother and Sion. I understand every word.

I clasp my hands to the sides of my head. "Stop arguing, and stop lying to me, both of you." I glare at Sion and then back to Máthair. "You're his mother?"

"I am mother to you both even though you are not of shared blood. There's no familial bond between you. Sionnach is my natural child, and you are the child created, then given to me by Finnbheara."

I am so sick of this Finnbheara Faerie King asshole being everyone's excuse for whatever the hell is going on. "What do you mean created and given to you? And how can you claim to be his mother and my adopted mother? Sion's two hundred years old."

Máthair's lips twist. "So, he's told you some."

Sion raises his arms. "I said that I had."

Lines etch Máthair's face as she looks between Sion and me. "You told her of your fate?"

I hate the way they're talking as if I'm not here. I counted on my grandmother for answers and instead, I find her living in a tree and as cryptic and obtuse as Sion on his worst day. "I know he's a wanderer, *fánaí*, Veil guide, whatever. I'm helping him with the soulfall—"

Relief crosses Máthair's face. "So, you believe?"

All the years of folktales and Faerie stories she'd tell me in front of the fire come flooding back. She was prepping me for the day when I'd be forced to take a leap of faith and let those words fly off the page into my lap.

"I accept St. Augustine's belief in what can't be seen, in doomed souls, and—" My eyes meet Sion's. "Him. Even though I want to drown him in this lake." I wait a beat to calm my tone. "I do believe his heart is true to his purpose." A swell of tenderness rises, but I bat it away before it muddles my thinking.

"Thank the powers of earth and sky," says Máthair. Not exactly the Catholic prayers of thanks she brought me up on. "Then you know this is his last chance to break the soulfall."

I nod. "Or he's stuck in the Glade of Chimes. Here."

Máthair's face slackens. "Failure of his duty to the spirits of others will bind his soul here forever."

"Is that so bad? This isn't a soulfall."

"It's not the land of dreams, my child."

I train strands of white-blond hair behind my ears. "Not *Tír na nÓg*."

"Aye." Sion and Máthair say together.

They stare at one another until Sion speaks. "Imagine being surrounded by the smell of bread baking or meat roasting every day of your life, but you aren't allowed a bite. All you do is starve day after day."

A bitter laugh escapes me at his metaphor. "Let me get this straight." I point to my grandmother. "Somehow, you messed with time and adopted me to help Sion free the souls to earn his ticket to *Tír na nÓg* or heaven?"

A look passes between them that makes my skin crawl. The creepier stories of changeling children click to the forefront of my memories. "Oh, no. Did this Finnbheara character snatch a baby from my real parents and stick me in its place? Is that why they gave me up for adoption?" A horrible thought occurs to me. Did a baby die so Máthair could raise me like one of her prized apple trees to save her real kid? Have she and Sion spied on me since I was born, waiting for me to ripen? My failed DNA tests flash through my head. "Am I not human?" I hate the tremble in my voice. "Am I a Faerie?"

Máthair breathes deeply, spawning tiny whirlpools in the water around her. "Finnbheara is a mercurial being. He's dawn light and the deepest of shadow, a star-filled sky and the wickedest of maelstroms. But a kaleidoscope of generosity and benevolence lie at the base of his tumultuous nature. Once in ten ages does the king summon essences from the earth to create a spirit such as you, child of swan and oak."

Eala Duir.

Swan oak.

"And that's supposed to give me special power to help the soulfall?"

Máthair's eyes drink me in with the familiar love I've sorely missed. "The spirit of an oak grants breadth of vision and self-confidence."

Finnbheara didn't put enough oak in his Eala recipe because I am neither of those things. I prefer the narrow lens of a safe and small life. The very thing these two ground to dust by forcing their agenda on me.

"And the swan—" Even through the shining filter, I see tears sparkle in my grandmother's eyes. "Has a powerful connection to *Tír na nÓg* and represents the compassion of the human soul."

The only connection I have with a swan is my ridiculous feathery hair. I dig my fingers into my arm to touch flesh and convince myself I'm real. "I'm supposed to buy my very existence was created via magical interference from Finnbheara?"

"Has your life not been a happy one, my darling girl?"

I flinch at the question. Up until Máthair was taken from me, my life was filled with happiness.

"I am the mother you were given. Finnbheara created your spirit, but you were born of flesh and are as human as any begun the natural way. I insisted it be so. For you to have compassion for humanity, for the souls, you had to live a human life."

Sion runs a hand along my arm. His touch is both comfort and confusion. My face flushes, recalling his embrace and the sweetness of our lovemaking. Those things were real to me. Despite mythical overtones and our out-there skill of bopping across centuries, we are flesh and blood and bone. I meet his gaze. "My parents were real people?"

He nods. "A barren couple. The woman was a welcome vessel. After your birth, Finnbheara adjusted their perceptions to shield you, then blessed those folks with many other children as thanks for bringing you into the world for our ma." Sion breaks eye contact. "They've no memory of you."

This is ludicrous. I bite the inside of my cheek. As crazy as traveling through time or souls falling or rising from a gray tower. Insane enough to possibly not be a lie.

I look back at the face in the water. "Why you?"

Máthair presses her lips into a tight line.

"Why did Finnbheara do this for you and your son?"

Sion curves fingers around my arm, tightening his grip as if I'm ready to fly off the rock ledge, and then meets his mother's eyes. "He loved her."

I yank free of his hold. Fury sparks in me, flames reviving a banked fire. "Finnbheara is your father! You liar. If he's a Faerie, so are you." Given all the weird he chose to tell me, why did Sion never admit to his Fae heritage? How would that truth change anything? His essence comes from whatever tree or animal is a chronic liar.

"He's not." Tiny cracks appear in the diamond shield from the force of Máthair's voice. They heal quickly. "Sionnach's father is not Finnbheara. The king loved me, and for a time, I bided with him in his lands. I was young, my head filled with visions of sapphire palaces and skies shining silver white, but I woke from the dream. I couldn't stay with him. I longed for a life rooted in the earth, and love that didn't shift with the changing winds."

The greenhouse. All the wondrous things growing under Máthair's touch were her tethers to a real life as dear to her as any magical kingdom. I search Sion's eyes, her dearest creation. I believe my grandmother loves me, but the feeling is tainted. It was born of her desperation to cultivate me into someone to save her real son.

These people—my grandmother and the man I began to let into my heart—by their own words admit I'm no more than a device. Finnbheara, the king of deception and mischief, fabricated me as a gift for the human woman he loved to allow the soul of her son to pass into eternity.

"Where does my future fit into this Faerie puzzle?" They're defining me as a non-entity, a token to be moved from space to space in a game between worlds above and below the earth. My life is a sham. I'm nothing more than a creature who belongs in a folktale—Eala *bán*, the white swan sent to chase away shadows and curses.

Sion's voice is laced with pain. "My ma accepted banishment here in exchange for Finnbheara giving her son a gift, a soulmate, *anamchara*, to aid my final chance to end the soulfall. You."

I rub both hands down my face. "Why is it your final chance?"

"I was a young man when my wound was killing me." His hand strays to the injury that lamed him. "I sent word to my folks knowing I'd never see them again. When Ma got my letter, she feared for my soul and pleaded to Finnbheara to save me. Even a king of *Tír na nÓg* has a limit to his powers." He lets out a long breath. "The bargain was struck to make me a Veil guide with two hundred tries to end the soulfall in my care so I could earn my place in the light. Ma thought it would be more than enough time for me to succeed." His eyes drift to Máthair. "When this time came for my one final go after much failure, my mother begged the king to aid me. For the love Finnbheara bore my mother, he allowed you to be by my side, giving me a true chance to succeed."

"You haven't tried to end the soulfall since I was born?"

He shakes his head. "I waited for you to be ready."

"If we succeed, then what?" My head swims with the crossover of reality and fantasy— reasons and subterfuge. The purpose of everything I've heard here benefits Sion, not me. I feel more alone than the day Máthair died. Their words confirm my purpose for coming to Ireland, hell, for even being born, was to become Sion's *anamchara*. "Do I blip out of existence once you save the soulfall and tootle down the great cosmic highway to your destiny?"

I scoot away from this manifestation of my grandmother. One truth rises above the rest as crystal clear as the diamond coverlet on the lake.

Betrayal.

Máthair never loved Ella or Eala or whoever I am for me. She nurtured me as a tool to help her son.

I glare at Sion. "Being a Veil guide is your perk from Finnbheara not mine."

Sion never valued me enough to share the real truth until I threatened to skip out. I'm trapped in a crumbling castle built upon a foundation of lie after lie after lie.

His cry and the *smack* of his palm against stone reverberate through the glade. "A perk!"

"Yes, a perk. You're not one of those poor people stuck in a soulfall, waiting for someone else to save them."

"Poor people? Have you not learned a thing? They're where they are for absent virtue, and I'm charged with fixing what they broke."

"Why did Máthair fear for your soul and strike a deal with Finnbheara in the first place?"

Sion's face shifts between anger and despair. "I've much to answer for."

I back away from the rock. My first impulse is to demand an explanation, but I shake my head to clear it. It doesn't matter. In what world, Faerie or real, does any of this motivate me to continue?

I put more distance between us. Is this a threat? Neither Máthair nor he stated it as such, but Faeries and the people who deal with them aren't known for being candid.

The fragrance of sweet clover imbues me with a sense of peace I absolutely do not trust to be genuine. Instead of joy at finding my grandmother, emptiness fills me, body and mind. The scant echoes of home and belonging rising in the glade are counterfeit.

"I will not be the disposable element in your cozy Loho family picture." The mushy reunion with Máthair I wrote in my head turns into a fractured whim. The grandmother I loved died in New York City. There was never anything to find here in Ireland but pain and treachery.

The stabbing in my chest is a truth I believe. My hundred thousand heartbeats are nearly spent. I've done my best to help Sion with the souls, but I need to do whatever is in my power to keep existing. The only way to achieve that is to run as far and as fast from this place and these people as possible.

I whirl to face my grandmother and the traitor on the rock. "I'm sorry for your curses and banishments, but I won't be part of your story anymore. Stay out of my life, both of you." I curl my hands into fists and press them to my lips. Knuckles dig into my jaw.

I am bone.

I am flesh.

I am real.

Sion holds out hands in supplication. "'Tis one final bridge I'm begging you to cross with me."

"Your lies destroyed that bridge in devastating purple and blue flames."

The overhanging rock hides Máthair, but the pain in Sion's expression transforms my heart into something as delicate as one of the sparkling, glass panes floating upon the lake. Through his green glass eyes, I see he is every bit as fragile. Gone is his brow-creasing frustration with me. In this final moment together, I know the cracks beginning in my battered heart end in his. The Veil sweeps around me, and I leave chimes and deceit behind.

In a handful of breaths, I'm leaning against the passenger door of the rental car inside the low stone wall surrounding Colleen's grandmother's house in Enniscorthy. Was it my own doing or Sion's that sent the car and me here? As I press a hand to my heart, waiting for equilibrium to kick in, a shadowy form blocks my path to the front door.

"Alone I see."

I gasp, prepared to bolt until I recognize Charlie in the faint glow of the porch light.

CHAPTER 22

THE COLLEAGUE

I read somewhere that you don't tremble when you're actively in shock. It's afterwards, when brutal awareness returns, the shakes set in. They wrack my body for the entire drive from Enniscorthy to our hotel in Dublin. Colleen is convinced my condition is related to my near tumble the morning after our Beltane bonfire. She insisted I let Jeremy lead the tour solo while I take a day to relax and recover. It wasn't a hard choice to escape into the oblivion of sleep.

Except there is no escape.

Sion inhabits every corner of my subconscious, damn him.

In my dreams, we travel together through the Veil. We trace the stars with outstretched fingers. We laugh. We make love.

Before I let myself drift off, I feared nightmares of melting Veil walls, foxes baring pointy teeth, and shadow villains, but only sweet memories of a ruined love visit me.

Am I conjuring these, or is Sion still manipulating my psyche the way he and Máthair have done my whole life with hidden meanings in folk tales, dream flashes, and shadow stories in the fire?

The knock on the hotel room door in late afternoon isn't loud but insistent. I channel my inner ten-year-old and pull the covers over my head in behavior unbecoming a college professor.

"Eala?"

My first instinct is to hunker down in my burrow of misery. The second is to escape out the window in case it's Sion, ignoring my edict to bugger off.

Leave me out of the rest of your crazy story.

My mind roves despite my efforts to hobble it as a discordant litany drones through my head.

Eala, you accept the soulfall and traveling through time, but easily abandon the souls because Sion and Máthair betrayed you?

I run out of usable oxygen and fling the covers off my head.

The answers you're looking for aren't always the ones you want. Tír na nÓg would be ashamed. Finnbheara will strike you down. There's nothing of the oak or the swan in you.

The more my mind or the persistent visitor hammers at me, the worse I feel. Instead of taking the hint, the knocking gets louder, but the voice is pitched too low to recognize. "Eala, are you awake?"

No accent, probably Charlie. After his midnight creeper performance last night, I'm not eager to hang with him alone in the land of the living even if it is at Colleen's behest.

If I ever was a part of the living.

"Stop it, Eala. You are alive."

"Pardon," says the muffled voice from the hall.

Charlie was none too happy about the dents in the car roof from Sion's tantrum at Leap Castle. Once I played the *we parted ways* card and told Charlie and Colleen that my *Irish fling*, their words, was staying at his uncle's instead of going to Dublin with us, nobody pressed me for details.

I call to the door. "How many euros do you need to pay for the damage, Charlie?" Lord knows I've got them. Why did Máthair bother to leave me a small fortune when she knew my days were numbered?

Here's a newsflash for Ma and *mac* Loho. I have no intention to put myself in the vicinity where I might go *poof* with the last of the soulfall. I'll never Veil travel again. I pray stepping away from Sion's insanity will reset my life—my human life. When I get back to New York, I'll carve a future in Kennard Park be it tenure-track or as a perpetual adjunct. The dreams I carefully orchestrate are the only ones happening from now on.

I pull the covers up to my chin as a shudder runs through me. What if I pissed off Finnbheara by quitting and he *poofs* me anyway? Dammit, I'm buying into my own paranoia. I am human. Nothing I heard in the Glade of Chimes matters. Forward motion is my sole option to prevent madness.

The Veil Sprites are so dim inside me, they're no more substantial than a stomach growling from hunger. Probably their way of being aloof. As far as I'm concerned, they can turn their sparky little backs on me and fly away. I will not return to their world, and without Veil juice, hopefully they'll fade completely. Even if they try to sting, I'm determined to leave the fantastic behind. I rub my feet between the sheets to warm my toes. Sion and the weird tree spirit of my grandmother have lost their Fae-bargaining minds, expecting me to continue after they pointed out Finnbheara stamped an expiration date across my forehead.

The voice gets louder. "It's Jeremy." He raps twice on the door. "Colleen asked me to check in on you while she's taking the Viking tour. Do you need a doctor?"

Shit. Colleen wasted no time in reviving the Eala/Olk initiative. It's my fault. I admitted Sion was a mistake, and she was right about Jeremy being the better choice. I intended to show that I appreciate her judgement by not encouraging a whiplash transfer of my affections to my colleague. I try for a casual tone. "She's a worrier. I'm doing much better. Thanks."

Maybe she's been right from the start. If only I could Veil travel back to the flight over here before Sion happened with Jeremy and his soothing voice. What a different trip it would have been by his side and not Sionnach Loho's.

"Glad to hear it. Are you up to joining me for dinner?"

An excuse doesn't rise to my lips. Maybe my subconscious is ready to trade life-threatening danger for a person who represents a measure of safety and the ability to erase my fear with gorgeous poetry. Another dose of his brand of calm is welcome about now.

"Sure. Give me an hour?"

He gives another double rap of acknowledgment. "Terrific."

When I emerge somewhat relaxed from a hot shower, Colleen lounges on my bed in our shared room. She leans back on her elbows, a knitted scarf with Norse runes draped around her neck. "Someone yummy is waiting for you in the lobby."

"He's a colleague, not a blind date." I remind myself she's looking out for my heart. I sit next to her and bounce the bed a little to lighten the mood. "We're sharing a meal. It doesn't have to mean anything, okay?"

She juts her head forward. "But it could mean something. Newsflash—no girlfriend. I pried." Colleen twists my shoulders and directs her energy to French braid my hair. She trills on. "Over a pint of Guinness tonight, he'll realize you're the woman of his dreams."

I keep my protests at bay. Colleen believes this is what I want. She's supporting me.

Sadness bubbles inside. I've been living in a dream with Sion, our connection, making love on the Leviathan, that final look we shared in the Glade of Chimes. I need to be practical and actually transfer my interest to calm and stable Jeremy. I've known Sion a handful of days, in a handful more, I can get over him. I will get over him.

Except, Sion wasn't some normal random man I hooked up with. He's—

Colleen tugs a little too hard in her attempt to make my hair obey. "Remember the poem we had to memorize back in high school? The Yeats one about finding our dream men."

I remember it all too well.

"But I being poor, have only my dreams;
I have spread my dreams under your feet;
Tread softly because you tread on my dreams.

Sion did not tread softly on my misplaced dreams of him, of a loving reunion with Máthair. He pulverized them beneath period boots from his Alfie tree's canvas bag. If someone cares, they have your back. It's clear to me now, my so-called partner shoved me into the path of flames and a shadow assassin because he knew I was expendable.

I should have known better than to buy into the illusion of a cosmically fated romance. Every time I've taken a risk with a guy, it ends in a sucker punch. With my love-struck stupidity for Sion, I've been acting more like Colleen than Colleen.

"La, you've had your Irish one-off. Fun, but not your usual sensible self. Think of tonight as a fresh start with potential for long-term. I feel it in my gut that Jeremy could be your guy."

"Yes, you've made that clear." I clench my jaw. She'd never reduce Sion to a one-off if she was aware of the good he was trying to do in this world. Ugh, why am I defending him? Is it *do-gooding* when it serves a personal agenda?

"Do you disagree?" she asks, one eyebrow raised. "If you do, I'm on your side."

My lungs deflate. "No. I can't argue he has potential." Maybe our spark hasn't happened yet.

Colleen grabs my hand and clamps it on her thigh, oblivious to my rising tension. "Check this new layer of chunkage. My boyfriend's been stuffing me with cottage pie, Guinness stew, mounds of potatoes, and life-changing sticky toffee pudding ice cream sundaes."

Her frame is as bony and lithe as ever. "You're imagining it."

She giggles. "At least it's happy fat. Did you hear me say boyfriend?"

"Quick promotion."

She coos, and I poke a fingernail into the mound of flesh at the base of my thumb to remind myself what's real. My best friend and I discussing happy fat and boyfriends is real. Jeremy Olk is real.

Colleen finishes my French braids and pulls me into a side hug. "Promise you'll keep an open mind."

My mind spent the last few days cracked open wide enough to drive a bus through. Snapping it shut feels like the safer option. "For you."

She lays a hand on my cheek. "For you."

I nod.

My fellow academician lounges on a comfy armchair in the lobby. Comfy, that's a good word to describe him. I could use some comfy and real. Spending time with a person who will answer questions without a dozen layers of sneaky is surprisingly appealing.

Jeremy stands to greet us. He moves so formally; I expect him to bow. Instead, he offers me his arm. When I take it, I swear Colleen exhales in relief.

The tiny local restaurant he chooses in Dollymount near Dublin Bay definitely fits the comfy scenario. Jeremy raises a spoonful of lamb stew. "Ah, a taste of home."

"Home? As in you're from Ireland?" I assumed he was Boston Irish.

He dabs sauce from the collar of his red turtleneck. "Yes. Not far from here, Loilgheach Mór." His Irish pronunciation is flawless.

"Your accent kicked into high gear there."

He laughs and repeats the name in an English-friendly version. "Lullymore. It's a bitty island, surrounded by a bog. Very timeless feel to the place."

The last thing I need is another dose of timeless. My feet are staying rooted in a world with jeans, sneakers, and graduate students.

"You don't need to Americanize it for me." I study the pattern on the bowl. "I enjoy Irish with authentic flair. Are you fluent?" A stab of longing for the lilt in both Máthair and Sion's accents hits me. It's now clear why Sionnach's voice reminded me of my grandmother's. In addition to genetics, he grew up hearing the same songs, stories, and scoldings I did. From the same person. I take a breath to prevent the thought from digging in too deep.

"My parents would disown me if I wasn't." He grabs the edge of the table with both hands. "How is your grasp of Irish?"

I hold back a snort. Since my association with Sion, my sketchy Irish has become more like a first language than second. Probably a nugget Finnbheara threw in my swan/oak mix to benefit his lover's son.

"I hold my own." Smiling, I share my go-to tongue twister in Irish. When I finish, I raise a finger and translate so he knows I've got the goods. "There is a boil on the back of the bishop's knee. But the bishop doesn't know there is a boil on the back of his knee."

Jeremy claps. "Nicely done."

I dip my head in acknowledgement. He launches into an anecdote about the evolution of Irish slang as his name rolls around in my head. Jeremy—Dr. Olk. I can't deny his intense academic vibe is alluring.

His next question returns me to the conversation. "Where did you pick up the mockery of the good bishop's plight?"

"It was one of my grandmother's favorites." Thoughts of Máthair's truth sour my rising good mood.

"Wish I'd known that jewel in seminary. It would have raised a few eyebrows."

"Seminary? You were going to be a priest?" The shadow of Sion's Father Colm nudges its way into my brain.

"For a minute and a half. My mother's dream. Grad school in Boston was mine." He lays a hand on his chest. "Academia always tugged hardest at my heart." His eyes fix on the window where a steady stream of people pass in front of the restaurant on their way home from work. "As you're aware, Ireland hasn't always been the most hospitable place for priests."

"There's an understatement."

His eyes dart to me, narrowing slightly and then relaxing. "Of course, Irish history bubbles in your veins." He mimes a check mark in the air. "I'm sure the subject arose in your doctoral research."

"I focused more on sacred sites and connections to druid and Celtic myths, not so much their Christian history." A pit opens in my stomach. Was my interest in that particular topic a niggle from Finnbheara for his entertainment?

Jeremy leans in. "I've always been intrigued by the rocky path of Christianity in Ireland, especially Catholicism. It's fascinating." He widens his eyes. "And terrifying."

I fix a look of interest on my face, preparing to agree with any suggestion from him. Getting closer to him may unearth hints about my future at Kennard Park University.

"In fact, my own dissertation back in the day was on the atrocities Cornwallis visited on the Irish."

A shudder runs through me. "That's dark."

He nods enthusiastically. "Oh, it is. Take pitch-capping for example." Jeremy crosses his arms and leans them on the edge of the table, suspending his face over the empty bowl. "Cornwallis found great pleasure in using the practice on priests. A cap was filled with hot, melting pitch—" The waiter stops by to light the candle between us. The flame makes Jeremy's teeth glow yellow. "Then it was lowered onto the head."

He mimes the action, closing his long fingers over the top of my head. When I startle, he pulls his hand away.

Gravelly undertones color his voice. "There was no surviving such an abomination of course, but the agony—" He reaches under his glasses to press a finger to the corner of his eye as if to blot away a tear. "Those few minutes of life ebbing away. Horrible." His warm brown/black eyes lock on mine. "To complete the desecration of a human life, they'd rip the cap off, exposing the brain and bringing on instant death."

If he thinks this story charms my scholarly interest in any way, he's mistaken. I squirm and peer into the dark corner of the restaurant, half-expecting to see Father Colm's shadow rise along the wall.

Jeremy pats my hand. "My mother would be appalled at my choice of meal talk. Forgive me." He folds his napkin and places it next to his stew bowl.

"Will you visit your mother in Loilgheach Mór?"

He casts his eyes downward. "No. She's been gone a long time."

The silence stretches while I try to figure out the right thing to say. His pensive pause at the mention of someone lost brings up a memory of the Máthair I will choose to remember, my grandmother, not Sion's deal-making ma.

Jeremy taps the table with both hands. "Would you care to explore a bit?"

After the pitch-capping story, I hesitate. I have plenty of my own ghost stories to fill any quota.

"We can stroll over to Bull Island."

This time the silence is my doing. I'm torn between kissing up to the guy who benefits my future on several fronts or returning to the solitude of my hotel room and attempting to define my reality. Memories, feelings, and my otherworldly activities of the past few days slosh through my mind. They need to be sorted like a deck of cards into proper suits so I can move forward. One certainty is that I will not be wandering through the Veil with Sion Loho in the oncoming Celtic day.

"Or if you're tired—"

"No." I cut him off. "We're only here a couple more days. I want to see as much as I can." Bailing on him right after dinner has the earmarks of a kiss off, not a kiss up to. I need to keep Jeremy Olk in my plus column.

I'm not used to the late onset of dusk. At home, it would be full night by now, but Ireland is farther north than New York. Jeremy switches into docent mode as we cross the wooden bridge onto the jetty of Bull Island. What doesn't this walking Wikipedia know?

I breathe in salty air and long to sit alone atop the steep rocky wall that sweeps down from the path to the bay, close my eyes, and imagine my blood communing with the waters of the Irish Sea. I pull the brandied melon scarf from my pocket. Its color reminds me of the brightness of Sion's hair in the Veil, and I stuff it away. It's taking a maddening amount of energy to act normal.

Jeremy regales me with tidbits from the tour I missed at Dublin Castle. I'm nodding and commenting at all the appropriate places, but my mind keeps flipping to where I don't want it to go—Sion and the soulfall. There are two nights left between now and Beltane. Will he be able to save the last two souls in time? Alone?

It's no longer my concern. Whatever might have started between us is not worth sacrificing the non-fantastical academic future I've invested in for so many years.

I kick a rock that careens a fair distance before flying over the edge of the walkway to land with a splat on the low tidal mush stretching across the Dublin side of the bay. When I add another "Hmm" to the one-sided conversation, Jeremy laughs.

"And I'm probably rambling on about things you already know, Professor Duir." His hand brushes the small of my back as he moves closer.

At the end of the jetty, we stand above a huge expanse of sand on the north side. It looks to be a quarter mile or more before gentle waves slide over the beach. I twist away and point off into the distance. "Is that a seal?"

He squints along the shore and then breaks into a smile. "A seal or selkie?"

I have no desire to dip into folktales and legends. "Nope, just a dog." I steer him back to the topic of Dublin Castle. "You were talking about wild, unsanctioned parties at the castle?"

He chuckles. "Wild and wilder up the scale to abject debauchery. Ah, the stories and shenanigans, including the theft of the Irish Crown Jewels."

I stop dead in my tracks. "The Irish Crown Jewels?"

"The scandal extraordinaire. Never solved."

Gears whir in my brain. I'm consumed with the need to hear more. "If I'm not mistaken, Arthur Vicars was accused of stealing them, right?"

He looks at me sharply.

I execute a casual hair toss. "They mentioned the jewels at the National Gallery tour but didn't finish the story."

"Mr. Vicars was assumed to be the culprit. Speculation abounds that he was shot down on the street the night of the theft to mask a worse scandal. There were saucy accusations such as the brother of a great explorer and even one of Britain's royal family being tied up in that salacious package of theft and depravity." He chuckles. "Imagine the gossip."

Shot on the street?

History *is* changed.

My heart races as the vision of Arthur Vicars's silhouette in the soulfall tower drives every other thought from my head. He didn't steal the jewels. I know he didn't, or he wouldn't be in the soulfall for losing his diligence after a lifelong effort to prove himself innocent. A lifetime cut short by the fiend in the Veil.

Jeremy returns his hand to my back. "I'm sure many a castle tower room or palace apartment has stories to tell."

Does Sion know about the explorer's brother and the royal family connection? When he goes back to repair time, following Vicars himself could be the worst of all possible false leads.

My mind strays to the soulfall, Little Harriet, Alaina Kennedy, Strongbow's squire, and the Earl of Rosse whose telescope showed me a moon lovelier than ever I imagined it to be. Those four souls are stardust and fireflies, basking in their chosen eternities.

"Shall we perch on the steps to enjoy the sunset?" Well-worn concrete steps lead down to the Dublin side of the bay. The rocks bordering them are littered with stranded seaweed left behind by the tide. At the base of the stairs, a couple enjoys end of day kisses.

A sense of Sion's soft mouth against mine ignites a longing that blows through my soul as fierce as wind off the bay. These moments need to back off. He and Máthair are my past.

Jeremy waits for me to settle before joining me in clear violation of my personal space. I want to welcome him in—to feel the thrill of possibility. Warmth. Want. Anything. Damn it. It's as if Sionnach used up my reserve of attraction, and I'm left dry and devoid of emotion. Bracing myself away from Jeremy, I create a small distance between us.

"To revisit the topic of your wonderful book, I must say I particularly enjoyed the parallels you drew between Celtic sacred sites and praised local, not just academically accepted folklore." He pushes round glasses into place.

"I had an edge being raised by—" I almost say my Irish grandmother but tamp down the urge to speak of Máthair. "With lots of stories." Since he brought it up earlier, I figure it's okay to pry a bit. "I wish Kennard Park would stop dragging their feet on the open permanent position."

His arm shifts so it rests on the step behind me. If I lean back, we'll be snuggling. "They'd be a fool not to take you, and they know it." A smile stretches across his face. "I believe a certain email will be coming your way soon, but you didn't hear it from me."

A thousand questions snap to mind, but I hold back. I don't want to put him in an awkward position. What I really want to do is leap up, shake his hand, bolt, and go home until Beltane has passed. Maybe then my psyche and emotions have a shot at recovering. Instead, I force a smile. "Grand."

"Have you considered cataloging the folk and Faerie tales you've dug up? Track their origins, hunt for regional connections, other versions. There's a second book in the making." He hums a few notes of an unfamiliar tune. "Don't leave out Irish sketches, extravagant plots flung outside the bounds of reason." He cocks his head to the side. "Ah, what a jolly world to immerse oneself in."

My life is an Irish sketch. I tap my temple. "You must know plenty of stories too."

His bottom lip curves into a neat little bow. "A fair amount, or should I say, a Faerie amount."

Faerie.

Before my brain has a chance to protest, my mouth blurts one of the questions bobbing in my head. "What's your take on Finnbheara?"

Jeremy scoffs, gaze pinned on the distance. "King of the Connacht Fae, or rather, the king of whim servicing." Fingers of slate gray clouds stretch over the bay, blocking their fluffier white cousins. "Dictator is a more fitting title for him. According to the stories, the fellow did whatever he liked whenever he liked."

What would Jeremy say if he knew he was sitting next to a product of the king's whim? Does Finnbheara keep tabs on me? My eyes drift to the clouds as a blood red shine from the setting sun overtakes one of the gray streaks. Is he watching now? Is Sion? I surreptitiously check the length of the jetty behind us.

My future colleague laughs. "Myths and legends do prey on the gullible." He claps a hand to his thigh. "Did you catch the news today? There was quite a brouhaha at a local castle not far west from here last night. Leap Castle, I believe."

I shrug my shoulders, playing dumb while I fight to keep my stew down.

"A flock of Catholic priests claim to have exorcised a druid spirit that was rumored to inhabit the castle for centuries."

I bite my tongue to keep from blurting Pwyll's name.

"The report said several coalitions of ghost hunters threatened legal action." He grunts. "Grandstanding for publicity." He curves his neck so he's looking directly into my face. "Do you believe in ghosts, Eala Duir?"

My nervous laugh is as fake as they come. The sky dims. I counted on hanging out with Jeremy to ground me after time-hopping and soul-saving, but our conversation of pitch-capping, Finnbheara, and Pwyll dispels my hope.

He lays a hand over mine. "Someone with your penchant, Eala, for

Celtic mysteries must have an open mind when it comes to things unseen."

Ghosts and Celtic mysteries are a smidge of what St. Augustine meant by *faith to believe what we do not see.*

"By the way, I'm happy to share Mr. Loho is no longer an issue."

My heart twists at the sound of his name. "Oh?"

"Colleen confided that he makes you uncomfortable, so I made arrangements for him to switch as the local expert for a different student tour."

Mention of Sion wrecks any potential for relaxing into this sunset moment with Jeremy. I need to get back to the hotel. The pain of Sion and Máthair's shredding of my life blocks out any effort to enjoy myself.

"I'm confident Sionnach's absence will make tomorrow's trip to Luttrellstown Castle more enjoyable for you."

I startle at Jeremy's use of Sion's real name, but then give myself a virtual face slap. I'm sure it was listed on Colleen's meticulous tour itinerary. As I watch the bay, fading light hits the water in lines of sugar white. I catch Jeremy gazing at me in an intense, non-blinking way.

"You'll fit in perfectly tomorrow at the home of a beautiful Guinness girl." His hand makes its way to a strand of hair blown loose from my braid.

I jump to my feet as our sunset chat officially leaves what's left of my comfort zone. What's wrong with me? Jeremy has been sweet and intelligent, the perfect combination. I want to connect with him, but there's a Sion-shaped wedge in the way. Maybe once we're away from here and back at Kennard Park, I'll be able to muster interest. "We'd better catch the bus. I promised Colleen I'd meet Charlie and her at the hotel before dark." I'm already hopping up the steps to the jetty.

Jeremy's long legs make it easy for him to join me. "Of course. When we return home, will you take me to your favorite restaurant in Kennard Park?"

Good, I didn't scare him off. Future. I must think of the future. There is a chance this man and our little college town can fill the hollow space my time with Sion created.

I sneak a sidelong glance at Jeremy. He's doing weird movements with his hands, grasping them and twisting. His tuneless hum fills the air, making me uneasy.

"Absolutely." I move far enough away so there's no possibility of touching. Again, my traitorous thoughts fade to Sion.

Sionnach.

My fox no longer.

An ache rises inside me. Was his tenderness under the moon a lie? I want it to be true. I'd like to preserve some non-tainted memory of our short journey together, even if it is finished.

My heart stutters and then resumes with a beat strong enough to bruise my chest. The beginning of the Celtic day strikes. Veil Sprites assert themselves and my soul dances with them, burning away my denial of the journey I abandoned and reminding me who I am.

Despite his frightening display when we lost Pwyll and his inability to be completely open, damn me, I so wanted to love Sionnach Loho. Yes, his motives were selfish, but his good heart and devotion to the grace of others was real. His lies batter my spirit, but the soul is a free thing apart from the rational mind. My soul found a home when his light called, but it failed me.

None of that matters. I'll never see Sion again. If Finnbheara plans for my future to drip away like the last raindrops caught on a leaf after a storm, at least I'll take the bittersweet memory of that brief moment in time where I did love a Veil guide.

Anamchara.

Jeremy is trying so hard to connect with me. I feel like a jerk for holding back.

Night shoos the last of dusk's glow. Is Sion travelling yet? I resent the guilt trickling down my throat, not for Sion, but the souls. Do I dare attempt to travel alone to Dublin Castle and try to catch the thief in the act of stealing the jewels? Arthur Vicars deserves to rise from the soulfall, not crash onto merciless river rocks. What about the last soul in the soulfall? I don't even know their story. Is it an easy fix or as convoluted as Strongbow's squire? Frost creeps up one vertebra after another until my entire core is glacial. To learn the last soul's missing virtue, I'd have to climb the soulfall tower.

A car crossing the wooden bridge we walk along rumbles like low laughter. I'm kidding myself. Without enough courage or my own *fánaí* tree with a handy bag of period clothing, it's impossible to travel. I don't even understand how I navigated the Veil back to Enniscorthy.

If I did.

Sion's always been the one to get us where we needed to go. His guilt probably drove him to send me to Colleen's grandmother's after the revelations in the Glade of Chimes.

I stare out the window on the short bus ride into Dublin, saying as little as possible. Jeremy, ever the narrator, explains Bull Island got its name because the Celts believed the noise of the wind blowing across its sands reminded them of a bull panting.

We hop off the bus near the quays on the River Liffey in sight of the Ha'penny Bridge. Lost in my messy head, I cut a path through the crowd on the sidewalk, leaving Jeremy behind.

"Eala?"

I let him catch up and pretend to be distracted by buskers livening the night with their Irish trad music. "Sorry, I'm just taking everything in."

"Please do." He meets my gaze with gentle kindness. This man is the essence of patience.

For half a second, I think about asking him if he's ever heard of the Glade of Chimes. The air around me shimmers with spectral light as if nature itself yearns to provide the answer.

Stop, Eala. There is only one safe path for you.

Flickers fall across the bronze sculpture of a tree rising from the concrete in front of a pub. A plaque near its base reads:

The yew grows to a very great age and is connected with the processes of death and continuing life. Yew - Loho

As deeply as I wish it were a bad dream incapable of leaving the scars I now bear, my time with Sion was as real as the street musicians in front of us.

Máthair taught me to view life as a series of lessons. What I learned on the shores of the glassy lake in the Glade of Chimes pressed the disjointed pieces of my life into a picture I'd never choose, but it's the one I've been given. Failed DNA tests, unknown parents, and the ability to travel through fucking time.

I am not what I seem to Colleen or Jeremy. My mind clears. It doesn't matter. I'm determined to create a future that conforms to the boundaries of reality. My days of being powerless, swept out to sea on a wave of someone else's obligations, are over.

I rest my palm against the trunk of the bronze yew, silently wishing my ex-partner success and ultimate peace. Sionnach Loho is on his own.

Reaching between us, I take Jeremy's hand.

CHAPTER 23
THE ANGEL

The twin turrets of Luttrellstown Castle are clad in blankets of velvet ivy. I wouldn't turn down a nice ivy wrap given the icy bite to the air. Between the towers, tracery as white and delicate as the finest lace covers Gothic-style windows. I fully expect Cinderella's glass coach to fly past me. The cornflower of today's Beltane Eve sky harmonizes with lilac spurs peeking out from under the grape Popsicle petals of violets along the walkway.

This cool color scheme from the stroke of an artist's paintbrush is perfect for the former digs of Aileen Plunkett, daughter to Arthur Guinness of the beer brewing dynasty. She's one of the golden Guinness girls Jeremy likened me to last night. Remembering the compliment sends a pleasant sensation through me. It's an encouraging sign I may yet be able to take charge of my future.

We enter a ballroom with butter yellow walls, white lacquered baseboards, and cornices. Maybe a nice cup of tea will mellow my still-agitated mind. Several long tables with wood polished to reflect the light are set meeting style to accommodate our group. White-gloved attendants standby, waiting for us uncultured Americans to settle onto the crimson leather seat cushions of ladder-back chairs.

"Do you want to sit closer to the fire?" asks Charlie. With sunlight blazing behind him through beveled glass windows, he turns to shadow. His dark arm extends slowly, reaching a finger toward me, and I jerk away. His shape and the gesture are disturbingly familiar.

"I'm fine here," I say, nodding across the table to the white marble fireplace.

Charlie reaches around Colleen and taps a goose bump just above my wrist. There's ice in his touch. "Your skin doesn't agree."

Unsettling thoughts writhe through my head as Charlie's silhouette grows and shrinks. Could Charlie not be what he seems? I'm not. Sion isn't. What's one more sham player in this Faerie game? The line between paranoia and caution bleeds into a sloppy blur.

Charlie whispers to Colleen, and she beams at him. I pull a sleeve down over my pebbled skin, and vow to control the crazy. Am I doomed to envision shadow villains around every corner for the rest of the trip? Charlie defended Sion that day in the pub. Why do that if he's the creep chasing Sion through the Veil?

Then again, if Charlie is the shadow priest, he'd want Sion close to track his movements through the Veil. Two new couples hanging together is the perfect ruse to keep tabs on your target. It was Charlie who found us coming out of the woods after my first Veil travel. Had he been waiting for us? He was the one lurking in the shadows in Enniscorthy when I returned.

Colleen pats my shoulder. "If you need to go back to the hotel, we'll go with you."

I lay my hand over hers. "I'm fine."

"You were crying in your sleep." A low sound rumbles in her throat. "When you weren't yelling. That's not fine. You should have stayed in bed."

Charlie ducks behind her to get closer to me, adding his two cents. "I'm happy to take you so Colleen can check out the rest of the fancy castle."

The thought of being alone with Charlie freezes my blood. "I don't want to miss more than I already have." I nearly say miss another Celtic day but catch myself.

Colleen shook me awake sometime after midnight. She'd slipped back into our room after her romantic rendezvous with Charlie. In my dream, Sion and I laid together in the grass at the base of the soulfall tower. The cries of the souls had vanished. He kissed me over and over to say goodbye because it was time to enter his banishment with Máthair in the Glade of Chimes. We peeled our clothes away until we stood naked under the full Veil moon. His hands brushed every sensitive place on my body, igniting a glimmering drop wherever they touched. The sweet quiver of Veil Sprites lingered within each spot until their collective light set my skin aglow. Sion's lips followed the path over my breasts then lower to where I'd taught him to pleasure me. Stroke after stroke of his tongue was relentless bliss. With each pass, I hummed notes of want. I held tight to his shoulders as his hot mouth brought me to climax.

He begged to learn more about making love. I lay back on the soft damp grass, bending my knees to teach him where his circling fingers could make me scream. After my release, I eased him down to draw the tip of my tongue along his ready cock until he begged to finish inside me. Just before I gave in to his wishes, I took him deep into my mouth, slowly sliding up to savor the salty pearl of his eagerness. We relished each other's bodies...until the cries of the soulfall tore us apart.

I woke to sweat dampened sheets, the smell of wet stone and river still in my nose as Colleen rescued me from the nightmare. Once she was asleep, I tried to purge my guilt from leaving Sion behind. I rationalized there's still one Celtic day left before Beltane. He has a chance to free the last two souls on his own. Maybe it's only the final soul that needs him. Vicars might already be free.

Then I remembered the priest.

Visions of pitch-capping, oily black shadows splayed across the stones of Leap Castle, and Pwyll being reduced to a pile of coffin splinters ruined any further chance of sleep.

I settle into my seat to end any further discussion of Charlie taking me anywhere, and field a few questions from grad students. One of the attendants reaches between us to fill China teacups. The elegance of his movement reminds me of ballets Máthair took me to see at Lincoln Center.

"This is fancy," says Colleen, earning a frown from our server. She whispers to Charlie. "I don't think he appreciates our group of uncultured Americans."

"Aye, we're naught but a passel of bowsey fools." Charlie's latest stab at an Irish accent and vernacular shows no improvement. Colleen shushes him and jerks her chin at Jeremy who delivers a *manners please* glare and takes his seat at the head of the table.

Even though I've pledged to see where things might lead with Jeremy, it's a relief to sit far enough away to avoid any more edgy tales of historic torture for today. Tiered trays overflowing with finger sandwiches of salmon and cucumber are set before us. Colleen goes straight for a hibiscus macaroon and feeds it to Charlie.

Before diving into today's lecture, Jeremy fusses with the red plaid scarf around his neck, then shoots me a smile that should make my toes tingle. I feel nothing. What the hell is wrong with me? Why can't I warm more to him?

I pound my thigh with a fist. I've got to give my conflicting thoughts some grace. Trauma recovery doesn't happen in one night. I appreciate he didn't try to kiss me on our date. I will not trade one whirlwind romance for another. Jeremy and I have time.

At least, I hope I have time.

Jeremy stands behind his chair, resting his hands on the padded back. "Aileen Plunkett was famed for glamour and her fantastic parties. When the twist was all the rage in the 1960s, she brought Chubby Checker here to Ireland to teach her crowd the dance."

Charlie breaks into an upper body version of the twist. He'd better leave that move out when defending his dissertation at Cambridge. I'm definitely losing it to think this gangly goofball is an evil priest chasing Sion through time.

Or am I?

I can't shake the image of shadow Charlie reaching to touch me.

Jeremy clears his throat and continues. "After Aileen's day, Luttrellstown Castle continued to be a significant map dot on the social scene with the wedding of a world-renowned soccer player and his even more famous rockstar wife in the old gate lodge." He removes his glasses, cleaning lenses while he continues. "My favorite bit of castle lore is that a very young girl named Aileen Guinness sat on the Wishing Seat here on the grounds and hoped one day this magnificent place would be hers."

His glance strays to me, and his mouth quirks into a smile. I turn away before anyone notices, locking my sight on the carving of a beatific female face just below the mantle of the fireplace. She's surrounded by sculpted rays of what must be heavenly light. I stare into the curved white eyes of a goddess or angel while a voice shrieks inside my head.

"You've abandoned them."

Are the words hers or mine?

Suddenly, the room blazes as the glass walls of the Veil overlay plaster. The angel's face turns to shadow beneath the sheen of prismatic streaks. Around me, sounds of student chatter and teacups continue, oblivious to the unseen realm hailing me.

Has the time come for Finnbheara to tear me from this world?

I grip the edge of the table as the angel's eyes begin to glow with blossoms of flame. Beneath her in the hearth fire, a miniature replica of the soulfall tower rises from burning wood: black, charred, desolate.

What am I supposed to see? Did Sion succeed last night or not? Will candlelight rise again in the window as those without restored virtue fall and fall and fall for the rest of eternity? Tears well in my eyes at the thought of Sion playing soulsongs for others and never one for himself in the Glade of Chimes.

I still, letting the dream flash play itself out. Is Sion sending this to me? Or is it the work of Finnbheara intervening to draw me back in to help his erstwhile lover, Máthair, and her son?

The soulfall tower's window fills with golden light. A silhouette steps into its frame and reaches arms to the sky. I recognize it.

Arthur Vicars.

"Believe what you will," it cries and steps into midair. No sparks ascend to the clouds.

The dream flash sends its grim message. Sion has not broken the soulfall. Now that history is jacked-up, it'll be even more difficult to connect Vicars with the right artifact.

The angel turns her fiery glare on me. A banshee, herald of death, screams in my head.

"Eala Duir, within madness always lies something real."

"Eala," says Charlie, his touch ripping me from the dream flash. He stands behind me with both hands on my shoulders, a dark visage against tall glass windows.

I do know this shape. It rose against Leap Castle's walls and within purple-blue flames. I pull away from him.

"La, you're panting?" Colleen rubs my back.

I must find Sion. Dammit, he is my reality inside madness. I've not only left him alone to face the shadow in the Veil that might be Charlie, but the dream flash proves Arthur Vicars's virtue is not restored.

Dread crawls up my spine like a long-legged spider. If I can't find Sion, I'll have no choice but to figure out Veil travel on my own. My eyes dart to the angel. She's as still as death now that her message has been delivered.

This otherworldly herald wailed a truth I must accept.

A thousand cracks run through my shell of denial until the pieces crumble at my feet. I was created to save Arthur Vicars and all the others. If I leave the souls behind, my spirit will wither and die with or without intervention from Finnbheara.

I must spend whatever time I have left to end the soulfall—with Sion.

Pushing my chair back, I rub my nose and stand. "Tissues." I quickly put distance between Charlie and me. There's bafflement on his face I want so badly to believe is genuine, but the cost of trusting him may be paid by Sion and the last two souls in the soulfall. "Restroom. Be right back."

Colleen looks from Charlie to me. "We're going to try to track down the Wishing Seat after tea. Interested?"

I want to drag her as far away from Charlie as I can, but what if I'm wrong? Standing there with his stilt legs and spiky hair, he looks as non-threatening as a pigeon. Sion will know how to keep Colleen safe if need be, another reason I must find him and fast. I say the thing guaranteed to make Colleen back off. "I promised to hang with Jeremy for the rest of the tour. You guys go ahead."

The Wishing Seat.

It may be folklore, but my years of study prove that deep within stories and tales are unseen truths a whole lot less far-fetched to me than they used to be. It's a place to start. Once upon a time, I'd have asked the Wishing Seat for life in a small college town with a Jeremy-type. That future disappears to join the billions of stars I'll never touch.

The soulfall is the light calling me.

Veil Sprites sizzle inside, awakening in a chain of tiny explosions from heart to fingertips. Glade of Chimes Máthair claims my swan essence has compassion for human souls. Compassion—one of the seven virtues blazing in my heart.

For Sion. For the souls.

Teacht orm.

Find me.

That compassion drives me to go after Sion and tell him what Jeremy said on the topic of the distorted history of Arthur Vicars. And to warn him about Charlie.

I scurry down the row of seats toward Jeremy. Instead of avoiding danger, I'm barreling head-on into it. Has my swan self-confidence finally kicked in, or have I caught Sion's impulsivity? My priority is to jump into the Veil and search for my partner. If only I could ask Jeremy for help, but he's the reason Sion isn't with us.

A sheen of tears softens my vision.

I'm the reason Sionnach Loho isn't here.

Jeremy sees my approach and breaks into a smile that fades when I close my fingers around the beige corduroy sleeve of his jacket. "Please keep Colleen from going off alone with Charlie. I'll explain—" I almost say later but switch. "In a few minutes." I need him to think I plan to come back. That should buy me a smidge of time until he comes after me. Enough to get away.

I dash from the ballroom before he has a chance to stall me. Forcing myself to walk, I take the quickest route outside. Once there, I pull the map of the castle from the pocket of my jeans to get my bearing and suss out the best place to catch the Veil. A patch of green designates an area of forest glen.

"Okay, Eala. There's your target."

If I jog, I'll reach the old gate lodge in no time. Surely, there are enough trees there to hide me while I summon the Veil. A dot on the map inside the glen marks *The Wishing Seat*. If Aileen Guinness Plunket could grab herself a castle by sitting there, I should be able to find a two-hundred-year-old *fánaí*.

Once I cross a small stone bridge, I'm at the edge of the forest glen. Thin drooping branches hide me from the castle. I'm ready to call the Veil.

To calm myself, I hum an old lullaby Máthair used to sing to me. While my hands reach to the sky, my mind reaches inward for the Veil Sprites, but they've gone quiet. I'd give anything to be able to understand what their reactions or stillness portend. For now, I visualize the spectral film of the passageway with its array of colors and close my eyes.

"Come to me."

The rush of the nearby stream fills my ears, and I imagine becoming a beam of light ready to drift through the seam between worlds.

Nothing happens.

My heart quickens not in the way of spent heartbeats but of panic. I fan my fingers in the air around me, searching for the filmy substance of my Veil, or the glass walls of Sionnach's Veil. Suddenly, I understand why his is glass. It's his brittle future, easily shattered. My passageway is pliable, eager to serve me. I'm ready for whichever answers my call. I'm prepared to even brave an undulating wall scorched with holes.

The Veil does not come.

Am I too close to the walking trail or the castle for it to show itself? Tearing across the jade carpet of lawn under a collection of mismatched trees, I search for a white poplar with green triangles climbing the trunk.

"Where are you, Alfie?"

Sion's *fánaí* tree isn't here. Lawn gives way to shrubs, and I lose the path completely.

Above me, sunlight leaks through a canopy of green patchwork. I try again to summon the Veil, but it's abandoned me. I call, "Let me in." No result. I collapse onto a patch of dirt dusted with leaves.

Why didn't I ask Sion more about the specifics of travelling? I don't even know if travel is possible this long before a Celtic day begins. I'm probably stuck until nightfall.

I bury my face in my hands and cry like the world is ending. It is. My world is disappearing with the tears falling between my fingers. The choice before me is to hide here in the woods or go back to the group and pray I can slip out alone when the Celtic day dawns.

I clutch Máthair's charm around my neck. "If you loved me at all, give me the strength not to give up." I try to stir the concoction of emotions inside me into a smooth mixture, but they refuse to blend.

Off to my left, I catch the *clip clop* of horses. Checking the map, I guess at my location and slink in the direction of the sound. The old gate lodge shouldn't be far off. I'll hide in the structure until sunset. If I find the Wishing Seat on my way, all the better.

I manage to wind through the underbrush to the path. Pausing to listen, I don't hear voices nearby. I make my way to a great stone arch rising above the road. The old gate lodge stands sentinel next to the chipped and worn stacked stones of a small tower. I feel as if I've stepped into the past without the Veil. Quiet and the absence of any part of the modern world settles around me. I navigate scrub and rocks to an arched doorway. It's a tricky step up, but I slink into the shadows of the gate lodge and freeze.

I'm not alone.

CHAPTER 24
THE WISHING SEAT

I n the corner, a rectangular niche is cut into the wall. A pair of slate slabs roughly a foot square form a rudimentary seat upon which sits the form of a man bent forward, elbows balanced on his knees, head resting on fists. He could be a sculpture, except for the stream of whispers flowing from his lips.

I keep still, hoping my entrance was quiet enough not to disturb what must be a prayer or a wish.

Is this the Wishing Seat?

If it is, I'll come back when it's empty to plead my case. Carefully lifting one foot at a time, I work my way backward. The man deserves the privacy he sought in this shrine of moss and rock. My fingers find the side of the arch. Two more steps, and it'll be as if I never breached his solitude.

The man rises, turning to face the seat so his back is to me. I pivot, stretching my leg to judge the long step down to the ground. His voice rises above a whisper as he kneels in front of the stone bench.

The words turn my spirit to glass.

"Bless her, great king Finnbheara, with the peace I hereby forfeit." The sun dips enough to cut through the low branches of the glen and illuminate the space. Light isn't necessary when the soul before me is as familiar as my own heartbeat. In Sionnach's outstretched palm is a tiny round ball, the size of the shooter marble I had as a kid. He kisses it, then bows his head to place his offering on what he clearly believes is the Wishing Seat.

Is he attempting to bargain with the Fae king for the freedom of his mother's soul?

Panic roars like stormy seas through my mind. Do Veil guides need an artifact for transit to their next place? If they do, I'm certain Sion is about to sacrifice his. I'm across the room as fast as the single beat of a swan's wing to snatch the ball. "Stop. Don't give away your forever."

Hair the reddish-brown of a hazelnut frames his shocked expression. "Eala."

I place it back in his hand. I've seen these in a museum. It's a musket ball.

I took a musket ball to the knee.

I close his fingers around his Veil guide key and squeeze his hand. "It's not time to give up. We have a hundred thousand heartbeats left."

He staggers back and collapses onto the slate cushion. "I never thought to lay eyes on your golden freckles again."

Whatever brought us together, Veil Sprites, fate, or the King of the Connacht Fae, I don't care.

I love this dear Irish boy.

Even if my passion outweighs his, I will stay with him to finish what we started. I try to assume a matter-of-fact attitude, but the flush flowing across my cheekbones gives me away.

Recovering enough to stand, Sionnach moves the two steps it takes for our bodies to be nearly touching. His palm against my cheek is as soft as moss clinging to the spaces between the square stones of the wall.

"When you embarrass, the color across your skin doesn't glow with the blood beneath, lass."

Veil Sprites twirl and float inside me, ballerinas across a stage. My heart flutters as I lay a hand over his. Why is it once you've touched someone, kissed them, caressed them, it's nearly impossible not to keep doing it?

He brings our joined hands to his lips. "'Tis the morning kiss of sunlight, waking the palest pink rose, amber and blush mix to a thing lovelier than dawn."

I slide my hands over his shoulders and lock them together under his curls. My fate, whatever moments I have left in this world where a sun does rise and a moon follows, will be tied with the soul in my embrace. I raise my face for a kiss, my oath to him, to Máthair, to the souls that will bind my end of days.

There is no kiss.

Sion takes my wrists and guides me away from him. His hands release me.

The rejection fractures my spirit, and pain compresses my chest as the truth of what I heard him saying moments before is confirmed. The musket ball was an offering, a prayer for Máthair's soul, not mine. If he wanted me, nothing I said in the Glade of Chimes would have kept him from coming after me.

I take a step backward and then another until my back meets stone wall. I've become the last Faerie story in my grandmother's repertoire. An Eala *bán*, the white swan will guide souls to their destiny and then cease to be. I'm a shell of life only entitled to artifice, not love. Finnbheara's Eala Duir is the means to an end in someone else's tale.

If Sion doesn't need or want me to help with the final two souls, then Finnbheara can damn well take me now.

I forbid my tears to fall. "I need to tell you two things, and then you'll be rid of me." I slide a foot closer to the doorway, praying I can get my information out and leave him before I dissolve back into the essence from which I was made. "Charlie might be the priest destroying the Veil. Don't ask me to explain just take me seriously."

Sion tries to speak, but I raise my voice above his, addressing the center of his chest to avoid his green glass stare. "Track down the explorer's brother. I think he's going to grab Vicars's spare key and steal the Crown Jewels. It's a hunch, but I wonder if you've retrieved the spare key too early. Maybe the theft of the spare key has to happen before it will work to free Vicars from the soulfall. Once the thief, whoever it is, has stolen the key, you take it back and give it to Vicars's soul. I believe that will confirm his innocence and restore the virtue of his diligence."

Before I'm able to slip around the corner and out of the gate lodge, Sion blocks my way.

"Please move. After Vicars is free, you'll save the last soul on your own. I've nothing more to say."

"It sure ain't all I have to say." He plants his feet and stands like a soldier ready to engage in combat. "You said your peace, now 'tis fair you hear mine."

"Fair!" I laugh and make a noise dangerously close to Sion's derisive grunt. "What in the name of the moon and Veil Sprites is fair about any of this?"

He's breathing heavily, and I expect the famous Sion Loho temper to explode any second. Instead, he scrubs hands over his face. "If fair is off the table, will you hear truth?"

My voice is low but steady. "Are you capable of telling the truth?"

The gold ring around the green of his irises flares. "I've kept this and that from you, but never lied." He grabs my hands. "And I won't lie to you now." Sion pulls me against his body. "Damn me more than I'm already damned, but I love you, Eala." He rests his forehead against mine, his skin as hot as a Beltane bonfire. "I am in love with you. It wasn't meant to happen. It makes us both as weak as the shell of a bird's egg still in the nest."

The blaze in his eyes heats my Veil Sprites to an intensity that brings on lightheadedness. Suddenly, his lips are on mine, rough and desperate. His tongue sweeps inside my mouth to capture all it touches as if to remember everything for eternity. My soul cries with joy. This is home—in Sionnach Loho's arms.

There's a loud *smack* as he abruptly ends the kiss. "The night I kissed you at Leap Castle, tasted your sweet breath of butter and honey, and witnessed your grace in saving the lad—I fell completely." He gazes at the chipped stone ceiling. "I've been falling in love with you for years as I watched the passion you invested in your life's work, your kindness to everyone lucky enough to be in your life, and a thousand other reasons. Damn me for it." His arms drop from my waist as he whirls to pace the length of the gate lodge.

I want to run to him and tell him I'm as damned as he if love is what damns us.

"Calling you to me was a mistake." He pulls at his hair as if to rip it from his head. "All those years, I sent dreams to test your mettle. They turned you into a creature of fear who crumbled when life got too big. I ruined you for the souls. And my weakness of heart has finished the job."

I slip along the wall to the arch. "If your faith in me is gone, then we're truly finished." I spin, gripping the stones for balance and ready myself to jump to the ground.

Sion throws his arms around me from behind, locking me to his chest as he drags me further inside the gate lodge. His voice is raw against my ear. "Did you not hear me at the seat, you damn woman? The mistake was tainting your life by bringing you into *my* failure."

He twirls me in his arms, bringing our faces inches apart. "I'm an arrogant bastard who resented you. I wanted to prove to Himself I could free the soulfall on my own. That's why I never told you the whole of it. The danger. My mother. Your fate." His fingers dig into my arms. "Did you not hear me beg Finnbheara to take my miserable soul and let you be? To grant you a life apart from the fate of the souls." He tilts his head to shout at the stone ceiling. "Curse his promise to my mother. If I'm to fail, I won't take you into ruination by my side."

He releases me and presses the marble-sized ball into my palm. "Here's the musket ball that lamed me. It's the key tying me to the soulfall as their guide."

The ball is warm in my hand. I was right. It's his artifact.

"Take this token of a soul who loves you with everything a man has to give of himself." Sion takes my face in his hands and kisses me tenderly. "And forgive me."

The walls of the Veil rise around him as he presses his fingers to his lips then holds them toward me in farewell.

He's releasing me from obligation. Breath catches in my throat. The gift is not Sionnach's to grant. The souls are as much in my charge as his. I was created by Finnbheara, King of the Connacht Fae, to walk through fire hand-in-hand with Sionnach Loho and light the path that leads beyond this life for those who cannot see.

It is the destiny I acknowledge—and choose.

Instead of watching the magic of the Fae take him from me, I throw myself into my fox's arms. The Veil stutters around us. My will to stay with him grates against his to free me.

When I was tiny, Máthair took me to a beautiful version of Peter Pan with Celtic music and magical Bunraku-style puppets floating across the stage. That's when Neverland became my forever dream. The moment of the play I'll never forget is when Tinkerbell is dying, and Peter says to the audience, "*If you believe in Faeries, clap your hands.*"

While keeping Sionnach in my grasp, I clap my hands behind his back slowly and then faster and faster.

"What's this? In the name of my ma's soda bread cookies, you've crossed over giddy to madness."

The mention of the cookies I, too, adore strengthens the bond I feel to this man. "I do believe in Faeries."

He captures my hands, gaze burning into mine. "I've told you before, I'm not a Faerie."

I bring our hands to my heart. I've found my Neverland.

"But I am."

I raise my face to his. "I believe. I believe it all, and I want it."

Our lips find one another. Every jagged edge of mistrust between us disappears. The harmony of our spirits remains. The kiss rises in fury until I taste blood from where teeth and lips dig into each other to prove we are living things, not phantoms in destiny's great game. We fall onto the stone seat. I'm rooted to Sionnach's lap. His arms lock around me. My hands grip the sides of his face, thumbs sliding across those wonderful ears he's always eager to hide.

I laugh and nuzzle his hand away when he tries to cover his ears with curls. "Don't." I drop tiny kisses around the curve of each non-pointed ear. "All this time, I assumed you were hiding Faerie ears."

His hand slides under my shirt to tiptoe along my spine until his thumb dips inside the back of my jeans as he traps my bottom lip between his teeth. "I wish it were morning, so I had proper time to love you."

"I second the wish." I cover his mouth with mine. I will make love with him right here on the cold stones of the gate lodge. "We may never have another morning, my love."

It's not only lust driving me but an intense desire for my *anamchara* to redefine my empty spaces. Finnbheara created me for Sionnach, but I've become more. We've become more. Together we are the spectral light of the Veil. We fall together into the chasm of desire.

I run my hands under his shirt to trace the muscles of his chest, sliding fingertips down the soft auburn patch at its center. He yips when I pinch his nipples and then laughs at his surprise. His hands rediscover my body, and I moan softly when he cups my breasts. He swiftly digs under my sweater to lift me out of my bra and takes one nipple then the other into his mouth. His teeth claim and pull until I'm ripe for him to suck hard enough to send me shuddering in violent waves.

He rubs calloused thumbs over my peaks to keep me pleading for more while his ragged breath meets the skin of my neck. "*Anamchara.*" Here, now, then, past, present blur together as we touch and kiss and want.

I stand before him and slide my jeans and panties to my ankles. Snatching his hand, I guide his fingers between my wet folds. Quickly introducing him to another nuance of lovemaking, I ride those fingers until they find their way inside me.

Sion's eyes widen. Between groans of disbelieving pleasure, he manages a few words. "We may not be alone for—"

Reluctantly, I pull free before I dissolve under the sensation of Sion's touch. Yanking his jeans and boxer briefs low enough to free his pulsing cock, I wrap my hand around it. "Remember what I said about no quick rutting?"

He releases a series of unintelligible syllables as I stroke faster and faster.

My words burrow inside breathless panting. "Sometimes... it's...necessary."

I lower my head to his lap and tease his tip with quick flicks of my tongue while I continue to trickle my fingertips up and down his length. I take more and more of him into my mouth, sliding my lips to replace my touch. He bucks his hips, thrusting across my tongue. When I feel his shaft begin to quiver against my lips. I give a long hard suck then release him.

In a flash, I'm on his lap, fitting my slick wanting over his hard cock. My knees grind into the stone seat, but I don't care. We need this joining to seal the promise to stay together until the end.

Sion drives into me while he moans, "Love, love, my love," against my ear. I thread my fingers through his hair, rocking against him as I clench around his powerful thrusts until he swells inside me and bursts with release. His cry echoes around the walls. I swallow them with a kiss then pitch my hips forward over and over, finally throwing my head back with an answering wail as I follow him into the absence of all things but each other.

We hold tight, waiting for the return of control over breath and body. Abruptly, the sun disappears behind the horizon. Its weakening light is our warning. Sionnach leans against the stones, panting. "I wish for a lifetime of days before Beltane."

I clear a mop of curls from his eyes and trace a finger along his bottom lip. "I don't know if this is actually the Wishing Seat."

"It'll do." Sion presses his lips gently to mine and lifts me to my feet. "I'm afraid, my love, time calls us." We're both wobbly as our liquid limbs regain form. With gazes locked as if that will ensure we won't be parted, we quickly reassemble our clothing. As layer after layer of shadow erases details of the gate lodge, Sionnach presses me gently against gray and black flecked stones. "I wish for time to claim your body and spirit beneath a waxing moon."

"With a million stars to bless us." We savor the taste of one another, demanding kiss after kiss until my blood sings with the oncoming Celtic day.

Finally, he sighs, folding me gently into his arms. "In all this misery and battle, you're my bit of grace."

As the final Celtic day to end the soulfall dawns, the eye of our storm passes. Once again, we stand ready to be battered by the ire of fate. I don't care. I'm the *anamchara* of a worthy heart. I vow to all the gods that ever were or ever shall be, I will fulfill my purpose hand-in-hand with my fox.

The Veil binds us together in its myriad colors. Sionnach raises my chin with a knuckle. "I've one more wish to ask of you."

I nod toward our personal wishing seat fading outside the mystical tunnel as we begin to travel. "You'd better hurry."

"Watch the soulfall to the end. Step outside fear and accept who you're meant to be."

The Veil pulses vibrant and alive without breaches or burning flames along the shimmering walls of our passage between today and yesterday.

"I promise to try."

The light in his eyes dims for a moment before his lips curve into a gentle smile. "I believe in you, Faerie girl." He claps his hands.

We fall into one final kiss. The Veil guides us. The thought of watching the last soul drop from the tower window sends shivers through me. Sionnach tightens his hold, never to let me fall.

I close my eyes and reach out through this path of mystery to the enigma of Finnbheara.

Mighty king, grant me life beyond the end of the soulfall with this man.

If there is power in the blessing of *anamchara*, may it find me. As our kiss deepens, so does my resolve to serve the last two souls, whether there's any left of Eala Duir afterward or not.

CHAPTER 25
THE LAST SOUL

Breaking and entering is not in my wheelhouse, but Sionnach is quite accomplished at it. I crouch behind a wing chair in Arthur Vicars's front room on Clonskeagh Road. The place is dark and empty unlike the first time we popped into 1907.

In my hand is a whistle. I'm supposed to blow it when our perp, who we suspect may be the renowned explorer's brother, goes for the kitchen cabinet where the second key is hidden. Sionnach swears that one long, loud whistle will bring the Dublin Metropolitan Police running.

He's gone to Dublin Castle to tip off Arthur Vicars about the impending theft. If all goes well, as soon as our target leaves the party to steal the key, Vicars and Sionnach will be close on his heels. I pray the Veil fiend hasn't anticipated or tracked us. It's imperative we've landed in the right moment to keep Vicars alive.

I'm already shaky when my next thought nearly shatters me. What will I do if we're forced to confront the evil, and it is Charlie?

Please let Colleen be safe.

My disappearance at Luttrellstown undoubtedly caused enough insanity for Jeremy to put the tour on lockdown. I regret what I'm putting both Colleen and him through.

I wish I'd been able to say goodbye to Colleen, an impossibility with

our last Celtic day already at hand. "I'm so sorry, C. I love you, friend
—sister."

I can't dwell on her life or my life after the soulfall. That's a guaranteed
road to madness.

Footsteps outside send me back into ready position. If the man heads
straight for the key cabinet I scoped out in the kitchen, I'll have a clear
shot to run out the front door and blow the whistle. The door creaks and
moonlight spills across the sill to reveal not one, but a pair of men
stepping into the room.

At first, I think it's Sionnach and Vicars but realize my error before the
door clicks shut. The two throw off their coats and collide in a passionate
kiss. I shrink behind the chair in case they turn on the light, but they fall
onto a sofa with no intention of flipping any switch but each other's.

"Are you sure Arthur won't be walking in that door?" asks a deep male
voice.

His paramour answers. "The fool's held up at the castle. There's time if
we're *royally* quick about it."

The men chuckle.

In a voice that could easily be described as regal, one of them says,
"Then kneel before me, knave."

My chances of escaping unseen are nil. Hopefully, pending sensual
activities will relocate so I can grab the key myself and leave through the
back door. That will at least keep one of the men from stealing the key.
It'll give Sion and me the chance to reset and Veil travel back to our
starting point for another try before the Celtic day ends. Let tonight be a
cautionary tale for Vicars to keep the second key in a more secure hiding
place. The whole changing history gamble is dicey, but we're out of time.

Unexpected silence falls over the room. "Did you hear that?" asks one
of the men.

I press a hand over my mouth. Am I the sound? Did I breathe too
loudly? I raise the whistle to my lips. Raising hell and running are my two
options if they discover me.

Both men scramble to their feet. The squeakier voice of the two
answers. "Grab our coats. I'll get the key to the jewels."

I hear what put them on alert—Sionnach's convincing English accent.

"I got a right good tip off, Mr. Vicars sir."

Out the window, a pair of shadowed forms close in on the house but not fast enough. The would-be lovers head for the kitchen at the rear of the house. My coward's brain warns me to lay low, but it's our last night. I can't lose this chance. I stand, blow the whistle, and run after the men attempting to steal the key.

"What in bloody hell?" shouts one of them, whirling to face me. He already holds the ornate key in his hand.

"Drop it," I yell. Grabbing a low stool from the corner of the kitchen, I swing it at his head. The crack to his skull reverberates through my body. He drops to his knees with a scream as Sionnach and Vicars burst through the front door, lantern held high. The thief's face crumples a split second before his body does. The key skids across the floor.

The door at the back of the kitchen hangs open. Sionnach, Vicars, and I glimpse the second man streak between buildings and disappear. The rumble of voices sounds from the street. Three policemen charge into the house.

Sionnach retrieves the abandoned key from under the table. He presses it into Vicars's hand. "Hold tight to both keys in your keeping, friend. Trust no one, and you'll save yourself."

As bodies crowd the kitchen, Sionnach pulls me into the shadow of a doorway. The moment backs are to us, we slip through time.

As soon as we enter the Veil, searing heat burns my skin and hair. I scream, raising hands to shield my face.

Ambush.

"Run," shouts Sionnach. Together, we tear down the narrow passageway of the Veil away from the raging purple-blue fire. He pushes me too roughly and I fly forward, unable to catch myself before rolling onto the carpet of faded turquoise orbs.

Behind Sionnach, a shadow steps through the flames. The figure of a priest stands tall and lanky like a grasshopper. Wind from the fire flaps his robe, raptor wings. Crackling noises deafen me as an ugly tear rips open the walls of the Veil. Through the breach, the full moon is close enough to blind, but it's all wrong. Its usually bright white surface is a sickly yellow surrounded by fraying red rings.

Sionnach lifts me into his arms, and we plunge through the wall of sizzling heat.

I expect to roll onto the familiar grassy slope beneath the soulfall tower. Instead, a wave of spitting froth smacks me in the face. The weight of my Victorian clothing pulls me underwater. After fighting my way up, I swivel to avoid getting battered by the next white plume, but the river's current jerks me forward. Familiar white moonlight pebbles across the surface of water. Substantial rocks embedded in the bottom of the river strike at my feet.

A break in the spray allows me a glimpse of an up-thrusting boulder ending in a familiar craggy point. I'm headed straight for the moss-covered tooth that lies in wait for souls at the bottom of the tower.

To my left, a slender finger of stone breaks through churning water. With a double arm stroke and a lucky push off the bottom, I'm close enough to wrap my arms around the pillar. Between my refuge and the riverbank, the trunk and branches of a fallen tree bob in the current. Its roots are embedded in the sheared-off face of a small rise at the water's edge. Between stone and tree, the current relaxes slightly. I frantically kick toward shore and manage to crook an arm through a soggy fork of branch.

I search for Sionnach. He's thrown his body across the rounded top of another boulder not far away. From the looks of him, it won't be long before the river sucks him back in.

"Sionnach," I holler, trying to be heard above rushing water.

He turns to my voice. The water between us is agitated and unwelcome, but he dives in. I twine the fingers of both hands as tightly as possible around the tree and stretch my body out into the river.

When his hands clamp around my ankle, our combined weight nearly causes me to lose my grip on the branch.

Sionnach grabs handholds of my dress and slides over the top of my body until we are sandwiched together in the cold sting of the river.

"Climb," he shouts, and grabs my waist. Together, we slither along slimy wood onto a strip of mud. The roots of the tree provide a rudimentary ladder to the grassy slope below the soulfall tower. Crawling away from the river, we cough until breathing is bearable.

I clear my river-ravaged throat. "Did the monster follow us out?"

We scan riverbank, woods, and tower. I reach out to the Veil to try to sense the bastard. All that comes is a tiny current running up my arms and the faint smell of lemongrass and spearmint.

Sionnach is first to let his guard down and collapse onto his back. "The fucker's not here," he wheezes, but then sits when he catches sight of my face. He runs a finger under my cheekbone. "You're burned."

A stripe of black darkens his forehead. "You too."

His hand probes tender skin.

I raise a tentative fingertip to my cheekbone and draw in air with a hiss. "Shit—stings."

"Oh, my love," he says and cradles me in his arms. We're both drenched. We shiver and cling to one another, stealing a moment. The full moon sits in its proper place above a familiar tree line. Not far off, a creamy pearlescent oval reflects off wet grass. The room at the top of the soulfall tower glows. I steel myself for the wailing.

Sionnach rises to his feet, extending a hand. "Climb the tower with me?"

I want to draw courage from the well of purpose in my heart. He expects me to join him to bid Arthur Vicars farewell and hear the last soul's story. My legs refuse to move. My hands shake so badly, I trap my fingers between my knees to steady them. The weakening of my senses, the sickness in my gut, signals the onset of crippling fear.

"I truly want to, but I can't." The salt from my tear sets off a throbbing pain across my burnt cheek. "I'm sorry. Forgive me."

He crouches before me, leaning in for a tender kiss. "You're not to worry." Sionnach stands and takes a few steps toward the tower, then comes back to me. A cheerless half-smile plays across his lips. "It's not a fear of the high places that plagues you." He shakes his head. "It's fear of falling from them." His bottom lip quivers. "And the falling I can keep you from." He blows lightly on my burn. "I'm sorry I cursed you with such fear."

The voice calling me into the skies over Times Square echoes through my mind—so clearly Sionnach's now that he's part of me. I'm not angry. I understand his impatience was desperation to help the souls. He meant no harm. I'm furious with myself for not being able to move past my fear even on our last night together.

We're destined to climb those stairs hand-in-hand.

At least I can do one thing he's asked of me. "I will watch the last soul. Come down right after, and we can finish this."

His face droops with exhaustion and a sadness so deep, the weight of it presses on me. He returns for another lingering kiss. The heat from our lips flows through our bodies, erasing the outer layer of chill from the river. When he begins to draw away, I trace his lovely full bottom lip with the tip of my tongue. He pulls me to my feet and presses the length of his body to mine, finishing the kiss I began.

I watch until he disappears through the bottom door of the tower. The wails from the soulfall cut through the night.

Bracing myself, I don't look away as the soul of Arthur Vicars holds a key aloft, then rises as earthly starlight. No matter what mess we've made of history, this time, Vicars's artifact worked. I'm witness to the man's unfailing diligence in professing his innocence until the end of his life. Soul and its virtue seek the heavens together.

I grit my teeth. The silhouette of the final soul grows as it nears the window. This last song of sorrow is unlike any other. It soars above the trees, deep and rich, infinitely more haunting than the ones that came before it. How can a requiem of such beauty belong to a spirit separated from virtue?

And then my heart steps onto the windowsill. Sionnach sings my name to the stars and falls into the night. His soul crashes against rock. Blackness of a spirit in agony drips down unforgiving stone.

"Sionnach." I scream his name and fly across the grassy slope. I mount the stairs of the soulfall tower without hesitation. My fear of climbing is nothing compared to the torment of losing him to the churning water or the Glade of Chimes for eternity.

"St. Augustine, let him be there." He's the last soul. Sionnach will fall from the tower over and over with no other spirits to delay him. Halfway to the top, my legs threaten to stop carrying me.

What if tonight is different? From Éostre, the equinox, until the feast of Beltane, the window of redemption is supposed to stay open. If the rules changed and Sionnach isn't in the tower room, I vow to hunt the rule maker through eternity. I press both hands to my heart. It still beats. If mine beats, I pray Sionnach's does the same.

His words echo in my heart. *"Step outside fear and hold tight to who you're meant to be."*

I force my body the rest of the way up the stairs and through the arch at the top. Firelight from the ring of torches set into the wall at shoulder height splashes across stone. Sionnach sits on the floor next to the window, head upon his knees. In moments, he'll rise only to fall again. I drop by his side, wrapping my arms around his body. *"Anamchara,* tell me your soul story."

His head sinks onto my shoulder. Lips move against the skin of my neck. "You climbed."

"You promised you'd never let me fall." I'm here higher than I ever imagined I'd go in this tower or anywhere. Through the window, I see the river and field far below. My body doesn't shake, there's no nausea. At the Leviathan, Sion's presence wrapped me in safety. Tonight, I took a risk for someone else and fear released its hold on me. Before I appreciate the absence of my lifelong burden, heaviness in my chest reminds me the Celtic day is not endless. "How can you be in the soulfall?"

"The guide is always the last soul."

I want to shake him. This is the worst of all his omissions. "You should have told me."

"I'm not to speak of it until the souls before me enter grace."

How can redemption and so-called grace be wrapped in such cruelty? If I'd known from the beginning Sionnach was the last to be saved, I never would have left him. Tests, lessons, what is the point when decent people are damned?

I rub my nose against his temple. "This is one cosmically screwed up system."

He closes his eyes and slumps as if the last of his energy was spent seeing me walk through the archway. "That it is."

I shake him and press my fingers into the sides of his face. "How do we save you?"

Flames from the wall torches soften the green in his eyes. "Maybe I shouldn't be saved. I'm the reason evil entered the Veil. If ever there were a sign some sins are not to be forgiven and virtues forever out of reach, we've seen it."

"Dammit, Sionnach. Don't you dare give up. I climbed the fucking tower. For you. Now talk."

He looks as if he's been stabbed through the heart. I drop kisses across his eyes down to the tip of his nose and end at his lips. I feel life bleed back into the flickering soul in my arms. "Please, my sweet fox."

He stares out the window. "You asked why Ma feared for my soul. I told you I turned spy for a bit of money to keep Ma and Da from starving. What I did send was more than an honest living would bring. Ma suspected I wasn't telling all. She had a sense for truth and lies."

Yes, my Máthair always did.

His chest rumbles beneath my touch. "I told myself, my reasons for leaving home were noble, but 'twas ambition that truly drove me. I stained the virtue of my intention to help my folks with glory seeking."

"But you did good things for Father Colm, right?"

"Aye, it was my job to keep the lads wanting to become priests anonymous until he could ship them off to Spain or the Holy Father in Italy." Torchlight shines off his tears. "A musket ball to my leg was all it took to break me and doom the good father."

In a panic, I reach into the pocket of my dress to touch the musket ball Sionnach gave me at the gate lodge. Thankfully, it's still wedged in a corner of fabric.

His breath stutters and catches. I stroke his curls. It takes a few minutes to calm him, but he's able to continue. "Father Colm was arrested on my word and killed. I got free and ran to my folks, shamed and broken. I couldn't even help Da with the fields 'cause of my useless leg."

The despair in his voice brings tears to my eyes.

"Da planned to indenture himself to get me and Ma to America." He slaps the side of his thigh. "One night, I left 'em without a word, only a letter of farewell, knowing they had clear passage money enough for two. Da could travel as a free man. No one needs the burden of a son whose cowardice destroyed a good man like Father Colm and those he would have led into a life of service. Dying from a festering wound was too good for me."

I hold his face in my hands, stroking his strong cheekbones. "Máthair wouldn't cut a deal with Finnbheara if she didn't think you were worth it."

"If I'd known of her past with the king and that such a bargain was possible, the letter with blessings for their journey and news that my end was coming fast would never have been written. Ma and Da would have sailed to America and not found out for years what became of me." A strangled sob cuts off his words.

"Sionnach, what virtue of yours is lost?"

I've seen so many emotions on this man's face, but the one he wears now breaks my heart. He's crushed. The hope that's driven him for two hundred years is gone. I lay a hand on the side of his neck. His pulse beats against my lifeline. "Tell me."

The golden ring around his irises has faded to dull brown. "Sacrifice." He stares past me. "A decent man would sacrifice himself and not speak Father Colm's name to the English. That wasn't the way of it with me. I failed." Creases stretch along the sides of his mouth. "I've traveled back and let the soldiers beat me and offered my life instead of speaking the father's name." He nods his head to the window. "But I never rise. I'm never free." His chin drops to his chest. "I wasted decades on myself that belonged to saving the other souls. My obsession with self-preservation robbed them of the devotion I owed them."

I lay palms against his breastbone. "If trying to change your history didn't work, there's another answer."

He lifts his head as if it were as heavy as one of the boulders in the river below. "This is a question that doesn't need your solving, my darling Eala. There's one reason Father Colm, as himself or Charlie or the other characters he's been, chases me through the Veil. He seeks rightly deserved revenge." He sits straighter. "As it should be. My earned fate is to spend eternity watching others sing their soulsongs and pass on, never to follow."

I shake my head. "This isn't right. Why would Father Colm try to keep you from saving souls? Wasn't that his life's work as well?"

He cradles my head in his hand. "That's why Finnbheara sent you. For them—the souls. Not for me. Now my ma will not live in eternal disgrace because her son's lost virtue kept others from finding theirs for so long."

The Máthair I knew would not be consumed with her own eternal disgrace. She lived for the people she loved. Her son. Me. She asked Finnbheara for a human child to raise and love in order to save Sionnach. It's my compassion for humanity, not any oak or swan essence that's shown me the way to restore virtue to the souls.

The virtue of compassion my grandmother taught me.

Warmth starts at my heart and radiates through my body. Veil Sprites incandesce. As if his gentle touch rested on my shoulder, St. Augustine's words come alive in my thoughts. *"Faith is to believe what we do not see; and the reward of this faith is to see what we believe."*

I pull the musket ball from my pocket. "You thought this was your key, didn't you?" He nods. "You believed if you went back and were killed to protect Father Colm, your soul would be at peace. If the man was as good and holy as you claim, he'd never trade your life for his. Much less chase you across time trying to damn the entire soulfall when you fail."

I take one of his hands in mine. "Restoring your virtue is to forgive yourself. The sacrifices you must fix are the ones you're holding that don't belong to you. Believe you're worthy of your mother's sacrifice. Allow Father Colm to be at peace for his sacrifice of giving his life to a cause he cherished. Let go of your guilt and shame. Celebrate his vision and own the good part you did play in it."

He sets his other hand on mine. "How?"

I run a finger across my burn. Sionnach can't dip inside a Veil in flames to parlay with the beast he thinks is Father Colm. And then it comes to me.

He needs to talk to Máthair.

Not the Glade of Chimes or New York City Máthair. His Ma.

"By going home. Tell your parents the whole truth. You turned spy because you loved them and wanted to save your family from starving. Confess your ambition if that's what clears your conscience. Repent your part in Father Colm's death and give your parents the chance to forgive you. You owe it to Máthair after what Finnbheara's favor cost her."

His gaze holds fast to mine. Slowly, I see the beginning of trust in my words easing the tension in his face.

A gust of frigid wind howls up the stairs, blowing out the torches in the room one by one except the flame closest to the archway. Sionnach puts his body between me and the stairs as a hand reaches in to snatch the single burning torch from its bracket. A figure raises the fire before him. Our visitor's black shadow flows in an unnatural direction outward from the flame instead of reflecting on the turret wall behind.

"A miserable worm like you, spy, does not deserve forgiveness."

I link arms with Sionnach to face the shadow priest. "Stop, Charlie. You don't understand."

"Charlie!" the priest bellows a laugh. "That dolt is who you think me to be?" His Irish accent is heavier, less fluid than Sionnach's. "Fools, the both of you."

At this, the priest brings the torch near his face. A red-eyed Jeremy Olk stands before us clad in the black cassock and robes of an eighteenth-century priest. "You don't remember me, spy, but your face burns in my soul."

"You're not Father Colm," says Sionnach.

The torch flames shift from the red orange of natural fire into the purple-blue flames of the hellfire destroying the Veil. "I would never profess to be such a great man." Olk shows his teeth. "A man whose flesh was parted from his brain because of you."

I shudder at the memory of the man I believed to be Jeremy Olk describing the pitch-capping practice of Cornwallis.

Olk catches the movement. "And you, damn woman, nearly sent this wretch to his reward." He stalks around the room as we counter his moves to stay as far away as possible. A finger with a nail bruised black points to Sionnach. "This man murdered Father Colm and the dreams of us all who wished to follow his work. I returned from Spain to serve my faith and found death." Olk spits on the floor in front of Sion. "You alone destroyed the good father's mission."

Sion's voice quavers. "I never laid eyes on you in Father Colm's presence. You're a demon sent to do the devil's work."

"I am Father Jeremy O'Neill, a disciple of Father Colm. It is you who carried out the devil's plan when you spoke my beloved priest's name to the English."

I twist Sion's sleeve in my hand as I stare at the monster. "How are you still alive?"

Olk's laugh sends the sensation of needles spiking into my flesh. "Finnbheara's not the only power open to dealings."

Sion's voice floats through the air. "Where there is light, there is darkness."

Once the Olk creature reaches the window, he stills, glancing into the night. "The Celtic day wanes before us." He waves the torch. Cool flames turn gray stone to muted sapphire. His voice oozes with the arrogance of the self-righteous. "Prepare to embrace eternal torment, Sionnach Loho."

My blood stirs as the air shimmers around Sionnach. He's calling the Veil.

Olk flicks a wrist as if shooing away a fly and the thin sheets of glass around us crack, then shatter, scattering multi-hued shards across the floor.

Sionnach moans. I press a palm to his chest and feel the weakness of his heartbeat. What has Olk done to him?

Backing away from the shower of glass brings me near the steps. I motion Sionnach behind my back to draw closer while I glare at the thing that was Jeremy Olk.

This will not be our end. My default is always to cower or run but not now. I will act for Sionnach, for myself to shed the bonds of timidity and fear that held me for so long. "No god will welcome you into heaven for hunting a Veil guide."

The tarnished priest reaches to light the closest torch with his own before he leers at us. Flickers of blue and purple race across stone. "Revenge is my heaven."

I point a finger at Olk's bloodshot eyes. "Revenge will lead you straight to hell." Grabbing Sionnach, I turn and leap into the center shaft of the turret. The monster's ignorance of my power to initiate travel allows us the seconds we need to escape.

As Olk bellows, the Veil plucks us from the tower.

CHAPTER 26
THE COTTAGE

We land in the Veil forest where Sionnach first introduced me to the other worlds existing alongside our own. He falls to his knees, face as pale as the moon, gasping for breath. In a flash, he grabs my sleeves and shakes. "You've got to go back. To your time, your life, your friends. We'll both die if you stay."

I cover his hands with mine. "This is my time, and you are my life." The *fánaí* tree is next to us. I reach into the bag of clothing and throw him a *leine*, vest, and britches.

He makes no move to transform from Victorian servant to peasant. "What are you about, Eala?"

"We'll both go to your parents. Make your peace, and your soul will be free." I grab the collar of his shirt to pull him in. "*Anamchara*, we will end the soulfall tonight." Any protest dies when I capture him in a kiss to emphasize the non-negotiable nature of my plan.

He returns the kiss with ferocity.

"Tell me how to travel to your parents," I say, trading my dress for a *leine* and skirt without hiding behind a tree. My near-naked body offers a sensual promise to be collected when we succeed. "Olk finds us when you call the Veil. If I do it, maybe he can't follow."

Sionnach strips to his boxer briefs. The contours of his body are beautiful in starlight. He dons peasant clothes in the space of a sentence. "I can outdo the bastard."

I want to argue, scared to death Sionnach is unstable this close to Beltane, but there's no time. We link arms and blast through the glass walls of Sionnach's Veil with a crack and land in the middle of rolling farmland.

He grabs my hand, and we race down a country road. "Over the next rise."

To my dismay, Sionnach limps, slowing our progress. I tell myself it has to be this way. His redemption must come after the musket ball lamed him.

A stone wall to our right curves with the path. Did Loho father and son lay these stones to mark family land?

As we crest a hill, the view knocks the breath from me. Not more than half a city block before us is the edge of a massive cliff. Beyond, the sea crashes over a wide stretch of rocky coastline. Off to our left, a finger of land stretches into the waves. At its far end, the flashing beacon of a lighthouse pulses through rising mist.

"Beautiful," I whisper to the road of moonlight sketched across the surface of the water.

"Here," says Sionnach, tugging me through a wooden gate. Tall wildflowers border a lane leading to a small cottage. A familiar smell of herbs and lavender wraps around me. I'm back in my grandmother's greenhouse.

Home.

Smoke rises from a stone chimney poking above a thatched roof covered with lines of rope. Moonshine silvers stone walls. White rocks outline windows that peek from behind a beard of ivy. Behind the house, two giant yew trees stand guard at either corner.

At the door, I stop. Once again, our actions are about to skew futures and pasts. If Sion's virtue is restored, does my existence become unnecessary? I've no choice but to move forward.

He takes both my hands in his and kisses them. "You ache to see Ma as I do."

My Máthair is on the other side of these wooden slats. Despite keeping the truth from me, I love the woman who faced down the King of the Connacht Fae to insist on my humanity. I will see this through with my fox. To restore his virtue is worth gambling my place in this life.

Sionnach raps on the door and then pushes it aside to usher me in.

The scene inside is a killing blow. The stench of soil gone to rot fills the cottage. Máthair, my grandmother—Sionnach's mother, stands atop a trestle table with a noose around her neck. Rope has been thrown over the rafters of the house to form impromptu gallows. My hands fly to my mouth as I recognize the man next to her. Timothy Yew—who will one day pose as Máthair's lawyer in New York—wears a matching noose around the ruddy skin of his neck.

"Ma. Da," cries Sionnach, bursting into the single room cottage.

His parents call, "Sionnach," in one voice. Father reaches out to son, but then grabs the rope around his neck to keep it from tightening.

"Far enough," roars Olk, one foot poised on the edge of the table, ready to kick it over and hang Sionnach's parents right in front of him.

Máthair and Timothy hold hands. Here is the man who bested a Faerie king for this woman's love. The man or spirit who, at my grandmother's behest back in New York, gave me the means to find my destiny.

How many spirits have walked through my life?

Martha O'Dwyer Loho is no more than forty. A woman I've only seen in the few black and white pictures she kept in a wooden box on the mantle above our fireplace. She drinks in Sionnach with wide green eyes banded with gold. I start, recognizing the same green glass eyes I now share with her son. She has the eyes of a *fánaí* who's wandered through the Otherworld with her Fae lover.

"Praises, we're blessed to lay eyes on you." Máthair passes a swift glance in my direction. She doesn't know me. Like the absence of Sionnach's limp when we traveled back in time, I haven't happened yet. The need for me hasn't arisen. Sionnach's human life hasn't ended with a missing virtue. To his parents, the man standing next to me with springy russet curls isn't the Veil guide he will become. Máthair's bargain with Finnbheara is in the future.

Sion shakes a fist at Olk. "How dare you enter my home."

"We opened our door to a man of God," says Máthair. "Not a red-eyed demon." For a heartbeat, I believe her expression might melt the fiend on the spot.

"Go now, Son," says Timothy. "And take the lassie with you."

Olk's cassock is splattered with mud. He grins. "You fools thought you could best me. The moment you called the Veil, I saw where you'd travel to try to salvage your wretched soul."

My throat constricts. I should have trusted my instinct and stopped Sionnach from guiding us here.

Máthair spits at Olk. "A thousand masses could be said for your soul, and it would still be as black as ash."

"A thousand masses won't save your son's soul either." He points a finger at Sionnach. "Your lad turned spy and condemned a good man, a priest, to torture and death."

Máthair's and Timothy's faces pale as they stare at their son. Emotions from disbelief to horror cross their faces.

Timothy is first to speak. "Is this true?"

Sionnach's shoulders collapse under the shame he's worn as a yoke for two hundred years. "I have the blood of a priest on my hands."

Olk growls through gritted teeth. "The confession of a blackened soul."

Máthair turns on Olk. "Do not speak of my son's soul." Tears brighten her eyes as she looks back to Sionnach. "Why did you do it?"

"Weakness, Ma. Cowardice."

Timothy watches his son. "Did you offer up the priest willingly, son?"

"Faith, no. 'Twas torture wrenched such words from my lips."

My heart threatens to stop beating at the thought of Sionnach being tortured at the hands of Cornwallis and his terror.

Timothy gazes intently upon his son. "'Tis wrong you've done."

Máthair shakes her head but stops as the rope chafes her throat. "Did you confess this betrayal to a priest?"

From behind them, Olk lets out a low laugh. "There is no absolution for your son's sin."

"Yes, straight away," says Sionnach to his mother.

Máthair pushes a strand of hair that's strayed in front of her eyes. "You should never have put your life in a world of such danger to send us money."

Timothy reaches a hand toward Sionnach. "I'll bless you, not condemn you, for taking on such a burden."

Sionnach lowers his head in deference. "Forgive me for choosing ambition instead of staying here and seeing you through hard times." He meets his father's eyes. "And for causing the death of a sainted man, bringing disgrace to your house, Father." Slowly, he turns and bows to Máthair. "To you, Ma—" Tears rain down the faces of both mother and son. "I thank you for the thing you'll be doing for me soon."

Olk growls as his gloating smile is replaced by gritted teeth. "Silence, priest killer." The bones of his face press against his skin as he teeters on the precipice of failure. He rocks the table, drawing cries of pain from the elder Lohos.

The room brightens from an unseen source. Olk gags and chokes. The air around us is charged with sweetness and warmth. Our tormentor forces out a breath, fogging the air around his head as his final assault threatens to fall apart.

The grace of forgiveness swirls through the cottage like a whisper of breeze through wildflowers. I feel the Veil acknowledge truths told—virtues restored. The last soul in the soulfall, my Sionnach, will rise tonight.

I take in the twisted version of Jeremy Olk. The whites of his eyes are filled with red, crisscrossed lines. His hair has no more luster than matted straw. The skin of face and hands is covered with wrinkles and veins like the bark of a very old tree. His voice is stone grating against stone. "It's time to bargain, spy."

Even the essence of forgiveness bearing down on him does not stop this creature in a priest's robe, blinded by his damaged perception of celestial justice. He will fight until he or Sionnach are destroyed.

Olk crosses to the front of the table. "Your soul for theirs. Come back to the tower with me and forfeit your grace, or I will force them to leap off the table and take their own lives." His laugh is soot and bile. "Suicide is a mortal sin. Do allow me the favor of tormenting their souls for all time in our shared purgatory."

Where Sionnach's arm touches mine, his muscles ripple, a dry branch catching fire.

With a roar of "Devil take you," Sionnach streaks past me and tackles Olk. In a few twists, Sionnach is captured in a headlock, his *leine* torn open. The tip of Olk's knife pierces the skin of Sionnach's left breast above the heart. A thin stripe of blood trickles below the blade.

I lunge forward, screaming, "No."

Sionnach groans in pain as Olk compresses his windpipe while pressing the dagger farther into flesh.

Olk shows his teeth. "No farther, Eala, or you'll forever bear the stain of these three ruined souls." I freeze, trembling with absolute helplessness.

My existence is defined by Sionnach's success in freeing every soul in the soulfall given into his care, including his own. How can I stand here and watch a soul-rotted Jeremy Olk drive a knife through my love's heart or kill my grandmother and Timothy Loho? What happens if Sionnach dies in this time? He will never become a Veil guide. Little Harriett, Strongbow's squire, the Earl of Rosse, Alaina Kennedy, and Arthur Vicars will be condemned to fall into disgrace for all of eternity. Olk's evil will triumph, and I'll bear the stain of more than three cursed souls.

Olk sneers. "You've played your part well, leading me to this Veil guide."

The accusation is a blow. "I didn't."

"Oh, but you did, stupid woman, even after your petty rift with him." My stomach drops. The man I knew as Jeremy charmed me, and then acted the hero to rid my life of the annoying local. His fabricated romantic advances, stories of pitch-capping and Faeries, were machinations to drive me back to Sionnach so he could follow.

Rage surges through me. The energy of the Veil vibrates beneath my feet, shaking the cottage floor. It's as if a crust of winter ice upon a river falls from my spirit. Planting my feet, I raise a fist. "Stupid, I am not." I am the essence of oak and swan created by Finnbheara, great King of the Connacht Fae. "And you are no priest. Your Father Colm would damn the fetid soul you've become."

Olk glowers with white-hot hatred, driving the blade deeper into Sionnach's chest.

Within me, Veil Sprites explode into a wall of flame. I am not helpless. I possess the power of human and Fae. It's time to embrace both. A lifetime of folklore and stories swirl in my head, quickly settling on the tale of a simple woman who sought the aid of a mighty Fae king. The story sharpens in my mind, showing me how to act.

I sweep a hand toward the cottage door. It flies off the hinges as I cry to the night. "*Éisteacht liom mo athair*, Finnbheara. Listen to me. For the love you bore this woman, grant me the power to overcome evil."

In the distance, lightning erupts above the horizon, spiking across the sea. On the farthest point of the peninsula, the lighthouse begins to spin faster and faster, as bolt after bolt of lightning pummel it. The structure explodes into a pillar of blinding white. Before the light stands a colossus clad in polished silver armor with a crown upon his head. He raises a stone shield as tall as the vanished lighthouse to the maelstrom of furious gray-black clouds above his shining helm. His other hand wields a gleaming silver sword, pointing directly at my heart.

I turn and bow to my king. Behind Finnbheara, a hundred shafts of light pierce the clouds to meet the sea. Each place they touch erupts in a geyser of hissing steam.

My hand tingles and then a cylinder of pure white light no thicker than my finger rises from my palm—passed from Finnbheara to me. I turn to Olk, who drops Sionnach and backs into a corner of the cottage, fear mangling his features. I level the light at his heart. "In the name of my maker, Finnbheara, I purge you from the Veil. I purge you from the earth. I purge you from the heavens."

Olk raises arms to block the light streaking from my outstretched hand. He attempts to shift from man into the conflagration of purple-blue fire he uses to infect the Veil. Snow white flames as delicate as strands of fine lace surround him, compressing the malignant fiend into a smaller and smaller mass. For a moment, golden light illuminates him like an angelic portrait, but he swiftly corrupts into a sculpture of ash. Wind screams through the cottage and Jeremy Olk's blackened soul flies through the open door, riding the night wind to Finnbheara's outstretched palm.

The king squeezes his hand into a fist and raises it to the sky. From between his fingers, black liquid drips into the sea. When the last of Jeremy Olk is consumed by the waves, Finnbheara thumps his chest and nods to me. King and lightning stream back to the clouds. The lighthouse resumes its solitary watch over the shore.

My head swims, and I clutch a chair to keep from falling. Timothy and Máthair escape their nooses and drop to the ground next to their son. Both adults stare at me with a combination of fear and awe, but Sionnach's face breaks into a pain-riddled smile.

"Ma. Da. This is Eala Duir." He reaches for me. "My love."

I rush to his side. While Timothy presses a wad of cloth against the bleeding wound in his son's chest, Máthair turns to me. A distant flicker shines at the back of my grandmother's eyes as bright as emerald glass. She pulls me into her arms, holding me to her heart with the same strength that carried me through life from the day I was born until the day she left me.

The love in her voice whose absence tore a hole in my heart flows through my body, repairing damage I thought I'd wear forever. "Then we love you too, dearest Eala."

Beside us, Sionnach's breathing turns ragged. Words shift into groans. Máthair transfers his head to her lap. "Tim, fetch my dandelion oil." She turns to me. "For healing."

Judging from the gray pallor of his skin, and the pool of blood on the floor next to him, my Sionnach is not going to heal in this time. I don't need to count heartbeats to know the end of the Celtic day draws near. I rip the kerchief from my neck and toss it to Máthair to replace the blood-soaked cloth over Sionnach's wound.

He smiles at his parents, straining to speak. "No man goes beyond his day, eh, Da?"

Timothy Yew, no Timothy Loho, the stocky farmer that sent me on my journey to find Máthair, lays a hand on the crown of his son's garnet-colored head. "'Tis not your day yet, *Mac*."

Not in this time and place, but it is Sionnach's last day. We must return to the soulfall tower before the day dawns so he can pass into forever. I trade places with Máthair and cradle Sionnach's curly head on my lap while she pours dandelion oil into the wound, tending to her boy for the last time.

I lean over and kiss her cheek. "I will take care of him, Máthair." I lay a hand on Timothy's sleeve. "I promise."

In front of the astonished faces of my grandmother and the man for whom she forfeited *Tír na nÓg*, the Veil enfolds Sionnach and me in radiant glory. We glide through time back to the soulfall tower.

The round room at the top of the turret is once again bathed in the glow of golden torchlight. Outside the window, indigo night fades to lavender, the precursor of dawn. Beltane has grabbed onto a trail of moonlight to draw itself over the world.

Sionnach sits next to me on the floor, patting his chest. The Veil works its magic, and the wound becomes a thumb-sized pink scar.

I grab both his hands in mine and kiss them. My tears wet his skin. "Will you go to Heaven?"

We cradle each other's faces. His lips trail from my temple to my mouth, claiming me with the joy of a soul finally unfettered. Sionnach's voice is raw. "I'll spend my eternity searching for your soul."

Rivulets of tears drench my skin. "Why didn't Máthair send me to you sooner?"

Sionnach gives a gentle laugh. "And you'd a opened your arms wide to me if I'd dropped in on any old Éostre and asked you to join me in Ireland to hop around time?"

I can't help but smile, remembering how I badly wanted to drop kick him the day we met in the Druid's Cave at Blarney Castle. I rise to my knees, pulling him up with me. We press our hearts together. "Don't leave me. I love you. There's nothing in this life or the next that will matter as much as you."

He buries his face against my neck. "I should have begged Finnbheara to change the bargain and trade eternity to stay one lifetime on this earth with you."

I grab fistfuls of his *leine*. "I'll ask it of him now. He's listening. Finnbheara came when I called to him at the cottage."

Sionnach shakes his head, his gaze drifting to the window. "My hour has come." He lays one hand over my heart and the other over his. "One hundred thousand heartbeats."

We fall into a kiss filled with the hundred thousand words we'll never speak to each other.

Sionnach whispers. "My darling. My love. *Teacht orm*. Find me."

I pull my grandmother's ring from my finger and slide it onto his pinkie. "*Teacht orm*. I will. I swear I will."

Helping one another to stand, we walk hand-in-hand to the window. I can't tell if the pain in my chest heralds the end of the Celtic day or the splitting of my heart. "Wait. You don't have a key."

His eyes glitter in the dying torchlight. "*Eala bán*, your compassion is the seventh virtue in this soulfall and my key." Our lips brush and then take each other in a last kiss filled with all the passion of future kisses that will never be.

Sionnach's voice is rough as he sings scattered phrases of the song, "An Eala Bhán," about a white swan, dreams, clasping hands, and promises fulfilled.

With the tips of our fingers still touching, he steps onto the sill. "Send me to the mercy of fate, *Anamchara*. I'm too weak to fly on my own."

I can't do it. The love of my life will not enter grace without me. As Finnbheara loved Máthair, I love Sionnach. I will follow him to eternity.

I send final thoughts to the air.

Goodbye, Colleen. I'm grateful Charlie is a good man. He'll love you. I know it.

Máthair's farewell letter to me promised—*Go and ye will be found*. I did, Grandmother. I found more than dreams. I found wonder. I found love.

I throw my arms around Sionnach's waist. The momentum carries us into the sky before Beltane's rising sun. His spirit blazes within my arms into flecks of golden light that cling to my body as desperately as my soul strains to keep him next to my heart. A flock of Veil Sprites bursts from my skin, flowering around his soul. I'm surrounded by the brilliance of my *anamchara* as whispers pass through my body. "*Teacht orm, Eala bán, find me.*"

My beloved's soul and the Veil Sprites flutter upward to chase the stars fading from the sky. I reach for them, begging all the powers of the earth and mystery to let me follow, but I slip downward away from the light.

This is my end. I've pushed fear aside and fulfilled the task I was created for.

Eala Duir will be no more.

The tip of my boot touches the rock that blessed or destroyed each spirit in Sionnach's soulfall. I hug my body, preparing to disintegrate into the sludge of a spent soul, but my arms float upward, lifting my body after them. Wisps of white feathery hair fly before my eyes, blinding me to the force that elevates me away from the earth. Then my arms accept the power of wind beneath them.

I fly.

Gold-flecked white wings beat in rhythm with my heart. Below me, the firelight of dawn streaks across emerald hills. With every stroke of my wings, I push the shadow of night from the land.

In the distance, I hear a symphony of chimes as the soulsongs of *Tír na nÓg* call me home. I'm bound no more by one hundred thousand heartbeats. An aurora of dazzling lights breaks through morning mist as the gates of my maker's Fae kingdom are thrown wide to receive me.

On my threshold of forever, a russet streak flashes through the rolling sea of green grass below my flight. Across the blessed soil of Ireland, banishing shadows from the ground as I chase them from the sky, is my fox.

One from earth, the other from sky, we enter the land of dreams together.

CHAPTER 27
THE EPILOGUE

I float through opalescent splendor. Ribbons wearing endless colors dance around me through a brilliant white mist. The spectral wonder of the Veil pales in comparison with the unparalleled beauty surrounding me. The delicate *ting* of bells accompanies strains of violins to mimic the song of a gentle spring breeze.

Tír na nÓg.

Soft currents beneath my wings keep me aloft as I slowly twist, searching this new horizon for Sion. Within me, Veil Sprites melt and spread throughout my being to fill my spirit with undulating warmth instead of their usual bursts of heat. I'm certain I will find him as soon as we pass through this threshold to our forever. For now, I revel in being joy personified, lacking fear or any other earthly weight of longing or want.

Until within a thunder strike, I hear the desperate cry of a fox.

The strands of color whip out of view as if wind has torn a flag from its mount. Veil Sprites reform within me, stinging until my consciousness begins to shift from ethereal bliss into reality. I plummet downward. My wings slow my descent enough to escape a painful landing.

When the mist peels away, giving shape to the void, my heartbeats quicken. Looming above me is the colossus I left only moments ago on the sea cliffs above the Loho cottage.

Finnbheara.

The light reflecting off his white-gold armor is as unforgiving as blazing sunlight. I shield my eyes and search high above the ground for the source of the agonizing cries my heart will always recognize.

Sionnach, my fox.

Thunder rolls again as Finnbheara speaks. "You dare guide this mortal into my kingdom. It is not his place."

Ten feet above my head, the king dangles my love. I reach for Sion, but Finnbheara drops him onto the sparkling silver and green grass. I fear for him. The creature hits the ground hard and rolls from the momentum. After a few yips of pain, Sion regains his human form.

I fly to him. As soon as my wing touches the flesh of his cheek, I become Eala the woman, not the white swan. Knee-length *leines* of thin beige fabric cover our nakedness.

Sion desperately clutches me tight to his chest. "Eala, my *anamchara*."

I splay my fingers across the sides of his neck, peppering his face with quick furious kisses.

Again, thunder rolls above us, and the tip of a gleaming sword as tall as a house is thrust into the ground next to us.

"Leave our realm at once, Sionnach Loho."

Without an ounce of timidity in my bones, I stand before Finnbheara, King of the Connacht Fae, the closest being I have to a father. "This man fulfilled your bargain. The soulfall is broken, its spirits free. You cannot deny him entrance to *Tír na nÓg* if it is his chosen destiny."

In a flash, Finnbheara discards the dimensions of a massive marble statue and telescopes down to the size of a tall man with lithe, corded muscles evident through his fitted, metallic tunic. He removes his helm, allowing waves of shimmering silver hair to cascade over his shoulders. Despite his now palatable proportions, waves of power still surge off him, crackling through the air. Sion and I take a step back.

"Our bargain was not with this man." The king narrows eyes that shift color from gold, to emerald, to lilac as he stares at Sion.

Sion gulps a lungful of air. I squeeze his hand hard to keep him from opening his feisty mouth and making our situation go from terrible to impossible.

The king stretches his arm with the grace of a dancer and points a long, thin finger at Sion. "Our affection for your earthly mother, *mortal*, allowed you to escape a fate in the Glade of Chimes. Give thanks for that and be gone." Finnbheara turns his back on Sion.

This time, I lay my palm over Sion's lips when he begins to speak and give my head a single shake. The fact that Finnbheara has not sent me packing gives me a drab of hope.

Without deigning to look at us, the king offers me his arm. "My child and I have much to discuss."

My—not *our* child. The king dropped the royal pronoun. Is it possible Finnbheara cares for me at all, or am I merely one more triumph in his existence of Fae trickery and bargains? He answered my call when my existence depended on it. This is my one chance to find out if I truly mean anything to him—my one risk to take—my last moment not to lose Sionnach for eternity. It is time to test if whatever I am has even a drop of Fae clout.

I shoot Sion a look I pray reads as *trust me*. Instead of taking the king's arm, I move directly into his path and drop into a deep curtsy before lifting my gaze to the mighty Fae. "Great King Finnbheara, I'd like to propose my own bargain."

Thank you for reading! Did you enjoy? Please add your review because nothing helps an author more and encourages readers to take a chance on a book than a review.

And don't miss more in the *Fae Destiny* series coming soon! Until then read more from Leslie O'Sullivan with PINK GUITARS AND FALLING STARS. Turn the page for a sneak peek!

Also be sure to sign up for the City Owl Press newsletter to receive notice of all book releases!

SNEAK PEEK OF PINK GUITARS AND FALLING STARS

You only get one parachute. There's no point packing two for a B.A.S.E. jump since you'll be pavement art before the second chute blossoms.

"Justin!"

Startled by a bellow from my jump leader/uncle, Timmer MacKenzie, my toe jerks to a stop half an inch above the trigger pedal of my launcher. Is his gray matter shredded, distracting me during a safety check? There's no chute on my back. One accidental tap on the business end of this launcher, and I'll be eye to eye with the flock of seagulls patrolling the Hollywood skies. I retreat onto the non-ballistic end of my perch. Peering over the edge of the Rampion Records Tower, I analyze the antics of the wind.

"Join us," Unc calls, teeth clenched in a P.R. smile. He hosts a cluster of reporters near the center of the circular roof. "Meet the rising star of the Slinging Seven."

Their faces morph into a collective portrait of panic as I leap more dramatically than necessary from launcher to the terra firma of the rooftop. After a salute to the Hollywood sign, a photo op my uncle will appreciate, I join the party. Pre-jump interviews are not my happy place, but keeping a smile on Timmer's face is essential. He leads our B.A.S.E. jump troop, giving the green light for my carcass to launch off skyscrapers, bridges, and cliffs in a wing suit.

"This Rampion Records Tower may rival Mount Olympus for acceptable jump altitude," Timmer tells the press jam sandwich. "Even so, I believe in enhancing the safety zone for my lads."

I sweep an arm across the roof. "Thus, the launchers."

"Your latest exhibitions of low altitude B.A.S.E. jumps have raised serious concerns," says a fresh-out-of-journalism-school reporter. He rocks a Channel Six pin on the lapel of a blazer clearly tailored for someone else. We get his type all the time: low man on the news roster, usually stuck with covering mudslides or C-list celebrity screw-ups.

I grunt at the question. Timmer's a walking archive of aerodynamics. His B.A.S.E. jump designs adhere to a superhuman canon of safety. Even Unc can't control the wreath of clouds descending on the tower. Humidity makes trickier conditions. My bangs congeal into a sweaty clump. Twenty-three is too young to die when you have plans, and I have plans.

"To you, B.A.S.E. jumping is an extreme sport. To me, it's a science." Timmer slings an arm around my shoulder. "Would I risk my own nephew's life?"

A grandfatherly dude slides square-framed sunglasses to the end of a nose in serious need of a good hair plucking. "Come on, Mr. MacKenzie, that kid can't be eighteen."

I wince at the familiar speculation my youthful image always dredges up. Satan's roadies have prepped a new circle of hell for Timmer's perpetuation of the lie about me being eighteen. My B.A.S.E. jumping talents at twenty-three are PDG – pretty damn great—but a fresh out of high-school dude rocking my moves is prodigy wonder boy territory, great P.R. fodder.

I keep my lip zipped over the deception. I'm not going to lie, it does not suck being a prodigy wonder boy.

Unc spins me to display the product emblems plastered all over my banana-colored wing suit. "Endorsements like these don't come from launching children into the sky. Justin jumps one-hundred percent legally."

The reporter's skepticism settles at the edges of his mouth. Metallic coating on his sunglasses turn my gray eyes silver as I catch my reflection. The gloaming breeze plucks strands of my tawny mane free from the generous layer of product I always apply before a jump. I'll have to retame those suckers to restore my roguishly hot vibe instead of the young and soft look Timmer prefers. I'd give my right nut to have a growth spurt on the spot. Sadly, thanks to MacKenzie short man genes, there probably aren't any in my future.

A gust of wind blows the press a tiptoe closer to the curved edge of the roof. Timmer and I hold our ground with matching "no big thing" expressions.

A babe in a raspberry-colored lady suit pushes toward me, eyes bulging with concern. Twitchy fingers alight on my shoulder. Next to my banana wingsuit, we're a fruit salad. Here comes the *concerned auntie* vibe.

"Justin, why take risks B.A.S.E. jumping with the Slinging Seven Troupe even for someone as enchanting as Zeli?"

I bite back a groan at the mention of the pop queen.

"Is glorifying her platinum record worth your life?"

Truth rumbles in my throat. *Yes, ma'am, B.A.S.E. jumping is worth the moon. It got me to Hollywood, the land of my music dreams. Dreams that will free me from Timmer's whims so I can make my own destiny.*

Timmer's glare scorches a hole in my suit, cueing the trained monkey answer he expects.

I open my arms to the clouds. "Who doesn't want to fly?" Every person on this roof does. I see it in the way their eyes brighten.

My stomach loops into a knot. Unc may piss himself when his prize canary asks to go AWOL. I've jumped off everything Timmer asked of me on our jiggy pathway around the country to make it here. My gaze drifts to the Hollywood Sign as I press toes into the roof of Rampion Records, the touchstone by which all music greatness is measured.

Tonight, this bird will fly off the Rampion Tower. Tomorrow, I dive into the audition for Rampion's annual singing competition, The Summer Number One. It's the U.S. Open of music, amateurs vs. pros, where Rampion Records dangles a chance for nobodies like me to go mic to mic with their current stable of rock stars. According to the Rampion P.R. machine – *Even the little people in this world have a shot at the Summer Number One dream.* This ammie is going to kick some serious pro ass and score a Rampion Records contract. I've got everything I need for the audition: demo tracks, my guitar, ass-hugging black jeans, and a sexy aviator jacket.

For the last five years, in every crappy rent-a-room the Slinging Seven have crashed, I've done dozens of online music courses. I study. I practice. I'm ready.

Unc laughs at one of the reporters he's chatting up, and I see Ma's smile here on the rooftop. Our signature MacKenzie smile packs serious wattage. I should know, I've busted it out often enough to sway, play, and dazzle females of the species.

Once I grab the top spot in the Summer Number One, my pile of gold for winning will be enough to snag my own digs here in L.A., the last place I remember Ma smiling. The cold burn of loneliness flares when I think of her and wonder if she's safe.

Clouds thicken as I watch the sun dip into the Pacific Ocean. I ignore a stitch of concern at the base of my neck as the jump difficulty ticks up a notch and think in my language of future Justin merch.

T-shirt moment: Music Dreams Sucker Punch Death.

Channel Six pushes in front of his colleagues. "Justin, does Zeli have a lock on the top pro spot in the Summer Number One?"

Lady Suit bumps her shoulder into mine. "Is Zeli your dream girl?"

My lips twist into a frown. Zeli is my nightmare.

Timmer digs his fist into my back, my cue to fix my pissy face. I manage to upgrade to a grimace dressed as a smile. By their winks and snickers, the reporters take my tension as embarrassment. I'd like to water cannon them all off the roof. I'm entitled to a dream girl, but it will never be the plastic diva with her bubblegum diluted pop crap. That chickadee is an affront to everything I love about music.

Unc hasn't run out of bluster. "It's an honor for the Slinging Seven to be part of Zeli's platinum record celebration."

My temple throbs. I'm more than half nuts to risk a concrete sandwich for that over-hyped female commodity with a pink guitar.

Don't stop now. Keep reading with your copy of PINK GUITARS AND FALLING STARS

And find more from Leslie O'Sullivan at
www.leslieosullivanwrites.com

Want even more from Leslie O'Sullivan? Read PINK GUITARS AND FALLING STARS and be sure to check out all the details on her website at www.leslieosullivanwrites.com

Zeli's signature pop diva sound and image are nothing short of magical—literally. Her fame comes with hidden costs, a curse that could ruin her voice forever.

Aspiring indie musician, Justin MacKenzie, is determined to kick it to the top of the Rampion Records' Summer Number One professional vs. amateur singing competition.

The favorite to beat in the annual televised contest is none other than the label's smoking hot superstar, Zeli, whose crazy extensions flow the length of a football field. Those ridiculous extensions, coupled with her bubblegum brand of pop, are an affront to everything Justin loves about music until a stolen kiss blazes into a romantic encounter.

Once inside Zeli's world, Justin discovers things are not as they seem. In their quest to allow the real Zeli, to step into the spotlight, the pair must confront the mysterious force behind the dazzle of Rampion's success. If these star-crossed lovers can't rally their own magic to defeat the darkness, they will lose everything—including each other.

Please sign up for the City Owl Press newsletter for chances to win special subscriber-only contests and giveaways as well as receiving information on upcoming releases and special excerpts.

All reviews are **welcome** and **appreciated**. Please consider leaving one on your favorite social media and book buying sites.

For books in the world of romance and speculative fiction that embody Innovation, Creativity, and Affordability, check out City Owl Press at www.cityowlpress.com.

ACKNOWLEDGMENTS

Love to my Company of Readers ARC team. I treasure your enthusiasm. I'm so excited to share my stories with you.

I am filled with such gratitude to all the readers, reviewers, book bloggers, podcasters, booktokers, bookstagrammers, and other social media friends who are so generous and encouraging. I love hearing your thoughts about the voices in my head that make it onto the pages of my stories.

Lisa, wonderful author, editor, and cherished friend, thank you for championing this story that's so dear to my heart, and sticking with me on this journey.

Tina, Yelena, and the team and authors at City Owl Press, you're all magic. Miblart – the gorgeous cover made me weep tears of joy. Laura T., P.A. extraordinaire, you are amazing!

To my fellow writers in the Storyteller's Syndicate, you're better comfort than all the mac & cheese in the world for keeping this solitary writing journey from being a lonely one. Special hugs to Lisa Edmonds for making the group happen.

My sweet daughter, Melissa, thank you for traipsing through the haunted castles, neolithic tombs, death-defying suspension bridges, narrow roads, graveyards, and so many other wonders of Ireland with me to research this book. I hope you've recovered from my terrifying left side of the road driving. Jon and Jane, who share my love of Ireland, I'm indebted to you for making my "must see" list for the Emerald Isle. Someday, we'll end up there at the same time.

To the folks and ghosts at Leap Castle and Charleville Castle who opened their doors wide to let me snoop around, I thank you. Seeds of this story were also inspired by the fabulous TV program, "Tales of Irish Castles," with Simon Delaney – highly recommend.

As always, family and friends (including Joe and Sandra who I dimwittedly left out of previous acknowledgements), I love you so much for your endless support.

And for the record, I do believe in Faeries.

About the Author

LESLIE O'SULLIVAN is the award-winning author of *Rockin' Fairy Tales*, an adult romantasy series of fairy tales reimagined, set against the backdrop of a fictional Hollywood music scene and *Behind the Scenes*, a contemporary rom com series that peeks into the off-camera secrets of a wildly popular Irish television drama. Leslie is a UCLA Bruin with a BA and MFA from their Department of Theater where she also taught for years on the design faculty. Her tenure in the world of television was as the assistant art director on "It's Garry Shandling's Show." Leslie loves to indulge her fangirl side at Cons.

www.leslieosullivanwrites.com

facebook.com/leslie.osullivanauthor

instagram.com/leslieosullivanwrites

tiktok.com/@leslieosullivanwrites

ABOUT THE PUBLISHER

City Owl Press is a cutting edge indie publishing company, bringing the world of romance and speculative fiction to discerning readers.

Escape Your World. Get Lost in Ours!

www.cityowlpress.com

facebook.com/YourCityOwlPress
x.com/cityowlpress
instagram.com/cityowlbooks
pinterest.com/cityowlpress

Made in the USA
Las Vegas, NV
14 July 2024

92298712R10184